TEN TALES OF THE HUMAN CONDITION

A NOVEL

BEN ERRINGTON

To my mother, Elizabeth.

For Star Wars, Alien, Indiana Jones, Jurassic Park and everything else that made me want to tell stories.

And of course, for always being there.

A BOX LABELLED SOCIOPATH

**THE VISUAL ACCOMPANIMENT TO
'TEN TALES OF THE HUMAN CONDITION'**

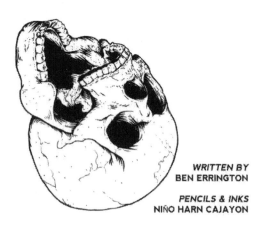

**WRITTEN BY
BEN ERRINGTON**

**PENCILS & INKS
NIÑO HARN CAJAYON**

Get 'A Box Labelled Sociopath',
the visual accompaniment to
'Ten Tales of the Human Condition' now!

"Today a young man on acid realized that all matter is merely energy condensed to a slow vibration, that we are all one consciousness experiencing itself subjectively, there is no such thing as death, life is only a dream, and we are the imagination of ourselves.

Here's Tom with the weather."

- Bill Hicks, 1989

CONTENTS

THE FIRST TALE - EVALUATE

1

It's quite possible that I am actually living the life I have always wanted. Perhaps this isn't the gruelling day-to-day procession of monotonous grief that I think it is. Maybe, after all this time and all of these doubts, I am actually happy.

I came into this without expectations, and I suppose in the end it has worked to my advantage.

I'm not a manic-depressive – I just convinced myself that I was because that's the person I wanted to be. I am nowhere near a nervous breakdown, I'm sure of that. In fact, I couldn't be further from one.

This smile on my face is genuine and I'm going to live each day like it's my last, making the most of every opportunity and reigniting the confidence that burned out long ago.

I'm back to my best and I'm ready to face the world on my own. I don't need her and I don't need everything she symbolises. I am a free man in a free world, and tonight I'm going to rediscover everything I have lost.

I have to forget every time that I doubted myself, every time that I felt like it was all too much and I couldn't cope. I have to forget that sometimes I wake up in the morning wishing I hadn't.

I am worth more than that.

I hope that I can be granted forgiveness for all of the shit I have caused, and somehow I can be washed clean of my sins; born again as a new man.

I have to start living for myself, that's the only way I will be able to claw myself out of this cavern of pitiful despair. Everything is gunna be okay, I'm sure of it.

I'm doing it again.

I'm lying to myself.

2

Growing up, we live our lives with thoughts of the future constantly hanging over us. One foot always aimed towards tomorrow, an eye of anticipation gazing at the horizon as it grows ever closer but never seems to arrive.

The images of our future selves are a seldom-seen ghost, hazy and cold, drifting in and out of focus. Our ambitions and dreams are all hinged on hope, hanging by a thread so delicate it can be broken by a thought, a breath or a word. That's why growing up can be so difficult, because no matter how well you think you know the world around you, you really have absolutely no idea. That's why it's easy to often feel lost and alone.

Change is something that happens around us, never to us. We are the same person inside and always will be.

We may think that we evolve as human beings, changing our thought processes to suit the situations we are thrown into, but that really couldn't be further from reality. We are the same throughout our lives, each action and reaction tapping into potential that already exists within us.

We don't adapt, we just are.

It's the external forces that affect us, emotionally more than anything else.

At one stage I even convinced myself that I had creditable expectations, but now I know that they are, and always were, redundant. Pointless and pathetic, not even actually there, just shrouded in a cloak of authenticity that can easily be removed where appropriate. Expectations are like that, so I shouldn't gripe.

I am, of course, only one man. I stand out as much a speck of dust floating on the crisp morning air, my form accentuated by the white glow of the sun.

I can make a difference, even if it is just to myself, but in order to do this, there are ten tales I need to tell.

It starts somewhere dull and detached, which is

perfect really, the very scene I need to put all of these words and thoughts into some sort of narrative, untangle the barbed wire from the inside of my brain, tearing every sharp point from the soft and wet flesh, and stretch it out before me so that it starts to make sense.

It ain't gunna be easy.

3

The bus I have been waiting for finally rolls into sight. My heartbeat increases as if a jump-lead has been rammed into the twitching muscle, sending an electrifying current around my body and into my blood. Each blood cell vibrates like a sex toy, transforming my entire body into a conductor of energy, causing my back teeth to bite together and my forehead to bead with sweat.

It is the rumble of excitement building up in me, the arrival of this chariot of public transport: it means something I have been looking forward to is now that fraction closer.

I feel relieved. I may not have much in my fragile world that makes me jolt with emotion, but this bus arriving after almost thirty minutes of waiting even makes a smile grow in the corner of my mouth.

I don't like waiting. As sure as the sky is blue. As sure as the grass is green. As sure as my father is a closet faggot and my mother is an irrepressible nymphomaniac.

All our lives we wait. The only thing that separates an incessant chain of tedious events is the waiting in between them. The dull brain-fuck of sitting or standing in the same spot for minutes, hours on end, staring at the flat discs of old gum on the concrete sidewalk or the floral pattern of wallpaper in a waiting room, staring so hard for so long that the pattern begins to work like a Magic Eye image from the back of a comic book.

The shapes and colours bleed together as your brain begins to grow confused and all recognisable logic falls away, causing your eyes to cross and normality to warp.

The walls of reality cave in and you hallucinate, a simple trip that can be ignored by blinking hard and rubbing your eyes with the back of your hand, but in the time that you are absorbed in the bending of familiar territory, you feel like the world could end and you wouldn't even notice.

Waiting really gets to me. Most of the time it turns out that what I have been waiting for was hardly worth the wait at all.

The silence and suspended nothingness enhances my emotive state, so if I am angry it makes the veins in my head inflate. They throb with pressure and feel like they could burst at any moment, flooding my skull with blood and killing me instantly.

But it isn't anger that I am feeling right now, it is the excitement that I have felt in my gut since late last night, throughout the hours of darkness and into dawn. Each moment that passes hurts my stomach with butterflies of anticipation and fizzes my body with carbonated blood.

The pending exhilaration begins to boil inside me, making my bladder feel tight. I need to pee, but I will have to hold it in at least for another forty-five minutes as my bus journey is just about to begin. Frustrating, yes, but the sting of needing to urinate twinned with the sweat on my forehead now running down the side of my face will keep me focused.

My mind strays for a moment as the bus pulls up to the kerb and stops with a hiss. My eyes dart up to the orange number '647' on the front of the vehicle and a cold scent, a mixture of stale fumigation from the mass of traffic growing around the city of New York and my oaky cologne fills my nose.

I think of each human being who stands around me at the bus stop, waiting like me. Insects living in the dank spaces under my apartment floorboards. They all swarm around my feet like a sordid cloud of meaninglessness, waiting to embark on the same day of their lives that they experienced yesterday. That is why they are different from me, because today will not be the same as yesterday for me.

It will be entirely new.

I have forgotten about my regrets and my guilt, but none of the faces that surround me have done so today. Their minds are filled with the same dull thoughts that have always lingered there. They are the same thoughts that will occupy them for years to come.

"Did he hear me asking him to stop?"

"Would anybody miss me if I wasn't here?"

"If I vomit up everything I eat, will I die?"

"Did I lock the front door?"

"Does anybody even notice me?"

"What shall I have for lunch?"

"Will the pain go away if I cut myself?"

"Can I ever forgive her?"

"Is this how my life will always be?"

They are questions that do not warrant an answer, at least not one that I care about. Words and thoughts clogging up the brain like wet leaves in guttering.

I stare at each person around me with keen eyes from behind my sunglasses.

The elderly man, hunched over and frail, puffing away desperately at a cigarette, like a dog gnawing the fat from a bone. He holds it tightly with stubby fingers, drawing in the smoke with cracked lips, gasping from the cancer rushing into his mouth and blinking like a baby in the new morning light.

His stale stench hits me as he turns to offer a smile, his teeth corrupt with yellow and brown. I return the smile, but widen my lips are much as possible to show my straight and white teeth, just so he knows that this is what a smile should look like.

I see the discontent flash in his eyes before he looks away, and it makes me feel good. He uses his free hand to pull the collar of his anorak up over his neck. I can see the bones of his fingers through his thin skin, stretched across them like cellophane.

Next, the teenage girl with her bad skin hidden by layers of black and white makeup, trying despairingly to rebel against normality while simultaneously blending in with every other forgettable face.

She gazes with empty green eyes at the ground, her mind no doubt plagued with thoughts of suicide so she can attract the attention she so desperately craves, for a reason she doesn't even know herself.

I know her type, I see her a dozen times a day. I already know where her life will take her. She'll end up latching onto some junkie scumbag, his lies of love for her making her life seem worthy of living for the first time. He'll take advantage of her lowly nature and manipulate her into somebody he can control.

She'll become an addict and a sex slave, the man she loves selling her skinny body (which would probably look quite attractive in the right clothing) to wretched skagheads.

She'll look back on days like today and miss them. She'll remember a dreary event like waiting for a bus and it will seem sweet and exhilarating. Her hollow shell of an existence will need to be filled, be it with despair or shame, anything to get away from the numbing horror of what she will become.

She is destined to die alone, malnourished and sickly, her body ruined from drug abuse.

Finally, there is the person standing closest to me. An obese woman staring at my head as if it is made of candyfloss, saliva gathering at the sides of her mouth, frothing as her tongue moves beneath her lips. Her stare is resolute, so much so that it bothers me, clawing into my soul.

She appears supernatural, like there is a demon lurking within her, the beast having been sent from another world to complete some profane task but now becoming distracted by me, of all the people in this fucked-up hole of a city. Her eyes tear into me and I can feel my skin begin to loosen on my face.

I break my defiant stature and shift my weight as she looks away from me. I look across at the back of her head.

She has a bad perm and an even worse dye-job. I think about grabbing hold of her wiry hair and thrusting her face into the side of the clear plastic bus stop, maybe breaking her nose and fracturing her skull, turning her podgy little face into a bloody mess, allowing the demon to be free from her body and have no choice but to return to the sullies of Hell.

I'm getting carried away. I need to keep my head firmly in the real world and stop this fantasising.

My wife tells me that almost every day. Perhaps, for once, I should listen to her.

The bus doors squeal open and the elderly man makes the first move to get on, dropping the stub of his cigarette and stomping on it as if it were a bag of dog shit on fire.

The obese woman struts forwards and the teenage girl skulks after her. For some reason the fat bitch waits and allows the girl and me on before her, which is either a genuine polite act or another chance for her to get a close look at me.

The familiar stink of the bus fills my nose, and I remember the days of driving to work with the roof down of my BMW, the wind thundering past my ears.

Those days are gone, and it's my own fault, of course, if we are distributing blame here. Half a bottle of aged golden rum, a six-pack of light beer and a couple of tequila shots with salt and lime apparently affect your ability to drive.

The cops didn't see the funny side, even if I did only run the sidewalk and collide with a concrete bollard.

For me, it was the best entertainment I'd had in a

long time. Nobody died, and my car was a complete write-off.

If anybody should've been pissed it should have been me. No more driving for me for two years.

Two fucking years.

It's for this reason and this reason alone that the bus driver gives me a nod of recognition as I pay for my ticket. If I hadn't crashed merely ten feet away from a pair of cops doing a late afternoon patrol, I wouldn't have to share this awkward and tiresome moment every morning.

The bus driver slumps over the steering wheel, his eyes lifeless and his chubby cheeks flushed pink. His navy blue blazer looks too small to contain his width, as it is splitting at the shoulders, revealing the white padding from within.

It is faded and discoloured, probably from the amount of sweat that has passed through it in the years it has been worn. His greasy black hair hangs in strands at the sides of his bearded face, disappearing beneath a Yankees baseball cap that is equally as discoloured as his jacket.

He looks a mess, and I know why. For one, he's lonely. There's been no companion in his life for as long as he can remember. That's why he attempts rapport with me on occasion – a thumb in the air, an over-the-top smile, a question or two and a comment on the weather. It's tragic.

He would be the happiest guy in the world (or at least on this bus) if I asked him if he wanted to get a beer and catch a game this evening.

There's no attempt at a social connection today; he seems more disjointed than usual. I know it's because all enthusiasm for life was sucked out of him when he masturbated before he left the depot, perhaps to the thought of a twenty-something brunette girl in denim shorts who raised her hand in thanks when he stopped at a pedestrian crossing a few days ago.

It's one of the first stops on this bus route, so the bus

is empty but for the three I have boarded with. The driver waits as we sit, and to my exasperation, the bloater of a woman decides to sit next to me as I take my place on a seat towards the back.

I exhale loudly in annoyance.

The bus smells like day-old vomit and the fatty sitting next to me smells like sour milk. I bite my lip in frustration, but it isn't hard enough to draw blood. I need to try my best to remain calm.

I breathe out slowly as the bus begins to move, trying my best to block out the world around me. I temporarily become an agoraphobic within my own body.

I struggle, especially as the elderly man sprays the stagnant atmosphere with the remnants of his breakfast as he sneezes, but I get there, and I feel my heart begin to slow as I calm, even as I suffer the weight of the obese woman's elbow and ass against my hip.

I take out my wallet from a pocket, flip it open and look down at the business card that can be seen through a translucent flap in the leather.

I have read this business card over and over again. The thought of it resting, untouched, in my jacket pocket kept me awake for several hours last night.

I read it again.

'Ryman & Jones Psychiatry. For a free hour of evaluation, call (866) 454-6607 to book an appointment or visit us at 228-232 West 16th Street. Compassionate understanding guaranteed.'

I focus on my excitement again, bringing it back to the centre of my mind and holding on tightly to it, because I know that I could lose it at any moment. As much as it feels good right now, I know it probably exists for all the wrong reasons.

It's always for all the wrong reasons.

4

I sit, perfectly still, on a plastic folding chair in the reception of the Ryman & Jones Psychiatry office. Surprisingly, my heart rate is slow.

The room smells of furniture polish and repressed memories, if you can imagine that, the sweat of guilt and unhappiness providing the bitter twinge in my nose.

The walls are stained yellow and brown with nicotine and the high ceilings make me feel odd, almost like I am a china doll within a child's dolls' house, being looked down upon by innocent eyes, my limbs stitched together with thread and my body full of stuffing.

I bring my hand to my forehead, but I do not feel the cold surface of white china, just the familiar touch of skin.

I gaze around the room at the pictures hanging on the wall. Supposedly peaceful images of sunsets, sun-bathed beach scenes and snow-covered landscapes.

The floor is surfaced by grey carpet tiles, which feel thin and old beneath my feet. I am the only client in this office today.

A young male receptionist sits across the room behind a large curved desk, his neck resting on a high-backed leather chair and his feet upon the table.

He holds a cell phone between his cheek and his shoulder, his chin juddering as he talks loudly to somebody on the line. His shirt is creased and his trousers too short for him. He wears white socks underneath old black shoes and a length of blue beads around each wrist. His hair is matted and messy, as if he has been out of bed for no longer than ten minutes after a bad night's sleep of a couple of hours after staying up late taking ketamine.

I throw him a livid look to let him know that I am unimpressed by his unprofessional and arrogant stature. I'm a businessman, and this sort of behaviour is unacceptable to me.

I would consider myself understanding, although not

laid-back: I lost that pathetic characteristic years ago. If this loser was working for me and he pulled any of this shit, he'd be out of the door, and he'd be lucky not to get my boot in his jaw.

"You know I love you, sugar-pie."

His voice is as annoying to me as his appearance, way too nasal for his own good. He shouldn't be successful with women in any way, but he seems to have some skank on the phone hanging onto his every word.

I can tell by the smell of his cheap cologne and the acne scars on his face that he was a loner in his younger years yet now thinks he's a big shot. He falls short of this illustrious title and is nothing but a self-assured prick.

"I know baby, but I'm busy tonight."

He speaks to the girl as if she is five years old. He blackmails her with saccharine words, making her feel special while no doubt screwing her underweight sister behind her back. No doubt she treats his skinny dick to a far more vigorous hand-job.

I take off my sunglasses so that he can see the irritation in my eyes. He glances up at me and his eyes stop dead. He shows his cowardly colours, quickly removing his feet from the desk and standing up awkwardly, almost losing his grip on the cell phone.

It slips in his grasp like a wet bar of soap.

The words he speaks to the girl on the phone, whose voice I can hear clearly as it is as nasal as his, now become harsh whispers.

He looks at me again, and this time I see the fear flare up in his eyes. He abruptly ends the conversation without so much as a "Bye-bye honey-bear", putting the phone into his desk drawer.

I even hear her last despairing words of "Are you even listening to me?" as he hangs up.

The kid offers me an anxious smile as he shrugs his shoulders, but he seems to lose momentum as they rise up and slink back down.

His hair has fallen across his forehead, which I can already see is beginning to bead with sweat. The look on his face tries to find common ground with me. A raise of his lip, defeated and dismal, says 'Women, huh?'

He expects me to return the look, but I don't let my incensed gaze falter one bit. He looks down at his feet as he bites his bottom lip.

I hear him say "Shit" under his breath.

I never used to be so efficient at making people uncomfortable, which I guess is as good a talent as any to develop over time. I can manipulate most situations in my favour because when human beings become awkward, they tend to hit the 'abort' button.

This usually causes them to revert to the easiest action to remove the tension as swiftly as possible, and if I have caused that tension, I can get away with almost anything I want.

It's a simple process.

I grind my teeth in frustration. I would enjoy toying with this inept idiot on any other day. But today I need to be centred and I need to be focused.

I breathe in slowly and let the scowl fade from my face.

A beep of an intercom on the receptionist's desk cuts the silence. The kid sits down onto his chair with a squeak of leather and fumbles around to click a button just below the intercom speaker.

I hear a delicate female voice, but from across the room I cannot make out the words. The kid nods to himself before muttering a reply. He looks towards me.

"Looks like you can go in now, Mr Gardener. Room Two."

I stand up, take hold of my briefcase from a chair next to me and begin to walk across the room, my shoes thundering on the carpet tiles.

I smile like a maniac at the receptionist as I pass his desk, and he widens his mouth uneasily in response, the fear more lucid in his eyes.

5

My name isn't really Mr Gardener; to use my real name would be stupid.

I place the palm of my hand against the office door. I bring my hand down to the doorknob and twist it, pushing away the barrier between rooms and laying my eyes upon Cassandra Jones for the first time.

She is standing in the middle of the room, presenting herself to me in a way that sends a shiver of anticipation up my spine.

Her hands are folded just below her stomach, and these are the first of her features I notice. I stand still for a few seconds as I admire her perfectly manicured and painted fingernails. Her fingers are slim and long, no wedding or engagement ring in sight.

I take in the rest of her. Her hair is long and sandy, hanging over one shoulder in subtle waves. She wears small black-rimmed spectacles on the end of her petite, rounded nose, shielding her powerful green eyes behind a gentle lustre of glass. Below this, her lips are pink and thin, smiling softly.

She wears a white short-sleeved blouse with frilled edges, as well as a black pencil skirt that seems slightly too small for her, emphasizing her pear-shaped form.

Her legs are bare and pale. Her shoes are heeled and made from some sort of lacquered pink material. They are perhaps a little too promiscuous for a professional environment.

She is younger than I had expected, mid-twenties more so than late. From the sound of her voice and her overall manner on the telephone, I thought she would have had at least a few more years of experience in this field, but no bother.

"Good morning, Mr Gardener," she says, her lips

barely moving as the words pass them. "My name is Cassandra Jones, we spoke on the phone."

I move forwards and stretch out my free hand, and she mirrors my action.

There is a clumsy moment as she realises that she has gone to shake with the wrong hand. She giggles like a kid and switches over to the correct hand.

We shake loosely for a second, neither of us really committing to it, the skin of her palm soft and warm. Our eyes meet and her smile grows wider, revealing her straight, white teeth.

She is slightly discomfited in her own skin, which I didn't expect, for she seemed so confident and proficient on the phone. The way she constructed her sentences was expert, and her eloquence was outstanding. She listened, and even if she was replicating empathy, she did it so well that I wanted to believe it.

Yet now she is jerky and nervous, but somehow, that's quite empowering. I feel a connection with her already.

"Please take a seat," she says as she turns away from me and walks around her desk.

I watch her for a second and I feel my lips go almost instantly dry.

I hadn't expected any sort of sexual attraction to her and I certainly didn't want it to be that way. She is much taller than I had imagined she would be and almost too beautiful. Her looks aren't extravagant and overly appealing at first glance, but there is something about her, quaint and sweet, that draws me in. Her scent fills my nose and the room. Violet and summer.

The office is large, wide and incredibly bright due to the far wall being almost entirely a window. It looks out upon the jagged horizon of New York, the mid-morning sky bleeding against the angular shapes of the gargantuan man-made towers.

The glass doesn't seem very thick. A human body

could shatter it if thrown against it hard enough. I could get some real distance with a run at it.

The flooring is flat granite tiling and the walls are vibrant with bold floral prints, lined with heavy-duty shelving and mounted with framed certificates displaying Cassandra's various qualifications and permissions to practise.

I spot a flat and long couch in the corner, next to a broad-leaved houseplant. A standard leather and velvet psychiatry couch, perfect for lying back on and fading away to the soundtrack of whale song and waves upon the shore while discussing Daddy issues and recurring feelings of inadequacy.

Cassandra's desk is in the centre of the room and is almost an exact replica of the one in the waiting room, but slightly bigger and with a glossy black finish. She sits in another high-backed leather chair and begins to tap the keys on her silver-cased laptop.

I see a reflection of me standing there in the gleam of the computer and notice that I look gangly and odd, like a teenager with no confidence.

I look away from it and take a seat in front of Cassandra's desk.

I place my briefcase flat on the floor behind my feet. I realise that I haven't said a word since I entered the office, so I clear my throat.

"Thanks for taking the time to see me today, Miss Jones," I say, doing my best to sound calm despite feeling my throat judder. "It is *Miss* Jones, right? I don't see a ring."

Cassandra looks up from her laptop and smiles kindly. She pushes her glasses further up the bridge of her nose and pulls her chair closer to the desk.

"You're correct, I'm not married," she says, the recognisable warmth from the telephone call returning to her voice. "But please, call me Cassandra. Formalities will be wasted here."

I return her kind smile. There are a few seconds of still silence and this helps my heart rate to level out.

"In that case, call me Jack," I say, but this isn't my name either. "I only get called Mr Gardener by salesmen, and nobody likes salesmen."

Cassandra laughs, but it makes almost no sound at all. She just breathes in sharply. I can tell it is a laugh out of habit more than anything else, for my comment was neither funny nor relevant.

I notice her eyes behind the lenses of her glasses, and I can already tell that she doesn't yet know what to make of me. I know that she is a woman of sympathetic nature because I wouldn't be here if she wasn't.

"Okay Jack," she says, pausing to look at her computer screen once more. "We touched a little on your problems when we last spoke, but I like to start these sessions with a clean slate."

I am drawn in like a moth to a bright light, flickering around her aura.

"Forget what we discussed and let's go into this with a fresh mind. It certainly helps me, as I seem to get a better understanding of people and their personalities by talking to them face to face. That way, I can help the best I can and offer the most applicable advice."

She leans forwards even more, placing her elbows on the surface of the desk and linking her hands together under her chin.

Her blouse rises slightly at the shoulder, revealing a tiny tattoo of a butterfly on her pale skin. There is some text below it, perhaps a date, but from across the desk I cannot make it out.

I realise I am staring and quickly snap myself out of it, blinking intensely.

"Okay, sounds good," I say.

Cassandra brings a pad of lined paper out of a desk drawer and places it in front of her. She takes a pen from an empty mug to her right.

She seems a bit lost for a moment, as if she is unaware of what she needs the pen and paper for. She looks up at me, then back down at the pad. She begins to tap the pen against the side of the empty mug, groans slightly, draws out an "Umm" and bites the insides of her cheeks.

"I'd like to get started with a simple question," Cassandra finally says, almost whispering. "Well, it will be as simple as you choose to make it."

She looks at me with intensity and I feel the hairs on the back of my neck prick up. I clear my throat once again and scratch my cheek.

"Why do you think you have come here today?"

Her question is delivered with swift precision, cutting into my psyche like a newly sharpened knife, exploding across my mind in colourful imagery, mostly smeared red.

I see a man that I loathe with a gun in his mouth, a single tear streaming down his face as the barrel of the weapon gets forced further down his throat, scraping against his teeth.

"Well, I'm not entirely sure," I admit, my voice sounding thin and lifeless. "I've never been to a shrink before, but I don't know what else to do. I've tried every method my doctor has suggested and every type of medication I could get my hands on."

I stop for a second to catch my breath.

"I think my problem is much deeper than I actually know. There's something that's affecting me deeply and I don't know what it can be. It's entirely psychological, I know that much."

Cassandra nods tenderly and marks the top of her pad of paper with a bullet point.

"Go on," she says.

I shift myself forwards in my seat.

"I am suffering terribly with insomnia and I have been for almost six months. I rarely sleep for more than an hour or two every night and a lot of the time I don't sleep at all. Pills don't work and I've read dozens of self-help books."

Cassandra doesn't look up from the desk.

"When I do get to sleep, I almost always wake up sweating and nauseated. I have a disturbing recurring dream."

Cassandra's eyes flick up at me and she studies me attentively. I can tell from the way she looks at me that the certificates on her wall aren't just for show.

I lean forwards even further and wait for her response. Her face is flushing pink.

"Well Jack," she says. "Insomnia is more common than you might think. It affects a lot of people, and like you, they tend to seek advice from their doctors, most assuming it to be a physical ailment rather than a mental one."

I press my lips together as I listen to her words. Her hands are now flat on the desk and I can't help but look at the swell of her breasts beneath her blouse.

"You are right for coming to see me to discuss the matter. It does seem like you are suffering rather badly, and I am sorry to hear that."

I nod in agreement and look away from her chest. I am not sure if she caught me looking, but to be honest I don't really care.

I can even feel myself beginning to get an erection.

"Insomnia can be caused by many different things," Cassandra continues, "and it comes it various forms."

I loosen the knot of my tie and pull away my collar from my throat, but I don't stop listening to her.

"It can be common amongst recent trauma victims or those who are under significant emotional stress. The human condition is delicate, and unless it is treated with care and attention, it can react in peculiar ways. Think of it as a flower that needs just the right amount of water and sunlight to keep going. The insomnia you are experiencing is simply your mind's way of telling you that something is wrong, and that can be caused by outside forces or maybe even subliminal thoughts. We need to get to the root of the problem."

I smile at her analogy, although thinking of my condition in comparison to a flower may not be the right thing, for there is nothing beautiful or exceptional about me.

Cassandra's words are articulate and poised. She seems to have settled, which makes me happy. She makes a note against the first bullet point on her pad of paper, yet I cannot see what is written from across the desk.

I feel obliged to make some sort of verbal reaction, but I cannot form a word. It comes out in a "Hmm".

She purses her lips and continues to try and evaluate me.

"Lack of sleep can cause hallucinations and delirium. This can filter into your dreams once you finally get that sleep you have been craving. Do you feel comfortable detailing this recurring dream to me?"

I look out of the window for a second, reminding myself how I had planned to reply to this expected question.

"Of course," I say. "Although it is a little weird and embarrassing. It makes me feel a bit queasy just thinking about it."

Cassandra smiles, trying her best to make me feel at ease.

"Don't worry, Jack," she says. "Take your time. Detail to me whatever you feel comfortable with. This is a safe place and I can assure you that I will not push you beyond the boundaries of security."

I begin to lose my erection as she reels off the clichés, but it's probably for the best.

"It involves my wife," I say, looking down at my lap. "She's on our bed, her legs spread wide. There's blood everywhere on the silk sheets, a huge puddle expanding every second."

I look back up at Cassandra.

"She's screaming in pain, her face and hair soaked in sweat. I assume that she has been attacked, maybe there's been a break-in and some son-of-a-bitch has panicked and stabbed her. As I get closer the pieces come together and I realise she's in labour. She's giving birth right there on the bed."

Cassandra nods as she listens, seeming to be unfazed by what I have told her so far.

"I try and do the right thing," I continue. "It's too late for an ambulance so I hold her hand tight and tell her to breathe, helping her through the pain. She is squeezing my hand so tight that it fizzes and burns, but I tell her over and over again that it's going to be okay."

I stop for a second and wipe the sweat from the bridge of my nose. Again, Cassandra's expression doesn't change. She doesn't even blink.

"I see the baby's head crowning," I say. "I feel my heart thudding with excitement, for I am about to see my child come into the world. I can barely contain myself. I start to cry. Happy tears."

Cassandra's face glows, and I see her eyes glaze over.

"But then I notice that something isn't quite right. My baby's head looks strange somehow. It's smaller than I expected and it's an unusual shape. My wife's screams are getting louder as the head comes out and the body quickly follows, slipping out into a bloodied slump on the saturated sheets."

I intake a large breath as if I am anticipating the climax of the story just as much as I hope Cassandra is.

"I let go of her hand and feel my jaw drop as I look down at what she has given birth to. It isn't a baby – well, not a human one anyway."

Cassandra listens, gripped. I know that I have paced the tale of my invented dream exactly right.

"It's a dog, a puppy, I'm not sure what breed."

I stop to gauge Cassandra's reaction.

Her smile is nervous and she clears her throat, not knowing how best to react.

I feel for her in this instance, for I wouldn't be sure how I'd react to something so bizarre.

"Now the tears are streaming down my face," I say, my voice louder. "No longer are they tears of joy, they are now tears of horror. I see the puppy moving on the blood-soaked bed, wriggling like a hairy slug."

Cassandra licks her lips.

"My hands are shaking and I look up at my wife, who has stopped screaming. She has a huge grin on her face. She actually looks happy to have brought such a creature into the world, ecstatic even. She asks me a question and it makes my skin crawl just remembering it."

Cassandra writes something else on the paper.

"She asks me 'Aren't you proud of our baby boy?' I feel vomit lurch up into my throat. I can actually taste it."

Cassandra turns her head at an angle, which makes me feel a little exposed.

"And then comes the worst part. The part that makes me not want to get back to sleep ever again. The part that made me come here today because I can't continue living my life when this haunts my every night. It makes me wonder if I am losing my mind."

I rise out of my seat somewhat, hovering, although I don't know why. Perhaps the restlessness I have in my bones from the build-up to this moment.

I see Cassandra's mouth open an inch.

"I grasp hold of the puppy with my quivering hands," I say. "I hold it by the scruff of the neck, making sure I don't look at its face, and I shove it back up inside my wife, using all of my strength."

I imagine the look on the face of my darling wife, her mouth upturned in agony.

"I force it back to where it came from, knowing that I am hurting her. Her screams return, much more severe, and she is telling me to stop, but I don't. She hits me and scratches me down my face, but I persist."

I imagine the pain of my wife's hands slapping into my face.

"She yelps like a dog, which is peculiar really."

I sit back down into my seat. I calm myself with laboured breaths, bring my voice back down to a regular level and place my hands on my knees.

"It's usually about then that I wake up."

Cassandra stares at her notes with wide eyes before taking her glasses off and placing them upon the desk.

"Right, well," she says, barely appearing to react to my extraordinary dream. "Abnormal and unusual dreams can plague a sleep-starved brain, so whatever is bothering you and causing the insomnia has a grasp on how the dreams are perceived. I guess the best way for me to come up with any kind of analysis is to first understand your relationships."

I blink and swallow hard. My mouth is dry.

"Your relationship with your wife, for example."

I look up at the ceiling, my eyes growing as dry as my mouth. I picture the face of my wife. The beauty spot just below her lip, her wide eyes and bold lashes. The chickenpox scar above her eyebrow, her cropped black hair angled against the cool bronze of her skin.

The treachery in her eyes, lies hiding behind them like pacing animals behind glass, forever in captivity and longing to be free.

I attempt to decide how best it is to reply to Cassandra Jones. I want to tell her that my wife is a deceitful, scheming, selfish whore.

"Well," I say, "my wife is absolutely everything to me. I love her dearly. We are very close and I'd most definitely say we have a healthy relationship. It's a positive and loving companionship and she's my soul-mate."

I show Cassandra my palms as I continue.

"We have a great sex life, which I think is important. I'm a lucky guy."

Sure, my wife's sex life is great. It's just not with me. I cannot even remember the last time I had sex with her.

I'd rather put my penis into a loaded bear-trap. I'd prefer to have a bloodied stump where my genitals once were than experience any level of intimacy with her ever again.

I can tell from Cassandra's tolerant nods that she is somebody who has been in love before; in fact, she is far from a stranger to it.

She has had her heart broken, more than once I would expect, and I am sure that she has broken other people's hearts. It's evident that she has had her fair share of both tragedy and elation; the tender understanding in her eyes proves that.

I can also tell that she is a sexually experienced girl, and I mean that to her credit. She is experimental and free more so than easy, although she could be damaged by past incidents, the details of which I do not know.

The low cut of her blouse does not suggest that she is in any way square when it comes to sexual activity.

Maybe the heartbreak forced her to build up a barrier and now she is the kind of girl who refuses to commit, or doesn't want a serious relationship at this current moment in time, her career more important to her than a partner.

"Any reason in particular why you think your wife would be the focus of such a distressing dream?"

I shake my head, trying my best to enhance the idea that my relationship with my wife is nothing short of a fairy-tale.

"I have no idea," I say.

"No unaddressed feelings or grudges? An underlying problem from the past, for example?"

I shake my head again, pushing out my bottom lip.

"So no tension between the two of you at all?"

"No tension at all," I confirm. "As I said, we are very close. If we ever have any issues we discuss them."

Cassandra jots down another note.

"Okay," she says. "That's good. Do you and your wife have any children?"

"No, we don't. It's never really ever been on the cards. We are both quite career-orientated."

Cassandra nods.

"And what do you do for a living, Jack?"

I scramble around for an answer.

"I'm a freelance journalist."

I have no idea why this profession is the one I go for, but it's better than the first two that pop into my head, which are zoo keeper and dentist. I know for a fact that my single-breasted black Armani suit doesn't make me look like I could shovel animal shit or poke around rotten teeth for a living.

"Really?" Cassandra says. "I wouldn't have expected it."

She's much more observant than I had expected. She impresses me more with every word. Again, I focus on the curve of her breasts.

"How come?" I say with a puzzled look on my face.

"The suit, the briefcase, the shoes and the way you walk and talk. It all screams a Wall Street exec. I mean that as a compliment, of course."

I smile, making sure I show her how good my teeth are. She's opening up a bit, getting comfortable. Getting me onside with compliments, which is not a method of psychiatric evaluation I have ever heard of, but perhaps that is the way she works. Some women like to inject an element of flirting into their practise; it helps them get ahead and be perceived as both approachable and highly authoritative. It wouldn't strike me as common in this field, but I'm not going to worry.

"I hope you don't mind me saying so," Cassandra utters, possibly realising that her comment may have offended, despite my smile.

"Of course not," I say. "I guess I believe that dressing the part is half the battle. Freelance journalism can be difficult, and getting respect for your art is important. If I turn up to a meeting with a contact or a client wearing slacks and a hockey shirt, I know I'm not likely to get hired. If I invest in something like this suit, people are gunna think I am somebody with confidence, experience and the means to get a job done."

I know that I have done nothing to suggest to Cassandra that I am anything other than a freelance journalist. If there was some doubt in her mind, I have all but eradicated that now.

"Okay," she says. "How about your wife, what does she do?"

"She's a teacher. Third grade."

I bring my right leg up onto my left knee and lean back on my chair.

"So, she's good with kids?" Cassandra asks.

"Oh, yeah. She's great. She just has no interest in becoming a mother and I think that's because she gets all the good parts of parenthood in her job, so she feels no need to have a baby herself."

"And you've discussed this?"

Cassandra mimics my lean back and rests the end of her pen against her bottom lip.

"As much as we need to. It's not an issue at all," I say.

Cassandra breathes out, almost in a sigh.

"I'm going to cut to the chase, Jack, but only to help you. I hope you know that."

She waits for me to say something but I don't.

"Do either of you have any problems regarding the conception of children? Or have there been any events in the past where a pregnancy has been, um, terminated?"

She paused just before she said that last word.

6

I see a shimmer of benevolence in her face and notice something I hadn't noticed before and I could kick myself for almost missing it.

Her make-up is heavily but well applied. It blends in with her skin tone and doesn't look like too much at all, but beneath the matt finish of her foundation I can see faint bruising below her left eye. The grey and purple of an injury that is now a few days old.

"No," I say. "No problems as far as I am aware. We use regular contraception and have been doing so for years. Since the beginning, I think. No abortions either."

I smile, trying not to appear patronising.

"I don't think the content of the dream has any real connotation. Regarding her giving birth, I mean."

"I understand," Cassandra says sensitively.

The bruising now seems clearer than ever and I cannot take my eyes off it. She has done a good job in concealing it.

Now that I have noticed it my head swarms with ideas of how it got there. The most obvious assumption to make would be a violent partner, or perhaps ex-partner.

Maybe a run-in about how low-cut her blouse is, the partner suspecting her of trying to seduce a work colleague. Jealousy is a fucker and conspires to make a paranoid, self-loathing moron out of the best of us.

It could have been an argument about who gets what during a split or simply a punishment she received for standing up for herself against a controlling thug.

Then again, it could be a fall, or a walk into a door. A fight with another woman in a club or even a mugging. Some Puerto Rican motherfucker could have elbowed her in the face while trying to steal her purse.

"How long have you been married to your wife?" Cassandra asks.

"Eight years," I answer without hesitation. "We were dating for only two years before that. Some say we rushed into marriage, but it felt right."

This is the truth, and it feels heavy and turgid in my mouth.

Cassandra nods and comes forwards in her chair, back to her original sitting position.

"Okay Jack, thank you," she says. "How about any recent traumatic events or ongoing stress? Any significant problems involving other family members? Or a situation at work?"

I imagine a fist crashing into Cassandra's face. I imagine tears running down her cheeks and smearing her mascara. I imagine her slumped in a corner, sobbing into her hands.

"Nothing I can think of," I say. "I've had a few stress-free years, especially when it comes to my job. Things are coasting along nicely. Nothing traumatic either, although I did nearly get hit by a truck last month while crossing the street, but the insomnia started long before that."

This statement is also true. Some knucklehead in a flannel shirt almost flattened me in his pickup because he was concentrating more on guzzling an extra-large soda than on the road.

I imagine Cassandra lying unconscious on the bathroom floor, a thin trickle of blood coming from her nose and running down her chin.

"And I don't really have any other family. I was an only child and my parents died when I was young, but we were never close anyway. My wife is all I have."

I know that I am not giving her much to go on, but I want to see exactly what she is capable of. She is trying, bless her heart, and she is doing well, but she won't get any deeper than she already has.

Cassandra makes yet more notes, which is beginning to bother me now. Our conversation so far has been placed into five or six scraps of written text, separated into bullet points.

That would be all she remembers of this meeting if I was to cut it dead right here. She may type it up and file it away somewhere, but in her head this will be just another simple exchange with a guy who can't sleep and thinks he has problems, when all he has is an overactive imagination.

I have learnt more about her in this short space of time than she has about me, and I'm not the one with certificates to suggest that I am qualified.

"Do you think the fact that your wife gives birth to a dog rather than a human baby has any substance behind it?"

I sneer at Cassandra's question and I think this is because the ridiculous nature of my lie hits me. I mean, a woman giving birth to a puppy? Shit, that's weird.

"I really don't know," I say, raising an eyebrow. "We don't have a dog, and never have. I don't think my wife even likes dogs."

I spit out my answer. She senses the impatience in my voice and I see her grimace slightly, screwing her eyes up.

The first client of the day, and I'm the most difficult of the week. Let's aim for the month. Screw it, the year.

"We don't have to carry on if you feel agitated," Cassandra says quietly. "I understand that your problem is affecting you and that it is of a sensitive nature, but I assure you that I am only trying to help."

I imagine her making herself sick after a big meal. I imagine her standing on a balcony, contemplating throwing herself off it. I imagine her driving on the freeway, edging her foot down onto the accelerator, speeding up and wanting to turn into oncoming traffic.

"What advice has your doctor given you?" she asks. "What meds have been prescribed?"

I realise now that she has given up on me. An hour of free evaluation, which we aren't even a fraction of the way through, and I am already being thrown onto the heap of losers who can't be helped.

She wanted my answers to be different than they were, just so she could grab hold of something to pin my insomnia on. Something to blame so that I don't feel so helpless.

Now it would seem she wants me out of her office and back onto the street, down into the depths to mingle with the outcasts, the racists, the criminals and the deadbeats.

I'll give her something to grasp onto. I'll make her remember me.

"I told you. Pills don't work," I object, feeling my brow furrow and my jaw jut out.

"I see that is the case, but I am interested to know what you've been put on," she replies, "I mean anything really. Sleeping pills, Prozac or... "

"Prozac?" I snap. "That's an anti-depressant."

"I am fully aware of what it is, Jack."

"So who said I was depressed? I can't sleep."

"I didn't say you were," Cassandra retorts, looking more at my chest than into my eyes. "I am simply asking if you have been prescribed anything, and in my experience Prozac is used all too often as medication for a vast amount of mental disorders."

I say nothing, urging her to continue.

"The treatment of depression is its primary use, yes, but it is also commonly used to treat obsessive-compulsive disorder, eating disorders, drugs or alcohol dependencies and even insomnia. I assure you that I am not accusing you of being depressed: jumping the gun like that is not something I indulge in."

I bite my lip and grind my back teeth.

"I am merely trying to help you get to the bottom of your issue, Jack," she adds.

"I can see what you're doing," I say. "You want to put a word against me. You want to stamp me with 'disorder' so that you can convince yourself that you have done your job."

Cassandra shakes her head. I see her bottom lip jerk slightly. Her voice is tainted with unease.

"Mr Gardener, I assure you—"

"Don't assure me anything, Miss Jones," I say, calm

and assertive. "I am not a manic-depressive and I don't need you to tell me that I am."

Cassandra's face has drained of colour. I can see that I am distressing her, but I continue with my onslaught. It's the only way I can make her understand.

"Mr Gardener," she continues, her voice croaking. "I am very confused. This is my job, and I am not trying to put you down or judge you. I am respectful of your problem and I want to help you. If you think that I am being unhelpful to your cause, I suggest we end the session here as I do not wish to cause offence or distress you in any way."

Cassandra is the model professional.

I feel my face going numb as I imagine her falling to her death after leaping from a high ledge, her spine smashing to dust and her stomach exploding.

"Tell me something," I say, toning down the displeasure in my voice. "Why do you choose to do this?"

I don't want to seem as manically confrontational as I perhaps am; that was never my intention. I lean back in the chair, drawing an air of serenity across us both. I fidget with my wedding ring.

"I don't understand," Cassandra replies. "What do you mean?"

I can't help myself.

"Why do you choose to evaluate the human condition in such a way?" I ask, loosening the knot of my tie even more.

She flusters, licking her drying lips.

"This is what I do for a living, Mr Gardener," Cassandra replies, her voice determined and tinged with resentment.

"You place everything into a neat little cardboard box, tie it up with a silk ribbon and label it with whatever you see fit," I say, ignoring her words.

"I am trying to help you," she repeats, eyes keen. "This is a free hour of evaluation that you sought out. I am not gaining anything from talking to you today and this meeting is not for my benefit. You are turning this into a disagreement between the two of us and it doesn't need to be that way."

I ignore her again.

"Whether it is 'sociopath', 'psychopath', 'masochist', 'schizophrenic' or 'addict', does labelling someone give you a better understanding of them?"

I stand up as I talk, my voice getting louder and a bead of sweat running down the side of my face.

Cassandra's eyes are wide and she sits perfectly still looking up at me, her hands flat on the desk.

"You fascinate me with your ignorance, Miss Jones," I sneer, saliva spitting out from between my lips.

Cassandra shakes her head in disbelief. It's only a matter of time before she wells up with tears.

"The human condition is temporary," I continue. "One moment, a being capable of love, rage, sympathy, apathy, mercy and causing unspeakable damage to those around them. The next, an empty vessel. Burned or buried and reduced to a memory."

I imagine Cassandra getting hit by a car as she rushes across the street, her neck snapping in three places and her body lying limp at the feet of a crowd that has gathered. I imagine her curled up in a ball at the foot of her bed, bawling like a newborn baby and begging for forgiveness.

I have completely loosened the knot of my tie now, and it hangs around my neck like a length of rubber tubing – something similar to the tubing I would attach to a car exhaust and attempt suicide with.

"Perhaps you want to talk to somebody else," Cassandra says, her bottom lip quivering somewhat. "We have several professionals at this centre who may be more to your liking. If you want me to—"

"We have something in common," I say, cutting her off but attempting to add a dash of compassion to my voice. "We are both hiding behind a disguise, something wholesome that cannot be corrupted. But for me, this disguise is transitory, yet I know that yours has existed for a long time."

I see that she is pondering my words.

"What disguise are you wearing, Jack?" she asks.

I laugh. It is over-the-top and I know that it makes her feel on edge, maybe even sick. Her face looks green to me now, the purple of her bruising diluted by her make-up.

I imagine her face and body decomposing ten-speed. I see her skin rotting away and her red flesh greying like old meat.

"My disguise is not of interest," I say. "It didn't take me long to work out the exact structure of yours, but now it's clear. I am sure you take time to maintain it, but I can see the sorrow beneath your cloak of skin. We are all the same inside, red and sodden, but on the outside the differences show."

Evaluating the human condition is my talent. I just needed to see it from a different perspective, evaluate my evaluations, I suppose.

I know exactly what makes up Cassandra Jones and the disguise she holds so dear. I can see by the dread in her eyes as I loom over her that she is scared of me and it's a look I know she has had in those beautiful eyes before, which is a shame but unsurprising none-the-less.

She has, or had, an abusive partner, somebody who makes, or made, her feel unworthy and unappreciated.

"I think we should end this session here," Cassandra says, standing up. "You came to me wanting help—"

"I do want help. I really do," I say, genuinely.

I see a flock of birds flying past the window and watch intensely as they form a shape that reminds me of something. Something that I have seen many times before but I cannot put my finger on what it is I see.

A brief sense of déjà-vu sweeps over me, and for a second I feel like I might faint. I steady myself on my feet and stare into Cassandra's eyes.

"Then what is the point of this outburst, Jack?" she retorts, anger in her voice for the first time. "Why are you aiming your animosity at me? This is the behaviour of a—"

A lunatic. A fucked-up lunatic who is self-destructing from the inside out and just needs a way of making it all okay. A lunatic who needs an outlet for his angst, a decadent head-case who is in danger of losing all familiar features of his soul to a hungry abyss.

"A projector. You're projecting much deeper personal problems onto the world around you. You're denying your own condition and it's causing you to lash out at people who aren't to blame. Like me, for example."

She moves her hair out of her face and I see the tears in her eyes, desperate to come down her face. I want them to, I am almost pleading with them.

Show me that weakness, Cassandra Jones.

"I know my condition, Miss Jones," I say, thrusting my forefinger in her direction. "I have evaluated myself and I have been evaluated by others. You need to face up to your own problems, because I can see through your disguise and I can see pain beneath it. Cheap make-up won't cover up the bruising on your face."

I see a single tear break free and run down her cheek, streaking the make-up on her skin as if it had been applied merely minutes ago.

My heart wrenches and I feel a moment of guilt, which makes me disappointed in myself. Her next words are choked and broken.

"Please leave, Mr Gardener. Don't come back here again."

I intake breath, letting it fill my lungs. I feel the sweat on my head drying.

Cassandra wipes away the tear from her face and stems her leaking eyes with her fingertips.

"I understand when I have outstayed my welcome," I

say, bending down and taking hold of my briefcase from under the chair. "I will leave, but please promise me one thing."

She looks up at me, her demeanour striking me as that of a little girl lost rather than a strong and zealous woman. I have broken her down: she was resilient, but a few home truths are capable of revealing the vulnerabilities.

I take a final look at the beautiful young woman standing before me and turn around. I walk towards the office door with long strides, and stop still just before I take hold of the doorknob. I talk without looking back at her.

"Don't go putting me in the box labelled 'sociopath'. I've been doing that to myself for far too long."

I open the door and walk through it. I hear her begin to quietly sob.

Cassandra Jones, you complete me.

7

My condition is pure, as white and clean as freshly-fallen snow. I am at one with myself.

I see that the receptionist has left his desk and the waiting room is empty but for me. I step behind the desk, reach down to the drawer and pull it open. I see his cell phone resting inside upon some paperwork and I take it out and hold it in my palm for a few seconds, looking at my face in the reflective surface of the screen. My eyes look dead.

I drop it on the floor and watch it land screen up. I bring the heel of my shoe down hard upon it, shattering the screen and smashing the phone into several pieces.

I am the cause.

I am the effect.

I am anarchy.

I am chaos.

I am a cool motherfucker.

THE SECOND TALE - INTOXICATE

1

On my walk from the Ryman & Jones Psychiatry office to the Morning Glory bar, I take hold of a pack of cigarettes from the inside pocket of my jacket and smoke three of them in quick succession.

I get some strange looks from passers-by on the streets as I suck down the poison smoke into my lungs, closing my eyes and putting my head back in exhilaration.

The nicotine calms my skin.

According to my wonderful spouse, indulgence is my vice. Yes, my wife, the same woman who is fucking my best friend behind my back.

Yes, my best friend, the same man who gives me advice on how to save my faltering marriage.

Indulgence isn't only my vice, it's my escape. I don't indulge myself with life's sweet nectars to get ahead or forget my problems. Indulgence is just really fun.

I walk into the bar and the scent of stale beer wafts over me. I feel nauseated for a second but it soon passes.

I take a seat on a stool at the bar, placing my briefcase on it, and get the attention of the middle-aged barman who is staring into space like a zombie with a slight tap of my finger on a plastic glass-drainer in front of me.

He rubs his eyes and saunters over. I can tell by his bloodshot eyeballs and the dark bags beneath them that he hasn't slept much the night before.

Perhaps due to a busy night at this bar, working hard to earn his dollar and keep his customers happy.

Perhaps due to being kept up by his wife snoring like an ox and him having to attempt to get some rest in an armchair in another room.

Or perhaps because he was out cruising in his custom Ford for a willing rent boy to suck his wrinkly dick until four in the morning.

The barman stops in front of me, his grey hair slick against his head and a filthy dishcloth hanging over one shoulder of his checked shirt. He nods in recognition at me and leans against the bar.

"What can I get you, son?" he asks. His voice is friendly but his face is not.

I look around the bar and realise that I am the only customer this morning. I snigger and hang my head.

"I'm feeling like some Bourbon. Maker's Mark."

The barman turns without a word and begins working on my drink, clinking some cubes of ice into a glass tumbler and pouring the liquid from the bottle carefully.

He slides the half-full glass (I'm an optimist) onto the bar in front of me without a word. I knock it back, barely giving myself time to notice the bitter flash of taste or the burn of alcohol in my throat.

Warmth spreads across my chest and my stomach turns over twice.

A television set hanging on the wall is showing a news story about six servicemen being killed in an explosion in Afghanistan. The woman reporting on it wears a grey trouser suit and looks as frigid as they come.

I am indulgent, I won't deny that. Whether it is alcohol, narcotics or sex, I indulge myself with whatever I feel suits, so when my pitiful and predictable human brain feels grief and depression, I can blur the edges of reality and make it all better again.

I'm not relying on my indulgences in any way and they don't make me who I am. I am not an addict, for if you took away my booze and my coke and my regular visits to a certain hooker I wouldn't lose my mind.

I wouldn't end up curled in a corner, sweating like a pig and chundering fresh air. I'd be just fine.

I continue to order the same drink at regular intervals of about five or six minutes. When I am at least halfway through the bottle, the Bourbon sticks to the roof of my mouth, so acidic that it tastes like gasoline swilling around my teeth and tongue every time I take a sip.

I feel my head doing loops and realise the alcohol is taking the desired effect.

The barman is watching the television from across the bar, doing his best to ignore my presence when I'm not asking for more Bourbon.

The news programme is now detailing a story about a cop who is being convicted after pornographic images of children were found on his home computer. His sentence is being reduced due to a plea of innocence due to intense stress suffered during his years of service to the force, which included a successfully-negotiated hostage situation that saved the lives of three young girls. Girls he no doubt fantasised about after he got his medal for bravery.

An elderly Hispanic woman with a cleft lip is being interviewed and says he should be castrated. I am inclined to agree.

I call the barman with a grunt and he lumbers over at an achingly slow pace. He sighs as he gets closer to me.

"Take it easy, buddy," he says. "Didn't you knock back enough yesterday?"

"Hair of the dog that bit me," I say. "It was a vicious little bastard."

I stand up from my stool and pick up my briefcase from the bar. I wobble on my feet but manage to steady myself before I appear too drunk. I pay for my drinks with cash and I'm tempted to purchase the remainder of the bottle, but I don't.

I smile at the barman and finish the drop of watery Bourbon left in my glass.

I walk out of the bar without another word. I blink into the bright light of day, staggering onto the sidewalk as my eyes adjust. A group of teenagers spread out around me, avoiding me like I have a deadly virus.

An ambulance whizzes past, the siren screeching like a terrible beast, tearing into my head like a well-sharpened scythe.

I feel dozens of eyes on me as my surroundings spin and my stomach grumbles. As I move down the street I stop and lean against some iron railings.

I retch before throwing up onto the ground. My lips go numb and I wipe them with the back of my hand.

The stink of alcohol and stomach acid reaches me and I heave once more, but nothing comes up this time. I look up with bleary eyes and see a disapproving driver of a cab shaking his head in disbelief. I can't help but laugh.

This is fucking hilarious.

2

I have sobered up a considerable amount after chucking up my guts. I walk along the sidewalk as I approach the west side of Central Park, trying hard to walk completely upright and not hunched over like an ape.

I scan the parked cars on the opposite side of the street and see the one I am looking for.

A jet-black 1976 HX Monaro GTS with a white racing stripe on the hood. It's almost the exact same car I owned at twenty-two years old, but this one has four doors. My racing stripe was red and the vehicle was my pride and joy.

I cross the street at the lights and approach the car with assertive strides. I open the passenger door and slide in, squeaking onto the leather seat and placing my briefcase on the floor by my feet.

I notice that my black shoes are a little scuffed and that the surface of my briefcase is smeared with something that is likely to be vomit.

The driver is looking in the opposite direction, scanning the street with unwavering eyes behind his tinted sunglasses.

It's this moment that I remember my sunglasses are in my jacket pocket. I take them out and put them on my face before smiling widely.

William Beckford turns around to look at me. His face is confused as he looks down his nose, but soon a smile appears, showing a couple of gold teeth.

His appearance does not strike me as that of a person who could afford such a classic car. His long hair hangs lank at shoulder length and it doesn't look as though it has been washed for at least a few days, maybe a week. His face is stubbly and sandy, his skin weathered and tanned, stretched across his skull like a thin layer of old leather. His chin juts out, narrowing into a point.

He wears a long black leather coat that drapes open, revealing a tight black vest beneath it. A gold cross hangs over it, drawing my eye up to his scrawny neck.

Without saying a word, he turns away, brings a ringed hand down to the gear stick, checks his mirrors and pulls away.

A rendezvous with this man has become almost a daily occurrence for me, as indulgence is most definitely his speciality. He is a narcotics dealer extraordinaire, but he didn't always have the illustrious title.

He used to be a rock star. He is originally from England, where he was somewhat successful and even something of a celebrity. He spent over ten years playing bass guitar in a hard rock band called Screamin' Suzie, and although relatively unheard of here in the States, they sold millions of records in their native UK and toured the world at the top of their game.

I know this because he recycles anecdotes about his time in the band like they were words spoken from the Messiah. I have no idea how, why or when he made the choice to cross the pond and try his hand at drug dealing.

I guess being in a successful rock group gives you access to hard drugs and all of the characters that come with them. William Beckford is a very erratic individual, somebody who is difficult to understand, even for me.

His foot pushes on the gas pedal eagerly and we coast along the street at a decent pace. I gaze through the low windscreen and see we are approaching gridlock.

"Christopher Morgan," he finally says. His voice is soft and puts me fully at ease.

The British accent has always done that for me; there's something enchanting about it. The tones are dulcet and the vowels prominent. It's eloquent, although I'm aware that not all British people speak like that.

"That's me," I say.

That really is my name. There is no need to use any fake names or aliases around this man.

"You been drinking?" William asks as he pulls up to the traffic jam.

A car in front has weaved into the melee and almost hits the Monaro. William slams on the brakes and thumps the side of his fist onto the car horn.

"Watch it, you cunt!" he bawls.

He mutters more obscenities before turning to back to me.

"I've had a few," I tell him.

He rubs the tip of his nose and laughs. I feel my stomach turning over some more, but a deep breath levels me back out.

"You truly are a crazy fuck," he says, honking the car horn again. "Not even midday and you're pissed up. I guess we've all been there, brother.

"I fell off the wagon and never got back on. I have respect for you, Chris. You're dressed like a superstar and acting like one too."

I look down at my suit and see that I have a similar smear to that on my briefcase on the lapel of my jacket.

"You'd have fit in during the eighties' rock 'n' roll explosion," William continues. "None of that Sunset Strip bullshit, the real deal."

I don't really have a reaction to William's ramblings, although they entertain me most of the time. Even when I hear a story for the third or fourth time, I always remain interested and hang on to his every word.

"Tell me something, Chris," William says as he drives forward a few feet before being forced to stop again. "What's the biggest problem for an atheist?"

I stare out of the passenger window and watch an elderly black woman walking along at an incredibly slow pace.

I turn back to William and let his words sink in. I know that he is a religious man, finding God at a similar point in his life to when he became a drug dealer. I don't want to offend him with any genuine answer. Perhaps his question is an intelligent exploration of my religious views and where I stand in terms of faith. But knowing him, it probably isn't.

It's probably another crass joke that I have no interest in.

"I dunno," I say.

"There's nobody for them to talk to during an orgasm!" William says, beaming.

I imagine a nun being bent over a church stall and fucked hard. I imagine a vicar jerking off while watching some choirboys at midnight mass.

My delayed reaction is making William stare at me in the rear-view mirror, so I shake myself free of my wandering thoughts and laugh loudly.

I try to tone it down but it turns into a bizarre and insane cackle. William shakes his head as he puts the car back into gear and moves forwards again.

"All right mate, relax," William says. "Don't have a haemorrhage. It's just a joke."

I immediately stop my laugh and eradicate any sign of amusement from my face.

William moves on swiftly, not dwelling on my peculiar behaviour.

That's why I like this man, for he doesn't judge me, no matter what I present to him. Whether it is my actions or my explanations, he always takes me at face value. He is a rare being in a city full of backstabbers and fiends.

"How you doing anyway, my friend?" he asks.

We take a corner, the traffic dispersing for several seconds.

"Oh, y'know," I say. "As good as I'll ever be. Just pushing the boundaries of my futile existence. The usual."

"Positive-minded young man," William says, smiling. "That's why I like you, Chris."

William again looks in his rear-view mirror, this time watching the driver of the car behind him with white-hot intensity.

"What's this fucking prick's problem?" he snaps. "He's right up my arse."

This man's ability to switch from calm and collected to wrathful in the blink of the eye has me watching him in awe.

"I need something new," I tell him.

He looks at me, nodding like one of those novelty dogs stores sell to stick on your dashboard.

"We all need something new, brother," he says. "That's why society is so fucked up. Everybody has the attention span of a gnat, and that's why the album at the top of the billboard charts is some faggot in tight jeans wailing about his broken heart. Nobody's got the capacity for a classic anymore."

I tighten my lips and scratch my face.

"Sorry mate, I'm on edge today. I've got a surveillance van outside my place and it's making me a fucking nervous wreck. Fucking Yank pigs thinking just because I'm not from this neck of the woods that I must be a terrorist or something."

I nod in understanding, but I am unsurprised at the fact the cops are watching Billy Beckford closely. He isn't exactly secretive about his business, and he is the kind of guy that takes exception to any sort of police attention.

He may as well have a neon sign constantly above his head, because I am pretty sure that everybody and their mother on this side of town knows exactly what his profession is.

"Shit, that sucks," I say.

"Damn right it does," William snarls. "Sucks a thick one. What I do may not be on the right side of the law, but I do it with charm and precision, not like some of the arseholes waving guns in people's faces and leaving bloated bodies in the river.

"I offer goods in exchange for cash, which makes me no different from Steve Jobs, right? God rest his soul."

The traffic becomes compact again as we pass over a pedestrian crossing. I am not sure where William is heading as it's in the opposite direction to his place and nowhere near the spots we would usually do business.

Perhaps he wants to do his deals somewhere else so the cops don't begin to notice patterns in his movements. I don't ask, however.

"So, something new?" William says. "I've got something in mind for you, my friend. You got most of that blow I got you yesterday?"

"Sure do, only had time for a couple of lines. Good shit," I answer.

"Great job, Chris. Cus that blow is gunna cook up a storm in a speedball."

"A speedball?"

I am still getting used to this drug-using game. I am quite obviously a new user, because I still feel confused by the lingo and the nicknames for the various narcotics. I certainly do not know what a speedball is.

William reaches into his coat pocket and fishes around for a second. He takes out a small package of heroin wrapped in several layers of clear film.

It is about the same size as a small chicken egg and he holds it out in an open palm. I take off my sunglasses to get a better look.

"Shoot this with the blow at the same time, same needle," William explains. "Mix it together but don't over-dilute it. Half and half, more coke if you're feeling nervous.

Coke's gunna speed up your heart rate and the junk's gunna try and slow it down. It's gunna feel like your whole body is getting dry-humped by every Playboy centrefold you ever had on your wall."

I may have to Google 'how to speedball' when the time comes so I don't screw it up.

"Don't worry about cash, Chris," William says. "What you gave me yesterday will cover this. Enjoy yourself, brother."

I take the bump of heroin from his hand and put it into the inside pocket of my jacket. It feels so light and flimsy in my hand, but it contains such potency.

"Thanks," I say.

I realise that William has no chosen destination for this exchange to take place. He simply wants to keep on the move, even if it does mean making the deal in the middle of such a gridlocked street.

We move off again but only keep going for fifteen feet before stopping. The traffic is getting to William, whose fingers tap furiously on the steering wheel.

"How's the wife, Chris?" he says as he scoops some of his dishevelled hair behind his left ear. "Still committing adultery?"

I look down at my lap and imagine my wife in a sex swing with my best friend sliding his erect penis into her. Her tits are bouncing with each and every thrust and she's screaming at him, telling him to fuck her harder.

Filthy whore.

"Yeah," I say. "The bitch sure is."

William Beckford is one of only two people I have told about my wife's cheating and lies, yet now I don't know why I did in the first place. It was on a day when I was feeling particularly livid at her actions and I needed to vent. William got in the way of it, and, unfortunately for me, he isn't the best for listening or offering sound advice.

The buddy in question is Adam Phillips, and he's a self-righteous asshole. We met in high school and moved on to study law together at the same university.

He has always been around, no matter what direction I tried to take in my life, holding on to me and always wanting everything I had.

I should have noticed a lot more about his intentions when he always asked about my wife with such interest, even when we had only just started dating. The way they looked across the room at each other moments after I shared my last dance with her at our wedding. The way my wife talks about him being a 'great influence' on me and how I should strive to approach my career with the attitude he does.

I even work with Adam at the same law firm, Charleston & Green. We are both criminal defence attorneys, but I know for a fact that Adam thinks he is a much better lawyer than me.

I expect he also thinks he fucks my wife better than I ever have.

The truth is he brown-noses all of the right people and steps on the toes of everybody around him, including me, in order to get ahead at the firm.

My wife is easily pleased so she would most likely be happy with whatever Adam is packing, even if it is four inches. I hope all he has is four inches, as it would look even more ridiculous once I castrate the motherfucker.

"I don't understand why you don't do something about it," William says. "Confront her, at least. I've told you, you can't go on like this. Bottling it up won't do you any good."

I sigh and look back up at William.

"I will do something about it. I'm waiting until the time is right."

I sit back in the passenger seat, cross my arms and feel the small package of heroin press against my ribs.

I realise that I need to put it somewhere safe, so I pick my briefcase up from beneath my feet and place it in on my lap. I snap back the clasps and pull it open.

I drop the heroin into the case amongst the various paraphernalia I have amassed in the last few days. A near-empty bottle of vodka, a pair of NYPD standard issue handcuffs, a can of luminous green spray-paint, the floor plan of my apartment, a cell phone, a switchblade, painkillers, the remainder of my cocaine in a clear plastic baggie, an electric razor, two pairs of socks, a digital camera, rubber gloves, a spoon, a lighter, several packs of cigarettes and a roll of one-hundred dollar bills tightly bound together with an elastic band.

I close the briefcase and place it back at my feet. After seeing the packs of cigarettes knocking about in the case I suddenly have a craving.

"You mind if I smoke, Billy?" I ask.

"Not at all," William says.

I go back into the case, take out a cigarette from an open pack and light it up.

3

I am not a coward. I am far from afraid, especially of confronting my wife and the pompous prick Adam Phillips.

I notice that William is now driving back towards where I met him before.

"You know where I stand, Chris," William says. "With women it's all temptation and punishment. Did I ever tell you about what my first fiancée Elaine did to me?"

He has told me twice already.

"No, you didn't," I say.

He smiles broadly, obviously ecstatic that he can tell another tale from his colourful past.

"Screamin' Suzie had a 'no wives or girlfriends' policy when we were on tour. The British press has taken to calling them WAGs these days, but mainly in connection to those pussy footballers, not rock stars."

William coughs.

"It was something we adhered to for a long time, but I had just got engaged to Elaine as we were embarking on the US and Canada leg of our world tour in 1991, even though you Yanks were never big fans of Suzie.

"She came along, with the permission of management and the band, of course. It wasn't long before I realised why we had the policy in place."

I notice that the story has expanded slightly since the last time I heard it. William has set the scene with a back-story this time, explaining why Elaine was on tour with him in the first place. Perhaps he knows he has told me before and he wants to keep me interested.

"We're in Toronto, relaxing backstage after a momentous show. Some groupie chick that I've seen once or twice before wants me to sign her tits. Chris, these are fantastic puppies. I mean, some of the best I'd seen in a long while. Amazing DDs that I would have buried my face between if Elaine hadn't have been sitting right there."

I am listening attentively.

"Elaine shows her disapproval. She hurls abuse at this groupie and has to be held back by some of the roadies to stop her tearing out her hair. I tell Elaine that it's no big deal. I tell her that it happens all of the time: I'm always signing tits on tour and it's just the way it is. This sends her off, she absolutely flips out."

William laughs as he remembers the moment.

I remember the time when my wife found some pornography websites on the browser history on my laptop. Nothing too bad, just a video of a violent gang bang and some pictures of a girl mixing a fruit smoothie in her rectum.

Women can be full of wrath when they want to be. It's actually quite terrifying.

"Elaine smashes a glass against the wall and leaves, calling me every name under the sun. I'm feeling stressed, so I drink my body weight and snort a couple of grams, just to take the edge off things.

"It puts a bad spin on the entire night and the latest I can party until is 4am. I head back to the tour bus to crash, still without any sign of Elaine at all.

"I would have been worried about her if I didn't think she could probably defend herself better than I could. She always had a mean right hook."

I feel my palms getting clammy and the hairs on the back of neck prickling against my skin.

"I get onto the bus and find Elaine there. She's naked on the red leather seats, legs akimbo, and some skinny little prick standing over her with his jeans around his ankles."

I open my mouth wide.

"The ugly fucker is no older than nineteen. I recognise him as the drummer in one of the support bands. 'Hell's Dentist' or 'Hell's Orthodontist' or something dog shit like that. I remember that he couldn't keep a beat to save his scrawny ass.

"Anyway, he's got his dick in one hand and a drumstick in the other. And I shit you not Chris, Elaine has got that fucking drumstick inside of her! My fiancée has got almost the entire length of it inside her pussy."

I feel my face warp into a twisted grin. It's so contorted that it hurts my face.

"Oh shit," I say.

William does a similar grin to mine, basking in my interest. He laughs loudly and clenches his right fist together and shakes it inches from my face in an odd gesture that I don't quite understand.

"Oh shit indeed, brother," he says, his voice cutting into me. "So, I didn't wait until the time was right. I acted at that moment on instinct, like a fucking predator. The little bastard turns around, his eyes wide. He's shitting a brick.

"He loses his hard-on in an instant. His little cock wilts like a fucking dying flower."

I feel my body judder.

"I grabbed him by the throat and threw him through the windscreen of the tour bus. And my fiancée, the love of my life at that moment in time, had to have an operation to remove the drumstick from her cunt."

He stares at me in the rear-view mirror for a few seconds. I feel the blood beneath my skin rushing around and reddening my face.

I want to laugh, but I try not to.

"I thought the bitch liked it rough!" William sniggers. I erupt with laughter along with him.

William pulls the car up to the sidewalk and I notice that we are merely feet away from where he was parked earlier. He turns the key in the ignition, stopping the engine. My attempts to stop laughing aren't working, and again I am smiling widely. He sees my smile and replicates it, happy with the fact that I have been entertained by his tale.

My mind starts to wander as William begins to talk again. Something about a paramedic and something else about being blind drunk.

He is rambling now. I guess that's what happens after years of substance abuse: the connection between your conscious mind and your mouth begins to falter.

"Can you get me a gun?" I say, cutting him off.

He stops dead and turns his head to me slowly. I imagine cogs and wheels beneath his face, making his eyes move from side to side and his mouth open and close.

"What?" he says, taken aback. "Um, sure thing, pal."

He looks up at the rear-view mirror, again checking the surroundings.

I see a man sitting at the edge of the park on a bench reading a newspaper. He glances up at the Monaro a couple of times within ten seconds. He is surely within earshot of us, and despite the fact that William hasn't noticed him, I don't point him out.

I don't feel nervous of any attention from the

authorities. I'm sure that William isn't as much of a focus to the police as he hopes he is. Long gone are the days where he couldn't leave the house without persistent attention, now he's merely a dealer, common scum to the cops. Traffic offences are probably higher on their agenda.

"Not me, though," William tells me. "I know somebody who can hook you up. Let me pull some strings."

I nod, showing my gratitude. I turn and notice that the man who had been sitting on the bench has gone.

"What you gunna do?" William asks. "Kill the bloke shacking up with your missus?"

I again imagine the barrel of a gun pushed into Adam's mouth, scraping against his teeth and choking him until tears stream down his face.

"I haven't decided yet," I say.

"Well, whatever you choose to do, make sure nothing comes back to me. I've got every cop this side of the city wanting to bust me for any slip-up I make. If I get something like that pinned on me I'm fucked. No bribe I offer is gunna get a Yank pig to turn a blind eye. So, as far as you're concerned, you've never heard of William Beckford. Got it?"

I take hold of my briefcase again and bring it up to my lap. I open the passenger door slightly and feel a rush of cold air come in.

"Got it," I say without looking at William.

"I'll be in touch," he says as he starts the car again.

I get out of the Monaro and step onto the sidewalk. I close the door behind me and begin walking towards Central Park, passing a group of cyclists and a woman walking six or seven dogs.

4

The world will keep on spinning, no matter what I put into my body. While my brain does somersaults and my heart thuds like a jackhammer, everybody else continues to go about their daily business.

When I see a homeless girl, sitting in the subway station with her flea-ravaged mutt and begging for whatever small change I have in my pocket, I just walk on by. I don't want to get close enough to her to see her rotting teeth and smell the stink of her unwashed hair and piss-stained clothes.

I slump down onto a bench and put my briefcase next to me. My arms are buzzing down to the elbow and my knees are rumbling with adrenaline. Every visual is tinged with abnormal colours and movement. William was right; the speedball is making me feel good.

I look around this area of Central Park with tapered vision as my eyes screw up from the midday sun. It is busy, full of families enjoying the warm weather and workers from the city spending their lunch hour on the grass. I would have shot up here in the sunshine but I felt like some brief alone time, so I chose a public restroom stall, even though it reeked of shit. Smells don't matter when the junk hits you.

I watch the people walking by. I am captivated by their floating heads and mesmerised by their distant words which crash into my ears and splinter my brain like the force of a club hammer crashing against rotted wood.

I recognise a face in the melee. An attractive female sitting against a tree at the far edge of the park, just next to a small hump in the ground.

It's Cassandra Jones and she looks comparatively relaxed. She sits leaning back and resting her head against the bark of the tree. She has an open book balanced on her knees, her feet together. She wears the same clothes as earlier this morning but with a coral cardigan over her blouse. Her spectacles are balancing on the end of her nose as she reads.

The strange thing is that I don't even know if I followed her here or not.

For the second time today I throw up onto the ground. I lurch forward from the bench so that I am on my hands and knees and feel the hot vomit come up from my stomach and splash onto the asphalt.

I wipe away the vomit from my lips with my sleeve and realise that my sunglasses have fallen from my face. I reach down to grab them as an elderly woman strolls along, passing by and bringing one clumsy foot down onto the glasses and crushing them to bits. I see them split in two and almost scream as the lenses shatter.

I look up, my mouth wide, as the stupid old bitch who has broken my four-hundred-dollar sunglasses looks down at me in disgust. A wrinkled look of disdain that makes me want to leap up and strangle her.

She turns away from me and continues on, without an apology and without a care in her slowly darkening world.

I leap up and yelp. It isn't a word, just a noise, but it gets her attention. She turns around and faces me. I want to scream and shout at her. I want to spit in her face.

"Hey," I say. "What's the biggest problem for an atheist?"

She continues to stare at me, her eyes scratching at my skin like shards of broken glass.

"There's nobody for them to talk to during an orgasm!" I screech, following it with incessant cackling.

The sound that comes from me is like nothing I recognise. I must look like a mental hospital escapee who has somehow acquired a fifteen-hundred-dollar suit.

She raises her middle finger and flips me off before turning around and walking away.

I laugh even louder and see a teenage girl and her older boyfriend, probably in his mid-thirties, watching me, their eyes wide as if they are watching a circus freak show.

They are on the edge of their seats and I'm the fucking star. I'm the fucking bearded lady.

I may be laughing, but something is scratching at my brain and clawing at the inside of my skull. It paralyses my senses. I am in the eye of the storm and it's stirring up my paranoia. Soon I will not be able to cope.

I sit back down on the bench next to my briefcase and look frantically to find Cassandra Jones. She has moved from where she was sitting, and soon I realise that I cannot see her at all.

A bizarre, light feeling of vulnerability washes over me. But even that, at this current moment, is intoxicating for me.

I take hold of my briefcase and place it on my lap. I open it and pull out my cell phone. I give myself a few seconds for my eyes to focus on the screen. I have kept it on silent all morning, so as to avoid any unwanted distractions from my meetings with Cassandra Jones and William Beckford.

I squint at the screen and see that I have twenty-nine missed calls.

5

I stumble down the busy street, trying my best to keep on my feet despite the ground beneath them feeling as soft as marshmallow and my legs feeling like elastic bands.

I hold a strawberry milkshake in a white paper cup in my left hand and my briefcase in my right. My tie hangs loose around my neck and three buttons of my shirt are undone.

I must look like an insurance salesman after a mugging.

Or an estate agent after seven straight sleepless nights.

Or a criminal defence attorney after a morning of heavy drinking and some copious drug-using.

I see a reflection of myself in a café window. I look like a zombie. My eyes are lifeless and my skin looks an odd shade of green.

I am judged by my mistakes, never my accomplishments. But my mistakes are not purposeful acts of sabotage and hatred; they are merely consequences of consciousness. Inevitable conclusions. That fucker called fate, I suppose.

I'm looking at the ground as I crash into a robust form head-on. Initially I think I have walked into a brick wall, but as I look up I see it is a heavily-built man with tattoos on his arms and piercings on his face.

"Watch it, will ya?" he bellows at me, flecks of saliva hitting me in the face.

I move and let him pass. I watch him pushing his way through the crowd before throwing the remainder of my milkshake at him. It hits him in the back and covers his head, neck and shoulders in pale pink liquid.

I think about running but for some reason I stay exactly where I am. The punch I receive floors me and feels like it comes close to breaking my jaw, but I don't feel much pain.

I lie on my back looking up at the sky and nobody stops to check if I'm dead.

I might be. I wouldn't know the difference.

6

I sit in the dark cinema theatre and feel the dull ache of pain overtake my jaw. The drugs and drink are running out of juice and I'm returning to my sober state. I will have to sort that out as soon as possible. After the movie, of course, definitely not before as I don't want to miss the previews.

I shovel popcorn into my mouth and rest my feet on the back of the seat in front. The theatre is almost entirely empty except for a couple canoodling a few rows behind me.

I feel restless as I wait for the advertisements to vanish from the screen and the lights to dim.

In this quiet my mind begins to wander again. It's hard to put certain things away in a locked room and forget where you stashed the key. I hold the key in the palm of my hand during every waking moment of my life.

The truth is that I have no idea who I am. Maybe I did at one point in my life, or had at least convinced myself that I did, but now I don't.

I feel rage and dejection, but it's a pale and watered-down version of both.

Am I having a breakdown? I wouldn't even know if I was.

Does having thoughts of torture and murder make me sick in the head?

Does wanting to punish those who have betrayed me make me evil?

The cinema screen flickers and the advertisement changes. The bright yellow blurs my vision and I put my hand in front of my face to shield it.

I look through my fingers and see that the advertisement is telling me about the 'insane and crazy prices' of Jolene's Used Cars.

I'm not entirely sure that I can buy into that. Insane is killing another human being and wearing their skin as a coat. Crazy is drinking your own piss for health benefit. I am sure that Jolene can't compare to that.

The advertisement fades away and the lights begin to dim. The couple behind me are kissing loudly. I can hear every move of their lips and every low groan as they get horny.

If they end up fucking in here I'm gunna be pissed. Or I could make a video of it using my cell phone and then post it on the internet.

I cannot remember the last time my wife kissed me passionately. Or the last time I caressed her breasts and pulled her closer to me. I can't remember the last time my wife told me that she wanted me. I can't even remember the taste of her saliva. Or the taste of the sweat on her chest.

7

Once the sun has gone down I decide to return to my apartment. It's the last place I want to go, but I have overdone it on the intoxicants and I need to rest.

I've had myself a few more lines of dope and drunk a large amount of beer on the doorstep of a convenience store around the corner from where I live.

The walk back is a blur, and I'm dry-heaving walking up the flight of stairs to reach the floor where my home is.

I pass a middle-aged couple on the stairs and they give me a look of recognition, but I haven't got the faintest idea who they are. I wonder where they are going at this time. They should be settling down for bed, perhaps with a hot mug of cocoa or some sleeping pills. Maybe they are off to a swingers' club.

I walk down the corridor and pass a couple of doors before reaching number twenty-three. I take out my keys and look for the correct one.

The amount of keys on this bunch has grown significantly recently as they now include the keys to a storage warehouse near the Hudson River and some keys I had cut for my office, Adam Phillips' office and a small apartment I have just started to rent near Chelsea, forty minutes or so from here.

Twenty-three Melrose House is my home, however.

I find the key and turn it in the lock. Every time I do this I expect my wife to have changed the locks and thrown my belongings out of the window onto the street below.

The door swings open and the first thing I see, to my absolute joy, is the scowling face of my beautiful wife who is sitting on a black leather couch with her arms folded and her cell phone resting on her belly. She looks as though she hasn't moved from that spot in hours.

The love of my life. The apple of my eye. My beautiful and perfect Jennifer.

Her cheeks are red and her cropped black hair looks dishevelled. Perhaps from a late afternoon nap. Or from a late afternoon fuck.

I close the door behind me and move over to the kitchen counter and place my briefcase on it. I notice a tear in the leather of the case along with various bumps and scratches.

The apartment is large and open-plan. This living area is sectioned off into a sitting area, a kitchen, a dining area and an area towards the bedrooms where a pyramid-shaped water feature stands along with other side tables and a cheap-looking stone sculpture of some haggard woman (a bizarre purchase of Jennifer's). The floor is white-marble tiled and the walls are a cool grey.

Various artworks are on the walls, including an abstract oil painting that Jennifer did herself a few years back. It always gets compliments, but it's a pile of shit.

I see myself in a tall mirror on the wall. I look like I've been trawling the desert. My eyes are red and my lips are dry.

I look over at my wife and she stands up, her cell phone slipping from her stomach onto the rug beneath her feet. I haven't seen the outfit she is wearing before. I think every item of clothing she has on is brand new.

She is trying to look younger than her years and she isn't doing a great job. She wears a marine blue crop top and a pair of tight black jeans. She also has two-inch heels and I can see that her toenails are painted impeccably, a similar blue to that of her top. How quaint.

"Where the hell have you been?" she yells at me, her voice like a buzz saw. "I've been trying to call you all day."

I say nothing and adjust my loose tie in the mirror. I pull the knot tight until it is tidy again.

"You knew Robert was briefing the new case today," she continues. "He's furious that you weren't there. You didn't even call to explain. What are you playing at?"

Jennifer has yet to use my name. In fact, she rarely does anymore. Perhaps it is to depersonalise me. Maybe she does feel guilt and that's her way of dealing with it.

I look away from the mirror and walk into the sitting area. I walk past her and notice she is also wearing a new perfume. The familiar springtime scent has been replaced by something far more exotic. I sit down in one of the reclining chairs and lean back. My spine aches, but it is nothing in comparison to the constant throbbing of my jaw.

I know I probably need to get to the emergency room, but right now I really cannot face hours in a waiting room surrounded by broken noses, shattered collar bones and genital tears.

Jennifer stands over me with her hands on her hips.

"You're a fucking stranger to me," she snaps. "I don't know what you're thinking. All this bullshit, day after day, it's ridiculous."

I breathe in deeply. The air smells like sweat and semen.

Adam has been here, there's no fucking doubt about it. I expect he has screwed my wife on the three-thousand-dollar couch. Human sweat will make the leather fade and crack, then the couch will be beyond repair.

"You're going to lose your job! You're so fucking pathetic."

I imagine them going at it on one of the kitchen worktops. Jennifer used to like the feel of the cold granite against her naked skin.

I imagine Adam shooting his load over the spot where I will prepare my breakfast tomorrow morning.

"You're an embarrassment!"

I imagine Jennifer riding Adam on the fur rug down by the decorative fireplace. She's screaming as she slams her thighs down onto him and begs for him to orgasm.

"… a fucking loser!"

I imagine them in the bedroom on the red velvet antique chair. She is lying back and he is on his knees, thrusting into her so her head bangs against the back of the chair.

It's a chair that cost me almost four grand from a boutique in Paris during our honeymoon. It cost a fair few dollars to get it shipped here too.

"… can't take this anymore!"

She used to like to give me head in the shower. I'll admit, she did look good with wet hair and my cock in her mouth. Now I expect she does the same for him.

"… even listening to me, you bastard?"

She used to like to have sex while standing up against the window overlooking the streets, her breasts pressing against the glass.

"… hate you! I fucking hate you!"

And out on the balcony while it rained, the raindrops splashing against her ass when I spanked her hard.

"… give up with us! I give up with you!"

Her arms are floundering around. She looks preposterous. How did I ever love this woman?

She leans in close and shouts, her hot breath on my face and specks of her spit hitting me in the eyes.

"Say something! You're clearly intoxicated!"

I clench my fists and jolt forwards.

"Intoxicated?" I bawl. "With what, honey? Despair? Hatred? Desire? Or just good old drink and dope? It sure isn't love, baby."

Jennifer backs away from me, her face white and her mouth wide. Her hands have come up next to her face and she is doing her best to feign fear.

"Why are you talking like that?" she says, starting to sob. "I don't understand where this marriage went wrong. I'm done!"

It's something that she has said to me countless times.

It went wrong the moment she decided to jump in

bed with Adam. If only she knew how it was that I found out, she'd feel so stupid. The secretive and deceptive streak in my wife was well and truly exposed that day. It felt like everything I had ever suspected of her came rushing out into reality like a nightmare given life.

"I give up with us!" Jennifer screeches and her voice crackles. "It's over, Chris!"

She uses my name at last. It sounds foreign and peculiar as it falls from her lips.

Never before has she said those words to me. We have been hanging on the edge of destruction for so long, yet neither of us has ever given it that push. For her to tell me it's over, after everything she has done to me, makes every ounce of muscle in my body throb with rage.

They may be words that I came to terms with long ago, but I have never heard them spoken in the dead and cold air.

It's over.

I lean back in my chair and close my eyes. I see the obsequious smile of Adam Phillips.

"I don't want you anymore," Jennifer says, calmer now. "I don't love you. You're a joke."

I open my eyes and lean forwards. Jennifer steps forwards.

I imagine her pulling a knife and stabbing me in the neck, slashing first but then plunging it deep. I imagine a geyser of blood spraying across her brand new clothes.

I imagine the homicide detectives examining the scene and calling my murder a 'crime of passion'. Jennifer will lie about how I made her life a prison and controlled her with sexual violence, and no doubt she'll walk free.

"Talking of which," I say, "I heard a joke today."

Jennifer slaps me across the face hard and fast. It stings and makes my whole face go numb. I see the instant stain of regret on her face.

I bring my hand up and hold my face. Pain spreads across it, warm and pacifying. This is the very first act of violence that has occurred between Jennifer and me. Never before has one of us raised a hand to the other.

Women, as well as men, initiate domestic violence. However, 90% of men who suffer at the hands of it will never tell anybody about it.

The main reason for this, of course, is embarrassment. There's nothing that does a decent job of symbolically castrating a man better than admitting you're getting hit around by your wife or girlfriend.

I should hurt her for all she has done to me.

I should make her scream.

I should make her cry.

I should make her beg.

I should grab hold of her face and push my thumbs into her eye sockets until blood streams down her face.

I slump back into the chair and close my eyes once more.

"I can't be around you anymore," Jennifer says, her voice sounding distant, like she is on the end of a bad telephone line. "I'm going to stay with Angela."

I say nothing. I hear her walk away from me and move towards the bedroom. I hear her heels on the hard flooring and then soft carpet of the bedroom before she slams the door.

She is talking to herself, venting her anger as she no doubt packs a bag.

I am glad she has decided to leave, even though I know that she will be back. If she does want this marriage to end, she wants me to do it. That way she can avoid all blame and absolve herself.

A few minutes pass before I hear the bedroom door open and listen to the tap of my wife's heels again on the tiled floor. I open my eyes a couple of millimetres and see her walking towards the front door with a large holdall in her hand. Her handbag is hanging from one shoulder and she has put on a dark denim jacket. She doesn't look back at me at all. She stares straight ahead, her hair bobbing up and down.

She leaves the apartment and I take a deep breath. I take out a cigarette and light it. I hold the smoke in from my first drag for almost thirty seconds before letting it out. My head goes light and the pain in my jaw pounds like a kid banging a toy against a wall.

Vengeance is fragile.

Vengeance is cold.

My marriage has been soaked in gasoline and a match has been struck and dropped into it. It has been left to blacken and bubble until it is no longer recognisable as something I once knew.

Jennifer has finally plucked up the courage to walk out on me.

Courage, something that is just as fragile as vengeance.

The human condition is sickening. We all fall into the same hole and struggle to get out. I am not perfect. I am far from it, but it is the fault of my wife that I have become the person I am today.

She has shaped me into this man. It is probably the only thing I should be thankful to her for.

We manifest our pain into many sins and vices; it's just the way we are. That doesn't mean we shouldn't be subject to the penalty for our actions. We live in a world where something as simple as lust can exhibit itself as sexual addiction, fornication, bestiality, rape and incest.

My wife has simply become engulfed by adultery. This has and will in turn, push me to commit unspeakable acts. Acts that I will not proud of by any means.

I am not a fantasist; I would see myself as more of a realist. I cannot live with the hand I have been dealt; it doesn't seem fair. I don't believe in fate: I believe we are all in control of our own destinies. Now that may sound like a line you've heard in a crappy daytime TV drama or a low budget action flick, but trust me, it's entirely true.

I should commit myself to the seven holy virtues

rather than these sins. Chastity, temperance, charity, diligence, patience, kindness and humility.

Who the fuck am I kidding? I won't be doing that anytime soon, because they don't mean shit to me.

THE THIRD TALE - VALIDATE

1

Repetition numbs the human brain to a state of uncompromised slush.

Once you see the same sights and hear the same sounds every day they become dull and meaningless, and so horrifically familiar that a tedious haze surrounds you.

I am awake at the same time every morning. I eat the same breakfast of scrambled eggs and granary toast. I listen to the same radio shows hosted by the same monotone-voiced Irishman. I wear the same colour tie and wear the same fragrance splashed on my neck and wrists. Today, I wait for the same bus with the same driver to take me across town.

I am back to my usual routine. Yesterday's destination has made way for a journey to my office at the Charleston & Green law firm, no doubt to face the wrath of my superior Robert Morrison, an attorney with over thirty years in the profession.

He is somebody who has mentored me in my years at the firm and stuck by me when I made controversial and hazardous decisions. My blatant disregard for the integrity of the firm, him and myself will come into question.

The case Robert was briefing yesterday was a defence for the young son of a wealthy property developer who had been accused of kidnapping a nine-year-old girl and keeping her at his residence against her will for over twelve hours.

As far as I'm aware, no allegation of sexual abuse or physical assault is in place, but never-the-less it doesn't seem like something I want to be part of. If Robert chooses me to represent the pervert I will have no choice. It is my job after all.

I am well and truly stuck in a rut in regards to my marriage and my job. It's tough to get out of it when you get there. Drastic action needs to be taken.

Last night was the first I have spent alone since I can remember. Sure, every night for the last few months Jennifer and I have slept in the same bed, but there has been such distance that she may as well have not been there at all. She would shrink away from me if I got too close and always be up and out of bed before I awoke.

I never miss her when I am away from her.

Right now, I am finding it hard to remember the exact vision of her face at all.

2

I go to a convenience store less than a block away from my workplace. Just before I go inside a middle-aged black man passes me, preaching the word of the Lord at the top of his lungs.

I step inside, walk up to the cash desk and look at the back wall for my favourite cigarettes.

The clerk standing opposite me looks me up and down, her top lip raised slightly. She looks about thirty. She isn't obese but she is quite heavy-set with thick curly hair and freckles.

She wears a red polo shirt with a nametag attached just above her left breast. It reads 'Katie'.

I see this clerk almost every morning and she always gives me the same look. She turns away and takes a pack of cigarettes from a low shelf and places them on the counter without me saying a word. She doesn't need to, because I buy the same thing every time I come in here. She leans to her left and grabs a pack of peppermint gum and puts it on top of the cigarettes.

She stares at me with dead eyes. Her face is filled with disinterest. Misery is crawling beneath her skin.

Repetition numbs the senses and blurs the faces of everybody until their features become pixelated.

"And a bottle of vodka," I say.

She turns around slowly and takes the smallest bottle of cheap-branded Polish vodka from a high shelf that is lined with cheap booze.

"Bigger than that," I grin.

She sighs deeply and grabs the next size up. I nod in agreement and pay her. She counts out my change slowly and puts it in my hand. I feel the cold sweat on her fingertips as our hands come together.

I turn away from her and walk towards the exit. I see a small glass panel on the wall; beneath it is stencilled black lettering stating 'BREAK IN CASE OF FIRE'.

I stop next to it and thrust my elbow into it, smashing it inwards. I feel shards of glass bouncing off my face.

The alarm sounds almost instantaneously. It screams and whirs, tearing into my eardrums. I walk out of the shop, clenching my teeth and trying my best not to burst into uncontrollable laughter.

3

I walk into the lobby of Charleston & Green and begin to clock the odd looks from my colleagues. Some young skinny and unattractive bitch (Judy? Julie?) coming out of the elevator looks at me as if she's heard a rumour that I worship the devil.

A balding middle-aged man (Greg? Graham?) looks at me as if he's heard that I'm facing a charge for an alleged rape. I see a Chinese woman in her thirties, somebody who is usually very friendly to me and tells me about her children, avoiding my gaze and walking past me swiftly.

I take the elevator up to the second floor and progress into the offices, passing desks and seeing that everybody is looking hard at paperwork or computer monitors – doing anything they can to avoid an exchange with me.

I take a corner and walk down a corridor. I don't see another person until I reach a room just before my office.

My secretary, a girl in her early twenties who has worked for me a few weeks, sits at her desk and stares at her hands as she applies colour to her fingernails. I told her not to do that at her desk.

There is something alluring about her, and while I have absolutely no intention of having sex with her, I look down at myself to check that I look presentable.

The charcoal grey suit fits me flawlessly and my shoes are polished to perfection. I notice a few minuscule shards of glass on my arm, which I brush off. This movement catches her eye and she looks up at me.

She looks at me wide-eyed for around three seconds and quickly packs away the bottle of nail varnish into her desk drawer. She then gets up awkwardly, banging her legs against the underside of her desk as she does so. She stands up straight, almost as if I am an army general coming to inspect her living quarters. She brushes herself down and begins to shake her hands in an attempt to dry the violet enamel on her nails.

She is very good at taking care of the way she looks, which pleases me very much. Not only because it is enjoyable to look at her, but also because it strikes me that she takes this job seriously. If she turned up to work here wearing slacks and a hockey jersey, I may not be able to stop myself slapping her around the head.

Today she is wearing a coral-coloured dress that is cut just above the knee. Over it she wears a formal white cardigan, which is buttoned low enough so that I can see the curves of her modest bust. Her skin is golden brown and her chocolate brown hair hangs in majestic curls to a little below her shoulders.

"Good morning, Chloe," I say.

She smiles gawkily, revealing her slightly large teeth. One fault perhaps, but her striking green eyes make up for that. I watch the beauty spot above her lip as her smile recedes.

"Chris... Mr Morgan," she says. "You're here, I mean,

you're back. I wasn't expecting you."

"Any messages?" I ask.

She bends down to her desk and moves some papers around. She looks up at me and shrugs her shoulders. She smiles again.

"Quite a few actually," she says. "This place almost fell apart without you here. I've got them all written down somewhere... let me see."

I step forwards and I can smell Chloe's perfume, despite standing almost six feet away from her. I imagine that smell on my bed sheets and pillow.

"I'll be in my office," I tell her.

She stops searching her desk and stands up straight again. She raises her hand and extends her index finger.

"There was one important thing," she says softly. "Robert, um, Mr Morrison asked me to tell you he wanted to see you as soon as you arrived. Um, *if* you arrived."

She swallows and clasps her hands together at her waist.

"Right," I say, coming even closer to her. "I can tell from your face that I'm in the shit. Correct?"

She doesn't say a word. She simply widens her eyes even more, tightens her lips and nods.

"It's not my place to say," she says, clearly embarrassed.

With everything going on around me, the hassle of receiving an ear-bashing from my boss and the possibility of disciplinary action, which would result in the loss of respect in my position in the company, would be an inconvenience.

But yesterday needed to happen, regardless of the repercussions.

I must imagine the face of Cassandra Jones in my head during everything Robert Morrison says to me. She is my silver lining. She is my oasis on the horizon. She is my fucking angel.

"Take the morning off," I say to Chloe as I turn

around. "Go shopping or something, buy some shoes. Get some coffee and relax."

I hear her mutter a response, but I cannot make out exactly what she says.

There is a good chance I will never see her again.

4

I feel the hairs on my wrists prickling up and my knuckles twitching. Never before have I been so close to murdering somebody, and it could be either of the two men sitting in this room with me now.

I am using all of my self-control to stop myself smashing in the skulls of these bastards.

Robert Morrison's words are patronising and cringe-worthy. Each sentence he constructs makes me want to tear my eyes out with my bare hands.

However, it is the person sitting directly next to me who is making my skin crawl all over my body like a layer of wriggling maggots. So close that I can smell the wax in his hair and the mint of the mouthwash he used this morning. Possibly to get the taste of my wife's sexual fluids from his mouth.

Adam Phillips sits in a wooden chair to my left, one leg resting on the other and his hands together on his thigh. He is wearing a similar suit to me, although the grey of the material is slightly darker. The knot in his black tie is fastened amateurishly and his black hair is over-styled and thick with product.

I wonder how long he spent in front of the mirror retouching it and making sure not one part of it was out of place.

His face is clean-shaven and smooth. It makes his face look ridiculous as his large chin protrudes every time he talks. His earlobes are enormous and hang at the sides of his head like fleshy jewellery.

We are sitting in Robert Morrison's office. He sits

opposite us and he has been talking for a few minutes.

Robert is almost sixty years old. A veteran at Charleston & Green and the person who oversees every single case that this firm takes on. He makes sure that it is in the company's best interests, both financially and in terms of image, to represent certain clients and make sure the values of the business are presented correctly.

But, all in all, Robert Morrison is a miserable old cunt.

He leans forwards onto his desk that separates us, his hands linked together. The liver spots on his skin make me want to throw up. He peers at me with cold eyes through his round spectacles.

With each word he says, his white moustache quivers on his top lip. It is stained at the edges with nicotine.

This office is almost three times the size of mine. It is decorated in light colours, pastel blues and cooling whites. It is minimalist, as if furbished by a designer with a love for over-simplicity and an abundance of storage solutions.

I am certain that Robert hasn't overseen the design of this office. He is as old-fashioned and strait–laced as they come. He is the human embodiment of woodchip wallpaper and linoleum flooring.

The wall behind Robert is mounted with a sizeable oak display cabinet. Framed photos and certificates of Robert's achievements line the top shelf, while expensive bottles of various alcoholic spirits sit below. Cognacs, Scotch whiskies and the like.

There is a framed golf club mounted near the bottom of the cabinet. It is a putter that belonged to a certain golf pro I have never heard of. I know this because he has told me on countless occasions about the moment he met his sporting 'idol' at some gala dinner.

Right now I am tempted to walk over to the cabinet, kick the glass inwards, take out the club and smack it around Robert's head.

His face is almost purple as he continues to rant at me. A plastic plant in the corner of the office catches my eye, something green and rubber that is pretending to be something it is not and can never hope to be.

I drift back into the conversation as I see Adam crossing his arms. He is nodding along to each and every word Robert says, agreeing with him like a faithful dog. I imagine the brown-nosing prick on his hands and knees, acting as Robert's footstool.

"It's just unacceptable, Christopher," Robert says. "Never in all of my years at this firm have I witnessed such blatant disregard for a client. In fact, you've let your colleagues down even more so."

I scratch my nose and fix my stare onto the top of Robert's balding head.

"But you know me, Christopher," Robert continues. "I'm an understanding man. I'm giving you a chance to explain yourself. I'm giving you a chance to give me a decent reason as to why you went AWOL on such an important day for this firm and why you didn't call into explain your absence."

I don't say a word. I can see Robert's lips twitching. He wants to strangle me just as much as I want to strangle him. I wonder how far I can push him before he decides to leap over his desk.

"You know exactly what my values are. Professionalism at Charleston & Green is number one, without a doubt. As far as I was aware, before yesterday's fiasco you felt exactly the same. This is completely out of character, Chris."

Again I don't say anything. I am completely still. My chest doesn't even move as I breathe.

"Jesus Christ," Robert says, anger now tainting his voice. "Do you not have anything at all to say for yourself?"

I stare into his eyes for a few seconds before opening my mouth.

"Not really," I say. "I was just having a bad day, I guess."

Robert clenches his teeth together.

"You are not bigger than this firm, Chris!" he shouts, rising out of his chair and pointing a finger at me.

I turn and look at Adam who is looking down at his lap. I'm sure I can see a glimmer of a smile.

Robert sits back down and sighs heavily.

"I have no idea what is going on with you," he says. "But this case needs stability. Do you have any idea what it took to secure it? And what rides on it?"

I do not get a chance to answer these questions. Robert continues after taking a split second to intake breath.

"After all the work we've put in to building a defence, you have the audacity to put the success of the case in jeopardy with a reckless thing like a vanishing act. Who do you think you are?"

I once again look over at Adam. I can definitely see a smirk building in his face. I'll wipe the grin off that slimy fucker's lips. I shrug my shoulders. I know that this appears arrogant and I can see Robert's teeth clenching together.

Robert is a common man of money with no other redeeming features. He doesn't have the looks or personality to get by. He has relied on hard work and a pathetic ruthlessness to get to the status he is at today. All the while making no true friends and being used by women who want to live the lifestyle that comes with him but aren't willing to make an actual connection.

He does little to help himself. He is not a victim, that's for sure. I know from my time working with him that he's a fucking bore, and he does nothing to steer away from that. Talking to him for more than thirty seconds about anything other than this law firm will leave you wanting to jump out of the nearest window and hoping that you are at least three storeys up so the impact kills you and not merely renders you paraplegic.

He wasn't always like this. When I first met him he

was quite the opposite, humorous and easy-going. It was almost as if I watched him decay and fall apart like dry rot from the moment I started my career at this firm.

"You won't be working on this case from today onwards," Robert says. "I can't risk the client being further disappointed. Charleston & Green need this, I need this. I had faith in you, Chris, but obviously I'm naïve."

When you venture into a career such as a criminal defence attorney, taking the higher ground and obeying your principles before anything else is completely disregarded. While I am far from a saint, the revolution that is happening within me could do without representing the paedophile son of a rich tycoon and trying to keep the little prick out of jail.

I'd rather lose my job. I'd rather allow Adam Phillips, who has already fucked me over in every way possible, to become the saviour and step in.

Adam looks over at me. He has fucked my wife and now he is about to fuck me. I clench my fists and feel the veins in my neck throbbing hard.

"Adam will take the reins," Robert continues. "He knows the case inside-out; I have every confidence that he can do the job well. More importantly, I can trust him to put the best interests of the client ahead of his own."

I doubt that very much. I cannot recall a moment in Adam's life where he has put somebody else before himself. He wouldn't piss on somebody on fire because he wouldn't want his shrivelled penis out in public. He'd watch them burn to keep his modesty.

Before today, I have always been superior in the company to Adam. He hasn't earned this chance. I have given it to him on a silver platter and he shouldn't be smug with himself at all. I am in control.

I have given it to him and I can take it away. All that Adam's future holds is pain; I can assure him of that. He will never get promoted at this firm, regardless of the outcome of this case. He will continue to wallow in his own filth and greed until the gangling arms of Hell come up into this world and drag his lowly form into the depths, teeth gnawing at his skin and tearing it away to reveal his true form. A coward, a fraud and a traitor.

He can flounder around in the lowest circle and wait there until I decide to join him.

Robert can tell that my mind has wandered and he slams his fist on the desk.

"I swear to God, Chris, any more behaviour like that and you are finished at this firm!"

I know that Robert hasn't had sex with his wife for years. He may be able to satisfy her financially, but he cannot do that for her sexually. While divorcing him may not be the best move for her, living with Robert turns her life into such a bland existence that money and security no longer appear at the top of her list.

His wife is sleeping with other men behind his back, no doubt, but that doesn't satisfy her in the way she wants. It isn't just the sex; it's the excitement that comes with it. The way it makes butterflies flutter in her stomach and her tongue go dry.

The adultery she is committing is different from what Jennifer is indulging in. In a way, I can understand the actions of Robert Morrison's other half, but for my wife, she just wants to cause me pain and break me down into nothing.

She doesn't care about being happy because she knows that she cannot achieve that with Adam. She is chaotic, almost as much as I am, in her train of thought.

She may have had a plan at one point, but she sabotaged it long ago. Now all that is left is me, watching from afar.

I don't believe that adultery is the ultimate sin. Sometimes it is warranted, no matter how selfish it may seem.

Jennifer and Adam are hedonistic and malicious, and it is for these reasons that I will not even consider forgiveness.

"Do you understand what I am saying?" Robert says.

I look up at him and rub my chin with my hand.

I want to tell him that I don't. I want to tell him everything I think of him and that I don't blame his wife for seeking out sex with younger men and acting out all of her sexual fantasies because he can't get it up.

I want to tell him that, if given the chance, I would fuck his wife and make him watch. I would want to see the loathing in his face as I make his wife scream in ecstasy.

"I do," I say.

Robert Morrison is stressed. I am his stress ball — to be squeezed in his hand.

He's the fucking projector, not me.

I'd be surprised if he still knows how to use his dick. I imagine him lying on his side in bed next to his wife, shame swathing him. Perhaps he even sheds a tear in these moments, realising that his inability to please his wife is another step towards inevitable death.

"I want you to take a leave of absence for two weeks," Robert says, earnestness in his voice. "Get your head together and sort out whatever it is that's bothering you. See a doctor, see a shrink; I don't care what you do. Just come back into this office in fourteen days with a clear head. I won't stand for any more of this bullshit, Chris. You'll be out on your ass."

I cannot predict where I will be in fourteen days. I know for sure that I will not be in this office grovelling to Robert Morrison and assuring him I have changed.

5

"Buddy, you need to be careful. You're gunna get yourself fired. Robert isn't fucking about with this. He hit the roof yesterday; I've never seen anything like it. You need to be careful from now on."

Adam's words of advice mean nothing to me. To the

untrained eye, he is a caring friend, looking out for me and trying his best to recommend the best option for my situation.

It's all another layer in his cloak. A cloak built up so elaborately that nobody can see through it to what lies beneath. Well, nobody but me.

"Where were you yesterday?" he asks.

We are standing a few feet away from the closed door of Robert's office, next to a water cooler, as people walk past, a few of them craning their necks to get a second look at me. Word of my absence yesterday must have got around quick.

A phone rings at somebody's desk about fifteen feet away and I long for somebody to answer it. The dull tone makes my stomach coil up.

I look down at my shoes and bite my lip. Every ounce of me is resisting the urge to hit Adam hard in the balls with the back of my hand.

"I had a few things I needed to do," I say.

This is the truth. My meeting with Cassandra could not have waited until another day; it had to happen then, no doubt about it.

There was a time when my career was everything. It was more important to me than my health, my relationship and even my happiness. Now that couldn't be further from the truth.

It lies at the bottom of a stinking pit, underneath a pile of resentment. It is no longer vital in any way.

"Shit, Chris," Adam says as he places a plastic cup beneath the bulk of the water cooler. "After all of the work we've put into the Ramirez case, you just don't turn up? This was gunna be your moment. Stepping up and getting that kid off was really gunna put this place on the map."

I really wish he wouldn't preach to me. I don't give a fuck. He's the last person who should be deriding my intelligence this way.

"Some things in this world are more important than creating intricate lies to prove somebody isn't a paedophile," I say coldly as I fill up a cup with water myself. "Throw him to the fucking lions."

Adam looks at me with a blank face.

"But that's what this job is about, Chris," he says. "You've managed to help a lot more unsavoury characters avoid some jail time in the past. What's different about Ramirez?"

"I just... I wouldn't expect you to understand," I say, drinking the contents of the plastic cup in one go.

The cold water shocks my body and makes me breathe heavily. I cannot remember the last time I drank something that wasn't alcoholic. I blink hard and shake my head.

"You don't seem yourself," Adam says. "I'm worried about you, buddy. I know you care about your career and I know you care about his firm. Something just isn't right."

This fucker doesn't care about me. He doesn't think about my well-being when he ejaculates into the face of my wife. He doesn't worry about how I am feeling when he is cleaning the residue from his penis of the lubrication he used while penetrating her in the anus.

"Are things getting worse with Jennifer?" he asks, not one muscle in his face flinching as he mentions her name.

I remember telling him about Jennifer and me drifting apart, back when I thought that she may have been seeing somebody behind my back. It was a time when I had the pieces of the puzzle in my hands but I hadn't put them together correctly.

I wonder if questioning me about my relationship gives Adam any sort of enjoyment. Even if it does, I won't let him revel in it.

I decide to make him as awkward as possible. I want to see him squirm like the eel he is as I lay it on thick. Up until now, I haven't given him any sort of sign that I am losing my cool. Sure, my relationship is in the gutter but

I'm not shitting razor blades about it.

I drop my empty cup and bring both of my hands up to my face. I groan loudly like I am physically in pain, perhaps with crippling stomach cramps. I screw my eyes up and gurn, my mouth upturning and my bottom teeth jutting out.

"It's terrible, Adam," I wail as I begin to create fabricated sobs. "Jennifer can't even stand to look at me anymore and I can barely even look at myself. I've fucked up my marriage and I don't know what to do."

I open my eyes slightly as I feel tears smear down my cheeks. I use my fingers to spread them down my face to emphasize them. I am good at this.

"I'm going to lose her, I know it. I'm so scared, Adam. She's screwing somebody behind my back and there's nothing I can do about it. I'm losing my fucking mind."

I see that Adam isn't reacting as I perhaps hoped he would. He is biting his bottom lip and looking at me with the face of a concerned friend, but nothing more.

I want to see the guilt in his eyes. I want to make him sweat.

I drop to my knees and sob even louder. I grab hold of his trousers at the knee like a slave desperate for mercy from his master. My head hangs low and the tears drop from my face onto the carpet below.

"Help me, Adam," I screech. "I'm a wreck. I can't take it anymore."

Adam looks around the office, seemingly embarrassed by my actions. He is troubled more by how he looks to his colleagues than my welfare. He speaks to me but doesn't look down at me, his eyes darting around.

"Come on, buddy, get up. Jennifer would never be unfaithful to you. You guys may be having some problems but she loves you."

If he calls me 'buddy' one more time I'm gunna smash his teeth in.

"She doesn't fucking love me," I whimper pathetically. "I don't think she ever has. Why else would she do this to me?"

Adam tries to pull me to my feet by grabbing me around the arms.

I resist and fall even further down onto the ground, my hands on the floor and my knees rubbing along the carpet.

"Chris, you know I'm no good with the marriage advice," Adam says while placing a hand on my back. "All I can say is that marriages have problems, but you have to do your best to work through them. Don't give up, Jennifer is worth it."

She really fucking isn't.

I have to try and stop myself from laughing in Adam's face. It's hilarious that he is trying to give me advice on my marriage when he is the one that fucked it up in the first place. It's a little like an incompetent terrorist trying to disarm a bomb that he planted.

"If she's cheating on me, I'll kill her," I say as I look up at Adam.

This grabs his attention. Now he is looking down at me and I see his pupils dilate.

He is giving himself away without saying a word. I can now see the guilt as clear as day on his gawping face.

"I swear to God, I'll kill her. And I'll kill the rat bastard she is cheating on me with. I fucking mean it."

Adam helps me to my feet and steadies me. I wipe away the tears from my swollen face with the sleeve of my jacket.

I don't think I expected any sort of confession or admission of blame from Adam. He's not that kind of man and, even if he was, that would throw everything out of sync and my redemption would be significantly delayed.

Adam would not risk putting himself in the line of fire. He would prefer to sit back and reap the rewards of his wrongdoings without facing them head-on.

I will teach him the meaning of consequences.

"Take these two weeks and do what you can to work this out," Adam says. "See a marriage counsellor, I dunno. Spend as much time as you can with Jenny. Maybe even take a trip together somewhere. It could help."

Every word that comes from his mouth validates my reasons for wanting him dead. Never before have I heard somebody other than her mother and I call her Jenny. Her friend Angela would call her it on occasion, but very rarely. Somebody incredibly close to her only uses it and Adam is giving himself away so obviously that I feel like a fool as I continue to play along.

I wonder how far the relationship between Adam and my wife has gone.

Are they in love?

Are they planning to tell me eventually?

Will they just move away without a word to avoid conflict?

"You need a cigarette," Adam says and takes one from a pack in his trouser pocket. "Let's go outside."

I look into his eyes and see a minuscule reflection of my face. I look swollen like a balloon, ready to pop at any moment and cover Adam's suit in brain matter and tiny shards of my skull.

"Chin up, Chris," Adam says. "Everything's gunna be all right."

I don't need a cigarette, I need deliverance, but that seems isolated in my head, surrounded by an ocean of agony that I need to fight my way through.

I am not yet fully equipped to take this on. A man with a task, no matter what size, is only as good as his tools.

I will have to wait for salvation, but I am patient, so, for now, I'll take a cigarette.

6

The end of the cigarette lights up and I take back. Smoke billows from the end and gets in my eyes, drying them out and causing me to screw them up. I cough, as my throat is even drier than my eyes.

A simple cigarette feels like it is tearing me apart. Perhaps it is the constant abuse of substances that is finally taking its toll on me.

I've been taking more drugs in these last few months than I have previously in my entire life. I'm catching up on lost time. Lost time wasted on careers, apartments and lovers.

William Beckford puts his lighter into his coat pocket and watches as I cough and splutter, smiling like an ecstatic child.

I rub my eyes and clear my throat. The smoke no longer hurts but soothes, as it usually does. The sweet grasp of nicotine holds me close, filling my lungs with black treacly tar.

I stand in the middle of William Beckford's small apartment kitchen, just over an hour having passed since I left my office at Charleston & Green, taking a few items from my desk drawers as I did so. Everybody watched me as I made my way out of the building, nattering quietly amongst themselves and debating about whether I had been fired or not.

There is a strange stale smell in the air; a mixture of a few things makes it fairly unpleasant to be standing in this cluttered and cramped kitchen. There's a frying pan on a hob at the other side of the room, filled almost to the brim with old bacon fat. It has turned yellow and solidified. A chrome bin stands in the corner, overflowing with trash that has been piled so high it seems impossible that is hasn't toppled. Cigarette packets, beer bottles and heaps of waste food threaten to fall onto the floor if disturbed even slightly.

The floor is sticky beneath my feet, the bottom of my shoe detaching itself from the linoleum with a gluey tear accentuates every move I make.

This kitchen probably hasn't been cleaned properly in years and I can't imagine William ever pulling on a pair of rubber gloves and giving the floor a good scrub.

This is probably why he never seems to wash his hair. Now that I think about it, the same stale smell that fills this kitchen is what fills my nose every time I meet with him. I thought it may have been his car, but now I realise that's the only thing William seems to keep clean.

I guess drug dealing does a lot to you, even if you used to be a rock star with women falling at your feet. It's a slippery slope and Billy Beckford has been on it for a long time.

"You've been overdoing it, brother," William says. "Choking on the fags is a definite sign of that."

William turns around and walks out of the kitchen. He is wearing a bright red bathrobe that is tied at the waist and matching slippers on his feet. On the back of the robe is a stitched image of a snarling bulldog holding a British flag. The dog is chomping on a lit cigar, which hangs at an angle from its jaws.

William still wears his sunglasses in the dull light with his lank hair slipped behind his ears.

We move into the living area of the small apartment. It's no bigger than twelve feet across and is stuffed with too much furniture for such a tiny space.

On each side of the room is a two-seater couch, both completely different in style and shape. A lounging chair sits next to one of them, the leather faded from black to a cracked grey.

There is a low, square coffee table in the centre of the room that seems to act as a makeshift dining table for William, as it is stacked with dirty plates, pizza boxes and yet more beer bottles. There is a chest of drawers in the corner that would surely belong in a bedroom; two of the drawers are missing and it is stacked with an enormous amount of junk, including a laptop with a broken screen, a few books, a huge glass bong and several cartons of Marlboro cigarettes.

The walls are discoloured and uneven. A few things hang on them, including framed gold discs of two Screamin' Suzie albums. There is also a black and white photograph of William with his band-mates standing in front of a colossal tour bus. They all have their hands up in the air and seem to be whooping with delight.

William looks exactly the same, not seeming to have aged a day in almost twenty years, and I think he is still wearing exactly the same sunglasses as in the picture.

The entire room is strewn with debris. The floor can barely be seen beneath clothes, newspapers, magazines and other waste. The couches are the same, with trousers hanging off the back and shirts balled up in piles. One has a bass guitar lying across it, although three of the strings are missing, leaving a solitary string looking lonely across the fret board.

William lights his own cigarette as he turns to me.

"I would say I'm sorry about the mess," he says, "but I fucking ain't!"

He laughs and knocks some clothes from the couch and onto the floor. He sits down in the cleared space and puts his feet up on the edge of the coffee table, the only edge that seems to be free of clutter.

I stand gawkily in the doorway, wondering where I will be able to sit down. I worry about sitting in something that will stain my jacket or treading in something that will ruin my shoes.

"Sit down, mate," William says as he takes back again on his cigarette, flicking the ash from the end of it onto his robe.

I feel my skin crawling simply from being in a room where there is so much mess.

"Just move some shit from that sofa," he says,

nodding at the couch closest to me.

I wait a few seconds and take two steps towards it, stubbing out the last of my cigarette on the wall when William isn't looking at me.

The bass guitar is across several black bags filled to bursting, which I try to pull out from underneath it. The instrument almost falls to the ground but I manage to grab it by the neck as William leaps up from his chair with a distressed yelp.

"Careful with that!" William says firmly. "That's a vintage Rickenbacker!"

I shake my head as I stand it up against the wall, cautiously making sure it stays propped up.

"It's got one string," I say in bewilderment.

"I know," William says, shrugging his shoulders. "It's not the strings that make it a vintage instrument; you can put any shitty ones on it. But the body, the craftsmanship, the beauty. You can't recreate or mass-produce something like that, it's a one-off."

I move the black bags onto the floor and create a flat area on the couch big enough for me to sit down on.

"Then why keep it laid across the couch with all this other shit?" I ask. "Have it mounted on the wall in a glass cabinet or at least in a protective case somewhere out of sight."

William sits back down before putting out his cigarette on the arm of the couch. I cringe at the sight of this as I sit down myself. My back is almost completely straight as I refuse to lean all the way back.

"Oh, Christopher," William says. "You bother yourself with these incessant insignificances. You don't have to conform to something you read in *Good Housekeeping* magazine or saw on a home makeover show. Just let what needs to be... well, be. Y'know what I'm saying, brother?"

I don't think I will ever be able to fully understand William Beckford. He has experienced too much of the world for me to be able to label him simply. His personality appears to be labyrinthine, despite appearing quite straightforward on the surface.

Although I haven't known him for long enough to consider him a good friend, I know that he is loyal and honest. He would never go behind my back and jump into bed with my wife, as Adam has. In fact, I expect he would rather castrate himself than deceive me as he holds certain values that he expects to be adhered to amongst men, even though he involves himself in such escapades as drug dealing, thievery and bloodshed.

"Yeah, I guess so," I say finally.

William roots around in the pocket of his robe to find a cell phone. He clicks some buttons and sighs.

I stare up at the mould on the ceiling and convince myself that I can make out a scowling face in the middle of blemishes in the paint.

"He's running late," William says. "Not like him at all. That's one thing I've learnt from the Russians in my time in New York, and it isn't what you'd expect. Not that they're cold-blooded killers, or that they have no sense of humour. It's that they are so fucking punctual it's unreal."

William coughs and hits his chest with the side of his fist. The cough converts into a laugh, which quickly disappears as he notices the concern on my face.

"Don't worry, brother," he says. "He'll be here."

I crack my knuckles and realise that I am still wearing my wedding ring. I hadn't even thought about removing it, but now, with Jennifer having actually taken the step to leave me, I should take it off.

It had become such a part of me that I didn't even notice it was there. A symbol of love and devotion, something that stands for so much that has been trodden on by hatred and duplicity.

I pull it from my finger and drop it into the inside pocket of my jacket. William doesn't notice as he continues to look at the screen of his cell phone.

"I'm not worried," I say.

William brings his sunglasses down his nose and looks at me over them.

"It's not a bad thing to have a bit of anxiety flowing through your veins, Chris. It's better for you than the junk. You should be worried, anyway. A Russian gangster will be coming through that door in a few minutes and you will be involving yourself in an illegal arms deal. Not an everyday occurrence for you, is it?"

William snorts.

I look across at him and shake my head.

"I remember the first gun I bought," William says. "I was only nineteen years old, full of resentment at the world and thinking with my bollocks. It was a 9mm Uzi semi-automatic machine gun. I could have gone for a standard pistol or something less extravagant, but that never even crossed my mind. I wanted the biggest and the best and something that would make whoever I pointed it at shit their pants. What a fucking twat I was."

I tilt my head and feign shock.

"You should be feeling the anticipation and fear tightly gripping your nuts right now. You wouldn't be normal if you didn't. I get it every time I go to conduct a risky deal or venture into the lion's mouth to discuss terms with a contact."

I shrug my shoulders.

"I'm okay with this, honestly," I smile. "I've just got a few things on my mind. I had a few problems at work this morning. I've been put on two weeks paid leave as they seem to think I'm not mentally capable of completing my daily tasks. They want me to get my head together."

William pushes his sunglasses back up against his face and shakes his head.

"You need to become your own boss, my friend," he says. "Nobody telling you where to be and what to do. No taxman, cash up to your eyeballs. It's an easier life. No bullshit boss, no bullshit colleagues. No bullshit."

I see Adam standing over me with a smirk on his face. I'm not going to be keeling over and letting fuckers like him root me like a dog.

"It's a rule I always followed when I was in the band," William continues. "Do what feels right and don't let the suits tell you what to do. You're the genius making the music and you're in creative control of everything you do. Don't let some faggot who thinks he's Mr Big Shot tell you what will get radio play and what needs to be mainstream just so you'll reach the sales threshold – that's not how it works. If you wanna write an eighteen-minute progressive rock song with a bagpipe solo and release it as a single, do it. I wipe my arse with three-to-four-minute pop songs. Just because his suit is pressed and his shoes are polished doesn't mean he knows shit about shit."

William looks at me in silence as I bite my bottom lip.

"No offence," he says.

I rearrange my sitting stance so that I am comfortable.

"None taken," I say. "It's a little bit more complicated than that with my job. I've worked too hard to get where I am to throw in the towel and take up dealing smack."

William laughs insanely.

"I'm not suggesting that, Chris!" he says, cackling. "Shit, you couldn't hack this game. It's a motherfucker. Every time you turn your head you see some vulture is ready to kill you for the gear in your pocket. Then there are the corrupted pigs who want to make an example of you and do all they can to force you into giving them a bigger cut of your profits than you take home so you don't get thrown in jail."

I nod in agreement, letting him wallow in his ego as I foresee the arrival of the Russian.

It's not as though listening to William's rants bothers me in any way as most of the time I enjoy them, but right now I can only concentrate on the meeting at hand. Even this morning's events seem redundant in comparison.

"… that's how you end up becoming a regular at the station and spending hours in a cell just for backtalk and refusing to be ass-fucked by some little prick who thinks that because he has a badge that makes you his bitch. I was kicking in skulls of guys like that while he was still sucking on his mother's titties and whining to have his shitty ass changed."

"… can't just roll over and be somebody's dog. We all came into this world in the same way, naked and screaming. Don't need anybody telling me they're better than me or looking at me like I'm a pile of horseshit. That's gunna get them in all sorts of trouble. I'll take them out of this world naked and screaming, the same way they came in."

"… seen the wonders of the world and been at the top just as often as I've been in the gutter. You won't meet anybody who has been through half as much shit as me and lived to tell the tale, and if you do, the tale won't be as interesting as I make it."

He is right on that one, I'll give him that. He knows exactly how to tell a story, and it's a talent that not many people have. He could stand up on a podium and have a few hundred people immersed in the images he weaves from the dead air for several hours.

There is something not quite right with William today. Beneath his skin I know that there is something bothering him, but he isn't letting me see it entirely.

He keeps me at arm's length, spewing his opinions and anecdotes like venom into my eyes.

"… fakers and faggots abusing the system because they think they are of a higher distinction than everybody around them. They haven't even lived. They've been cooped up in their tiny box for so long that reality itself has become a fucking sludge for them. Hell, reality couldn't care less. It forgets them as easily as I do. I don't need a post-it note on my fridge door to remind me who they are."

William lights up another cigarette and I see his cell phone drop onto the ground as his legs jolt. He is so animated as he talks it is fascinating.

I look down and watch the blue light of the cell phone screen disappearing beneath a few empty packets of cigarettes and some crushed cans of soda.

"… desperate for some sort of recognition in a world where you can only make it to the very top if you suck the right dicks and forget everybody you hold dear. You've got to be a real cunt to do that, let me tell ya. You'll end up with blood on your hands and, at some point, it may even be yours.

"If you can live with yourself after all of the toes you've stepped on and you don't mind leaving your house every morning with one hand on the butt of your gun, then I wish you the best of luck. But you're gunna need eyes in the back of your head if you ever want to feel safe in this city ever again."

I can't tell whether he is talking directly to me or just thinking out loud. He seems spooked, and that really isn't like William Beckford at all.

"… get me started on those gun-spinning wannabe mobsters with their crowbars in one hand and their dicks in the other, stupid motherfuckers. If they swing their balls around for long enough they're gunna hit somebody and that's when things really start to get messy."

Three hard knocks on the front door cut off William mid-flow and he stops dead. His mouth hangs open wide before morphing to a wide grin. He points at the door with his thumb and whispers like an excited schoolgirl who has just heard the latest gossip.

"That'll be him," he says almost inaudibly. "Remember, I'm only the middle man. Whatever happens, however things pan out, I wasn't involved in this."

I nod as I stand up, straightening my tie.

"Oh yeah, better warn you," William says, slightly louder this time. "He ain't gunna be happy that you're here, so if he gets a bit edgy, just follow my lead."

He leaps across the coffee table and steps towards the door, one slipper coming off as he does so. He puts it back on and takes hold of the door handle as there are three more knocks on the door.

"What the fuck?" I say fretfully. "You didn't tell him I was gunna be here?"

"Nah, no point. He wouldn't have come. Keep cool though, pal. Just don't ask him when he left the Soviet Union, no jokes about his weight and don't look him directly in the eye."

7

William opens the door and the Russian stands still behind it, taking up almost the whole of the doorway with his colossal form. He looks down at the ground for a few seconds before looking up with acute blue eyes. He stares at me without taking an inch of notice of William.

He is incredibly overweight, his stomach hanging out in front of him like a balloon and several chins resting on the collar of his t-shirt. He wears a black suit jacket over this t-shirt, which is bright yellow in colour and must be big enough to fit three or four average-sized men inside.

His head seems perfectly round. He has jet-black hair that is receding considerably and a thick handlebar moustache above his upturned mouth. His eyebrows are as thick as his facial hair and pointing downwards in a scowl that matches the one I convinced myself I could see in the mouldy ceiling above me.

The anger on his face is so overstated that all he needs in addition to his purple-tainted face is steam discharging from his ears and he would be the perfect epithet of an enraged antagonist from a cartoon show for kids.

He steps forwards and both of his shoulders rub against the sides of the doorway. He mumbles something in Russian, and this is when I notice that he is carrying a hefty aluminium case with both hands out in front of his stomach.

"Andrei!" William says, his voice cutting the atmosphere like a samurai sword through flesh. "Good to see you, my friend!"

The Russian looks up at William, the look of displeasure on his face quite obviously making him uncomfortable. He makes no attempt to come into the apartment, which he turns his attention to with another cutting look.

"Come in, Andrei," William says as he stretches out his arm, showing the way into the apartment from the open door.

The Russian doesn't move. He just locks his gaze back onto me. I can feel my heart rapidly beating, so much so that my ribcage feels as though it is made of toothpicks and will collapse at any given moment.

"I thought I told you, none of your fucking friends here when I come over," Andrei snaps.

His Russian accent is not as thick as I had expected it to be. It's Russian, that isn't hard to notice, but it has a slight New York drawl, which is odd.

"It's okay, Andrei," William assures him. "Not a friend as such, one of my customers. I can vouch for him. He needs a weapon."

Andrei turns his head and for a second I think he is about to walk away.

"Even better," he says in annoyance. "Not a friend but one of your fucking customers. I'm not selling a piece to some junkie, Beckford."

William puts a reassuring hand on Andrei's left shoulder. The Russian looks at it as if a bird has taken a shit on him.

"This bloke ain't a junkie," William says. "An occasional user, yes, but not a junkie. Trust me on this one, Andrei. Look at his fucking suit. No junkie could afford to dress that way without mugging some Wall Street cocksucker."

Andrei seems to take a few seconds to deliberate on his next move. I feel like I could strangle William for being so flippant in his disregard for offending such a dangerous man, and, even worse, dragging me into the firing line.

"I don't care, Beckford," Andrei says. "A simple phone call to warn me of the proceedings would have been courteous. I told you last time, another stunt like this and I wouldn't be dealing with you anymore."

This time Andrei turns his whole body away from the doorway. William slams his hands down at his sides like a child who has just been told he can't get have an ice cream.

"Don't be such a drama queen!" William laughs, but I can see from a bead of sweat on the side of his face that he is exceptionally nervous. "I'm always good for business, you know that. Don't disrespect me in front of a customer, Andrei."

Andrei stops dead and turns back to William. He leans over and places the aluminium case on the floor just outside of the apartment. Then he steps inside, which seems to shock William, as he steps back with a jerk and knocks the back of his legs into the coffee table.

"You want to talk to me about respect?" Andrei sneers, his teeth clenching together. "You have no respect at all, not even for yourself. Just look at the pigsty you live in. You expect me to come to this shithole and help you out? You don't even show any consideration for the position I am putting myself in."

William backs off even further, raising his hands in front of him as if to defend himself from Andrei's words. I am still like a statue and I don't even think I could move my legs if I wanted to.

"Andrei, please," William implores, "you've known me a long time. I ain't gunna make excuses for my lack of thought, that's just the way I am. I am sorry if I've made this difficult, I haven't intended to. I'm trying to help out an acquaintance. Quit the hard man act and let's get down to business."

"I've heard it all before," Andrei continues, his eyes narrowing. "I'm sick of your empty apologies. You think I'm a pushover? I cannot just sit back and let this happen over and over again. You were sorry last time and the time before that."

For the first time I can see William for something other than brash and esteemed, which is what he puts himself across as. I can see the fear in his eyes, even beneath those shades, and that shows he is lower down the food chain than perhaps he believes.

"Just calm down, Andrei," William says, his voice overly nasal. "Let's discuss this and work something out."

"I am tired of your voice, Beckford," Andrei growls. "You're a fucking nobody. I will not be made to look like a fool by a nobody."

Andrei reaches into his jacket and pulls out a gun. I recognise it from movies I have seen as a Beretta pistol, 9mm, something like a standard police issue weapon, although I'm not entirely sure. I suppose that movies don't always have small matters like that correct.

In any case, the weapon looks tiny and inferior in Andrei's hands, so much so that it doesn't even make me feel afraid when I see it. I am more interested in the look in Andrei's eyes as he points the gun at William's head. He looks as if he is pointing a remote control at the television.

William raises his hands like a bank clerk during a robbery. His mouth is open wide and I can see his jaw shaking violently. I feel like a mere observer at this confrontation, as if I am watching a live reconstruction of a murder. It feels abnormal to be watching this unfold, as if the men standing before me are elements of my imagination.

"Shit, mate," William says to Andrei, his voice quiet. "What are you doing?"

Andrei's face doesn't falter.

"I could shoot you down here in your home just for disrespecting me," he says. "Nobody would care. I doubt anybody would even notice you were gone. Then I could turn and put two bullets in the chest of your friend. He wouldn't have told anybody he was coming here, so that's two worthless motherfuckers scratched from the face of the Earth."

William says nothing. His hands are shaking sadistically.

"You are a pathetic excuse for a man and I will be doing this city a favour by stamping you out. You are vermin and it is a miracle that you haven't been exterminated already."

William looks over at me, his face full of terror and uncertainty.

"Andrei, please," William utters, his voice reduced to a squeak, just like a rodent. The vermin Andrei has accused him of being.

Andrei turns his head and I start to plan a possible escape for the moment the Russian executes William. I could move quickly into the kitchen and, if I am quick, I could open the window and leap out. It's a risk and I may break my ankle, but it's better than being shot dead in this fucking apartment.

However, with the mess in this room and in the kitchen, my escape could be hampered. Even with the obese lumbering blob coming after me, he could be swift enough to catch up and put a bullet in my back. I'll be damned if the last thing I see is the discoloured walls of that kitchen and the last thing I feel is the cold linoleum floor on the side of my face.

"You stupid fucker," Andrei says, the anger drained from his voice.

He drops the gun from William's head and puts it back in his jacket. A huge smile appears on his face and he begins to laugh, a huge bawl that slams into me and makes me feel so relieved I could rush across to him and kiss his portly face.

"I'm pulling your leg, Beckford," Andrei says between chuckles. "Your face, you should have seen it. You really think I'm gunna just kill you? Holy shit."

William looks over at me. He keeps his arms raised and I can see his bottom lip trembling.

"I expected you to give back as good as you got," Andrei says. "Beckford, the years are getting to you."

William finally puts his hands down by his sides. He begins to laugh awkwardly and playfully pushes Andrei in the chest.

"You motherfucker," William says, his voice crackling. "You know how paranoid I get. You really had me going."

Andrei laughs louder still and looks over at me. My face feels as if it is made of varnished wood and I try my best to join in with the laughter, but it's hard to change to that from fearing for your life in several seconds.

"My wife told me to lighten up," Andrei smiles.

Andrei and William embrace in an inept hug. William takes off his sunglasses and wipes away the mist from the inside of the lenses before putting them back on his face.

"You've got a fucked-up sense of humour, Andrei," William says.

I can hear the confidence returning to his voice. It was interesting to see a glimpse of the real William Beckford beneath the garish exterior he creates.

Andrei turns and leans over to pick up the aluminium case. He turns back and uses his free hand to knock the junk from the top of the coffee table. I see a half-full mug of old coffee fall from the edge of it and disappear amongst the mess on the floor.

Once the surface of the coffee table is bare, although stained with various unknown substances and blemished with burn marks, Andrei places the case onto the table with a clunk.

"Fucked up, maybe," Andrei laughs, "but I don't like

missing a chance to make you squirm."

William glares at me, his eyes radiating through his sunglasses.

"Close the door, Beckford."

William quietly does what Andrei told him to. The door closes with a click and William walks around Andrei, back to his seat on the far couch.

"This isn't the perfect place to conduct business but I suppose it will do," Andrei says to nobody in particular. "Let's get down to it."

8

I sit back down in my seat and wonder if Andrei will need to find somewhere to sit down himself. William hasn't offered him a seat, perhaps due to his irritation at Andrei's cruel skit from a few minutes ago.

Andrei is a big guy and I can't imagine his legs wanting to continue to support his weight for much longer, but he seems okay for now. He is looking over at me with his arms across his bulk of a chest.

"Don't talk much, do you?" he says to me.

I realise that I haven't said a single word since the Russian came into the apartment. My brain has been working overtime and hasn't had the chance to conjure a word that would be relevant. I look over at William and see him lighting up another cigarette, the lighter shaking in his grip.

"The polite thing for Beckford to do would be to introduce you," Andrei says as he looks towards William.

William sits in silence before realising what Andrei said. He jerks forwards and blows a stream of smoke from his mouth.

"This fine gentleman is Christopher Morgan," William says. "He's everything I wish I was. Sharply dressed, charming and a mysterious son-of-a-bitch."

I stand up and offer my hand to Andrei.

"Nice to meet you, sir," I say.

Andrei takes my hand and makes me feel like a small child as he shakes it.

"Andrei, please," he says.

He taps his index finger on the surface of the aluminium case as I sit back down.

"I don't usually do deals with strangers, but if William trusts you then I guess I don't have anything more to go by. I will ask you to forget my name and face when you leave this room, as I will do yours."

I nod to show that I will, but I can't help but think that it would take a serious head injury to make me forget the face of this man, especially after my first impression.

Andrei turns his attention to William who is cracking open a can of beer. I have no idea where he got it from and I can only think he had one in his robe pocket or that somewhere there is a small fridge within the debris of this room.

"I come all the way over here and you haven't offered me a drink or a smoke," Andrei says, the antagonism returning to his voice. "All the while you sit there supping away like a baby on his mother's tit."

William swallows his first glug of beer.

"Sorry, brother," he says quietly. "You want something?"

Andrei turns and smiles at me. He seems to be able to turn the anger on and off like the flick of a light switch.

"No, I'm fine," Andrei says without looking back at William. "But an offer would have been greatly appreciated."

William shakes his head in disbelief and continues drinking from the can. I smile at Andrei, showing that I am entertained by the mockery he is bringing upon William.

"I would guess that you have more in the manners department than my friend here," Andrei says to me. "Anything Beckford had died long ago, the drugs zapping away the part in his brain that tells him to be considerate and courteous."

William sighs gently.

I feel a cool breeze against my face coming from the slowly spinning ceiling fan, which I notice at this moment for the first time. It isn't really needed, as today is a significantly cold day for late summer.

Soon it will be fall, a time of the year I look forward to. It signals change, something that I must take on in my life, more so now than ever. As the leaves drop from the trees I will see all that has done me wrong falling into a chasm and out of my sight.

"You want a weapon. This correct, Chris?" Andrei asks me.

"Yes, that's right," I reply.

"I won't ask what for, that's not important. I've been doing this for long enough to know that when people buy guns they need them for one of two things."

I sit in silence not knowing if I am supposed to guess as to what these things are.

"Protection or revenge," the Russian states.

I see the face of Adam Phillips, smiling as he receives a text message from my wife telling him exactly what she plans to do to him when she sees him later tonight. It involves sitting on his face.

"Whatever it is, I've brought along three wonderful examples of personal weaponry."

Andrei snaps open the clasps on the aluminium case.

"I don't mean to make that sound like a sales pitch," he says as he opens the case, "as these babies sell themselves."

I lean forwards in anticipation as Andrei reveals the weapons inside the case, which are displayed on top of a layer of cut-out grey foam.

They look faultless and brand new, as if these are the display models and once I choose one Andrei will fetch it for me from a back room and it will come in a cellophane-covered box.

"Three sexy ladies," Andrei says.

I stare at each of them with intensity. I imagine how I would look holding one of them in my hand. It's such power for a man to possess: the hand of fate is taken hold of and twisted until the bone splinters and breaks.

"First up we've got the Glock 26 9mm pistol," Andrei says as he points to the first gun. "This is the sub-compact variant. It's got a few special features that separate it from the rest. Very short barrel, as you can see, paired with the slide. Magazine is a ten-round double-stack, which basically means it's quick-firing and you can pop off more shots before you have to reload."

Andrei looks over at William who seems to be concentrating on something on his cell phone.

"For more information on firing quickly ask Beckford, or any one of the hookers he's fucked in the last month," Andrei says with a grin.

I laugh and realise that William hasn't heard the quip.

"Next is a true classic," Andrei says as he moves onto the second gun. "The Ruger Mk III, which is perhaps an acquired taste but a certain favourite of mine. It's a .22 long-rifle semi-automatic pistol with some fantastic additions to an original design. It has a 6.875-inch barrel, adjustable rear sights and an internal safety lock. A great weapon to have for both long and short range, probably one of the only weapons on the market that can be used for both effectively."

I move my eyes onto the third one and this really takes my eye. It looks like something Clint Eastwood would carry in a holster during a desert standoff in the midday sun.

"Last, but certainly not least, we have the Colt Python premium American revolver. One thing you Americans did get right, and although it can be typecast as a weapon that only cowboys and rednecks carry, I can't fault it. It's one of the only things on this planet that I would say is a perfect example of engineering. We've got a .357 Magnum cartridge and a six-inch barrel. It has superior accuracy and smooth trigger pull, although you've got to watch yourself with the recoil."

I stare down at the Colt Python and feel my hands growing clammy as I am desperate to take hold of it.

"I can see the look in your eye," Andrei whispers, "like a man who has been locked up for twenty-five years and has just gone to a strip-club. Want to hold this baby?"

Andrei removes the revolver from the foam with the tips of his fat fingers. He spins it around so that the butt of the gun is facing me.

I don't need a second invitation. I take hold of the gun and feel the outstanding weight of it in the palm of my hand. I bring it up to my face and can see a reflection of my look of awe in the shimmering barrel.

The cold grip of death stands for something so strong, yet can be such a burden. I will not let this weapon be a burden to me. I must think of it as something that has been missing from my life and has now completed it. A part of me that has finally been returned, although I have never seen it before. The missing piece.

A word of enquiry to a contact and as soon as the next day I am holding a Colt Python revolver.

William seems to have shaken the shock from his system and is trying to waffle on with yet another anecdote, this time with Andrei the unassuming audience.

"Did I ever tell you about Annie Parker?" William asks him.

He has told me, that's for sure. It was one of the first things he said to me when he found out I was married.

The Russian has left me alone with the gun. I wonder if it is loaded.

What would stop me turning around and blowing half of Andrei's skull away?

How about shooting William in the face so that his sunglasses shatter and a gaping red mess replaces his eyes and nose? There's nothing at all to stop me doing that.

These murderous fantasies spill across my mind, slurring with the loud words of William. For a few moments I feel comatose standing here with the gun in my hand. I know that neither of them are watching me. I look at the thick barrel of the Colt and wonder how it would feel lodged in my mouth.

Of course it isn't loaded.

"… backstage at a Screamin' Suzie gig at the Hammersmith. First time I met the girl, massive fan and apparently followed us all over Europe when we were touring. Anyway, she starts spouting all of this romantic poetry bullshit, telling me that I'm her lost soul mate and that she has finally found me. It scared me shitless."

This weapon is my choice for sure. There is a certain glamour surrounding it that has captured me. I feel like an insect writhing in its silky web, unable to free myself and giving in to being trapped.

"… shows me a tattoo on her hip of my name. Fucked up, I know. She's cute, don't get me wrong, but not really my type. She's way too skinny, wears too much make-up on her face and this whole worship scenario isn't really doing it for me, if you can believe that."

I will need to develop my ruthless streak if I want to make it work.

I can't stand motionless as I did when Andrei pulled his gun. My best idea was to run and try and escape through the window, which is quite dismal.

"… as drunk as an Irishman on St Patrick's Day and exhausted from the show, so I tell her to get lost. I just want to smoke some weed and go to sleep. I don't even want my dick sucked, which is rare, even by this enthusiastic young lady."

I bring the revolver up even closer to my face and press the end of the barrel against my teeth. My trigger finger shakes as I place it against the side of the gun. I wonder what smell it will make after it has fired.

Gunpowder, flint, bonfires, sizzled human hair. I am

looking forward to finding out.

"… rejection seems to drive her insane. She starts sobbing and grabbing hold of me, begging me to make love to her then and there. I make sure she gets the message, telling her I'm not interested, but then things really get out of hand when the bitch pulls a gun on me!"

William's words fade into the background as I place the gun back down in the case. I see Andrei stand up and come back over to me, all the while William continuing to ramble on with his story. A story that I know how it will end.

"Which one makes the biggest hole?" I ask.

Andrei laughs heartily and bumps against me with his rounded stomach. He smells like woodchips and spicy cologne.

"That would be the Colt," he says, his voice deep and cutting against the wailing tones of William, who I can hear saying something about how the gun Annie Parker pulled wasn't loaded.

"Exit wound the size of a watermelon," Andrei says, showing me how big it would be by gesturing with his hands.

"Then that's my choice," I confirm.

Andrei nods and closes the case.

"And a good choice it is, Christopher."

The Russian puts one of his substantial arms around my shoulder and pulls me close. I feel fragile as I stand next to him, for his mass makes up about three versions of me.

"I only take cash, I hope that's not a problem," he says into my ear. "I'll include a few things with the weapon, including ammunition and the oil and cleaning utensils for the chamber. I can also give you a holster if you like. We'll sort out the formalities of payment once we have had a toast to our first deal."

Andrei looks over at William, who is standing and flailing his arms as he gets to the end of his tale.

"… and after all that, I fucking married her!"

Andrei's brow furrows as he pulls me closer still, my head burying into his jacket.

"Beckford, get us a drink so we can celebrate a fine first deal!"

William exhales, almost in a child-like huff, steps through the trash on the floor and makes his way to the kitchen.

Andrei speaks into my ear and I feel his hot breath against me.

"Remember, Christopher. Forget my face and forget my name. Don't get trigger happy, at least not for a while. This city may sometimes feel like the Wild West but it really isn't. I'm counting on you."

He lets go of me and puts out his hand. I shake it for the second time as William comes back into the room with two cans of beer in one hand and an already-open bottle of red wine in the other.

He hands one can to Andrei and another to me. The can is warm but I feel obliged to join in with the merriment.

I open the can and warm froth spills onto my hand. Andrei does the same and raises his can high in front of him. I follow his lead, as does William, but only after drinking a few mouthfuls of the wine.

The cans clink together with the glass wine bottle and Andrei clears his throat.

"To trustworthy business partners and the beginning of something beautiful," Andrei says loudly.

"And to my wife," William adds, "the crazy groupie bitch."

THE FOURTH TALE - MEDICATE

1

The next hours are spent drinking copious amounts of cheap warm beer, terrible red wine and snorting enough coke to make my entire face go numb and feel like it may melt away, like a marshmallow when put into a flame on the end of a pointy stick.

Andrei doesn't indulge as much as William and I do, just knocking back a few beers before he makes his excuses and leaves. Not before I finalise the payments for the gun, of course.

He leaves me with the Colt Python, which I place carefully into a leather storage flap in my briefcase. I decided not to buy a holster for the weapon, because, as Andrei said, this city may sometimes feel like the Wild West, but it isn't. Walking around with a revolver in a leather holster may be a bit too much.

I see the sun beginning to set through the murky apartment window and realise that I have killed a lot of time doing not very much at all.

I watch a flock of birds moving swiftly across the setting sun and place my hand on the window, just to feel closer to them. They are free, and how wonderful it would be to soar above the city and watch the circus of life from afar. Feeling the warm air beneath your wings, holding you up like a colossal and buoyant cushion. I would give anything to be so high and not have to worry about falling to my death.

I stare out of the window for so long that the sun is almost out of sight, now just a dull orange glow smeared across the horizon creating yellow and red blotches in my vision.

I look around at William who has fallen asleep on the couch, his head resting awkwardly on the couch arm and his mouth wide open. Saliva dribbles from his mouth onto his chest near where an empty wine bottle rests.

I pick up my briefcase from near the door. I decide not to wake William as I move silently out of the apartment, closing the front door behind me.

I am late for a rendezvous and I hope that she won't be too mad at me. She shouldn't be angry in any case, because, after all, I'll be paying her for the pleasure of her company.

2

I feel invisible more than ever as I make my way to the apartment of Kacey Ross. It's a walk of several blocks and I move silently through the young night as the seeds of destruction and vice begin to bloom into depraved flowers.

The oddballs and perverts come out in this city at night, as the light of day blinds them and reveals their obvious imperfections, like a tribe of underground Vampires that haunt the landscape with their secret and sickening existence.

They don't even notice me as I drift by them as the red mist of sleaze clouds their eyes, something I can keep at bay. The only thing we have in common at this time is the familiar bloodlust.

I arrive at a large steel-panelled door as I hear three distant pops, perhaps a car backfiring or a drive-by shooting, I can't be sure.

There is a square metallic panel to the left of the door with a grubby keypad and a speaker just above it. Names are scrawled on the wall next to the box with numbers against them and above that are various pieces of poorly-spelt graffiti. The only word that seems to be written with some level of intellect is the word 'whore', which is smeared largely in white paint. There is another attempt at spelling this word a few feet above it, in a sentence that reads 'hore lives hear'.

I walk up two concrete steps and press the two buttons on the keypad that connects me to Kacey. After three dull beeps I hear a muffled answer that I cannot understand, and then I hear her clear her throat before she puts on her sexiest tone of voice.

"Hello?" she says.

"It's Chris," I reply, looking behind me as a couple of teenage girls pass by.

"Honey, you're late."

"I know, I'm sorry. I got caught up with something."

I hear her sigh softly, but she is playing with me. I already feel myself calming just from the sound of her voice.

"I forgive you," she says. "Come on up."

A low buzz comes from the speaker and the lock on the front door clicks. I push the door open and walk into the lobby of the apartment block, a stale smell filling my nose, a mix of urine and something else that I cannot identify.

I stroll across the lobby and pass the elevators as two men come out of one. I don't look at them as I move through a doorway onto the stairs and begin to stride up, taking two steps at a time. I move up to the second floor, the stairwell narrow and cold.

Two drunken women pass me as I am almost at Kacey's apartment, the sour smell of an abundance of cheap beer pouring off them, probably a similar aroma to what I must have. They cackle and mumble, getting too close to me for comfort, bumping into me in the hall without an apology.

I speed up as I hear the cackles descend into the stairwell, and just as I am about to knock on the front door of Kacey's apartment, it opens and I see her peering from behind it.

She smiles at me and her eyes light up as she beckons me inside. I step into her apartment and she closes the door behind me, pulling a chain across near the top of the door.

Kacey Ross is a vision of beauty, and something as simple as her delicate scent drags a veil of tranquillity across me. She stands in the hallway of her small apartment, her hands linked together at her waist.

She doesn't say a word. She just stares into my soul as I look deeply into her eyes and down at what she is wearing. She has made a lot of effort for me, as she usually does, and this makes me feel pleased.

Kacey is short, only a couple of inches taller than five feet. She has golden brown hair that is shoulder length, and it is tied at either side in pigtails. Her skin is a similar golden brown due to her African-American roots. She has wide green eyes that are framed by dark lashes and incredible, full lips.

She wears a set of pink silk lingerie, which includes a bra with lace floral edging and matching underwear. She has fishnet stockings on her legs that are cut off at the thigh, a few inches above her knee. On her feet she wears black stilettos that add about four inches to her overall height.

She has impeccable curves, which is exactly what I like about her body. Her hourglass figure strikes me as nothing short of perfection. I want to take hold of her and run my hands all over her body, and I can feel myself edging towards doing that, my hands becoming clammy with anticipation.

"You gunna come in or stand out there all night?" Kacey says, words flowing from her gorgeous lips like honey from the edge of a spoon.

I step in through the door without a word and Kacey's scent almost overwhelms me. Already I am forgetting everything that has plagued my mind and I am falling into a cavern of bliss that I will never want to drag myself out of.

Kacey Ross is a medicine for me; somebody who helps me battle the clawing hands of the ailments that threaten to put me down. She is the escape I need, never more so before now, and when I am with her I can forget everything else on this planet.

When she looks at me I feel as though I am the only man she wants and the only man she has ever been with. I guess that means she is just damn good at her job, but I don't care. I want to be made to feel like that, and it doesn't bother me that it is a creation. I try to forget that when her lips kiss mine.

She is determined and feisty, and that is a fresh breeze that runs through the alleyways of a place where many people accept what they are given and curl up in a corner to die. She is a fighter, and despite the fact that she is in a profession that she does not enjoy – except these appointments with me, or so I hope – she is always striving for better.

I admire that, perhaps because for so long I was one of the people that coasted along in a life that gave me nothing back, no matter how much I put in. For years I thought that was how life was, but it was the first time I met Kacey that I began to truly question the fabric of my dreary existence.

Back then, I had never met anybody like Kacey, let alone had somebody like her in my life. She has helped me through many difficult predicaments and helped me overcome fears. She can see beyond a face, deep into the essence that makes someone the person they are. She can root out the corrupt and the malevolent and put reason to it, and this is something I was inspired by and it certainly helped as I began to do the same.

All you need is a keen eye, a range of experiences and a simple base of logic. With those three components, you can work out a person's emotions, wants, needs, motives and even their secrets.

She helped me piss into the wind without getting wet.

Beyond this, Kacey is kind and understanding, so much so that I do not feel as though I am bulldozing her with my problems when I tell her about my cheating wife and my bullshit job. I know that she has enough crap to deal with in her life, but she still has time to listen to me and give me advice.

She has witnessed the worst of human society and this fascinates me. To have seen all she has makes her the person who stands in front of me right now: any more or less would make her somebody completely different. She has been left in the middle, a person who complements me flawlessly, diluting my neurotic and cynical elements and making me feel altogether more human. The connection between us both is unquestionable.

"Luckily I'm a patient girl," Kacey says as she turns around and walks a few feet down the hall towards the bedroom, my eyes fixating on her round ass.

The other doors leading to the living room, kitchen and bathroom are firmly closed. I know that she hates working from her home, but in recent months it has become the safest and most rational place for her appointments, and that really is saying something considering the characters I have seen on occasion during my ascent from the ground floor to this apartment.

I watch Kacey's buttocks bounce as she walks. She turns left into the open door that leads to her bedroom and I follow close behind her like a faithful dog. I clunk my briefcase into the wall, her body taking up my attention and blurring everything surrounding it.

Kacey's bedroom is dark but for a small table lamp in the corner of the room. It stands upon a table that is covered with make-up and hair products. A long mirror is against the far wall, along which runs a rail with Kacey's vast collection of clothes crammed onto it. In the centre of the room is a double bed which has red silk sheets stretched over it and a scattering of pillows beneath a black leather headboard. There is a small window above this headboard that is hidden by curtains, only a dull light coming through them.

The rest of the room, which doesn't have much floor space due to the size of the bed, is strewn with clothes, shoes, hairdryers and various other electrical items. It is nowhere near the level of disorder that William Beckford's apartment is, but it is chaotic enough to give the impression that ten girls have been getting dressed and styling their hair in here. What floor I can see seems to be old wooden floorboards that are stained with drops of white paint.

"I've been looking forward to seeing you, Chris," Kacey says as she walks over to the bed. "I haven't had the best day."

She turns around and sits on the edge. She brings one leg up and rests it on the other. Her eyes look even more vivid in the dark of this room.

I place my briefcase on the floor just inside the door and loosen my tie. I smile softly at her from across the room, hoping that my presence makes her feel half as exultant as me.

"Same here," I say. "It's been pretty fucking awful actually. You okay?"

"I'm fine," she responds. "Same shit, different day. You know the drill."

I slide my jacket off onto the floor, pull my tie off from beneath my collar and unbutton my shirt about halfway.

"How's Kieron?" I ask.

Kieron is Kacey's three-year-old son. I know that he is the driving force behind Kacey's strength of mind and want for change.

Perhaps she wouldn't be the way she is without him. I've never been a father so I wouldn't know what effect on the psyche it would have to become a parent. I suppose it would alter your values considerably.

The fact that Kacey is a mother may be another reason that I find her so compatible. I never had a mother figure in my life in any recognisable way, just a dirty old hag with more interest in booze and sex than parenthood. I am certainly not looking for any sort of replacement, I'm not a narrow-minded fool, but to see somebody who has such unconditional love for a person empowers me no end. I have never felt that for anybody and I don't know if I ever will.

"He's fine," Kacey says. "Gunna take him to the zoo for the first time tomorrow. He's gunna love it."

I do not know where Kieron is during these appointments. I have never asked. I expect he stays with a family member or a close neighbour.

She glides her hand across the surface of the bed next to her, gesturing for me to come and sit down next to her.

"How's the wife?" she asks.

I slide my shirt back and off. I watch Kacey's eyes flicker over my chest and stomach. Her lips glisten and I feel mine tingle in anticipation of kissing them.

"She left me," I say.

The words come out of my mouth but I don't really think about them at all. I am working on autopilot, my mind only really being able to concentrate on the beautiful vision of a woman wanting me to move closer to her. However, at the mere mention of it, thoughts of my wife start to filter into my mind.

Kacey's mouth opens in shock, but I see a look in her eye that suggests she expected it. I have confided in her regarding the deceit of my wife, over and over again.

"After all this time," I say as I unbuckle my belt. "After all of her lies and everything she has done. *She* left *me*."

Kacey tilts her head.

"Hardly seems fair," she says.

I pull my belt off and drop it to the floor as well. I am close enough to feel Kacey's warm breath on my bare skin as I sit down next to her on the bed.

This room shouldn't exist. Only a few feet separates this haven from the gloom and depravity outside the apartment door. This place glitters like a treasure chest full of gold; it's warm and calming while outside grows grey with mould and cobwebs.

"It can't be how this ends, Kacey," I say as she places her hand on my thigh. "I'm not finished, not yet. She can't get away with it, I won't let her... "

"Ssh..."

Kacey cuts me off and places a finger upon my lips. I stop in my tracks and any rambling thoughts about Jennifer fade away as I taste Kacey's skin. She leans forwards and kisses me hard on the lips, her tongue flicking in and out of my mouth. It's a perfect kiss, something that I have wanted all day.

In fact, I have needed her more than anything else all day. As soon as I taste her lips I begin to melt away and I know that it won't take long for me to drift into a state that I wouldn't be able to reach with any amount of drink and drugs.

Euphoria.

3

Kacey lies across me, her naked body entwined with mine as she sleeps soundly, her warm breath on my chest and her heart beating against my ribs. The sex has left me feeling sombre, as the still and tender embrace is all that is left after the passion has gone, faded into the night.

My sweat has dried on my face and body and my muscles feel exaggerated after the exercise. The temporary escape has driven a bolt of sanity into my brain, and although it has been well received and no doubt enjoyable, I know that it will not last for long. It will soon dissolve within my brain fluid like aspirin in water.

Kacey stirs and I run my hand through her hair, smelling delicate vanilla fragrances as it moves through my fingers.

I haven't been able to sleep myself and I don't know

why. It may be the loud voices that pass by her front door every few minutes, or perhaps it's the screeching tyres in the street below.

I wonder if Kacey is dreaming, and if so, what images are there within her mind. She obviously trusts me enough to fall asleep when I am here, despite me only being another customer.

I hope that she recognises our similarities. She is trapped, just like me, as the walls have closed around her and her only hope lies with the possibility of escape. Maybe that's a big difference between her and me, because I don't want to escape. I want to regain control.

Adultery is Kacey's sin and it lies at the core of her condition. External forces can push a person like her towards such a life, and while I do not know the details of what led her to become a prostitute, I know that the decisions she made were right at the time and I do not judge her for that. It set her on a path that has eventually crossed mine and I am eternally grateful that it worked out that way.

She awakes slowly with a gentle groan and looks up at me, her chin resting on my chest.

"What are you thinking about?" she says.

I look down at her and smile.

"You," I say.

The saccharine words that we exchange make me cringe. She kisses my chest softly.

"I doubt it. There's bound to be more pressing matters swimming around in that brain of yours. I know how you work."

I look up at the ceiling. A dog barks in the alleyway that is next to this apartment.

"I can't believe she left you," Kacey says, pressing the side of her face against the area of my skin she previously kissed.

I sigh deeply. Jennifer's face is just a haze in my head now. I can't make out her features, and maybe I don't want to anymore.

"Love is too fickle, Chris. I don't think any relationship can ever be untouchable, not these days. They'll all come to end, none will last. I've been told that I'm the only one and that I will be loved forever, but it's only until something that seems better comes along. Love is a lie, and that's because people are selfish. I don't want to make you feel worse, honey, I really don't. But it's the truth."

She isn't making me feel worse. She needn't worry about that. She is completely right.

Love is too fickle. It is pale and weak, an anaemic vicinity of the human condition, too easily poisoned by the virus of greed and lust. I have let this virus infect me and I have embraced the contamination. Greed and lust are now just as much a part of me as the worst of this human race. I have been bitten and now my flesh is beginning to rot away as the curse takes hold.

"It's okay," I say. "I know what you mean."

"I've learnt that you can never really rely on anybody but yourself, and that's exactly the way it should be," Kacey says. "You can't put your faith in somebody else when they have urges and desires. You're not in control of that. Shit, you're not even in control of your own."

"I know, but I just thought it would be different. I never thought I could make my marriage work, but with everything she's done to me, I wanted to be the person to walk out. I think that's the least I deserved. A chance to strike a line through the years I have been married to her and get some closure."

Kacey lifts her head.

"Sometimes we don't get that chance. You have to move on and do your best to put it behind you. I know that may seem difficult, but it's the only way you'll be able to forget her."

"I need closure, Kacey. Her walking out of my door isn't how this ends."

"I hope you're not thinking of doing anything stupid," Kacey says, cutting me short.

I look at her for a few seconds as she waits for me to respond. A few possible words run through my mind but I don't say any of them.

I turn my head away from her as she sits up.

"Chris, for fuck's sake, she cheated on you, yes. She put you through all of that shit and ended up walking out on you. It sucks, sure, it's a fucking travesty. But honey, you have to take the higher ground."

Kacey leans forward and kisses me on the forehead.

"At least I've got you," I say.

She looks at me and I see a flash of uncertainty across her face. It's a look that suggests to me that she's been in this situation before, where she thinks a client is falling for her and sees the husk of a relationship as something more than just sex.

I regret saying the words instantaneously, as that's not how I feel at all. I'm not deluded.

I know that all the time she has devoted to me has only been because I am paying her by the hour. I am glad that I have her, even in the way that I do, and I want her to know that.

I am not in love with her, but there is a connection, and while it isn't necessarily a devoted and tender connection, it's a connection none-the-less.

She listens, she sympathises, she opens up to me and she gives me guidance, however unintentional that may be. I have received more psychological help from Kacey than I did during yesterday's meeting with Cassandra, and she's the one with the qualifications and certificates on her office wall.

"Chris, listen," Kacey says.

"I'm not in love with you," I snap, desperately trying to reverse her train of thought.

The confusion is even more apparent on her face and I sit up with a jolt.

"I didn't mean it like that, Kacey. I'm not some obsessive idiot who thinks this is any more than it really is. I care for you, yes..."

"I... didn't think that, Chris, it's just..."

She loves me. She's been falling for me ever since I first met her and she's been dying to tell me but always held back because I was married and, although unhappy, she could see that I wanted to make my marriage work.

"I'm leaving New York."

I feel like a bucket of ice cold water has been thrown over me. My chest flips over. She can't leave.

She means more to me than I ever allowed myself to know. I think I've been looking in the wrong place for my recovery. She's sitting right here in front of me.

"What? How can you... When?"

Kacey puts her hand on my knee. There is a chill in her fingers and I move away, realising that this may seem like a childish display of resentment.

"In a few days, Chris, maybe sooner than that. I have family in the Midwest and I've been thinking of moving out there for some time. When I came to New York I wanted so much more than what I've ended up getting. This is far from the life I want, and now that I've got Kieron I need to do what's best for him. I can't raise a child here, I'm sure you can understand that."

My mouth goes dry. My skin tingles and my tongue goes limp.

"But... "

"I need to start over, Chris. I care for you too, but it's not enough to keep me here."

I feel light-headed for a second.

"Please, Kacey, you can't," I splutter, "I need you. You can't leave. You're the only reason I haven't jumped in front of a bus. Let's just talk about this. You know what I'm going through, how can you—"

"Your problems don't belong to me, Chris!" Kacey retorts loudly. "I've got my own, and I need to do what's best for my little boy."

I feel saliva gathering in my open mouth.

"Shit, I can't—"

"This, what we have, it's good," Kacey says, "but it's not real. We barely know each other, that's the truth of it."

I swing my legs out of the sheets and onto the ground. I stand up quickly but I have no idea what my intentions are.

I can't just walk out without resolving this; I may never see Kacey again. I catch a glimpse of my naked body in the nearby mirror, my flaccid penis limp against my leg.

"Bullshit," I snarl, "I'm not just another fucking customer and you know it."

Kacey wraps the sheet around her body and stands up, coming closer to me. She takes hold of my hand, which is convulsing wildly.

"Don't make this any harder than it already is," she says, putting her free hand around my back and pulling me next to her.

She drops the sheet and her naked breasts press against my torso. I wrap my arms around her and feel tears collecting in my eyes.

She is my medicine. I do not know what I will do without her.

The moment is dragged back to the bitter grip of reality by three thunderous thumps on the front door of the apartment. They are so riotous that I expect the door to smash inwards from the outside force.

Kacey's body jumps with each bang and grabs hold of me even tighter, her nails digging into my skin.

"Open this fucking door, Kacey!" the male voice at the door yells with unyielding frenzy.

"Oh no," Kacey says in a distressed whisper, "please, no."

Three more thumps on the door are delivered at an even more incensed pace.

"Shit, Chris, you've gotta hide," Kacey says as she lets

go of me and begins looking around on the ground for her clothes.

"What?" I say, refusing to keep my voice down, as she seems to be doing. "Who is it?"

Kacey finds her underwear and steps into it before pulling it up.

She looks alarmed, so much so that I can see her bottom lip quivering.

"I know you're in there!"

Kacey gives up on looking on the floor and moves over to the clothing rail that runs along the wall. She pulls a short-sleeved fur coat from the middle of the rail and slings it over her shoulder, slipping her arms into it and pulling it closed at the front. It doesn't seem to have a button, and although it covers her breasts initially it soon reveals them as she turns and walks forwards.

"Open this fucking door!"

She stops in the bedroom doorway and turns to look at me, as I am still standing at the foot of the bed, nude and perplexed.

"Just... stay in here," Kacey says, before walking out of the room.

As soon as she is out of sight I move, scanning the bedroom floor for my clothes. I see my underpants in a ball near the foot of the bed. I put them on quickly.

"Don't make me kick this fucking door in!"

"I'm here, Gio, for God's sake," Kacey's voice trembles.

I stand still as I hear her opening the front door. My feet are planted to the spot as I listen to the commotion in the hall.

Whoever this Gio is, he pushes the door inwards as Kacey begins to open it. I hear her shriek as the door swings open and smashes against the inside wall.

"Let go of me!" Kacey yelps.

I hear a thud, perhaps Gio pushing Kacey up against the wall. This is followed by the front door slamming closed.

"Janine says you're leaving!" Gio shouts.

Kacey doesn't respond. I can only hear her groaning, perhaps struggling in Gio's grasp.

I walk forwards, making sure the various items on the ground muffle my footsteps. I step across my trousers and shirt and lean down to get to my briefcase. I am so close to the open bedroom door that I can see the shadows of the two people in the hallway just a few feet in front of me.

"When were you thinking of telling me?"

I watch the shadows dance on the carpeted floor of the hall and I see Gio raise his fist and bring it down across the side of Kacey's face.

He grunts as he lands the punch, before steadying Kacey, who almost falls from the blow. I tilt forwards until I can see Kacey pressed up against the wall. Her head hangs like that of a rag doll, Gio holding her up by the neck.

I can see flecks of blood beneath her nose.

"Before or after you paid me what you owe?"

I see tears flowing down her face as she gasps for breath. I snap open the clasps on my briefcase as quietly as possible.

"I should fucking kill you—"

I reach into it with steady hands, making sure that I make no sound that would alert Gio.

"Worthless fucking bitch—"

I breathe in and out three times, slowly.

"… not leaving, I can guarantee—"

I stand up and stride into the hall, making sure my footsteps draw immediate attention to me.

"…ugly cunt."

I catch Gio's eye and he turns his head towards me. I raise the gun to the same level as his head, making sure he sees exactly what I am holding in my hand.

His eyes widen and his hand drops from Kacey's neck, but I'm not giving this fucker a chance to reach for a weapon.

I pull the trigger of the Magnum revolver, the flash blinding me for a second and lessening the upshot of the enormous bang that erupts from the weapon.

I don't even see the impact of the bullet that rips into Gio's face, tearing half of it from his skull and swathing the ceiling, walls and door behind him with thick blood, brain matter and other gunk.

By the time I blink so that the flash is out of my sight, I can only see the corpse of Gio slumped in the corner of the hall, blood spewing from his mess of a face and soaking his navy blue sports tracksuit.

There is no twitch from the body, just a stillness that creeps up my spine. A bolt of excitement, fuelled by the adrenaline and enhanced by momentary vindication.

I see Kacey slump to her knees. She begins to sob frenziedly, her hands covering her face. I can make out some words beneath the grief.

"My God..."

I lower the gun, feeling a dull ache in my elbow from the recoil as I fired the shot.

If I hadn't pulled the trigger at that moment, he may have reached for a weapon of his own and blown me away.

That must have been the reason: there had to be a reason. I wouldn't have stepped into the hall with the intention of executing him.

I step forwards and lean over Gio's sunken frame. I use the barrel of the revolver to open his jacket. I see a pistol tucked into his waistband and that gives me all I need to know. It was him or me, and the outcome has been the one I would have preferred.

"Who was that?" I say, my voice crackling like a bad radio signal.

Kacey's breathing is frantic.

I assume that the sight of me holding this huge gun may not be helping, so I place it on the floor next to Gio

127

and step over to Kacey. I sit down next to her and put my arm onto her trembling shoulder.

I see spots of Gio's blood on her fur coat and what looks like one of his teeth.

I think about how precognitive I was to load the gun before I left William's apartment.

"Fucking… killed him," she burbles.

I cross my legs and see smears of the blood on the bottom of my feet. I can already smell the sour decay of death that mixes with a thin yet potent smoky veil.

"There's so much blood," Kacey says.

"Who was that?" I repeat.

"This is bad – fucking bad," Kacey sobs, ignoring my question as she did the first time I asked it.

I have just fired a gun within an apartment block that is full of people. Despite the time, Gio's raised voice would have been heard, as would have the disturbance once he got into Kacey's apartment.

Perhaps some people would be used to such occurrences on a regular basis, but to hear a sudden bellowing gunshot followed by the quelling of such disorder would surely alarm even the most contemptuous individual. It can't be long before someone calls the police and an officer or two come knocking.

4

I place both hands over Kacey's and feel her warm tears between her fingers.

"Kacey, please calm down," I say.

She parts her hands and looks at me, her eyes red and her cheeks flushed and wet from the tears. A bruise on the side of her face is gaining depth and looks fairly painful.

"Calm down?" Kacey says, clenching her teeth. "Calm down? You shot him, Chris. Shot him! Are you fucking crazy?"

I look over at Gio's corpse, which seems to have

slumped further down into the corner.

A pool of blood is growing beneath him, soaking into the carpet and getting darker with each pint that I excrete from the body.

"I… he was hurting you."

Kacey swings her arms wildly and hits me in the face and chest. She wails, her mouth open wide and her eyes circled black.

I grab hold of her by the wrists and hold her tight until she stops.

"We're fucking dead," Kacey whimpers.

"Kacey, come on," I say, shaking her.

I stand up and try to bring her with me, but she refuses to budge. She's like a dead weight but I manage to get her to her feet by pulling hard on her wrists and steadying her once she is upright.

I put an arm around her waist and begin to lead her into the bedroom so that she cannot see the gore-covered corpse sitting morbidly in the hall.

"You don't understand," she says, dribbling.

I manoeuvre her across the bedroom floor and drop her onto the bed. She falls backwards as if she has no bones in her body.

I stand at the foot of the bed in nothing but my underwear and decide that now would be a good time to get dressed. I gather up my clothes from the floor as she continues to moan and gripe, but I don't listen to what she is saying.

"I do understand," I tell her. "That bastard was hurting you. The stupid fucker was thinking he's a big man by laying his hands on you. Not so brash and aggressive with a bullet in his face, is he?"

"You're… insane," she says, writhing around on the bed.

"I'm not insane. He hit you, what else was he going to do? He had a gun, was his next step to shoot you?"

I slip on my trousers and put my shirt on. I start to

button it up while looking around on the floor to make sure that any item I have brought into Kacey's apartment leaves with me. I pick up my socks and pull them onto my bloodied feet.

"He's like that," Kacey says, the tears not yet relenting. "He's got a short temper. Fuck, I can't believe he found out."

Her eyes widen and she stares at the ceiling.

"*Fuck*, I can't believe he's dead!" Kacey says, her voice going high at the end of her words. "What are we going to do? I can't get put away for this, Chris. My son, Kieron, fuck. He can't grow up without his mother."

I finished buttoning my shirt and lean over to pick up my tie before slinging it around my neck.

"I killed him, Kacey, me. I'll face the consequences, but I promise you it won't have to come to that. We have to get out of here, right now."

Kacey sits up and stares at me turbulently.

"This is my fucking apartment, Chris! There's a dead body in the hall."

I slip on my shoes and tuck my shirt into my trousers before fastening my belt.

I can see what I've done. That's one thing I most certainly am not: deluded. I have filled my head with fantasies of murder for so long now that it has become part of me, and now that I have committed murder for the first time I am finally waking up from my neurotic slumber. I am not panicking, unlike Kacey, perhaps from the terrible shock. It's not every day you see a man's head explode in your own home.

"Where did you even get that gun?" Kacey says, not far from hyperventilating.

"It doesn't matter."

"Of course it does!"

"A friend, William Beckford. He sells me drugs now and again as well. What does that even matter?"

"It's a fucking cannon. Shit, Chris. It's ridiculous."

I'm fed up of this bullshit now. We need to leave.

"Get dressed, get some things together, not much, and be quick," I say as I put on my jacket and brush the lint from it.

"Don't tell me what to do, you prick!" Kacey screeches as she jumps up from the bed.

She walks towards me and I grab hold of her, stopping her in her tracks.

"No, Kacey, I will tell you what to do. I'm not staying here just to give myself up for that worthless fucker, and neither are you."

Her face is close to mine, so much so that I can feel her breath on my skin when she talks. I see her jaw wobble.

"His name is Gio Rigo," she says.

"*Was* Gio Rigo," I correct her.

She shakes her head in disbelief.

"Who was he?" I sneer. "A boyfriend? A client?"

Kacey looks away from me and I loosen my grip as I notice the tips of my fingers turning white.

"He... he *was* my boss."

I let go of her completely.

I should have guessed, really. The sportswear, the jewellery, the slicked-back hair. He reeked of a maggot that would take advantage and manipulate vulnerable women. He obviously liked to use his fists to keep them in check because his brain couldn't do that work for him.

"Good riddance," I mutter.

Kacey looks back at me with her mouth so wide I think I can see every one of her teeth.

"You just don't understand, Chris," she says.

"I've already told you. I do understand."

"No, you don't. Gio, he's not somebody you can just shoot dead. His friends, his family, they aren't nice people. That's why I didn't tell him I was leaving the city; I couldn't risk the safety of me and my son. Fuck. Janine, the stupid bitch. I shouldn't have told her."

I sigh deeply and begin to slowly pace the room as she stands motionless.

"So what would you prefer?" I ask. "Is it these friends of Gio coming after you? Or is it gunna be spending a few years behind bars as an accessory to murder? Kieron will grow up without you and no doubt resent you for abandoning him at such a young age and it will cause damage that will never be able to be undone."

I stop and look at Kacey, who is looking down at the ground with a detached look on her pretty face.

"You can cut all ties and escape. There's no chance some volatile low-lives will have the mental capacity or patience to track you across the country."

She says nothing.

"He was just a pimp, Kacey. Who can he know?"

Again, she doesn't respond. Her eyes flicker as she deliberates her options.

"You'd be surprised."

I close my eyes and breathe deeply.

"Well, I don't care. Get dressed and get some things together, or I'm gunna have to drag you out of here half naked and I'd say that would attract more attention to us than I'd want."

5

I leave the bedroom and scope out the rest of the apartment while Kacey gets dressed. I walk into rooms I haven't stepped inside before, my time in this apartment always confined to the bedroom.

I don't put on any of the lights, just look towards windows and doors for any sign of a possible route out.

There is a window at the back of the living room that leads out onto a small balcony that has a fire escape leading off from it and down onto the alleyway below.

It looks dark and out of sight down at ground level, which makes it the best choice for an exit. Walking out of the front door and down the main stairwell of the apartment building could give potential witnesses a good look at my face, and that's hoping that they didn't as I made my way here.

I hear Kacey sobbing quietly in the bedroom as she moves around.

I feel my stomach sink as I realise that my fingerprints will be all over the apartment, and, unfortunately for me, the police have my prints on record due to my recent drink-driving offence. They'll be looking for Kacey but there would be nothing to tie me directly to her since nobody knows of my visits to her.

I move from the living room to the kitchen and begin to look for a cloth and some sort of cleaning product. I open a low cabinet to my left and strain my eyes in the dark to see what's inside. I see an iron and a bottle of drain cleaner, but nothing more than that.

I open the cabinet door next to the one I have already opened and see a few dishcloths bunched together behind a bottle of antibacterial spray and other cleaning products.

I grab a cluster of dishcloths and the cleaning spray. I pull the trigger on the bottle and add some of the cleaning product to the cloths before moving out of the kitchen and back towards the bedroom.

I clean the doorknob on the bedroom door, although I cannot remember touching it today. I walk into the bedroom and see Kacey, now fully dressed in what seems to be black velour trousers and a yellow crop-top, hunched over a small opened suitcase. She has piled clothes inside it and also a small leather-bound book, perhaps a photo album.

She is talking to herself as I look around the room.

"What the fuck do I take?" she mutters, taking in breath sharply, quite obviously still distressed.

The room smells terrible, but then I remember the bloodied corpse in the hall. Strange how something like that can slip the mind. The stench of death is taking over this place already, no doubt because Gio's bowels have given way.

I clean the doorknob on the inside of the door as well as the edges of the door, just in case. I clean the edges of the furniture in the room, finding it hard to remember exactly what I have touched. I clean a mug that sits atop a chest of drawers and move over to the bed and clean the top of the bedposts.

Kacey turns towards me, her eyes puffy and red.

"What are you doing?" she asks.

"Never mind, just finish what you're doing and be ready to leave. We're going down the fire escape in two minutes."

"The fire escape?"

"We can't walk out of the front door. We'll get down to the alley and cut back towards the park. Once we make it through there I'll get us a cab and we'll go to my place."

"Jesus, you can't be—"

"No time for arguments, Kacey. Two minutes."

She shakes her head and continues to pile her belongings into the suitcase. I walk out of the bedroom and clean off the doorknobs to each room I entered. I clean off the edges of the cabinets I opened in the kitchen and walk back out to the hall.

I remember that I knocked on the front door but I can't risk opening it for any reason, so I put it to the back of my mind and step over to the revolver that I left on the ground after I fired it.

I lean over and pick it up before tucking the gun into my waistband. I take a final look at the death mask of Gio Rigo and the blackening pool of blood beneath him before joining Kacey in the bedroom once again.

I pick up my briefcase from the floor and bundle the cleaning spray and dishcloths into it and clasp it shut.

"Time's up," I say.

"Chris, please, I haven't even looked in the living room. There may be things I need in there. I've got clothes for Kieron but I need to find more. I can't just leave, not like this. Maybe we can get rid of the body and—"

"No fucking way," I snap, cutting her short.

She bites her bottom lip with renewed anxiety. I feel bad for shouting at her, but now is not the time for these discussions. We can talk about what we 'should've' and 'could've' done for hours at a later date and I am sure we will.

"Let's go."

6

I make sure that Kacey opens the window in the living room that leads out onto the balcony. I hold my briefcase close to my chest like a newborn baby as she struggles to lift her suitcase up to the window.

She glances back at me, visibly disgusted at my lack of an offer to help. I don't understand why she has packed so much. She won't need it. It's all gunna need to burn if she wants to run away to her new life.

Once she is out onto the balcony I follow her out of the window, leading with one leg and making sure that my hands do no work to help me out. She turns to close the window behind her but I throw her a momentary look that convinces her to leave it.

My stomach wrenches as I hear a distant police siren, but seconds later I realise that it's fading, too far away to start with and even further away now.

We make our way down the fire escape slowly, my eyes darting around the streets I can see at the end of the gloomy alley. I make sure that each step I take makes as little noise as possible on the steel steps. Kacey makes no such effort, each of her steps shaking the fire escape as her suitcase clangs against the metallic framework.

Kacey sniffs and sobs, continuing to struggle with the case. We reach the bottom of the fire escape and step onto the asphalt, our shadows lurching onto the ground like labouring giants. She turns and looks at me, her make-up smudged and her mouth upturned.

I see somebody walk across the mouth of the alley in front of us and my right hand reaches for the gun in my waistband.

I remove my hand from the gun and place it on Kacey's shoulder.

"Which way?" she says.

"I told you, we follow the alley until we come out at the opposite side of the block. Then we'll move through the park and find a cab."

I turn and walk away from the mouth of the alley with Kacey following close behind me.

"I have to get to Kieron," Kacey says.

I pretend not to hear her. That's something I hadn't taken into account, and right now it's something we can't risk. We have to get away from the scene of the crime and get our heads down. A dash to anywhere other than my apartment is too risky, and although I know that Kacey won't be happy about it, we have to leave Kieron where he is until it is safer to get him.

"Chris, did you hear me?"

Again I ignore her, focusing only on the windows above us, looking for a watching eye.

"Did the gunshot make you go deaf? Answer me!"

Her raised voice makes my blood boil. I have no idea how somebody can be so brainless, no matter what distress they have been through.

"Be quiet," I say in a harsh whisper without breaking my stride.

"But... my baby," she says gently.

"Let's go to my apartment and talk about what's best to do when we get there, okay?"

She is silent again, seemingly not happy with my decision.

My heart thuds faster than I ever thought possible as we reach the end of the alley and walk out onto the street.

We cross the street, which is empty but for a group of teenagers sitting on a bench less than twenty feet away. There are no moving cars, which calms me somewhat, but my hands twitch, ready to pull out the gun if need be.

The transition from the murk of the alley into the brightly lit street eradicates this calm. I feel as though eyes are in every window, staring down at me as the streetlamps shine down upon me like a spotlight.

The teenagers look over at me and Kacey, quite possibly making a mental note of the direction we are heading in so that they can tell the cops when they ask.

I scurry across the road, my hand trailing behind me, urging Kacey to keep up. She whimpers, following me as I step up onto the sidewalk and move quickly into the park. I am grateful for the returning darkness and slow my pace to ensure Kacey stays with me.

"This is fucking crazy," Kacey says breathlessly.

The park seems to be empty, which is exactly what I wanted. The darkness is thicker than anticipated, which makes it difficult for me to see too far in front.

"We can't just run," Kacey continues, "that's not how it works. You can't kill somebody and get away with it. That may be how it happens in the movies but it's nothing like real life. There's always evidence and there are always witnesses. We may as well hand ourselves in."

The brisk wind sends a chill up my back.

"Don't start spouting that bullshit, Kacey. I know that you're scared, and there's nothing I can say to you that will take that away, but we're not giving up. There's no reason for us to be caught."

In this time of trauma and discord, I am beginning to see exactly the person she is. Irrational, deluded, panic-stricken. We have much more in common than I ever thought we did.

"The hard part is over," I assure her. "We made it out of your apartment and we're never gunna go anywhere near there again. My place is quite a way from here, so as soon as we get there we're safe."

I look over my shoulder at Kacey, who is looking down at the ground as she drags her suitcase along the footpath. We are almost out of the park, which is barely a block wide. I hope we have no trouble hailing a cab.

"I won't feel safe until Kieron is with me."

"Where is he?" I ask.

"He's with a friend of mine, in Brooklyn."

I stop dead in my tracks.

"Brooklyn?" I say.

"Yeah, he usually stays with an old roommate of mine a few blocks from here. But she was busy tonight so he had to stay with a girl who used to work on the streets with me, back before I did all my business from home."

I shake my head in disbelief.

"Fuck, Brooklyn?" I repeat.

"Yeah," Kacey says. "Look, I can go and get him myself. Give me your address, and once I've got him I can join you there."

As we approach the edge of the park, a car drives across us, slowly enough to keep me attentive. I rub my thumb on the butt of the revolver, my palms growing sweaty and the hairs on my back prickling.

I hold my breath until it gets far enough away. Once I can no longer see the tail-lights, I exhale.

"Too dangerous. I'll have to get him for you."

I look at Kacey as the golden glow from a nearby streetlamp reaches her face. I can tell from her quivering lips that she is trying to put together a sentence in response.

"I'm scared, Chris," she says.

I take hold of her hand as we cross the street. There's no need to say anything more to her, not now.

I am sure I would be scared as well if I wasn't running on the adrenaline that's coursing through my body. I've got no time to sit down and be frightened of the shadows in the dark and what terrors they hold for me.

I killed Gio because he hurt Kacey, and I will justify that to myself until the day I die. He didn't deserve to live merely to go on and abuse other women in the same way he did her.

As we cross the street and round a corner I signal a cab, which swerves around to us and stops. Once we get in the back and I tell the driver where we want to go, I look back over my shoulder and out onto the New York street, as if mentally picking up any breadcrumbs that I may have dropped that either the cops or these friends of Gio Rigo would be able to follow.

THE FIFTH TALE - DEVIATE

1

My apartment is dark and cold. It feels alien as I step inside, the way it would if I had been away on vacation for a couple of weeks.

Kacey slams her case onto the floor next to where I have placed my briefcase and walks over to the couch and sits down, her arms crossed and a scowl on her face.

I know that there will be no talking to Kacey while her son is still in Brooklyn, so I begin to make plans as to how I will go and get him.

Brooklyn is a fair way, meaning I will have to cross the bridge which will make the journey total close to an hour, depending on what mode of transportation I decide on. It's almost one in the morning, so a car is going to be my best bet.

Jenny's run-around is locked up in the garage basement of this apartment building and if I'm going to be making a habit of breaking the law, I may as well start to run with it.

I've already killed a man tonight, so driving illegally doesn't exactly strike me as pushing the boundaries and risking it all.

I sit down next to Kacey and she turns away from me. It's so dark that my eyes are finding it hard to adjust, which makes reading her expressions tricky. I would turn on a light but I don't want to advertise that anybody is home.

"You have to stay here while I go and get Kieron," I say, trying to make my words sound as far from a command as possible.

"You don't know where he is," she replies.

I place a hand on Kacey's knee.

"You gunna tell me?"

She shakes her head and shifts away from me. I know

she'll never forgive me for what I have done. She had an escape route from the life she hated, a tunnel leading to better and brighter things. I've pulled a trigger and filled the tunnel with concrete so that not even a small beam of that bright light can be seen.

"If anything happens to him, I'll kill you," Kacey says without looking at me. "You have to give me your word that you'll bring him back here, safe. I won't accept anything less. You owe it to us."

I stand up and walk over to the kitchen area. I open the fridge and take a bottle of beer from inside. I turn around and hold the neck of the bottle against the edge of the granite kitchen worktop and press the palm of my hand down on top of it hard and fast. The bottle top pops off and I bring the beer to my lips, drinking down the entire contents in one go.

"You've got my word," I say, wiping my lips. I have the urge to belch but I restrain myself.

I need a hit of some sort before I leave. The harder stuff isn't gunna be a good idea, but maybe a couple of lines, just to focus me a little.

"He's in an apartment in Bushwick, above a Puerto Rican deli," Kacey tells me. "It's in North East Brooklyn, which means when you get off the bridge you've got to—"

"I know Bushwick. Not inside out, but I know how to get there. Write down the address for me."

I open a drawer to the left of the fridge and find a pad of lined paper. I search in the drawer to find a pen before walking back over towards Kacey on the couch and handing the items to her.

"It's on Bushwick Avenue," Kacey says. "The girl's name who he's with is Naomi. I'll have to call her and let her know you're coming to collect him."

Kacey writes down the address on the pad, tears off the sheet of paper and holds it out to me. I take it, fold it in half and place it in my jacket pocket.

"Okay, the phone's in the bedroom if you want to use

it."

Kacey doesn't respond. She resumes staring into space.

"Don't tell Naomi about Gio," I add. "It will only complicate things. Tell her I'm Kieron's godfather or something. Don't let her dig. If she asks questions give her as little as possible."

As Kacey goes to the bedroom to make the phone call I dig into my briefcase and find what cocaine I have in there. I go into the bathroom, cut up a couple of lines and snort them from the surface of the flat white sink.

My head jolts with white electricity and it flows all the way down to my fingertips.

I come out of the bathroom and can hear Kacey talking on the phone in the bedroom. She sounds distressed, which probably doesn't help matters, but I can't really expect much more from her.

She's a hooker, not an actress.

I return the remainder of the coke to my briefcase and find the box of ammo for the Colt Python.

I tip the box over so that the bullets spill out over the contents of my case. I remove the revolver from my trousers and open it so I can see the empty chamber, which used to be home to a bullet that is now in Gio Rigo's skull. I take hold of one bullet from the briefcase and reload the gun before snapping it closed and returning it to my waistband.

I scoop up six more bullets and put them into my jacket pocket, which also contains Naomi's address.

I make sure I have my apartment keys in one trouser pocket and I assemble the rest of the items I'll need in the other. I pick up my car keys from a ceramic dish at one end of the worktop, still unmoved from when my ban was put into place, and find my cell phone in my briefcase before closing it and fastening the clasps.

2

A few minutes later, Kacey comes out from the bedroom. She walks back over to the couch with her head hanging low. Once she sits down I walk over next to her, but she doesn't look up at me. There is an awkward exchange of words, where I ask Kacey if she is okay but she misunderstands me, as if she wasn't even listening in the first place. When she asks me to repeat myself I decide against it, realising that it isn't worth my time right at this moment.

I turn and walk towards the apartment door. Once I am a few inches away from it, I turn and see that Kacey is looking directly at me, tears yet again streaming down her face.

"Stay here," I say. "Don't answer the door if anybody comes knocking."

I open the front door and move out into the night, closing it behind me as I hear Kacey's soft voice calling after me.

"Just bring back my baby."

3

I reacquaint myself with the silver Mitsubishi Lancer, running my hands around the steering wheel and gazing at the dashboard intensely.

Once I get the engine running I sit back and absorb the familiar hum of the vehicle, a soft vibration on the back of my neck and a distant hiss as the air conditioning gets going.

I click it off before it blows cold air in my face, as this night (or early morning as I guess it now is) is way too bitter for that, despite it being late summer.

I am so glad that this wasn't the car I damaged when I decided to drink myself over the limit and go for a relaxing drive. If I had done I probably would have felt a lot worse when I had my mug shot taken at the station. Luckily it was the shitty run-around I had decided to purchase as a second car for Jennifer and me.

This was never the car I had expected I would end up driving, and I most certainly didn't want it to be until Jennifer convinced me otherwise. To other drivers, I know that it seems pretentious and unnecessary, but Jennifer fell in love with it back in the day when I would do anything to please her, even put my dignity aside and forget the bad points of owning a car such as this.

I worried about growing into exactly the kind of person who would own a silver Mitsubishi Lancer, taking on all the pompous elements of the car and rising to the expectations of an observer. I managed to eliminate these worries in time, persuading myself that I would be ridiculous to think that I need to pigeonhole myself just because of the car I choose to drive.

Returning to this car after such a long time spent having to rely on the freak-show-on-wheels that is the public bus service feels so good I could cry tears of joy.

I pull away from the spot in the garage, my head filling with bullshit about tyre pressure and the level on my fuel gauge rather than the matter at hand.

I reach the automated shutter and brake hard. I sit and wait for about fifteen seconds, my foot twitching on the accelerator and my fingers drumming on the dashboard. Once the shutter is fully open I speed out onto the street, screeching the car around to the left and increasing the momentum as I begin to drive straight.

This really is the city that never sleeps, as you hear all the time when people describe this monster of a place. Even at this hour, and sometimes especially at this hour, the activity on the streets and the noise erupting like a geyser on every corner continues as if it were the middle of the day.

I am cautious as I make my way towards Brooklyn Bridge, keeping an eye on the pedestrians as I pass them as well as the vehicles that follow or pull up beside me.

The gun chafes against my crotch and all I want to do is take it out from my pants and place it on the passenger seat to my right. But I know that I need to keep it out of sight.

I hold no power to stop Kacey leaving New York, not now at least. Come to think of it, I doubt I did at all, even before I blew Gio's face to bits.

But back then I may have done my best to convince her to stay. It would have been a completely selfish act, something I know I wouldn't be proud of, but I need her, so much I find it hard to come to terms with. I would have gone as low as to have begged on my knees until she changed her mind, because her leaving would sentence me to death, at my hands or at the hands of another.

I would sink into the gutter and be the son-of-a-bitch who puts himself before the wellbeing of a single mother and her young son.

If anything, I now need to put any feelings I have for her aside and give her the push she may well need to do the right thing. She's terrified, and so she should be.

Terror grips the human condition and shakes it until every sense of reality is warped and shredded. She won't be thinking straight for a long time, and I need to make sure that I regain the correct amount of control in this situation so that I can send her on the right path.

She needs me to keep my head upon my shoulders, even if only temporarily, so that I can protect her and assist her every need.

I must keep my head on my shoulders. No running into Brooklyn like a headless ghoul.

4

The remainder of the journey, which takes me across the bridge into Brooklyn and on towards Bushwick, is uneventful. I make good time, less than forty-five minutes, which pleases me.

After the initial burst of paranoia followed by the usual tricks my brain does when it is backed into a corner, I manage to concentrate entirely on driving and figuring out the best route to get to my destination, for speed purposes, within the limit, of course, as well as low-key, to avoid the eyes of somebody who may be watching closer than before.

I can't remember if I have been to this neighbourhood before, but the buildings and streets look distinctly familiar. I look up at banners hanging all of the way across a high street I turn into, which I saw is Bushwick Avenue from a sign not far back. The banners are adorned with flags, which I can make out to be the flags of various Latino countries of origin, including the Dominican Republic and Puerto Rico, amongst others.

The street is lined with darkened shop fronts that represent this place as a multi-cultural area. I see hair salons, convenience stores, food markets, restaurants, takeaways and oddly a couple of shops that seem to specialise only in bicycles.

I haven't yet looked at the address on the piece of paper in my pocket, but as I approach a crossroads I notice a sign above a shop on the left side of the street and I know that it is the place. It's about thirty feet in front of me but I can read the words 'Homemade Puerto Rican Cuisine'.

I slow down the car to almost a standstill, letting the vehicle coast down on the slight gradient.

I won't stop too close, but I also need to make sure that the car is not so far away that a quick getaway will be impossible. I turn right at the crossroads and drive fifty feet before stopping so that I am out of sight of the Deli.

I park in front of a derelict Chinese takeaway that has wooden boards where it should have windows and, above these, a discoloured sign with broken Chinese scripture.

I can feel the adrenaline within me now. It feels like a

ferocious torrent of water: a white-water rapid making my heart feel like it's the size of a football and my muscles spasm with an unknown current.

I switch off the engine and exit the car with an eerie speed, locking it behind me and making it across the street before I even notice I am on my feet.

I look around behind me and take mental pictures of every face I see. Walking in the same direction as me is a bearded man with a shopping trolley full of plastic bags and other junk, although he doesn't look homeless, as his tweed jacket looks pressed and his black jeans look fresh from the washing line.

To my left, on the side of the street I walked from, is a pair of twenty-something Latino girls, rapping and hollering at a hip-hop song that is blaring from one of their cell phones.

I turn back to face where I am walking and clock a tattooed man with a bald head. His eye catches mine and, for a second although it feels more like ten, I feel my heart grow cold, certain he is looking at me because he knows exactly what it is I have done and what I am here to do. It is in this second that I am sure he is about to pull a gun or a blade and come at me, but he doesn't and removes his gaze from me.

I step up the kerb and feel myself speeding up. I lift up the bottom of my shirt so that the butt of the revolver is revealed and press the bottom of my palm against it. I rub my eyes with my other hand and blink hard a couple of times to clear my vision. I round a corner and after a few more feet I am almost opposite the Deli.

To the right of the shop front there is a dark brown wooden door, the paintwork scratched and faded.

Before I cross the street, I reach in and grab the paper from my jacket pocket, the cold bullets rolling around my fingers as I reach for it. The number of Naomi's apartment is 450.

I fold over the paper in my hand and cross the street,

striding with purpose and now squeezing the butt of the gun. Once I get close enough to the brown door I see three bells on the wall next to it, showing me that there are three residences above the Deli. Numbers 448, 449 and 450.

I look to my left and then to my right, making sure that I am not being watched, from street level at least.

I press the bell on 450 and hear a shrill noise somewhere a couple of floors up. I wait almost thirty seconds before pressing again, and the lack of activity coming from behind the door and the windows above makes a cold bead of sweat appear on the bridge of my nose. After what I think is another thirty seconds, I press the bell again, the noise seeming louder than the first two presses.

I hear a noise directly above me and step back so that I can get a good view. My neck cranes upward and I see a window open two floors up. It's pretty dark, but I can see a girl poke her head out slightly and it's fairly palpable that she thinks I can't see her.

The head disappears and I think about calling after her, but realise that I would have to be fairly loud for her to hear me and that could get half of the street twitching their curtains and looking out to see the source of the disturbance.

I continue to wait, looking all around constantly. To somebody watching, I must look significantly suspicious. I'm gripping the gun so tightly now that my fingertips have lost almost all feeling.

I think about kicking in the door, but I compose myself and soon my patience pays off as I hear footsteps growing louder on the other side of the door.

Just to be safe, I pull out the gun and hold it behind my back. My middle finger rests lightly on the trigger.

I listen as a bolt is unlocked and a chain pulled across the door. After another couple of clicks, the door opens a few inches and I see half of a female face staring at me from within greying obscurity.

"Who are you?" she asks me, sounding every bit as Brooklyn as she should.

"It's me, Chris. You gunna let me in?"

She looks me up and down, the light catching a piercing on her eyebrow.

"Who sent you?" she asks.

I put the gun back into my waistband, but this time behind me so that it is out of sight of the girl. I hold out my hands, not necessarily to show her that I am not armed but as a sign of calm, ensuring her that I am not an enemy.

"Kacey," I reply. "Come on, she told you I was coming. I'm Kieron's godfather."

She looks me up and down again.

"Never knew the boy had a godfather. She ain't mentioned you before. She wasn't making much sense on the phone, sounded scared and upset, like she'd been crying. You're on the Rigo payroll, aren't you? Working for Gennaro? Or Gio?"

I recognise a name but I don't flinch.

"What? No. Who?"

She looks down at the ground as if her answers lie there. She stutters as she tries to get her next lot of words out.

"W-what if I don't let you have him? W-what if I just close this door?"

I look around again, my patience wearing thin with this girl. I feel exposed out in the open as it is so I won't argue with her. I need to encourage her to open this door, and quickly.

"Kacey wants me to take her son to her," I say calmly. "There's no need for you to stand in the way of that. Trust me, open the door, it's the right thing to do."

She closes the door and I expect to hear her remove the chain, but after a few seconds she opens the door again. I grind my teeth.

"Is she okay?" Naomi asks me.

"She's fine. She just wants her son."

Naomi closes the door and removes the chain before opening it all of the way. I move quickly into the doorway and softly close the door behind me.

With the light from the street removed it is almost pitch black inside and I can only just make out the shape of Naomi in the darkness.

She moves and I follow her along the corridor. As we head towards a staircase my eyes start to adjust, helped by a faint orange glow coming from a light a floor or so above.

The staircase is narrow as we climb up it, me following closely behind the girl. I can now see that she is short and fairly plump, dressed in a thick pink robe with matching slippers.

She is Puerto Rican, as far as I can tell, although I can't be sure as my eye isn't keen for telling the nationality of individuals. Perhaps it's the fact that her home is above a Puerto Rican Deli that's throwing me off.

Her black hair is tied back tight in a ponytail, which seems overly hair-sprayed despite her being apparently dressed for bed.

As she follows the bend on the staircase taking us up to the first floor I see that her face is also caked in make-up, which I hadn't noticed before when she came to the door. Her eyebrows are thick and seemingly drawn on, while her lips are shiny with pink lip-gloss.

She has several piercings on her face, in addition to the one on her eyebrow. There are small silver studs in her nose, above the left side of her top lip and in both of her ears, one in each lobe and at the top of the ear.

"He's asleep, been so since about eight," Naomi says. "Poor little boy's exhausted. Must've been the trip across town. Kacey don't make a habit of having him stay with me, and I'm glad of it. Ain't got much patience with kids, but I try."

We reach the first floor. The landing is scattered with

various junk, including an old mattress and a basket overflowing with newspapers. The carpet is thinning and sticky under my shoes.

"How come Kacey's never mentioned you before?" she questions.

We turn back on ourselves and ascend another flight of stairs to the second floor.

"I moved to Europe a few years ago. Haven't seen Kacey in a long, long time. Back here on business, so thought I'd pay her a visit. She probably hasn't mentioned me because we're not as close as we used to be."

Naomi looks back at me over her shoulder.

"Close enough that she trusts you with her son though, right?"

I stroke the side of my face, which is rough from the build-up of stubble.

"I suppose so," I say.

We make it to the top of the second flight of stairs where there is a small landing and a single door that is open a few inches.

I look over the banister back down to ground level as Naomi walks into her apartment. With her back fully turned I remove the gun from the back of my pants and return it to the front for easier access if I need it.

The hallway inside Naomi's apartment is narrow and cold, the dull paintwork and discoloured ceiling highlighted by the bright white glare from a fluorescent strip-light that runs down the middle of it.

The light hurts my eyes and almost instantaneously makes me feel tired. I look down at my hands and see that my skin looks deathly pale, almost to a degree that I can see my bones.

The hallway is puzzlingly long. It seems as though we walk further than the length of the entire building before we reach a door at the end. We pass two doors on the left, both of which are closed, and one on the right with is fully open and lit only by a television displaying nothing but static on the screen.

I slow down and notice a man sleeping on a couch in front of the TV. He is young, perhaps early twenties, and is wearing nothing but a pair of white briefs and is snoring quietly with his mouth wide open. His chest is covered in tattoos and he has long black hair hanging over his face.

Naomi opens the door at the end and I follow her into an undersized bedroom, where I can see Kieron sleeping in the middle of a double bed which takes up most of the room.

He is curled up in a ball with his face buried in a pillow. He wears bright green pyjamas and seems to have kicked his blanket off onto the ground.

"I'll get his stuff together," Naomi says, looking at me face-on for the first time since I came into this building. "Most of it's in the other room."

She leaves the bedroom and walks into the room with the sleeping man, who I am assuming is Naomi's boyfriend, or even a customer, if Kacey's description of how she knows the girl is anything to go by. However, she certainly doesn't seem like the kind of girl I would want to pay for the pleasure of her company.

I am alone with Kieron, who is breathing deeply and soundly. I've never been in close contact with kids, so I may be a little out of my depth, but I suppose I can use common sense. He's over three years old, so at least he's toilet trained and eating solid foods. No need to worry about making up bottles with formula and he won't need to be transported everywhere in a baby stroller.

I walk around the side of the bed. The last thing I can be doing is taking my time. I need to get out of here: no more waiting around.

I lean over and scoop Kieron up into my arms, cradling him and placing his sleeping head on my shoulder. He stirs but doesn't wake up.

I crouch down and grab his blanket before wrapping it around his legs. I look around the bed and on the floor for something like a soft toy that would help calm the boy once he wakes up and is confused to see a stranger and not his mother.

As I move the pillow on the bed, I hear a distant thud from below. A low rumble that sounds like a ride-on lawnmower follows it, but I then notice that my ears are playing tricks on me.

The noise is footsteps, belonging to more than one person for sure, running up the stairs. I am frozen to the spot, even though I am trying my best to move. It seems as if it takes whoever I can hear only a few seconds to reach the second floor, but I know it must be longer than that. By the time the footsteps are so loud I can hear each one perfectly, the front door to Naomi's apartment is kicked inwards, hinges and splinters erupting from the doorway and the feeble hunk of wood collapsing to the ground.

I spin around and manage to hide behind the open door of the bedroom before I get the chance to see anybody come inside, which means I haven't been seen.

I hold Kieron close to my body with one arm and use my spare hand to pull the revolver out from my waistband. I cock the weapon and clutch the gun up by my face, take a few deep breaths and, holding them, silently listen as the intruders enter Naomi's apartment.

There are a few slow steps as somebody steps over the broken door. I hold my head against the wall so that I can see through the tiny gap between the bedroom door and the wall.

The angle the door is open at doesn't let me see far down the corridor, so I can't assess how many assailants there are. I listen closely to the slow footsteps again and would guess only two if I was pushed. Perhaps one more, but I hope not.

I hear Naomi come out from the other room, her footsteps closer and softer due to the slippers on her feet.

"What the fuck are you—"

I hear a clashing of fist to face and a high-pitched yelp. Naomi then screams, but it is suppressed and soon turns to a choking sound.

Somebody is strangling her and I hear whoever is doing it growling like a beast.

"Where's your whore-friend?"

The male voice is full of aggression. His accent and attitude is similar to that of Gio; perhaps he's a family member or at least of the same Italian American ethnicity.

Naomi cannot answer his question as she is busy gasping for breath.

"Huh?" the male voice continues. "Can't hear you, whore! Where's Kacey? Where's the other fucking whore?"

Naomi is hit again, a hard slap. She carries on wheezing as the hands around her neck persist with garrotting her.

Kieron begins to wake, rubbing his closed eyes with his hands and grumbling as his head moves from side to side. I hold him closer to my body, hoping this will soothe him and ease him back to his slumber. The noise coming from the hall obstructs what I hope, and the pummelling noise of my heart coming through my chest doesn't help either.

"I'll look for her," another male voice says, significantly calmer than the first.

I hold my head against the wall, my thumb twitching against the throttle on the revolver. I thumb it back as quietly as possible as I turn my head to try my best to see through the gap in the door.

I hear what must be Naomi dropping to her knees, panting insanely and beginning to sob. The angry man has gone quiet as his associate opens the doors that were on the left side of the hall as I walked down towards the bedroom.

"Empty," he says, coming out of the first room.

"Please don't hurt me," Naomi begs.

I slowly edge the door closed, only an inch or so, so

that I can see down the corridor.

I see a scrawny man with scruffy black hair and a wispy moustache walking into the second room to his left and coming back out only a few seconds later.

"Bathroom," he says.

I move the door slightly more so that I can see the other man, who is standing over Naomi. She is on all fours on the ground, breathing heavily and bawling like a child who has lost her mother.

The other man is much more powerfully built. His limbs are thick and long and his shoulders are broad. His neck is wide, and his head looks like an oddly-shaped boulder resting on top of it. He has a receding hairline and greying stubble on his face. He wears a tan leather jacket, which is faded on the elbows, and light denim jeans.

"I'll hurt you as much as I fucking want," he says as the scrawny man passes behind him and walks towards the living room that Naomi came out of.

Seconds later I hear a scuffle, a few punches being thrown and a dull clunk as somebody hits a wall. I hear a yelp of pain and somebody muttering a series of curses.

I see the scrawny man's back as he comes out from the living room, his body shielding my vision so that I cannot see the others in the hall. As he spins around I see that he is grabbing a young man by dark greasy hair and pulling him along the ground, his legs and arms thrashing and his mouth open wide in torment. It is the man who was sleeping in front of the TV.

The scrawny man hits the long-haired man hard in the back of the head and he slumps onto the ground just behind Naomi, looking pathetic and horrendous lying in only his discoloured briefs.

"Is this the motherfucker?" the burly man shouts at Naomi.

Naomi continues to snivel and snort on the ground, her face buried in her hands.

"Did this worthless piece of shit kill Gio?"

The long-haired man rolls over on the ground so that he is on his back. He seems only semi-conscious, and his eyes are wide and confused as he looks up at the intruders.

The burly man grabs Naomi by the hair and pulls her head back.

"Answer me!"

He spits in her face and slams her head against the wall. I feel like a distant spectator, perhaps watching this on an old grainy VHS tape on a black and white TV.

"I... don't know what you're... talking about," Naomi whimpers.

The scrawny man kicks the long-haired man in the head and I see a spray of blood come from his mouth.

"You know what?" the burly man says. "I'm gunna make this real easy."

He produces a 9mm pistol from his jacket and fires a shot downward, the flash from the gunshot illuminating Naomi's desperate face. The long-haired man wails in agony, his knee a red mess, blown to bits.

Kieron's eyes open wide, the gunshot dragging him from his sleep. His face is a picture of chaos as he looks at me, and I know exactly what's coming next.

I'm a stranger, and for a three-year-old to wake up next to a stranger after such a loud noise must be a traumatic experience, I can understand that.

I wish it didn't have to be that way, because he's about to put both of us in a shitload of danger.

Kieron begins to cry, his mouth as wide as his eyes, kicking his legs to get away from me. I hold him even closer with a solid grip so that he cannot move, my attention diverted away from the men in the hallway for a second.

During this second they have been alerted to the presence of somebody in this bedroom. I see both of them looking down the corridor towards the door, the shrieks of agony coming from the long-haired man fading into the background like ambient noise.

One thing remains on my side. My presence is not clear, for the only noise coming from this room is that of a crying child. I still have the element of surprise.

I push back from the wall and shift myself to the right so that I am in the doorway and directly in the line of vision of both of the assailants.

I straighten out my arm, lift the gun and fire off three shots in quick succession, my eyes not once blinking so I see where the bullets hit.

The first shot hits the scrawny man in the thigh, a bad shot perhaps, but I think I pulled the trigger before I raised the Python fully.

The second does better, hitting him in the neck and almost certainly killing him. I see him already falling to the ground as I fire off the third, which hits the burly man in the chest, just off centre to his right.

I move out of the doorway as quickly as I stepped into it, cradling Kieron's head as the burly man begins to fire his gun is response. The bullets fly into the room inches away from me, the pops from his pistol sounding pale in comparison to the massive roaring bellows of my revolver.

I drop to the ground as the bullets follow me, hitting the wall as I duck behind it, dusting me with plasterboard.

The burly man continues to fire until the clip in his pistol is empty, the low click followed by the sound of him falling to the ground with a despairing grunt.

It's difficult to distinguish the sources of the moans and groans of pain coming from the hall, but I can have a guess.

The wet gurgle and choke, similar to that of somebody being held under water, comes from the scrawny man as blood spills from the wound in his neck and fills up his mouth.

The low snarl, which is beginning to break into a desolate howl, comes from the burly man as he struggles to find another clip to reload his gun. I know he won't have the chance to, as he is also almost undoubtedly going to die from his wound, the revolver having created a cavity in his chest.

I have to admit I am shocked he managed to stay on his feet and return fire after such receiving such a fatal injury.

Behind these noises I can still hear the long-haired man groaning from his wounded knee, although this injury is nothing compared to the lethal mutilations I have inflicted on the two friends of Gio Rigo.

Naomi is crying, but it is muffled, probably because her face remains in her hands, the poor girl too terrified to look at the extent of the carnage that has unfolded.

"Fuck!" the burly man screams before growing quiet.

Kieron is also quiet, the fear and shock of the last few seconds and the loud gunshots causing him to bury his face into my jacket and shudder hysterically.

I stroke his hair to offer some sort of respite.

I wait for a while until I hear the gurgling from the scrawny man cease. I know that he is now dead, but I am not sure about the burly man. He may just be quiet as he goes into shock, but I didn't hear him reload his weapon so it should be safe to come out.

I stand up and press my back against the wall once again, my nose filling with the dust from the plasterboard that is littered with bullet holes.

I move into the hallway with my gun leading the way, aiming it down at the dead body of the scrawny man as I step over him, blood soaking him from the bottom of his chin all the way down to his groin.

The long-haired man looks up at me from the ground, stopping his complaining for a few seconds as I pass, not sure whether to be afraid of me or not.

I move onto the burly man, who also seems to be dead. His eyes are still and staring at the ceiling, a gun clip in his left hand and his pistol resting on his stomach, a few inches down from the hole in his chest.

I step over him, shielding Kieron's eyes from the corpses and avoiding Naomi's stare. She starts to say something but I manage to block it out, focusing only on the open doorway to her apartment with the broken door splintered on the ground in front of it.

I move out of the apartment and onto the stairs, looking down as I hurry my steps, ready to shoot anybody who stands in my way. I feel a blast of exhilaration as I race downwards, almost as if I am enjoying myself.

I've just killed the second and third people of the night, and I'm enjoying myself? Fuck, things really are getting out of control.

I reach the ground floor and hear Naomi shouting after me from above. I can't make out the words, so I ignore her.

I exit the building and quickly look to my left and then to my right, holding the gun out with every intention to pull the trigger. I see nobody and no longer care about having the gun in plain sight, so I start to jog across the street, holding out the weapon like a priest would hold a crucifix out to protect himself from a horde of Vampires.

Kieron sobs quietly, probably hoping that this is all a nightmare and that he will soon wake up to the familiar face of his mother. My ears ring from the gunshots and I can't even imagine what they did to the little boy's eardrums. He must be petrified.

I decide to offer some words of reassurance as I round a corner and see my car parked on the opposite side of the road.

"It's okay," I say. "Don't be scared, I'm taking you back to your Mom. You'll see her soon, I promise."

The boy continues to cry, so I turn my attention to the streets before me. I can see a few people roaming, but there doesn't seem to be anybody that would be a significant threat. Nobody is interested in me with my Colt Python cocked and loaded as I make my way to my car.

I look around to see if anybody is following me as I

cross the street and walk up beside my car. I open the back door and place Kieron inside on the back seat. I pull the blanket up from his legs and cover him up to his shoulders with it. I secure him with a seatbelt.

I close the door softly and open the door on the driver's side of my car. I climb in and open the glove box, place the revolver inside and push it closed.

I sit still and silent for a few seconds, looking around for anybody waiting to strike.

The cops aren't on my tail, that's for sure. I would have seen or heard a squad car and may have had to indulge in a high-speed pursuit, which would be stressful, so I am glad I have avoided it.

Gio Rigo's friends managed to stumble upon me, but I think that was pure luck. Once they knew Gio had been killed in Kacey's apartment they asked some questions and found out that Kieron was here with Naomi in Brooklyn.

They made their way here because it seemed like a possible place Kacey would have fled to.

I have to hand it to them; their detective skills have proved to be successful. It was just the way they went about their business once they got to their destination. For a start, they were way too loud. Breaking down two doors on their way meant that I knew they were coming, which gave me a chance to prepare myself and ambush the fuckers.

Kieron has stopped crying and seems to have fallen asleep, and I don't blame him. I could close my eyes and drift off just as easily as he did. But I will have to wait until I get home before I can get my rest. I turn the key in the ignition and pull away from the spot in front of the barren Chinese takeaway.

I've done right by Kacey, doing exactly what I promised I would. I've rescued Kieron from the clutches of the bad guys and I can't wait for the praise Kacey will heap onto me as I return him to her.

I'm a fucking hero.

5

I make it back to my apartment building and into the basement garage even faster than I completed the journey in the opposite direction.

I forget about keeping my eye on the speed limit this time, perhaps no longer fearing the attention of the police. I don't want to seem overly confident, but I am sure there is no way the murder of Gio Rigo can be linked to me. And as for the deaths of two pieces of disposable muscle in the district of Bushwick, Brooklyn, no doubt the NYPD will see it as drug-related and leave it at that.

I can't see Naomi and her long-haired friend giving a fully accurate statement, and in any case, I saved their lives, so they owe me. Even if they wanted to describe me to the cops, I'm just a man in a suit, and neither of them knew my—

Shit, I told Naomi my name was Chris. Kacey could have given more information than that over the phone, perhaps my surname. Fuck, I hope not.

Perhaps I can get Kacey to call Naomi and explain the whole situation and get her to feed the cops some lies. But then again, almost an hour has passed. The police may already be at the scene of the crime, collating all of the information and looking for evidence. Naomi may have already told them to start looking for a man in his thirties with short, cropped hair wearing a black business suit carrying a three-year-old boy in his arms. She got a good look at me, as did her friend.

In fact, Naomi wasn't entirely convinced that I was Kieron's godfather. She was worried by Kacey's tone on the phone and was without doubt very suspicious of me, even though she let me into her home.

She shouted after me, but I ignored it. Fuck, why did I ignore it?

She might think I was kidnapping the kid and had

Kacey locked up somewhere, tied up and gagged. Plus, the burly man had revealed that somebody had killed Gio Rigo. So Naomi could tie a name and a face to three murders and two potential kidnappings.

Jesus fucking Christ! I have to go back. Maybe convince her otherwise, or if she doesn't want to listen, kill her. Her friend too.

He's already taken a bullet in the knee so he may have passed out from the pain. I could just put a bullet in his head and wipe out the image of my face from his brain.

I'm panicking. I'm going to go upstairs to my apartment, reunite Kacey with her son and tell her we're going to a motel somewhere. I'll satisfy her that it's the best option and that in order to escape this we will need to run.

This is never how I wanted things to be. I have taken a departure from my intentions and now I do not know if I will be able to get myself back on the straight and narrow. This night has taken the faces of Jennifer, Adam and Cassandra out of my head and screwed them up into a ball before jamming them back in.

For some reason, as I take a sleeping Kieron out from my car and hoist him up so that his head rests on my shoulder, all I can think of is that from this moment on, I will never be able to stop running.

6

The look on Kacey's face as she takes hold of Kieron and squeezes him tight is a beautiful picture. She doesn't look at me at all, just dashes over from the couch as I walk through the door and seizes hold of her son, kissing him on the cheeks.

Kacey turns and walks with a sleeping Kieron and sits back onto the couch, rocking back and forth with her son close against her body.

It is now that she looks at me, her eyes small from the

amount of tears she must have shed.

I stand awkwardly, my legs feeling heavy. I expect her to deliver her thanks at any second, but soon I realise that she won't be giving me a word of gratitude. This doesn't even put us back on an even keel, I can already tell.

She is relieved that I have returned Kieron to her but does not think that I deserve admiration for it. She's probably right. She has no idea that the amount of shit we were in before bears no comparison to what we are in now. She went to pieces at the knowledge of Gio Rigo's death, so I am sure that she wouldn't react much better if I told her that I also killed two of his connections.

I'll keep her in the dark, that's the best place for her.

Kacey begins to sing softly into Kieron's ear, the tones drifting over me and soothing me somewhat too.

I will let this temporary peace envelope me, but not for long. Luckily Kacey is packed and all I need is in my briefcase, which remains on the kitchen worktop right where I left it. I think I will grab some clean t-shirts and some underwear while I am here, for I have no idea when I will be back.

I stand and watch the vision of magnificent maternal attention that is unfolding before me; something so natural and delicate happening in the middle of a rampant torrent, the cold rain battering against my face and the wind lashing at my skin.

I have to do my best to protect both of them, whatever the consequences. They need me, and now I know that I need them.

I look over at them, my legs wobbling. I feel as though I could fall over at any second. I swear that I see Kacey mouth the words "thank you" but it's probably just a trick of my mind in this darkness.

7

It doesn't take as much as I thought it would to

convince Kacey that the best thing to do is leave my apartment and get to a motel.

She's startlingly receptive to everything I say and, although she doesn't say much herself, seems to have calmed down noticeably. She doesn't resist at all, maybe because she's exhausted from the events of the night so far and can't wait to get to sleep, hopefully to wake up and realise that everything has been a twisted dream.

We gather up what we need and leave the apartment promptly and quietly without Kieron waking up and without Kacey having second thoughts. I look around the apartment before I leave, closing the door and locking it behind me.

That may be the last time I ever see that place, but it may be a good thing. It was never a place where enjoyable times were spent and it doesn't hold fond memories for me. When I think back to being there with Jennifer all I will remember is that it's the place where I was betrayed.

8

I have never stayed in a motel before, but I rack my brains and come across a memory of a former work colleague telling me an interesting story about a place on the way to New Jersey, just off the interstate, where he used to go to get away from his controlling and manipulative wife.

He would tell me about meeting women in bars and taking them back to this motel, screwing them and then calling a cab for them to leave. Sometimes, depending on his level of success and how satisfied he was with the sexual performance of these women, he would venture back out after sleeping with one girl to meet somebody else, if there was enough time left in the night.

It was always a tale that intrigued me, and even implanted the first idea in my head that I could use no-strings sex, in addition to drink and drugs, as some sort of escape.

The fantasy of this lifestyle soon began to seem out of reach and merely a mirage when I heard that this colleague had lied somewhat regarding the exact nature of these illicit liaisons.

Another colleague, who was much closer to this man than I ever was, announced to us one day that his wife had hired a private detective to follow him when he was staying out all night. Turns out he was actually meeting and having sex with gay men in their twenties after cruising various bars.

On three occasions where he was followed, the private detective had told his wife that this man had participated in sex acts with seven different young men, including one occurrence where he was with two of them at the same time.

Apparently there were photographs to prove this and the wife filed for divorce as soon as she could, signalling that the man would be sure to lose almost everything as he had signed a prenuptial agreement that put his wife in a decisive position.

That man never came back to work, obviously too ashamed and embarrassed to show his face in a place I now know as disloyal and judgemental, so clearly a smart choice. He couldn't even trust one of his closest friends at the firm, who told the entire office as soon as he got word of what had happened.

He lied when he decided to tell me of his adultery, perhaps so that he could somehow justify his sexuality to me and even to himself. Truth is, I never suspected him of being homosexual and I believed every word he said. I had no reason not to. He seemed to be confiding in me and I found that strangely stimulating.

I just hope that he wasn't lying about the whereabouts of this motel, because I am hinging a fair amount of hope on getting to it and putting the incidents of this night behind me. I need to sleep, and I feel like I could do so for a full week once my head hits a pillow.

I look in the rear-view mirror and adjust it so that I can see Kacey and Kieron huddled on the back seat, both of them in deep slumber. I am glad that Kacey has been able to rest.

Seeing a man with his brains splattered all over the inside of your front door could keep you awake, or at least aggravate your conscience by assaulting you with nightmares, but Kacey seems to have drifted off rather peacefully.

I follow some signs for New Jersey and memories are dragged into my head from back in the years when I used to visit my parents.

I never liked New Jersey and always wanted to get out of there and move to the big city, despite my father having aspirations for me to do exactly as he did and start a family, spend the rest of my life stewing in the same twenty-mile radius and retire a bitter old man.

I know that I must be close as I pass an industrial estate and a twenty-four-hour gas station, which although lit up seems to be completely empty, a gaping void as it approaches four in the morning.

The motel appears around a corner and I feel warmth in my stomach, or maybe relief, as I pull into a parking space in front of it and shut off the engine.

I decide to let Kacey and Kieron continue to sleep as I get out and walk along the sidewalk in front of the ground floor rooms, then cross a small courtyard to reach an office just before another lot of rooms, this time with a staircase leading up to the second floor.

I have a thought dash into my head that shows a television on in the motel office with an image being displayed of my face, an artist's impression of me, and a news story about three murders and two kidnappings. They are warning anybody to avoid approaching me as I am most likely armed and dangerous, but to call the police immediately if I am spotted.

As I push open the glass office door with a creak, I see that the television behind the low counter is showing a game show rerun, some old show from the late seventies, and not the news.

There is a middle-aged man sitting on a chair, his bald head so far back that his long nose points almost directly upwards. His mouth is open wide as he snores stridently, the thick-rimmed glasses on his face vibrating each time he breathes outwards.

I walk forwards and place my hands on the counter, looking around for a bell or something that can grab this man's attention.

I don't see anything, and I don't really feel like being polite, so I slam my fist hard onto the surface of the counter.

The noise jolts the man awake and his glasses slip from his face as he sits up. He pushes them back on and looks at me in disgust.

"Just need a room for the night," I say.

The bald man scratches his head like a confused cartoon character. He looks around on the counter for something before taking out a pen and a clipboard from a drawer.

"There ain't much of the night left," he says, his croaky voice breaking as he jots down a date and time at the top of a form attached to the clipboard.

"I still want a room, regardless of that."

He looks up at me, squinting through his glasses.

"Costs the same as a full night, mind you," he sneers.

He looks at me expecting a response, as if this information will put me off and I'll let him get back to his snooze.

"Fine," I say, barely moving my lips.

He looks back at the form, filling in a few more areas with the pen.

"On your own tonight?"

"No, I'm with my wife."

The bald man looks up at me with a juvenile grin on his face.

"Sure ya are, buddy."

"Sorry?"

I am so tired that I start to think that maybe I should sleep in the car. It may be too much effort to get a room with this clown standing in the way of it.

"Your wife, eh?" he says. "Don't worry, son, I've seen it all working here. Especially the night shift, know what I mean?"

I raise an eyebrow.

"It's not your wife you bring to a place like this. A working girl maybe, or a secret affair. I've seen it all. Rent-boys, cross-dressers, married women with men young enough to be their sons, even grandsons on occasion. All they want is a cheap room and it's not my place to ask questions."

I turn away from him and look at the television as he continues.

"Yeah, seen it all. There were even a couple of murders here once, and would you believe it, in the same room. Don't rent that one out anymore of course, just use it for storage."

I turn back to him, my eyes wanting to burn a hole in his pale liver-spotted skin.

"You see, a motel can be a breeding ground for the dishonest and it's fascinating to see the lengths people will go to so that they can keep their secret away from prying eyes. It's insane how often—"

"Please, shut the fuck up and give me a room."

The bald man stops in his tracks and fills in some of the remaining sections on the form in uncomfortable silence.

I drum my fingers on the counter as he turns the form to me, pointing at the relevant sections for me to fill in.

I use a fake name, the alias of Jack Gardener that I

have used before, and pay up-front for one room in cash.

I don't say thank you to the bald man and walk out of the office once he has handed me the room key.

9

I take Kacey's suitcase and my briefcase out from the trunk and find our room on the ground floor not far from where I parked the car. I turn the key in the lock of the door and kick it open gently, the smell of old tobacco, sweat and cinnamon filling my nose.

I place the luggage inside the door and search around on the wall for a light switch. I click it on and blink as the bright yellow light from a bulb in the middle of the ceiling comes on. The room is fairly undersized, with a double bed against the far wall. The carpet is a faded brown and the bedspread is a slightly lighter version of this same colour.

I walk out of the room and back to my car. I open the back door and stroke the side of Kacey's face. She opens her eyes and looks at me so removed from herself that I could be a ghost and she could be looking straight through me.

I pick up Kieron from the back seat and carry him into the motel room, placing him on the bed and pulling the blanket that is wrapped around his legs up over his shoulders. He stirs slightly but doesn't wake.

As I turn back around I see Kacey standing in the doorway of the motel room. She looks around the room with a frown and a distinct lack of interest, like a thirteen-year-old girl looking at an eighteenth-century art gallery.

"You okay?" I ask her.

"Fine," she says, looking at her feet.

I walk over to her and reach out, trying to hold her and offer some sort of reassurance. She moves away from me, walking around me and over to the bed. She sits on the edge of it, looking over at her sleeping son.

I watch her for a minute or so before I step out into the car-park and use my keys to auto-lock the car from a distance.

I stand there for a while and watch the empty street that runs by this motel. I wait for a car to pass, but nothing comes along. At this time of the morning, anybody who wants a no-strings sexual encounter at a secluded motel will probably have already had their fill and is now sleeping soundly, maybe back in the arms of the person they made their vows to.

To have and to hold, to love and cherish, to admire and adore. All that fucking bullshit. The priest may as well just hold the phonebook at the altar and read from that, it's equally as relevant.

I narrow my eyes and watch as a fox emerges from an area of undergrowth across the street. It dashes out into the road, something small moving in its mouth, kicking and wriggling as it tries to break free from the fox's jaw. I can't make out what the animal is. It could be anything from a squirrel to a kitten or even a fox cub. If that's the case, the adult fox could be carrying its young to a safer place or taking it somewhere to eat it. Cannibalism within the family unit. I am not sure anything could be more stomach-turning.

I turn around and walk back to the motel room, closing and locking the door behind me as I go inside. I pull the chain across the door, take off my jacket and put it over the back of the armchair. I place the motel key on the ground and sit down.

Kacey has fallen asleep next to Kieron, her head buried into the pillow. I stand up and walk across to the bed. I pull the bedspread up from one edge and cover Kacey up to her lower back.

I walk back across the room and switch off the light so that the room is dark except for a thin streak of light coming in from a gap in the curtains. I sit back down into the armchair, take hold of my briefcase and find my cigarettes inside. I feel guilty for smoking in the same room as a sleeping child, but I need the nicotine intake as I can't remember the last time I smoked.

I get carried away and smoke four, one after the other, my head feeling light and my heart slowing to a normal pace for the first time in hours.

I close my eyes and feel my body growing calm, the armchair swallowing me up.

THE SIXTH TALE - COLLABORATE

1

Jennifer holds out a hand for me as I fall backwards from a cliff edge and towards the raging waters below. There's a look on her face that suggests she isn't distraught to be seeing me fall to my certain death, but it's not obvious delight.

Somewhere in-between, as if she can't make up exactly how she feels about losing her husband.

The tips of her fingers stroke along my palm like the legs of a centipede as I reach out for her help. I try my best to grab hold of her wrist but she slips through my grasp like a rattlesnake, escaping the fate that I am about to face. I see jagged rocks at the shore below and I know that soon my spine will be smashing into them and my head obliterating like a full balloon.

I slip into an empty space, but it doesn't feel as though I am falling down. It looks to me as if Jennifer, her feet planted firmly on the cliff edge, is soaring up into the black sky, disappearing from my sight like a raven in the dark.

I scream after her, not a word, just a noise, my lungs burning and my throat feeling as though it is full of razor blades.

The jagged rocks wait for me below, the frothy sea crashing around them. I hear a distant ringing in my ear, something between a siren and an alarm.

I feel my body burst as my form ceases to exist, my bones shattering and my muscles ripping apart like wet paper. Every fabric of my being becomes a dark stain in the water, the furious sea smothering everything I ever was.

I will never be able to get back what I once had. Lost forever in the gloom, forgotten instantaneously and not even mourned. She watches me from the sky, between the stars with a cloud beneath her feet. I want a tear to fall down her cheek but she simply turns away and fades like a ghost. I would shed a tear myself but there's nothing left of me, only this thought, and a secluded memory, washing up on the shore.

2

I wake up and I am bemused to why my clothes aren't soaked and sticking to my body, and this is followed by a confusing moment where I have no idea where I am, the dark motel room unfamiliar and my body aching from an uncomfortable sleep in an armchair.

I sit forward and an intense pain twinges in my neck. I groan and twist my muscles, trying to ease it. The room is dark but I can tell that it is now morning as a beam of light bleeds through a gap in the curtain.

It is only now that I notice Kacey and Kieron are no longer sleeping on the bed across the room. There is a sign that they were there, the sheets on the bed ruffled and creased, but now they are gone.

I stand up quickly, blood rushing to my head. I feel like I could faint as I pull the curtains at the window. Vivid light floods in and I screw up my eyes as it feels like acid being poured into my face. I turn around and see that Kacey's suitcase is gone. I stride across the room and open the door to the bathroom, hoping to find Kacey giving Kieron a bath in the tub. The room is empty, and as I spin around I realise that the motel room key I placed on the ground before I sat on the armchair is gone.

I sit on the end of the bed and put my face into my hands.

I wanted to start a new life with her, and she's walked out on me like this? I thought there was something there, beyond the sex and common courtesy she showed me. I was convinced that I could make a go of it with her, become a father to little Kieron. We could both leave this city together and forget everything that dragged us down. She could learn to love me if she didn't already: it happens all the time.

I stand up and walk over to the door, opening it wide so that cool air rushes in against my face. I imagine Kacey and Kieron walking over to me from across the car-park, perhaps carrying some breakfast that they'd gone out to get.

I convince myself that I'm being overly optimistic, which really isn't a trait of mine at all.

I am now in this alone, as I had intended to be in the first place. I never expected to have three deaths to my name at this point, but there's nothing I can do about that now.

Those men are dead and they're gunna remain that way. If I look at Kacey as more of a burden then I can encourage myself to believe that I am glad to be rid of her.

I find it hard to even believe myself. I've become so distrustful that I even see myself as a potential fraud. If I was somebody else I would probably be the same.

I turn away from the open door but have to double back as I notice that my car is gone.

Fucking bitch, she's taken it.

She took the keys from my jacket pocket while I was asleep and stole my fucking car.

The whore has stolen my car and it had my gun in the glove box. That's one step too far for me. When I catch up to her I'm going to smash her skull in and take back the weapon I did so much to get hold of. The weapon I used to murder Gio Rigo and two of his associates. The weapon I wanted to use to exact my revenge on those who have put me in this position. That's it, I've decided.

Kacey's going on the list.

3

I take out a certain amount of my disappointment on

the shitty motel room, kicking my foot through the bathroom door and punching the walls so hard that the skin on my knuckles splits and bleeds.

I pick up the armchair and throw it across the room, smashing a hole in the far wall. I think about smashing the window, perhaps with the television or maybe with my head, but I decide not to.

It's only now that I notice the digital clock next to the bed that tells me it has just gone ten. I have slept for almost six hours but it feels like a lot less.

I pick up my briefcase and look around the room for anything else that belongs to me before leaving the motel room and slamming the door behind me. As I walk away, I look back to see a few twitching curtains in the windows of the other rooms as people peer out to see who has caused all of the noise.

It's me, Christopher Morgan, that crazy bastard you've seen on the news who killed three hapless gangsters and kidnapped a prostitute and her young son. But don't worry, the girl has escaped my clutches and taken my car! She's got one up on me and it's only a matter of time before I am brought to justice.

There's probably a helicopter in the air scanning the city for me. You won't have to worry much more, innocent people of New York. My rampage will soon be brought to an end.

The average man who went berserk and ended up being shot by the police as he was a danger to himself and others. The newspapers will have accounts from those who knew me well, all slander about how they knew I'd lose my mind one day and that they thought I was capable of blowing up from the moment they met me.

A story fabricated by Jennifer about an abusive relationship and my threats to kill myself if she left me. An interview with Adam where he portrays me as narcissistic and neurotic, a paranoid wreck that stumbled from day to day and could only get from morning to night with the help of drink and narcotics. Not far from the truth, granted, but coming from that cunt it's unforgivable.

I won't be letting that fucking happen. I'm on the move and I won't stop long enough for anybody to catch me. It won't be me lying dead as the faces of those who have deceived loom over me. Oh no, it will be quite the opposite.

I pick up the pace as I leave the motel behind, the building growing smaller as I walk down a slope and beneath the freeway. I can't walk all of the way back into the city because that could take a hell of a lot of time, and time is something that I don't have right now.

I continue to walk for about ten minutes, passing under the freeway and making my way towards the gas station that I remember passing early this morning on my way to the motel.

There only seems to be one car on the forecourt, a red Chevrolet Cavalier, parked near the front of the station near the pumps. It's empty as I expect the owner is inside paying for the gas.

I cross the street and approach the station, a few cars passing by but not pulling in as I make my way towards the Chevy.

I have never hotwired a car in my life, and I'm pretty sure it would take longer than the time the owner will be spending in the station. I hang back for a second and watch as somebody comes out the station and walks towards the car.

I sidle up behind the man, who is white, mid-twenties and dressed in baggy jeans, an oversized black t-shirt and a baseball cap.

I wait for the right moment, as he opens the car door on the driver's side, before racing towards the man, my briefcase raised above my head and my eyes wide like a wild man.

He turns at the last moment as I bring my briefcase down on his head with a colossal wallop, knocking him backwards against the Cavalier. I watch as he crashes forwards onto the ground, his arms breaking his fall and his cap slipping off his head. I kick him in the ribs to make sure he stays down, snatch the keys from his hand and jump into the car.

Once sat in the driver's seat, I place my briefcase on the passenger's side and lower my head, put the key into the ignition and turn it until I hear the engine hum. As I look back up to see the road ahead I turn to see the car owner is back on his feet.

The car door is already open about an inch, but I don't move my hands from their current position. I wait for him to lean down to open the door himself before swinging my left leg out and kicking the car door into his face. I kick again so that it hits him in the chin, just as hard as it did on the nose. I already see blood as I leap out of the car and I manage to take hold of both of his wrists as he tries to hit me. I thrust my head into his already broken nose, feeling the sinew crushed beneath my skull and flecks of blood splashing onto my cheeks.

The impact of the headbutt sends flashes of pain across my head but I shake them off as I clamber over the Chevy owner as he falls to the ground again.

I look down at the bleeding man on the floor, his nose bent to the left horrifically. His eyes are closed and he is uttering a low groan.

I notice that in the scuffle he has dropped a gun and not even noticed. It's a standard 9mm Beretta pistol, nothing special. Not like the enormous bellowing Colt Python revolver that has been stolen from me. This weapon is not even in the same league as this pea-shooter. But it will have to do for now seeing as I am temporarily separated from the Colt.

I look over at the gas station and see an Asian man standing inside at the counter with a telephone receiver pressed to his ear.

I flip him off as I place the Beretta in my waistband,

the gun feeling light and feeble in comparison to the weapon I was carrying around last night.

I get into the car, close the door and pull away from the gas station before edging my foot down on the accelerator and heading back into the city.

I need to get my head together and put my next move at the forefront of my mind. There are several people I need to visit and put to judgment. Today is the day I have been waiting for and building up to for so long in my head.

The days leading up to this, my appointment with Cassandra Jones, a liaison with drug dealer William Beckford, my wife Jennifer leaving me, my meeting with Robert Morrison, the false concern from Adam Phillips, my purchasing of a weapon from Andrei Pasenov, an evening of passion with Kacey Ross, the murder of Gio Rigo and the drive to Brooklyn to collect Kieron – all have been preparation for what is to follow.

First up, as it was when these tales began, is Cassandra Jones. She is the delicate flower that I now need to get on my side. My appointment with her as Jack Gardener was the groundwork I needed to put in. She is to be my collaborator, my partner in crime. And we're gunna tear New York City a new asshole.

4

My memory is split into several pieces and I find it hard to remember exactly where the office for Ryman & Jones Psychiatry is. I was only there about forty-eight hours ago, but already this area of the city looks alien and bizarre, like I have taken a wrong turning and somehow ended up falling into a wormhole that has teleported me to some alternate dimension.

I feel as though every pair of eyes on the New York streets is looking directly at me. As if this red Chevrolet Cavalier has a neon arrow flashing above it, similar to a sign that would be advertising a titty bar.

I may as well be honking the horn as I pass through, screaming at the top of my lungs out of an open car window, grabbing everybody's attention.

I think I'm on the correct block after about thirty minutes of driving around, but I'm still struggling to pinpoint exactly where I'm going. I take the card out from my wallet that displays the telephone number for Ryman & Jones.

I pull into a side-street and stop the car. I place the card between my lips, turn off the engine and climb out, dragging my briefcase out like a dead weight and crossing between a traffic jam over to a bank of payphones on the other side of the street.

The fog of congestion gets in my eyes, the fumes burning my skin. I feel as though it could slip off my body, falling down into a bloody wet mess at my feet.

Somebody shouts at me as I squeeze by a taxi but I ignore it. I use my ears to direct me rather than my eyes, the slow rumble of car engines showing me that a car won't hit me as I cross.

I step up onto the kerb, bump into some pedestrians and approach the payphones. I drop my briefcase on the ground with a clunk and take the card from between my lips. It's at this moment that I realise I don't have any change for the phone.

I turn away from the payphone and approach the first person who is coming towards me on the sidewalk. It is a young white man, early to mid-twenties at best, wearing a similar suit to one I would have chosen to wear when I was his age with aspirations to be an attorney.

His hair is short and black, and his face is cleanly shaven. As he gets closer he looks younger than I first thought, perhaps young enough so that he isn't yet able to grow hair on his face.

He has an earpiece in, one of those Bluetooth headset things, which are mostly used by the ostentatious and naïve. I wave in his face to get his attention.

"Hey, buddy," I say. "Got any change? I need it for the phone."

He ignores me and almost walks through me, but I move out of the way at the last moment. He is talking to somebody through his earpiece, not even clocking my existence as he passes by.

I walk behind him, my feet almost kicking at his heels. I call after him again, hoping that the reason he didn't see me was because he is so enveloped in the conversation he is having.

"Hey!" I yell. "I'm talking to you! I need change for the phone!"

He doesn't turn around and acknowledge me, which makes me realise that he's an ignorant pig. I lurch forwards and slap him across the head with the palm of my hand.

He turns around instantly, looking at me with wide eyes. It's the kind of look I would give a homeless person or crackhead who's hassling me for money.

I'm neither of those things, so this little prick should have more respect.

"Have you been that bad-mannered all your life?" I ask him, my arms gesturing violently.

"Sorry?" he says. His voice is small, like a rodent's.

"I asked if you had change and you just walked by. You didn't even look at me. Are you blind? Can you not see me standing here?"

"I..."

"It's fucking rude. Common courtesy, motherfucker. I'm not Robert Mugabe."

He looks down at his feet like a naughty child being told off for saying a curse word.

"Sorry."

He repeats the word 'sorry', but now it's in an entirely different context. I feel like a father disciplining his son. This man is ignorant *and* a pushover. Whoever his father actually is they did a really bad job of parenting him.

"No, not you, some guy came up to me," the man

says quietly.

I am confused for a second and then realise that he is talking into his Bluetooth headset.

I don't really think before I feel my arm lunging out, ripping the headset from his ear and smashing it against the ground.

I look up at the man, who stares at me like I am a grizzly bear.

The card has the address of the psychiatry office in black italic letters beneath the telephone number. It's something I knew was there before but somehow managed to forget.

Shit, I'm a fucking trembling mess. I even managed to forget the fact that I have my cell phone with me. What a fucking tool. I've roughed up a complete stranger for a couple of quarters for no good reason.

I look back up but see that the man has walked in the opposite direction, much faster than he had been strolling before.

"Sorry!" I call after him, but he doesn't turn around.

I walk back to the bank of payphones and pick up my briefcase from the ground. I begin to walk back to the Cavalier and stop dead in my tracks, watching as a beautiful woman trudges along the opposite sidewalk, her golden hair tied back in a bun.

She looks distinctly miserable, her head bobbing up and down like a doll's would if carried by an erratic toddler.

Cassandra Jones was meant to be walking along this street at this very moment as I stand nearby and I was meant to meet her.

5

I cross the street at a pace that makes sure I am about twenty feet behind Cassandra as I step up onto the sidewalk. I look over my shoulder as I pass the red

Chevrolet, making a mental note of its location.

The cops will be looking for a car of that description once the guy I stole it from reports the incident. I imagine by now the questioning is done and the police have a fresh idea of my face. They're putting the pieces of the puzzle together, linking the description of me given by Naomi and her friend.

There are hundreds, even thousands, of Chevrolet cars in this state, and a good portion of them are Cavalier. A red Cavalier wouldn't stand out like a sore thumb and the chances of a squad car coming down this street looking for the vehicle is a million to one.

As are the chances of a cop spotting me amongst the wealth of men in their thirties dressed in suits. Granted, I no doubt look like shit, but I will do my best to blend in.

I notice that I am getting closer to Cassandra, whether it is because she has slowed down or that I have sped up, I'm not sure.

I feel like a wild animal stalking an unknowing prey, cold sweat materialising on the back of my arms.

I wonder what kind of box she decided to put me in after our meeting. I know that she would have done that, because that's exactly what she is qualified for. Whatever kind of effect I had on her she would have felt obliged to come to some sort of conclusion as I left.

I would hope that the box she put me in wasn't labelled with homicidal maniac, and if it was, shame on her because she should have alerted the authorities immediately.

As that didn't happen, I can at least hold on to the fact that she may have seen a shred of normality, perhaps even humility, in me.

There are two types of murderers – it's as simple as that. Forget trying to put every single offender into their own category so they can be 'understood' by the shrinks and the families of those they have killed.

Whether it's a serial killer, a one-off crime of passion,

an act of revenge, genocide, or even an assisted suicide, the one thing that separates the two types of murderer is intent.

It's whether the taking of human life was predetermined or not that splits the killers down the middle. Those who get up in the morning with the knowledge that they will commit a murder are different from those who don't realise that they are capable of such a thing until they are looking down at the still corpse at their feet.

Cassandra Jones would have done her best to put me in either one of these camps, but I'm not sure that she would have been happy with the outcome either way.

I don't even fully know where I would fit in. Sure, I have had murderous fantasies for a while now, but I suppose I never really thought about whether or not I would be able to follow them through. The deaths of Gio Rigo and his two cronies weren't predetermined as they collided with my path against my will, my actions only an effect once their cause had interrupted my stream of consciousness.

I see the killing of Gio as an act of protection for Kacey Ross and the killings of his associates simply as self-defence. They would have put a bullet in me if I hadn't done that to them first.

Would I trade in being in a body-bag in the downtown morgue for my current situation? No fucking chance.

Cassandra stops dead as if I have called her name.

Shit, did I call her name? I don't even know.

I was following behind her but my mind was wandering so perhaps I wasn't in full control of my lips and voice-box. If I have called her name I must be developing some strain of Tourette's syndrome because I certainly didn't mean to.

I stop as she slowly turns around, her eyes locking onto me. I can tell that she has been crying and she looks notably distressed.

The sudden appearance of me doesn't seem to have offered her any sort of respite, only added to her woe. Her face is full of twisted confusion and even belligerence.

"Are you following me?" she demands.

I notice that she is wearing similar clothes to forty-eight hours ago, only the shades are slightly different. She has on a dark grey pencil skirt and a faded yellow blouse with a black jacket.

Her face looks so different with her hair tied back, her beauty even more apparent and the streak of delicacy I saw in her revealed even more.

I find it hard to form a response. I stand in silence and she begins to walk towards me.

"I saw you in the park as well, not long after our meeting," she says, her voice louder now as she is just a few feet away from me.

The make-up around her eyes is smoky and smudged, previous tears leaving their mark on her face.

"You're following me. Did he put you up to this?"

I shake my head slowly, not knowing what else to do. I expected her to be much more shocked to see me. I should be asking all of the questions, not her.

"Of course he did," she sneers. "This is exactly the kind of fucked-up thing he would do. Well, you can tell him that it's not working and I'm not fucking scared of him, not anymore. I'm going to the police and he can try his manipulative bullshit on them."

She turns away but I call after her. My voice is small and quiet.

"Wait."

She looks back at me, her mouth downturned and tears welling up in her eyes.

She is trying to be strong but I know that it isn't something she finds easy. Whoever she is referring to has taken advantage of her amiable qualities and broken her down.

"Nobody put me up to this," I say, sincerity coating my words. "I saw you from across the street. You looked upset, and I was a bit concerned following how our meeting panned out the other day. I was going to catch up to you, just to see if you were okay, and offer my apologies."

She blinks liberally and looks me up and down. She has no reason to believe me based on my previous actions. I could quite easily be a hired hand who has been paid to rough her up.

"I know I look like shit," I add, "I've had a difficult couple of days. But I'm not who you think I am, whatever that may be. I came to you needing help and I acted inappropriately, for which I have since felt terribly guilty. It looks like you have problems of your own so I'll leave you be. Trust me, I wasn't following you. It's coincidence that you walked by when I was making a phone call across the street."

I see her face change and realise I have implanted a seed of faith in her head.

I may have frightened her at our meeting but it would seem that at this moment I am the lesser of two evils in her eyes. Whoever is tormenting her is at the forefront of her worries right now.

"And what about at the park?" she says.

"I don't remember seeing you at the park. I had the rest of the day off work and I was killing time. Again, if you saw me there it was coincidence. Strange how many times you see somebody you recognise in a city this... vast."

She rubs her eyes with the back of her hands, removing the last remnants of tears from her face.

"So, I'm sorry," I say. "Have a good day."

I turn around and begin to walk away from her, feeling dejected for at least five seconds as I don't hear her call after me, at least not right away.

"Wait."

And there it is. Her voice sounds almost identical to how mine did when I said the same word a couple of minutes ago.

I stop and twist my heels as I turn back to her. I much prefer her hair down to this tight bun her hair is in.

"Listen, I appreciate the apology," she says, coming over to me as I stand rooted to the spot. "I didn't mean to be rude, but I've had a pretty nightmarish last few days myself. I guess at least we have that in common."

Somebody bumps into me as they stride past, but I hardly move an inch. I feel as it would take a wrecking ball to knock me to the ground.

"I understand."

I look at her skin, searching for the bruising beneath her eye that I had noticed previously beneath her well-applied make-up. It seems to have cleared up completely, or she has found a much better way of concealing it.

"I hope my conduct didn't have a hand in the nightmare," I say.

She laughs.

"No, not really. I was upset and a bit... astonished at how quickly you changed from calm to irate, but after a few hours I got over it. I guess your insomnia must be really getting to you. It wasn't personal and I know you weren't purposely lashing out at me."

I had forgotten about telling her I couldn't sleep. I had forgotten about telling her about the dream where my wife gave birth to a dog. All I could remember was the sound of her sobbing as I closed her office door.

"And before you ask," she says, "I didn't think of you as a sociopath."

She looks at me in a way that makes me feel warm and cold inside at the same time. As if my lungs are burning and my stomach is filling with liquid nitrogen.

I offer a smile but I want to take hold of her and kiss her deeply. I want to place my hands in the small of her back and pull her close.

"If you're not busy, Jack," she says, her lips seeming to move in slow-motion, "how about we get a coffee?"

I'm Jack Gardener. Cassandra Jones wants to get coffee with Jack Gardener. Fucking jackpot.

"Sure, I'd love to."

Cassandra Jones, for now at least, is the only woman in the world.

And as for the person who bruised my beautiful Cassandra's face, fury will rain down upon you with the force of a freight train, so you'd better find somewhere to hide.

6

We walk for a couple of blocks and most of that journey contains small talk and not much more. I am already delving into her consciousness and looking closer at her condition without having yet asked any prying questions. Although we walk side by side, she insists on looking me in the eyes as we talk, which slows our pace to a great extent.

We reach a coffee shop on a corner, one I haven't seen before, and walk inside. A bell signals our arrival and the rich smell of coffee fills my nose.

The shop seems to be empty apart from us and a young woman at the counter. Her head is low and I guess that she is reading something out of our sight.

Once we have our hot drinks we sit down in the corner of a seating area near a window. I see the girl at the counter eyeballing me as she did when she made our coffee, as if she recognises me or perhaps finds me attractive.

Right now, I'm Jack Gardener, so there's no way the crimes of Christopher Morgan are attached to me. Even if my face is on the national news and there's a police manhunt happening right at this moment.

I know I'm not in any trouble. Sitting here with

Cassandra is all I need to be thinking about. She is the light of my life.

Jack Gardener is untouchable.

"… been in here before?"

I catch the end of Cassandra's question, but it's enough so that I understand her.

"No, don't think so," I respond.

"Well, get ready to be blown away," she says. "This is some of the best coffee in town."

She blows on the edge of her mug and takes a sip. She tightens her lips before smiling, a gesture for me to try.

I lean down and mimic her actions, blowing on the liquid before taking some in. It's overwhelmingly hot, but I manage to swallow before spluttering.

She raises her eyebrows as if to say 'told you so', but I only find the coffee average at best. It would be a lot better with a dash (or generous glug) of rum.

"It's good," I lie.

We sit in silence for about twenty seconds, Cassandra continuing to take sips from the steaming cup between her hands.

"No freelance journalism today then, Jack?" she asks.

Cassandra is right on the money and I wonder how much else she has remembered about the guise I am taking on.

"I'm, um, taking some time off," I say.

Better to be vague than sensationalist and risk appearing fallacious.

"That sounds like a perfect idea to me," Cassandra says, staring into her coffee cup. "I need a vacation, something like two weeks. Just to get away from it all and get my head together."

I nod, wrapping my hands around my mug and letting the warmth from the drink fill my palms.

"I've had a few problems with an ex-partner," she continues, "some threatening phone calls and e-mails, you know the drill. He didn't get the message when we broke up and I don't think he ever will."

I nod again, not quite knowing what to say.

"God, what am I thinking?" she says, bringing a hand to her face. "I don't even know you. There's no way you want to hear all this."

I stretch out an arm and offer her a comforting hand on her wrist. She looks at me from between slender fingers.

"You can talk to me," I say. "And the least I can do for you is listen."

She smiles and brings her hand down from her face.

"It's hard trying to separate my bullshit problems from the problems I hear about every single day of my life," she says, her gaze moving away from mine and out onto the New York street. "It's my job to listen but I never feel as though anybody listens to me. I can't switch off that part of my brain that tries to rationalise everything and calculate the source of a dilemma, you know?"

I really do.

"Just because I have these qualifications, that doesn't mean I'm an emotionless bitch. I have feelings and I can be pushed over the edge as easily as anybody. Am I making sense?"

You sure are. I know the edge of reason as well as the back of my hand. I've been there and back, and now I'm so far beyond it I can't even remember what it looks like.

"I'm not the kid who walks into his classroom one day and blows all of his friends away with an assault rifle," I say, "but I'm prone to the odd outburst. I can't keep everything bottled up all of the time. I'm just not that person."

I imagine a hail of bullets tearing through a group of kids, their white shirts growing red and holes darting across a classroom wall.

"I think that's part of the reason I lost my cool back at your office," I say. "I try to keep things bottled up but it has the tendency to explode at the wrong moment."

She looks back at me, her eyes dazzling like gemstones. I feel a shiver between my shoulders.

"I..."

Tell me everything about this ex-partner. I want to know what makes him tick. Everything from what he has for breakfast to how he performs sexually.

"Did he hit you?" I ask.

She swallows hard and looks down at her lap. I know the answer before she even says it. She clears her throat.

"Just once," she says. "Never during our relationship, only afterwards. He was collecting some of his things from my apartment and we got a bit heated. He wasn't willing to finish the relationship and that was all I wanted. He was shouting so much and then he, um, forced himself upon me..."

I grip her wrist harder.

"He didn't," she murmurs, "but I think he would have. I scratched his face and that's when he hit me. It was so hard it felt like I'd been smashed in the head with a rock. I could tell he regretted it because he left straight away."

I bite my bottom lip and imagine Cassandra on her back on her living room floor, her skirt riding up and her underwear around her knees.

She is holding her face as it begins to swell and the throbbing pain begins to take over.

"And what about the threatening calls? And the e-mails?" I ask as an elderly couple enter the coffee shop.

Cassandra drinks more from her coffee cup and I follow suit, not wanting to reveal that I find the drink bland and milky.

"He tried to call me the day after it happened but I ignored it," she explains. "He called my cell non-stop and then began calling the office, but I told the guy on reception to say I wasn't there.

"He left a handful of messages on my cell phone answer service, the first of which were apologising and telling me he would do anything to win me back. After two or three of those they started to get much more aggressive, until the last one he left said he was going to kill me if he ever saw me again."

I tense my jaw and feel my face growing hot.

"The e-mails were more of the same. I didn't even read a few of them."

She pulls her wrist away and places both of her hands under her chin, clasped together in a prayer-like fashion.

"I'm not even scared," she says. "It's anger more than anything. I just want him to leave me alone. I should go to the police. He's threatened to kill me, so they must be able to help. Put a harassment order in place or something."

I look into her eyes and see a tiny reflection of myself sitting across the table from her. I look haggard and my skin looks paler than it ever has.

"Jesus, I can't believe I'm telling you this," she says before taking in a large breath.

I reach forwards and take hold of both her hands in mine, knocking my coffee mug in the process and splashing some of it onto the table.

I cradle her hands within mine, as if my hands are a spacecraft escape pod and hers are the last remaining living astronaut.

"I can help you," I say.

She shakes her head, each minuscule freckle on her nose reminding me of a star in the black sky of an unforgiving space.

"What do you mean?" she asks.

"Don't go to the police," I insist.

She looks at me as if I am speaking a foreign language. She must have expected me to fully agree with her and urge her to go to the cops. That wouldn't be the best option regarding the current circumstances.

"Let me deal with it," I continue. "Listen, if you go to the cops then yes, there are grounds for placing a harassment order.

"It will be a warning though, because words or threats aren't seen as crimes. He won't be spending any more than a few hours in a cell before getting the injunction thrown at him.

"He'll sign it, claiming he was feeling emotionally unstable and it was out of character for him to behave that way. But trust me, it's just gunna add fuel to his fire. There's no physical barrier between him and you with a harassment order, so what stops him breaking into your apartment and stabbing you fifteen times?"

She stares at my face for at least thirty seconds without blinking. Is she imagining a knife piercing her body over and over again?

When she finally blinks I see her eyes glaze over and glare at me with renewed intensity.

"B-but..." she stutters. "Surely going to the police is the right thing to do. What are you even suggesting, Jack?"

"Sending a message," I say. "Something to make sure he doesn't bother you again."

Cassandra opens her mouth wide before it turns into a broad, yet ill-at-ease smile. She chortles yet she clearly isn't amused. It's more of a laugh out of disbelief, I would say.

"What kind of message?" she asks awkwardly.

"Nothing sinister," I insist. "He's obviously not much of a man, so if threatening you makes him feel big let's see how he reacts when faced with me.

"I dunno, maybe we can say that I'm your new boyfriend. Show him that you've moved on and that whatever he does there's no chance of you going back to him."

Cassandra's mouth narrows and I see a flicker of uncertainty in her eyes.

"Hmmm, I'm not sure," she says.

I hope I'm not coming across as a sadistic freak and I hope even more that she isn't thinking of protecting this bastard. If he has told her that he wants to kill her, then he should be dealt with accordingly.

"It's up to you, of course," I say.

I turn and look at my reflection in the dull surface of the window next to me. I look as though I haven't slept in a week and that I must've got dressed in pitch black darkness with clothes I found in a dumpster.

I feel only vaguely cognizant and like I could fall into a coma-like state at any second. I need something to eat. It feels like a lifetime since I last had a decent meal. I feel empty in many more ways than one.

"It seems a bit irresponsible," she says, her tone distancing her from me. "I mean, I'd feel much more confident if I let the police deal with it."

"Then that's your decision," I say. "If you're happy with worthless pieces of shit like this guy doing exactly as they please without repercussion then all power to you. Who I am to judge or question?

"The inconsiderate and senseless always tread on good people in this world, and their excuse is always the same. They want an easy life, so they follow the rules. That's what makes them a good person.

"They would give five bucks a month to a charity just so they aren't harassed by a guy with a clipboard at their door and they can tell their friends that they are contributing to making the world a better place.

"They would give over their purse or wallet the second a thug brandishes a knife to avoid the unwanted confrontation. Why? Because it's the right thing to do. Just like calling the cops and reporting your ex-boyfriend is most probably the right thing to do."

Cassandra looks at me in a similar way she did when I was ranting in her office. I wouldn't say I am ranting now, just on a rampage of a different sort. A rampage where I want to convince, not confuse, and pull Cassandra into the same train of thought as me.

I know she's capable of it, but she needs to let go of her apprehensions. She wants to punish her ex-boyfriend for what he has done to her as much as I do.

"I'm not insane, Cassandra," I say, the words falling out of my mouth without me thinking about uttering them. "I'm a progressive thinker."

Cassandra breaks through the ice of her wary stare and smiles at me. I feel my bladder aching – I need to piss.

"I don't think you're insane," she says. "I never did. You're mesmerizing, that's for sure. Mesmerizing and passionate. It's a good combination. Refreshing to meet somebody like you and not have my brain numbed by depressed fools with insignificant problems. I wish I was like you."

I snigger like an inept teenager on his first date with the hottest girl at school.

"It ain't so great being me."

Cassandra puts her cell phone away and I wonder if anybody has called mine. I can't remember the last time I checked it but I can't imagine the likes of Jennifer or Adam being desperate to get hold of me for any reason.

I wonder if they woke up this morning feeling any different.

"I feel like I know you better than I actually do," she says, tapping her fingernails on the side of her empty mug. "I don't really know anything about you. You're sat here listening to me as I tell you something I haven't even told my mother or my best friend and you're basically a stranger."

Jack Gardener isn't a stranger. He's your shoulder to cry on and the hand to guide you out of the gloom. He'll pull you out of the way of a speeding car and take a bullet to the chest so you don't get hurt.

"Well, if it helps in any way, I'll give you some more," I say. "I mean, I think you know the boring stuff. Job, relationship status, etc."

I need to give Jack Gardener some hobbies and interest to broaden the scope that I am looking at him through. Cassandra is attracted to the dangerous element of Jack, as it is something she hasn't experienced in a long time. Her recent relationships have been dull and abrasive, bogged down by jealousy and destructive strategy.

She knows that I am a married man, yes, but has that stopped the bud of attraction from blooming into a flower in other instances? I know the answer to that question all too well.

"I'm a lateral thinker as well as a progressive thinker," I say, drawing in Cassandra by lowering my voice. "We were put here on this world to do something interesting, not fall into obscurity as statistics and blank faces in a crowd."

I take a deep breath and imagine Cassandra standing naked at the foot of my bed. I long for her to be lying next to me but she's standing there so that I admire her, scanning over every inch of her body so that I can appreciate the touch of her skin once I finally get to experience it.

"I think you're right," she says.

I knew she would.

"About what?"

"About sending a message."

7

I use the bathroom in the coffee shop to have a piss that would probably have filled up a bucket.

I turn on a tap at the sink next to the toilet and drink from it for at least thirty seconds.

I am glad that I have brought my briefcase into the bathroom with me because I suddenly feel the urge to take some cocaine.

I have been taking fewer drugs than usual over the last twenty-four hours, probably because my time is being taken up by other incidents that are far more interesting than roaming the streets like a homeless dog.

I'm running low on the nose powder and I use about

a third of what I have left, dabbing a small amount onto the back of my hand and jamming it up my nose. I snort three similar amounts of the drug before returning the pouch to my briefcase.

I take my flick-knife from the case and tuck it into my sock. I readjust the Beretta in my waistband as it has fallen low before closing my briefcase and retying the knot of my tie, which has been hanging around my neck like a dead snake since I left Kacey's apartment.

I look at myself in the bathroom mirror and rub away the remnants of the coke from my nose and top lip. I splash some cold water into my hands and then onto my face. I slap my cheeks several times until I see them turning pink and then return to Cassandra, who has stood up from the table and looks ready to leave.

She walks up to me and stops a couple of inches from my face. I expect her to lean in and kiss me hard on the lips, but she doesn't.

"I know what you were doing in there," she says, her warm breath against my neck and my hands twitching as they fight the impulse to touch her.

"You do?" I say, looking around the coffee shop to see that the girl at the counter is busy serving a woman in her forties and the elderly couple seem to have left.

"Yeah," Cassandra purrs, "and I want some."

I feel an excited twinge in my stomach as well as a sexual thrust in my crotch.

Almost as if this feeling signalled Cassandra, she places her hands over my penis, stroking it lightly and pushing me backwards towards the bathroom.

We go inside and Cassandra closes the door behind us, locking it with a bolt that I didn't use when I came in here on my own. I notice that I didn't flush when I had a piss so I pull the handle on the toilet cistern to get rid of it. She probably thinks I took a shit.

Cassandra unzips me and puts her hand into my pants, caressing my semi-hard penis harder and bringing her lips close to mine.

She doesn't kiss me, just takes my bottom lip into her mouth and sucks on it.

I put my briefcase onto the sink without turning my head away from Cassandra, who begins to flick her tongue into my mouth and jerk my cock harder.

I am almost fully erect when I grab hold of her wrist and pull her hand out from my trousers, not wanting to climax. She pulls her face away from mine and licks her lips.

Jack Gardener is a married man but that doesn't stop Cassandra. Monogamy is a practise with threadlike boundaries, and if there's one thing I have learnt from everything I have experienced, it's that.

"I want you," Cassandra says softly, her lips gleaming and causing me to salivate. "But I want to get high with you first," she says, so quietly that I have to read her lips to understand her.

I hope she's not an undercover cop and this whole event is happening so that she can bust me. That would be entrapment, I'm sure of it. Anyway, getting busted for drugs when I've killed three people would be ludicrous and on the same level as getting pulled over because my car has a smashed tail light when actually I have the corpses of two teenage girls in my trunk.

"Okay," I say.

I take out the pouch from my briefcase and thumb it around in my hand. There isn't much left, I'd say about enough for two lines each. I close the briefcase and pour the powder out onto the leather surface of the case.

"Need a credit card or something?" Cassandra whispers in my ear.

I look at her and nod. I can't be entirely sure but I would say that this may be one of Cassandra's first times experimenting with recreational drugs.

I'm sure she's smoked hash or something in her college days, but I can't imagine her jamming her nose full of coke in a hotel bathroom while one of her girlfriends shrieks with delight.

If this is her first experience of cocaine, I'll give her the whole clichéd mainstream show.

She finds an American Express card in her purse and I take it from her. I cut up four lines in the middle of the briefcase, trying my best to make sure they are all around about the same size. I pass the card back and she runs her index finger along the edge of it, scooping up a tiny amount of the coke and rubbing it into her gums. Maybe this isn't her first time.

After putting the card back into her purse she takes out a single dollar and begins to roll it. The note is fresh and crisp, sounding like leaves breaking underneath boots as she handles it.

I lean back and watch as Cassandra takes the lead, sucking up the first line. She looks up at me as it hits her, rubbing her nose with her thumb. Her pupils dilate and she's down on her second line before she gets a chance to compose herself.

She snorts and sniffs, scratching the bridge of her nose as she passes the rolled-up dollar to me.

I follow suit, drawing in both of my lines in quick succession. I make sure I clean most of the coke from the surface of my briefcase with my fingertips, rubbing it into my gums before passing the dollar back to Cassandra.

I feel the euphoria hit me as Cassandra starts to touch my cock again. I put my back to the wall and steady myself on the edge of the sink as Cassandra takes my penis out from my trousers, working me back to an erection.

She unfastens my belt and unclips my pants, which makes me panic for a second as I remember the gun in my waistband. It begins to slump behind me so I press myself against the wall to keep it from falling down my trouser leg or onto the floor.

We embrace in a kiss, my hands roaming free over her body, caressing her hips and ass as I pull her close to me.

She uses her free hand to guide me up her skirt and between her legs, my hand pressing against her vagina. Her cotton underwear is soft and the warmth of her crotch increases my passion.

I move my mouth down from her lips and onto the white skin of her neck, running my tongue up and down her throat as she exhales in delight, her grip becoming tight on my penis.

I hitch up her skirt so that is bunched around her waist before removing her underwear, pulling it down to her knees and watching as she steps out of it.

I return my hand to her pussy and feel the bare skin against my fingers for the first time. It has been recently shaved, perhaps a day or so ago. I slowly push two fingers inside her, watching her face as her mouth opens wide.

I continue to kiss her deeply as I move my fingers around deep inside of her. She sucks on my tongue as I push upwards against her g-spot and begin to gain momentum as she thrusts herself against me.

She loses her grip on my cock as I push her towards orgasm, her legs shaking and her fingernails digging into the skin on my arms. Her mouth opens wider still as she holds her breath, the thrusting slowing down.

I can tell that she wants to scream, which makes the intensity of her orgasm greater as she stifles it. She takes short and sharp breaths, rocking back and forth on my fingers until she stops.

She kisses me softly, pressing her head against mine and reaching down to my hand. She brings it up to her mouth and sucks the two fingers that have been inside of her. She then kisses me again so that I can taste the sweetness of her pussy.

She leans down and takes the tip of my penis into her mouth, flicking her tongue around the head before pushing down and taking most of its length down her throat.

She gets onto her knees and works my cock with both her hands and her mouth, sucking hard for several minutes until I cannot hold back anymore.

I ejaculate into her mouth as I hold onto the bun her hair is tied back into. I can't help but groan loudly as I do so, the orgasm so strong that it empties my mind for its duration.

I feel Cassandra swallow and ease her mouth from my penis. She puts it back into my underpants and zips up my trousers before refastening my belt for me.

My head spins and flashes with electric blue, the recipe of a cocaine high and an intense orgasm superlative and staggering.

Cassandra leans over and picks up her underwear before stepping into it and pulling it back on. Is this the moment she shows me her police badge? No fucking way. Cops don't suck the perps like that.

I notice beads of sweat on the side of her neck. I bring my hand up her and pull her head close, kissing her once more before unbolting and opening the bathroom door.

Cassandra slaps my ass as I pick up my briefcase and step through the doorway. I swear she feels the Beretta I am concealing.

8

We walk out of the coffee shop and I clock a suspicious look from the girl at the counter. Maybe it's Cassandra's flushed cheeks or the bulge in my pants that reveals it, but the girl knows exactly what we've been up to in the locked bathroom. Well, maybe not exactly, but she has definitely got the gist.

We move out onto the street and Cassandra turns the subject of conversation back to her ex-partner, as if the drug-taking and dick-sucking that took place inside didn't even happen at all.

She is telling me where he lives and what subway station it's best to get off at if we want to pay him a visit. She seems to be energized and agitated, although I know it's probably the coke.

I hear her mention his name, Joshua, but I am not listening to what she is saying about him. She walks on ahead of me as I take out my cell phone and press a button in the centre so that the screen lights up. I have had it on silent again and since the last time I looked at it I have just one missed call.

My heart sinks a little, which is pathetic really. I wanted everybody I know to be frantic with worry and trying to get hold of me, texting me messages of distress because my face is all over the national news and the broadcasters are warning the public not to approach me.

I check the call and it's from a cell phone number that I don't recognise. I notice an icon at the top of the screen that shows me I have an answer-phone message that I haven't yet listened to.

Cassandra continues to walk on ahead and doesn't look back at me as she chatters about something. I hold the phone to my ear.

"… one-bedroom place and it's so small it's like living in a prison cell—"

"YOU HAVE ONE NEW MESSAGE…"

"… not claustrophobic but—"

"RECEIVED ON…"

"… mould on the walls and ceilings—"

"AT 11:44 AM."

"… rather sleep on the streets—"

"TO LISTEN TO THE MESSAGE PRESS 1."

I zone out until I can't hear what Cassandra is saying. I press down the 1 key on my phone and I hear somebody breathing heavily down the line.

"Hello?" a male voice says, obviously confused. The idiot doesn't seem to realise he is leaving a message.

"Christopher, it's Robert," the voice continues.

"Robert Morrison. I hope you're well. I thought I'd give you a call to check you're okay after our meeting yesterday. I hope you understand why I took the action that I did and that it isn't a personal attack on you in any way. You're one of the best lawyers we have at the firm so I hope we can put recent problems behind us when you come back from your leave of absence."

It sounds as if he is driving while leaving this message, which is exactly the kind of tactless stupid thing this old fucker would do.

"Adam told me you were a little upset and I just thought I'd reassure you that your position at Charleston & Green is safe. I feel like we didn't leave yesterday on the best of terms, so I was wondering if you were free for a spot of golf this afternoon. It'd just be a chance for us to overhaul our professional relationship and move forwards.

"I will be at the Bethpage State Park Golf Club, which is in Farmingdale, from about two o'clock. It's on Quaker Meeting House Road, which isn't far from the Republic Airport. I'll just be hitting a few holes on my own, so you're welcome to join me. See you there or call me back if you can't make it. Thanks Chris, take care."

I end the message and place my cell phone into my trouser pocket. I call after Cassandra who is edging towards a crossing.

"Cassandra!"

She spins around and looks at me from down the street, gesturing for me to catch up to her. I break into a jog and look up at a clock on a store sign that shows me it is almost twelve-thirty.

"I was talking to myself," she says as I slow down to a stop in front of her. "What were you doing?"

"Nothing," I say. "Daydreaming."

"The subway station is two blocks that way," she says, pointing east.

She looks like she might vomit.

9

I follow her as she leads me to the subway station, not much conversation happening between us apart from the occasional fleeting look. She looks happy, which in turn makes me feel rather ecstatic.

When I saw her barely an hour ago she was in tears and looked as if she would be willing to leap into the Hudson River, and now, with an intake of coffee, coke and an orgasm, she looks on top of the world.

I zone out until we are on the subway train and try my best to begin some sort of conversation with Cassandra but cannot seem to progress from small talk. There's nothing stilted about our exchanges but it's apparent that both of us have other things on our mind.

"Is this a good idea?" Cassandra asks, her hands gripping onto a metallic rail in front of her seat on the train.

I look around the carriage and see that there are several other passengers with us, most of them sitting at the opposite end.

I see an African-American family, parents with three young boys and a teenage girl. The boys are loud and screech wildly as each of them plays with their handheld game consoles. The girl sits quietly tapping away at her phone while the parents stare at theirs.

Some other people sit around this family, most of them with looks of displeasure on their faces, the noise being made quite visibly bothering them.

"It's the only idea," I say. "Got a better one? He'll never be out of your life if you do anything but this."

I feel like the counsellor with all of the framed qualifications and I imagine Cassandra stepping into my office like a bleak figure of melancholy, needing my help and hanging on my every word.

"Back at the coffee shop," Cassandra says, "I know you're married, Jack. I don't know what came over me. I haven't been myself at all recently."

"It's okay," I console her. "It was as much my fault as it was yours. And anyway, I wasn't exactly truthful during our meeting. My relationship with my wife isn't what I'd call flawless, even though I made it out to be that way. It's actually a fucking disaster, but I felt stupid admitting it. I know lying about that was ludicrous."

Cassandra looks down at her feet.

"Don't worry," she says. "Sometimes it's much easier to avoid the truth."

I expect she's heard some outlandish stories over the years, some even more unbelievable than my fabricated tale about my disturbing bestiality pregnancy dream.

The subway train draws to a stop and Cassandra stands up, holding out a hand to me like an assertive mother.

I take hold of it and let her lead me from the train and onto the platform. A rush of warm air comes up from below my feet and causes me to screw my eyes closed.

When I open them Cassandra is leaning in to kiss me, so I close them again and let her lips press against mine. I have the urge to touch her breasts and lose the ability to control myself, both of my hands coming up and caressing them.

I open one eye and see that a small crowd has gathered next to us, consisting mostly of a group of children who appear to be on some sort of field trip, as an adult in a fluorescent vest is trying to ferry them away from us, our behaviour inappropriate for the eyes of minors.

10

"So where does he live?" I ask.

The streets appear unnaturally quiet as we pass a street vendor and move along a road where abandoned buildings and warehouses seem to be all that there is.

It's like we have stepped through a portal from one dimension to another, and in this dimension the majority of the human race has been wiped out by a mutated strain of an airborne super-bug.

"He lives in a studio around the corner," Cassandra explains. "It's a converted loft above this warehouse that used to make shoes in the twenties and thirties. Sounds a lot more glamorous than it actually is; it's a shithole. He rents it off a friend of his, who charges an extortionate amount for such a small place."

"There's no going back now," I say, striding next to Cassandra with my hand in the small of her back, pushing her along slightly.

"Just sending a message," Cassandra says almost inaudibly and indirectly.

We round a corner and enter a side-street, following the footpath up to a large cast-iron gate. The gate is open and we pass through it moving into a courtyard that is littered with junk and various discarded kitchen appliances.

The courtyard is surrounded with steel fencing, and at the far side there is a storage unit that is rusted and discoloured, no doubt having been there for a couple of decades.

I follow Cassandra as she walks across the sandy ground towards the warehouse. I can see that there are three floors from the broken and boarded-up windows.

The dusty orange brickwork of the building doesn't suggest that it's the same masonry used to build this place back in the twenties and thirties. It looks as though a renovation has been attempted, perhaps in the eighties or early nineties, which may have been the time the loft was converted into a studio, meaning the brickwork isn't as old as the building itself.

A steel flight of stairs, which looks like an even more recent addition to the structure, runs up the outside of the building on an angle from ground level up to the top, where there is a pine door with something scrawled on it in black marker-pen. From down here it looks like measurements, perhaps from when the door was cut from a larger piece of wood.

"Here we are," Cassandra says softly.

"That door up there?" I ask, pointing towards the door at the top of the steel steps.

"Yeah."

Cassandra puts her hand on my forearm. I place my hand upon hers and stroke my thumb on her wrist.

"Don't hurt him," she says with a look of earnestness on her face.

I look beyond the make-up on her face and see the faint purple of the bruise beneath her eye. It has almost gone now, but I can imagine how it looked when it first appeared after the fist smashed into her face.

"I won't."

She lets go of me and I walk to the bottom of the steps, putting my briefcase down on the ground and looking at my reflection in a ground floor smashed window.

My face is fractured into several pieces, each image of myself appearing different from the others. It is as if each version of me holds an individual element of my personality. It is now that I have to choose what elements to keep and what elements to discard.

Jack Gardener isn't this fucking complicated. He's the alpha male and he doesn't take any shit. Cassandra Jones is falling in love with him and I have to do everything I can to make sure that he doesn't lose her. He's what I need to be in order to succeed.

I slowly walk up the steel stairs with Cassandra following a couple of steps behind me. Once I reach the top I turn and take one more look at her, her face as pale as it would be if she had lost a close friend to terminal illness, before banging on the wooden door with the side of my fist.

I listen as somebody moves around inside, scuttling

like an insect. It's the sounds of somebody rushing to answer the door when they know it's the cops and they have crack-rocks on their kitchen worktop and need to hide them quickly.

A lock clicks and the door opens wide, Joshua standing in the doorway like a hulking stone figure. He's a fucking monster, built like a football player who has pumped himself to the brim with steroids. A boulder-like head sits on the top of broad shoulders, his arms hanging by his sides like hunks of granite.

He's at least six feet tall, but it isn't his height that makes me feel tense; it's the fact that he's almost as wide as the doorway.

He stares at me with the green eyes of a reptile, sneering with a sloping mouth, his chin jutting out and his forehead furrowing, each line on his head looking like a groove dug out from his skin with a shovel.

"What the fuck is this?" he mocks, revealing his straight white teeth as he smiles.

I notice he has at least one gold tooth near the back of his mouth. I imagine prising it out with a pair of pliers, blood filling his mouth as his tongue thrashes around like a dying fish.

"My name is Jack Gardener," I say. "You're Joshua, right?"

He glares at me like I have insulted his mother.

"Who the fuck is this, Cassie?" he says again, switching his attention just over my shoulder to Cassandra.

"Listen, you cunt," I growl. "Leave her alone. No more phone calls, no more emails, nothing. You got it? This is your first warning and if I have to deliver a second one I won't be doing it with words."

My last sentence sprints from my mouth like an athlete false-starting. It's only when I hear it that I realise how fucking stupid it sounded.

At least now I've come to understand one thing about Jack Gardener: he's no good at intimidation.

"Is this guy for real?" Joshua laughs, discounting me and looking back over at Cassandra.

I can't quite tell what age he is, but I would guess he is only mid-twenties, although it could be younger than that. He is wearing a hooded sweater with the logo of some university I do not recognise, which perhaps adds to his vision of youth. Cassandra was most definitely the older woman when in their relationship.

"You told her you'd kill her the next time you saw her," I say, gritting my teeth. "So what's stopping you?"

He steps forwards and I expect him to throw a punch. I steady myself and get ready to duck out of the way if a fist comes towards my face.

"This is none of your business," he says. "Keep your nose where it belongs before I break it."

I step forwards so that there are only a couple of inches between the two of us. He doesn't flinch but I know he is thinking the same thing I was a few seconds ago, but I can assure him it won't be me who lands the first blow.

"So you'll let your fists do the talking again, will you?" I deride. "That really is the best way of dealing with things, isn't it? If things don't go your own way you pound on them until they do."

Joshua looks down at the ground, perhaps weighing up the pros and cons of smashing my teeth in.

"I'm Cassandra's new boyfriend, so it is my business. Consider yourself cautioned. Do the right thing and back the fuck off, or you'll come to know what a wrathful castigation feels like."

He looks up at me and I see a fierce look light up his eyes. I've got him, and I know what it is that has snared him and is now dragging him in.

"Well, you've moved on pretty fucking quickly, haven't you?" Joshua says, the red from his eyes moving onto the skin on his face.

Cassandra remains silent. I need to twist the knife.

"She said she hasn't ever felt as horny as she did with me. She told me about your needle dick. You're a selfish and terrible lover, apparently."

I feel his breath against my face.

"She finally knows what it's like to be satisfied and that's thanks to me. Not some pumped-up kid with the girth of a ten-year-old and the stamina of an old man with a respiratory disease."

Joshua looks at me blankly. I turn to gauge Cassandra's mood and then he hits me, hard in the side of the head and the ear, dizzying me but not knocking me from my feet.

Joshua's fist is loose and his hand is slightly open, slamming into my head. My ear wails loudly and becomes the focus of the pain, my skull bearing the brunt of the punch and my feet spreading my weight to stop me from plummeting down the steps.

Cassandra is screaming as another fist hits me in the same part of my head, this time taking me down to my knees.

This punch connects better, almost knocking me out, as I feel myself drift into brief unconsciousness.

I see Joshua's face close to mine, screaming something at me that I cannot hear. My ear drums have ceased to work, as have my limbs as I try to raise an arm to stop him hitting me again. I see her trying to pull him away as he kicks me in the stomach, knocking the wind out of me.

I cannot stop myself being knocked down and the force of the kick sends me falling down the flight of stairs, my head hitting the steel at least three times as I plunge, my arms desperately trying to grab hold of something to stop my descent.

I roll like a stunt-rider falling from a motorcycle, the world spinning around frantically and Cassandra's high-pitched screech providing a hellish backdrop to my agony.

My whole body feels broken as I hit the sandy

ground. I will be surprised if I haven't fractured any bones.

I push myself up from the ground with my hands, my legs wobbling as I stand, like a new-born lamb stepping up not long after birth. I look at my hands, which are both grazed and red raw. I bring them up to my head and press them against my wounded skin, crushing pain spreading across my throbbing skull. I feel a split in my head, and when I look at my hands they are saturated with blood, the gash pulsing vigorously and leaking with fluid. It's fucking beautiful.

I turn around to see Joshua charging down the steps, Cassandra not far behind, continuing to shriek and plead with him to calm down. I take a few steps backwards as he approaches, catching the reflection of myself once more in the broken window. My face and neck are completely soaked with blood, meaning I hardly recognise the person I see. Motherfucker got me good.

Joshua runs into to me and knocks me to the ground with his shoulder. I hit the floor hard and my neck snaps backwards, the blood from my wound getting in my eyes. He hits me hard in the face and it may have broken my nose as I hear a sickening wet crack. He raises his fist again and I see his knuckles stained with my blood. Cassandra is behind him as he stands over me, her hands wrapping around his arm as she tries to restrain him.

Joshua turns to her and shoves her in the chest, knocking her to the ground. When he turns back to me I spit what blood has got into my mouth into his face, smiling insanely to rile him up some more.

This kid must really have underlying issues regarding how he deals with his temper, because this is fucking priceless. His face is purple as he wraps his hands around my throat, strangling me so hard that every ounce of air seems to be sucked out from my lungs.

I can't even choke and my trachea feels like it might be getting compressed to the point of being lethally damaged.

Joshua's teeth are clenched together and his eyes are screwed shut, using all of his strength to quite literally choke the life out of me.

Fuck, that's right. This prick is going to kill me. He's going to strangle me until I am still and lifeless just because I said he had a needle dick.

I bring my knees up from the ground and push them into his chest, but I know that I do not have the vigour to push him off. He's leaning down upon me and he's got gravity on his side, which puts the odds entirely in his favour.

I reach for my ankle and manage to pull down my sock, the switchblade falling into my open hand. I manage to flick out the blade using one hand, knowing that I only have seconds left before I am out cold.

I grip the knife with my palm and thrust my hand upwards, the sharp blade stabbing into Joshua's neck.

I push the knife in even more as his grasp around my neck loosens, his eyes becoming wide and full of terror as he realises what I have done.

Flecks of his blood splash onto my already-wet face as I take a huge breath, air filling my lungs.

Joshua removes his hands completely from my throat and stands up, the immense anger draining from his face, which changes from purple to white in a matter of seconds.

He brings one hand up to the weapon sticking out of his neck and flaps around, his eyes full of panic, trying to take hold of it. He cannot seem to seize it as he slumps down onto the ground, whimpering like an injured dog.

I cough and take rapid breaths. I smear the blood from my eyes and mouth, sitting forwards and hacking up saliva onto the floor.

I look and see Cassandra clambering to her feet, her expression all too familiar. It's exactly the look Kacey Ross had on her face when she realised I had killed Gio Rigo.

"You're bleeding," she says, gasping for breath as her

eyes dart from my bloodied head to the gurgling Joshua on the ground less than six feet away. "Shit, he's bleeding," she adds, before covering her mouth as she notices the flick-knife sticking out from his neck.

Joshua is growling like a beast and I can tell that he is not sure what he should do with regards to taking the knife out from his neck.

I'm not an expert, but I'd guess that he would be better off leaving it where it is.

"Jesus," Cassandra wheezes.

I continue to cough, the saliva coming up from my gullet now tainted with blood.

"He was gunna fucking kill me," I pant. "He pulled out the knife and I managed to push it back towards him. Shit, he was gunna stab me in the face."

"Fu-fuck you," Joshua says, blood bubbling up from his lips as he writhes around.

Cassandra shakes her head in disbelief.

"He's a fucking animal," I say as I manage to get to my feet.

I feel like I've been in a high-speed car accident and I have just been pulled from the wreckage, shards of glass in my face and my spine twisted from the impact.

"See what he's capable of?" I snap.

I touch my head again and survey the damage with the tips of my fingers. The wound is still leaking blood but I can tell that it will stop soon; there won't be a need for stitches. The blood is already clotting around the edges of the gash but it may help if I find something to tie around my head.

"Fucking psycho," I say, spitting more blood onto the ground.

Joshua burbles a response but it cannot be heard as the blood seems to be drowning him.

"He's the sociopath, Cassandra," I say. "This is the prick that's turned your life into such a prison."

Cassandra looks at me as if I am not really there, just

an apparition that has appeared to guide her through the next few minutes.

"Escape."

I pull out the Beretta from my waistband and offer it to Cassandra, holding the weapon by the barrel.

She may have never seen a loaded gun in her life, and here I am holding one out to her and urging her to grab hold.

"Holy shit, Jack," she utters.

I shake my head, feeling a single drop of blood running down the side of my face.

"Escape," I repeat.

"What do you expect me to do?" Cassandra replies, her voice cutting out halfway through the sentence.

"Don't act like you don't know."

She shakes her head as if she is avoiding a swarm of bees.

"You need to kill him."

I reach forward and take hold of her hand, forcing the gun into her grasp and closing her fingers around it.

I can see tears building in her eyes. She can't crack, not now.

If she doesn't do this then I will have no need for her. Be my collaborator, Cassandra, I trust you to do the right thing. This is your moment of redemption.

"Fuck, Jack, he only hit me once. He doesn't deserve to die."

"It would have been me," I say. "Nothing stopped him wanting to plunge that knife into me. He needs the push. Pull the trigger Cassandra, send the message."

The tears begin to stream down her face as she sobs.

"I'm not a killer."

She looks down at the gun in her hand.

"We're all killers," I say. "When we refuse to donate money to kids in Africa, we sentence them to death. When we don't recycle and we leave the tap running while we brush our teeth, we're sentencing the whole planet to death. In this day and age it's acceptable to kill, not necessarily right, but acceptable. This isn't one of those moments. Now, it's right."

I look down and point at Joshua, who is holding his neck with both hands and staring up at us both with dread in his eyes.

"No," Cassandra says, tears falling from her face and onto the pistol.

"It's either him or me. You either put a bullet in his fucking face or you put the gun to my head, pull the trigger and kill the person who has helped you get his far."

She shakes her head, the sobs getting louder.

"I can't!" Cassandra screams, her face red and tight.

"Make the choice!" I scream, louder than her.

I step towards her and grab hold of her wrist. I bring the barrel of the gun up to my face, just underneath my chin.

"Pull the trigger and it'll all be over."

I close my eyes, knowing that at any second a bullet could tear through my brain and kill me, eradicating everything I have ever thought and smashing the images of everybody I have ever loved into a thousand tiny pieces. Every memory I have ever had will be blown out into a bloody mist.

All of the work I have done will have been in vain.

The gun presses even harder against my chin as I listen to Joshua's continuing gurgles and chokes.

"Why?" Cassandra bawls. "I don't understand!"

"Him or me?"

Joshua has pulled the knife out from his neck with a jolt, a spurt of blood squirting out onto his chest. I hear him cry out.

"Do it!"

I hear a groan behind me as Joshua pulls himself to his feet. I open my eyes and turn to look at him, pulling my chin away from the Beretta.

The wound in his neck continues to spew out blood

as he comes at me, the knife raised out in front of him.

I raise my hands in a useless act of defence and watch as two gunshots are fired off in rapid succession from next to me.

One hits Joshua just below his left armpit, and the other in the side of the head, jerking him to the left before he drops to the ground with a slam.

The knife falls from his hand onto the ground and I step over him before he is even still, looking at the bullet hole in the side of his head. His eyes are wide and white, no longer full of anger, just a removed emotion, like they are marbles instead of eyeballs.

His body has slumped in a contorted way, his legs bent underneath the rest of his body.

I look back at Cassandra and see that she has dropped the Beretta to the ground.

I knew she could do it.

"What's next?" Cassandra murmurs coldly.

"Thank you, Cassie," I say. "For everything."

11

I pick up the pistol from the ground and return it to my waistband before walking over the flick-knife and scooping it up. I put it into a jacket pocket, not caring about what damage the blood will do to the silk lining inside.

"We have to leave," I say.

"Where do we go?" Cassie replies instantly.

"Anywhere but here."

Cassie walks over to join me and takes hold of my hand, ignoring Joshua's twisted corpse at our feet.

"Jack, I'm scared," she says, her bottom lip shaking.

"Of course you are. It'd be silly if you weren't."

I squeeze her hand to reassure her that I will be here to guide her and protect her until every fear she has is as dead as her ex-boyfriend.

"We'll go back to where I bumped into you this morning," I say. "We'll go to my car, which is parked around the corner from the coffee shop, and we'll take it far away."

Cassie tilts her head to one side.

"We're gunna go and play some golf."

THE SEVENTH TALE - EXASPERATE

1

We move quickly from the scene of the crime back to the subway station, Cassie dragging her feet like a stroppy teenager, constantly looking down at her hands as if they are stained with blood.

Of course they aren't actually stained - she didn't get close enough for that to happen - just figuratively.

She will be like this for an hour or so at least: the initial shock of having killed somebody, somebody she knew fairly well, will linger like an unwanted visitor.

I take hold of her hand and speed up my walk, imagining a man walking his dog through the courtyard of the converted warehouse and finding Joshua's body, his pet sniffing around the wet blood on the ground.

He will take out his cell phone while he struggles with the dog pulling hard on the lead as it attempts to lap up some of the blood, dial 911 and report the death to the cops. It's an obvious murder, he will testify, the victim having a laceration in the neck and two bullet wounds, one in his side and one in his head. Either that or a spectacular suicide.

We wait for the subway train in silence. I make sure that Cassie stands in my sight and no more than a few inches away from me. I don't expect her to run as soon as my back is turned, but I need to be completely prepared for the possibility of that.

It was my lack of preparation that led to my car being stolen by Kacey Ross, the cowardice overwhelming her.

I cannot do this alone, I know that now. I need Cassie Jones and she needs me.

I begin to notice odd looks directed at me from passers-by. The daily commuters look at me as if all of my skin has been removed from my face and each fibre of my muscle is exposed and both of my eyes are hanging by a gory thread out of my skull.

I bring my hands to my face and feel the sticky surface of my skin, relieved to feel that it's still there. I look at my hands and see the blood on my fingertips, remembering that my face is soaked and my teeth are yellowing with blood.

I have been walking the streets looking like the survivor of a car-bomb blast. I drag my palms down over my face, but the blood is drying. It will take more than this to remove it from my skin.

"Look at me," I say to Cassie. "I look like a fucking zombie. I'm covered in blood."

Cassie looks up at me with one eyebrow raised, as if she is completely oblivious to my horrific appearance.

"Yeah," she says. "You split your head open on the stairs when you fell. Lots of blood, but the wound doesn't look too bad though."

"I must look like a fucking loon," I snigger.

Cassie looks around as if just noticing the other people around us. A middle-aged black woman is gawping at me with her mouth wide open. A tall white man a bit older than me is walking behind her and does a double-take as he clocks me in his peripheral vision.

"Wash your face or something," Cassie says.

"Now you tell me. Did you not think me walking around like this may have been fucking ridiculous?"

"It's not my fault. I'm a bit shell-shocked, Jack."

I see more people starting to look over at me and soon it even feels as though a crowd is gathering. I look down at my suit and see flecks of blood all over the jacket. I have no time to get it dry-cleaned, and if I let the stains sink in it'll never get clean.

"If a cop sees me we're screwed. Shit, it's post 9/11, Cassie. If I had a beard people might think I'm a fucking shoe-bomber."

Cassie shrugs her shoulders and I have an overpowering urge to push her from the platform onto the subway tracks.

"Where's the bathroom?" I ask.

Cassie looks around for a sign as I focus my attention on the black woman, who seems to sense that I'm not happy with her staring me.

She closes her mouth and slowly turns around.

Cassie tugs on my arm and points behind me. I spin around and see a sign for the toilets with a red arrow pointing away from the platform and back towards the entrance.

"Wait here," I say, turning back to Cassie. "I'll only be a minute or so."

I feel a tug of worry in my chest as I walk away, hoping to the high heavens that Cassie stays put and doesn't decide to jump on a train and leave me behind.

I speed up and look down at the ground as I follow the arrow to the bathroom. I round a corner and turn left just before the steps leading up to ground level. I push the bathroom door inwards and look up as I step inside.

It seems to be empty, which is perfect. There are three stalls at the back of the bathroom and only one is closed. It may have an occupant but it doesn't matter, as long as I don't have eyes on me while I wash the blood from my face.

I step towards the sinks lining the left wall of the bathroom, my shoe heels clicking loudly on the tiles. I look back at the stall, the thought of somebody sitting in there listening to me suddenly beginning to get to me.

I lean over, one knee on the floor, and crane my neck so that my head is a few inches from the ground. I struggle to keep this stance as I look for the sign of feet under the stall.

Unwittingly I place a hand on the ground to steady myself as I see a pair of white sneakers with bright orange laces facing me.

Just a kid, maybe a teenager or someone in their early twenties, I can gauge that much. As long as it's not a cop, security guard or some prick with a stick up his ass who would run and tell somebody, I'm golden.

I stand in front of the sinks, placing my briefcase at my feet and look at myself, my reflection striking up an unrecognisable vision.

I look like the dazed and broken form of a natural disaster survivor, somebody you would see on a news report. I could have just climbed from the rubble after an earthquake or dragged myself from a truck following a high-speed collision.

My face is covered in blood but patches of my skin can be seen through the cloak, as if the blood drying is causing it to thin or soak into me. The wound on my head doesn't look as bad as I expected it to, but the blood it has spewed has travelled down to my face and onto my neck, staining the edge of my collar and splattering onto my tie.

I'm not a doctor, but I can tell that my head wound needs some sort of attention. I'm not sure about stitches, as it would still be bleeding if that was the case, but maybe just a bandage to wrap around my head and stem the flow of blood if it decided to start again. I don't want to aggravate the wound too much but I can't risk looking like an undead monster, which is exactly what I look like now.

The red of my face brings out the cold white in my eyes and it sends a shiver down my aching spine.

I twist the tap on and watch the jet of cold water spill into the aluminium sink. I cup my hands and gather the water in my hands, already seeing a tinge of pink in the liquid.

I lean over the sink and splash the water onto my face, the temperature of it taking me by surprise for a second and causing me to gasp. I gather more water in my hands and repeat the process, looking down at the blood-stained sink as the red stream runs down the plughole.

I use the palms of my hands to scrub against my skin, running them up and down my face, along my forehead and on my chin. I use my knuckles under my face and around my neck, not caring about getting my collar soaked with water.

There is some resistance from the drying blood as I scrub but soon I can tell that most of it has been removed.

I look up at the mirror and see my face has all but returned to normal, except for a few stains of red around the edges of it. I scoop up some more water from the continuously running tap and splash it around to make sure the blood is completely gone from my face and neck.

The contrast from the red to the white makes me look terminally ill and I'm not sure what version of my face I'd prefer to look at.

Is it the red skull of death that represents the real Christopher Morgan or is it this pale visage? And whichever one it is does that mean that the one left is the true face of Jack Gardener?

Fuck no. They're both me. Jack only exists for Cassie's benefit.

The face that's looking right back at me now is me and I have to accept that it's the face that will always be staring back at me when I look at a reflective surface. I can't change who I am, and sure, in years to come it'll be older and greying, but the same face none-the-less.

There won't be anything I can do now about my stained suit, tie and white shirt. I'll have to live with it. I'll be the guy who has been painting his son's bedroom red and accidentally got some of the paint on his clothes.

Yeah right, because you paint wearing an expensive suit, you fucking moron.

I look around the bathroom for a first aid kit, but I have no idea if they're stored in public restrooms like this. I don't see one so I suppose I will have to find something else to wrap around my head. I would use my tie but I don't want to look like some drunken man-child on the way back from a school reunion that turned into an all-night party. It may seem insignificant, but I do have some pride left within me.

I'd rather run the risk of bleeding out until I faint than walk around New York looking like a monumental cunt.

I touch the edge of my head wound with one finger, grimacing as a bolt of pain hits me. I take one final look at myself, brushing down my suit, straightening up my tie and flattening my hair. I pick up my briefcase from the ground and turn away from the mirror.

I glance back at the closed stall door as I approach the bathroom exit, realising that I didn't hear a sound from whoever is in there.

He's either the shy type, waiting until he is left alone before he can go about his business, or a fucking pervert, masturbating himself in silence, ignoring the existence of me in the bathroom and edging closer to orgasm.

Dirty fucker, I should kick the door in and hang him by his orange shoelaces. But I won't, because Cassie is waiting for me, and I've already been longer than a minute or so.

2

I walk back out towards the platform, looking through the moving crowds for a sign of Cassie where I left her. I mistake two or three people for her and it's only as I get closer to the platform edge that I realise she isn't there.

A subway train slows to a stop as I approach, the doors opening with a hiss and people beginning to push their way on.

My eyes dart around as I look for Cassie, my heart pounding and my dry throat tightening.

Fuck, Chris, you never learn. Dead bodies freak out the ladies and if you take your eyes off them for one second they're gunna make a run for it.

Nobody finds a killer cool anymore, it's a fucking turn-off. You forced her to shoot that man and now she's gunna run to the cops.

You're going away for a long time, Chris. A long, long time.

I see her head outside a kiosk across from me, standing next to a bearded man who appears to be talking to her. She is looking away from him and up at an advertisement about sexually transmitted infections on the wall.

I push my way through the crowd and try to catch her eye by waving my arm in the air. She is fixated on the poster so I bring my fingers up to my mouth and whistle loudly to get her attention.

Everybody but her seems to look at me and dozens of frowning faces bear down upon me. The noise I made may have been me yelling racist abuse for the reaction it seems to have got.

I continue to barge through the crowd, growing anxious about the subway train leaving without us. We've been at this station too long as it is; we need to get moving.

I part a stationary elderly couple just in front of where Cassie is standing and place my hand on her shoulder. The bearded man next to her looks at me with disbelief, as if I am the stranger interrupting a private moment between him and Cassie.

"Fuck off," I sneer at him.

He looks away from me instantly and down at his feet.

"Cassie, the train," I say.

She glances away from the advertisement and up at me.

"Sorry, I was daydreaming," she says, looking over my shoulder as the last of the train's passengers board.

I take hold of her hand and pull her back through the dispersing crowd, speeding up to make sure we manage to make it onto the subway train before the doors close.

She looks back at the kiosk where she was standing,

perhaps at the bearded man who was possibly trying to hit on her or perhaps at the STI poster that drew her in so intently.

It might be the bright colours and the flashy lettering that keeps her fixated or it might strike a chord because she had gonorrhoea once. She might even still have it.

We step onto the train and the door closes a few seconds later. It is busy, packed almost to the brim with people, their faces blurring together and my nostrils filling with various stale odours.

We have to stand, and we decide to do so against the surface of the closed doors.

I don't want to look directly at anybody, especially at those closest to me. If I do I may be inclined to headbutt somebody, especially the motherfucker just behind me who is breathing down my neck.

The journey isn't too long, so I should be able to go the distance, but if somebody ends up with a broken nose I won't be held accountable.

3

"I need to get a few things. It'll only be a quick trip."

Cassie raises her lip in a bemused scowl.

"You're confusing me, Jack. You're talking nonsense. First you mention some bullshit about wanting to go and play some golf and now you want to go to a home improvement store?"

She's talking to me like I'm an idiot. There's no need for her to be so condescending, not now. If this is the way our relationship starts then there's only one direction it can really go: down the crapper.

It's during these early stages that we should be complimenting each other and telling heart-warming stories about our experiences, snare our lover with a thought that we really are near perfection and implant the idea that we are made for each other.

After a few months you can let your true colours show. Dust away the glitter and reveal the growling tar of every resentment and disappointment.

"I need to pick these things up, I won't get another chance," I insist. "Look, I know you're worried, I understand that. Let me take the lead and everything will be fine."

Cassie exhales loudly.

"But surely we need to get somewhere and lay low. Fuck, Jack. I just killed my boyfriend and I did it for you."

I raise my hand to signal her volume has exceeded what I believe to be acceptable. The street is quiet but there are a few people gathering on a corner across the way.

She may have said it too loudly but I feel content with what she said.

She did it for me. She killed Joshua for me.

"Ex-boyfriend," I whisper. "You said he was your ex-boyfriend."

Cassie nods and looks around before lurching forwards and kissing me hard on the lips. I hold her by the hips and pull away from her after a few seconds.

"Trust me," I say. "We won't get caught. We're in this together so we need to work together. We're a team now, and teams have tactics. We'll lay low when the time is right, but for now, there are a few more things I need to do."

"I trust you," Cassie mouths, her voice not working.

What I intend to do isn't beyond me now that I have Cassie by my side.

The authorities will be on my trail, and right now I'm making it too easy for them. I need to move faster and throw a curveball out there to ensure I'm not caught before my bidding is done.

That curveball will be taking up the offer of a game of golf with Robert Morrison at Bethpage State Park Golf Club. We'll drop in on a home improvement store on the way and perhaps pay a visit to a pharmacy to grab a bandage for the wound on my head.

Once all of that is out of the way I am ready to get started. The preparation will be done and then the fun can really begin.

I have exhausted my balanced disposition and embraced the take-no-shit-make-no-excuses. When life gives you lemons you smash them down into the ground with your fists until your knuckles are bloody and grazed and the wounds sting as your hands are covered in lemon pulp and juice.

"You did it for me?" I ask as we continue to walk, approaching the coffee shop we were in earlier.

"Well, yeah," Cassie says. "But for me as well, I guess."

"You did the right thing," I assure her.

"I hope so."

Cassie looks over at the coffee shop entrance as if everything that happened in there earlier today is returning to her mind and she is experiencing it all over again.

"I really do."

4

The Chevrolet Cavalier is in exactly the same place as I left it, and the only difference is that it has a parking ticket tucked under a wiper on the windscreen.

Not my fucking problem.

I walk over to it and take it out, rip it to pieces and let it fall to the ground like confetti.

"I hate those," Cassie says. "They'll fine you tenfold if you don't pay."

I open the passenger door of the Cavalier and nod for Cassie to get in.

"I don't care," I say, "it's not my car."

Cassie climbs in without a word and I slam the door behind her, stepping out of the way of a cyclist as he comes towards me.

I watch as he cycles away, not once looking back as way of an apology. I should catch up to him, knock him off his bike and break his teeth. He isn't wearing a helmet so if he breaks a vertebra as he hits the ground it'll be his own fault. Safety first.

As I walk around the car and open the driver's door to get in the Cavalier, I notice a balled-up item of clothing on the back seat. I reach over to it and grab hold, pulling it apart and seeing that it is a grey hooded sports sweater with a zip up the middle and a black Nike logo emblazoned on the breast.

I put my briefcase on the driver's seat and slip off my blood-stained jacket. I fold it over my arm and sling it onto the back seat before pulling the grey Nike sweater over my head and yanking it down over my body.

It's a decent fit and will do the job of keeping me in the shadows. The cops will be looking for a suited lawyer carrying a briefcase with a crazed look in his eye. He will be armed and dangerous and should not be approached.

I would drop the briefcase as well but there are too many important things in there. I suppose I'm just not willing to discard necessities that could possibly get me pinched.

Like this car, which I'm certain has been reported as stolen. I won't be going to the trouble of torching it. Once it has served a purpose I will leave it at the side of the road and it will be picked up for a parking offence and not because the plate is registered as stolen.

I move the briefcase from the driver's seat into the back and sit down, closing the door behind me.

"A new look?" Cassie says.

"My suit had blood on it. It'll draw too much attention to us. This may be New York but if we walk around looking like extras from *The Texas Chainsaw Massacre* we'll have the heat on us before we can even tee off at Bethpage."

I start the engine and Cassie puts her hand on my thigh, her fingers edging close to my penis.

She's a fucking animal, this girl. I would never have expected it. She's everything I wanted her to be and more.

"You okay?" I ask.

"I'm just perfect," she says, almost pouting as she does so.

I want to have sex with her right now. I want to tear off her clothes in the back seat of this car without caring how many pedestrians walking by look in and see our naked flesh.

I should have fucked her in the coffee shop bathroom. Maybe that would have suppressed this desire to a manageable intensity.

"You unquestionably are," I say as I pull the Chevrolet away from the sidewalk and straighten it up on the road ahead.

5

Luckily there is a Home Depot store on route to Farmingdale, which is a place I haven't been to before. However, I manage to find my way there at the beginning of the journey once I get from Manhattan to Long Island as I stumble across signs directing me to the Republic Airport.

I have a route-planner application on my cell phone, but I haven't used it before and I don't think now would be a good time to start.

Plus, I don't want my cell phone signal to be traced and allow the cops or feds to hack into what applications I am using. That would give them the information as to where I am heading and they could send a unit over, perhaps even beat me to my destination.

They might want to send a SWAT team if that's the case, because I'll take hostages and fire blind shots at them before I let them take me down.

"Cassie, you ever been to Japan?" I ask.

She doesn't look at me as she takes a long breath inwards. I wouldn't quite call it a sigh but there is something dismal about it.

"No."

"Did you know that there are over thirty thousand suicides in Japan every year, which amounts to over eighty a day. It has the highest suicide rate of any country on the planet and its capital, Tokyo, has the highest people to square mile ratio of any city in the world. I'd love to take a trip there."

She looks at me and for a second she reminds me of Jennifer.

"They pack onto their subway trains like sardines. They do this every day, and when they're done with work they return to tiny apartments no bigger than the average American dining room. If they miss their train they've got to spend a night in a sleeping capsule at the station, which is basically a fucking coffin with cotton sheets."

She turns away from me and watches the traffic as we slow down.

"The human condition is claustrophobic, and if we are in too close proximity to one another, it wants out. It's a natural reaction. We're like horses, Cassie. We need the open plains, not a fucking pen with a wooden fence. We need to roam free."

I pull into the car park of Home Depot and tell Cassie to stay put while I go into the store. I take the keys with me but make sure that I don't lock her in. If she wants to run away then so be it, but Kacey Ross is the last bitch who is stealing a car from me.

I look back at her as I approach the Home Depot store and see her gazing out of the window, an impassive look on her beautiful face.

Once in the store I stride around with my head down, pushing my way through the ridiculous amount of people that fill the wide aisles.

First up, garden power tools. In particular, a chainsaw. I go for a recognised brand and model because I am easily swayed that way as an eager consumer.

I purchase a spare fifty-six-link chain, just in case, along with any accessories I think I might need. I pick up a bottle of chainsaw oil, some protective gloves and debate taking a chain sharpener, but decide against it. I certainly won't need one, especially with a spare chain that I can use if the first one gets blunt.

A sales assistant lingers as he watches me make my choice, but I give him a red hot glare and he moves away and starts talking to a woman in her forties who is across the aisle looking at garden shredders.

I move away from the aisle with my chainsaw and highjack an empty flatbed trolley from a man who is distracted by his wife's complaining as they look at a brochure displaying various lawnmowers.

I place the boxed chainsaw onto the trolley and begin to walk down the central aisle of the store. I spot a stand displaying thick black gaffer tape and pick up two rolls as I pass it and put them on top of the chainsaw.

I move down the store until I find my way to the paint department, making mental notes of the labelled and numbered aisles to make sure that I'm not missing anything.

Firstly, I find a small single paintbrush, only about one inch wide with thick black bristles. The type of paint I need isn't important as long as it's black. I pick up a small tub of chalkboard paint at a section that seems to store only specialist paints and decide that it will do the job.

I go further down the store to an aisle for electrical accessories and select some large cable ties about twelve inches in length.

Next to this aisle is a large section for household power tools, in which I find a standard drill with a pre-charged battery back.

I move out of this section and continue down until I

find an aisle with a ridiculous amount of various types of rope. I settle on a twenty-foot length of blue nylon that is wound onto a plastic spool.

I walk beyond the plasterboard and up to the rectangular sheets of plywood that are stacked on the ground. The sheets are way too big for what I need, but I remember seeing a sign as I entered the store saying any sheet materials can be cut down for free.

I pull out one sheet of plywood and balance it on the surface of the flatbed and manoeuvre around the end of the aisle to find an attendant standing in front of an industrial saw.

There don't seem to be many safety precautions in place as the middle-aged bordering-on-morbidly-obese man cuts the sheet of plywood into four almost identical pieces.

I pile up the sheets of wood next to all of the other items I have amassed and turn back on myself and walk towards the exit.

As I approach it I see a stand with small first aid kits displayed, which reminds me that I haven't visited a pharmacist to get a bandage and doubt that I have time now.

I pick one up, add it to my other items and pass through a 'NO EXIT' gate, keeping one eye on a security guard who is standing along a row of ten to fifteen cash registers, each seeming to be operated by a petite old woman.

I pull the trolley out through the automatic doors and exit the store without a word from a staff member or fellow customer.

I return to the car to find Cassie sitting in exactly the same place with the same detached look on her face that she had when I left.

I open the trunk of the Cavalier, take a few minutes to put the chain on the chainsaw and fill it with oil and gas from a small canister I find on the car's back seat, which saves me an awkward siphoning job. Once that's done I put all of my purchases inside, except for the first aid kit which I keep in my hand.

I adjust the back seat so that the plywood can fit and slam the trunk closed. I kick the flatbed trolley out of the way of the car and into the path of an oncoming pickup truck. The truck sounds its horn but I ignore it, climbing into the Chevrolet and starting the engine.

"Get everything you need?" Cassie asks, perking up slightly.

"Sure did," I say, holding out the first aid kit. "Can you help me bandage my head?"

Cassie nods and takes the kit from me, opening the plastic lid and taking out a roll of bandage.

"We really need to clean that wound," she says as I lean forward and let her examine the damage. "I don't understand how it stopped bleeding. I'm sure it needs stitches."

"We don't have time. Just wrap the bandage around as tightly as you can."

Cassie nods again and unrolls the bandage, wrapping it around my head, pulling it tight against the wound.

It stings but I don't struggle, letting her fasten it with a knot once it's been wrapped around a few times.

"Will that do?" she asks.

I look into the rear-view mirror. I look like an idiot wearing a bandana, tufts of my hair sticking up from beneath it and flecks of blood already appearing through the surface of the bandage.

The wound has been disturbed, a fresh flow of blood now seeping from it. It'll soon stop though.

"For now," I reply. "Thanks."

I reverse out of the parking space and approach a jam at the car park exit. I sound the horn for no real reason, the loud noise making me jump even though I was expecting it.

I feel Cassie lean in to me, her warm breath on my

cheek.

"I understand," she whispers.

"Understand what?" I question.

"What you said before. I thought about it while you were gone. We're horses, not sardines, right?"

I smile widely.

"Right."

6

The first time I met Robert Morrison he struck me as the kind of man who could get a table in any top restaurant without a reservation and who could convince any woman that he was the best lover on the planet.

He oozed confidence from every single pore and had a swagger about him that wasn't at all arrogant, which gave him that extra ounce of respect that set him above everybody else.

He had charisma and he had experience, which was the perfect combination for what Charleston & Green wanted to achieve at the time. It was a firm on the brink of great things and I knew that it was going places as soon as I found out that Robert was at the helm. With a captain like that, there was no way the firm was ever going to be in danger of going under. It had potential and a man who was nothing short of a visionary was developing it at a rapid pace.

He wasn't a good-looking man, and he certainly isn't now, but that didn't hold him back. He didn't need a chiselled jaw and dazzling blue eyes as it was the words that came from his mouth and the positive atmosphere he created with his presence that set him apart from the rest.

I respected him, and respect isn't something I have ever dealt out cheaply. You have to really warrant that respect if I am going to show it to you and I don't think that is ostentatious on my part in any way. It takes time to build a level of respect, and I don't care if you're a police officer or a judge or a criminal defence attorney, I won't bow my head and call you "Sir" until I am sure that you deserve it.

On the contrary, if I think you don't deserve it there's nothing stopping me telling you what a sanctimonious prick you are and that if you were on fire I wouldn't piss on you to douse the flames.

Robert Morrison had my respect, which it took a while for him to gain, but he lost it incredibly quickly.

The man I first met disappeared rapidly beneath a swathe of misery and pessimism, his passionate ideas and positive outlook dissolving like aspirin in water.

It was all because of his wife, as far as I am aware. I can identify with that and understand exactly what a strained relationship rampant with infidelity can do to a man, but he rolled over and let her destroy him.

He let the depression crush him until he lost every ounce of what he once was, and that's fucking unacceptable. We are all in control of our lives and shouldn't be backed into a corner; we should pick up a stick and fight our way out.

Robert Morrison lost every scrap of fight he had left in him and that's what makes him the pitiable excuse for a man I am on my way to visit now.

If he knew what was coming for him and why, would he have acted when he needed to back when he found out his wife didn't love him anymore? Would he have tried harder to sexually satisfy her to reignite their relationship?

I don't know if he would have. I don't even know if she would be worth the effort.

I look over at Cassie who has fallen asleep, her head leaning against the car window and her blonde hair hanging on her shoulders.

She let her hair down not long after we left the Home Depot store and I am finding it hard to stop looking at it. I want to run it through my fingers and inhale its fragrance, maybe even wrap it around my hand and pull it tight. I need to concentrate and keep my eyes on the road.

The journey has taken much longer than expected. Why the fuck has Robert Morrison decided to play golf at such a distant location? Farmingdale might as well be in New Zealand with all the effort it seems to be to get there.

It's already gone two o'clock but I am sure I will make it before Robert finishes at Bethpage. There would be no need to travel all the way there without the intention of playing more than a few holes.

After we crossed the East River on the Williamsburg Bridge and got to Long Island, after the visit to Home Depot of course, we made our way to the town of Oyster Bay, where I continued to follow signs for the Republic Airport for a while and took a few blind turnings once I realised that I may be going off course.

After feeling like I was lost for the best part of an hour, I saw a small sign for Bethpage State Park, which I followed into Farmingdale. Bingo.

It's a mystery as to why Robert would come here. Perhaps he grew up in this village and holds it close to his heart, or maybe he likes escaping the city for a few hours and forgetting that his wife is being rooted by a young man she met on a dating website where she advertised herself as an 'adventurous cougar'.

I round a corner and follow a long road down until I see a perimeter of trees that must surround the park. I reach the end of the road and pull into a courtyard that leads up to a stone-walled clubhouse with an elegant oak porch entrance.

I stop the car and climb out, cold air rushing against my face. I leave the Beretta and the switchblade on the driver's seat, knowing that I won't be needing them. I am sure the golf club doesn't frisk its visitors and members, but I don't want to be walking in armed to the teeth.

I decide to leave Cassie sleeping in the car. She doesn't need to be part of this next step and she needs to reserve her strength for the hours ahead.

I lock the car this time and walk up towards the clubhouse entrance, my feet crushing the gravel on the ground and my legs feeling unsteady after such a tedious and lingering drive.

I hope they let me in. From the waist down I am surely acceptable for an establishment such as this, but they may have rules on non-members turning up in hooded sweaters with a blood-stained bandage wrapped around their head.

If they refuse me entry I'll walk in anyway, and if they try to physically stop me I'll throw some punches and split some heads.

I step up onto the porch and get some odd looks from two greying men as they leave the clubhouse, although one of them holds the door open for me.

I step inside and walk up to the front desk where a middle-aged woman in a navy blue trouser suit is sitting, her eyes locked onto me from behind spectacles every step I take across the polished wooden floor.

I look around, seeing a glass door leading out to a restaurant/bar area and a large open area behind the desk that leads out to the courses.

I can see many people standing around another desk at the far exit, possibly hiring clubs or a golf cart, of which I can see several parked along an embankment outside.

"Are you here for a conference?" the woman at the desk asks, peering down her nose and over her glasses.

Behind the desk and around the sides of this large entrance room are glass cabinets displaying various trophies and framed photographs of top golfers. Amongst these I can see an image of Tiger Woods spraying champagne and smiling widely, a banner above his head stating that he is the 'US Open 2002 Winner'.

"Excuse me, sir?"

I stare at a bronze statuette of an eagle in flight on top of the desk. It's about three feet high and the craftsmanship is dodgy.

I don't understand why such a terrible piece would be on display. It's the first impression of mine for what Bethpage State Park Golf Club represents, and so far it's a pile of pretentious bullshit. Everybody is dressed like eccentric British aristocrats on vacation and it makes me feel queasy.

"Sir, are you here for a conference?"

A fucking conference?

"Um, no. I'm here to see Robert Morrison. He invited me down to join him on the course, although I am a little late."

The woman's wrinkles are terrible. She looks as though she's spent too much time on a sun bed and now it's making her skin look like the cracked surface of clay earth during a drought.

Her hair is grey and thinning, styled loosely into a curly halo. Her make-up is applied thickly and poorly, her lips an appalling shade of bright pink. The foundation rests on her crinkled skin like a layer of dust that has built up on an old leather suitcase that has been left in the attic for a decade.

"Okay, let me take a look."

My appearance doesn't seem to bother the woman at all, which is strange.

She taps away at a keyboard and looks at a computer screen that isn't visible from where I am standing.

"Mr Morrison is currently on the Green Course, sir. I don't see a note for any guests of his to be arriving, but if you like I can get a member of staff to take you up there. It isn't far, over the west ridge and past the tee-off for the Yellow Course."

I stare blankly at her. I am guessing that the colours represent how difficult the courses are, although I can't be sure.

"Or if you prefer you can rent a cart and drive up there yourself. You'll need a full driving licence and—"

"Okay, I'll do that," I interrupt. "Thanks."

"Will you be needing clubs? You can hire them for a rate of—"

"No, no clubs."

She looks up at me from the computer screen and smiles.

"Thanks for your help," I say.

"You're welcome, have a nice day."

I walk away from the desk and look back at her, half-expecting her to contact security on a radio or press a panic button under her desk, but she doesn't.

She just takes out a paperback novel from somewhere and begins to thumb through it, not once following me with her eyes as I make my way out of the building.

The members of the golf club don't treat me with such tolerance, most of them staring at me, even a few of them pointing as I pass by.

I don't see one other woman. They all seem to be men of a certain age, only a few below forty.

One elderly man, who looks in his late seventies, pulls hard on the sleeve of a younger man next to him, perhaps his son, and whispers in his ear and gestures over at me. I show them both the middle finger and mouth the words "fuck you". They stand in shock with their mouths open as I move out of the clubhouse, across some wooden decking and towards the golf carts on a grassy mound.

I can't walk to the Green Course from here and I definitely can't rent a golf cart. I stand around for a few minutes watching people return to and leave the clubhouse.

A golf cart pulls up next to me and an overweight man with a flat cap gets out, leaving a bag of clubs in the back of the vehicle as he walks towards the building but doesn't go in. He looks around and lights up a cigar, which I'm pretty sure is against club rules as I remember spotting a sign asking members to refrain from smoking on Bethpage State Park property.

He turns his back to me and I walk over to the cart,

happy to see that the fat bastard has left the keys in the ignition. I jump inside and watch as a tall man in a navy jacket, the same shade as the woman at the desk was wearing, walks up to the overweight man and seems to tell him to put out the cigar.

The fat man pleads his innocence with waving arm gestures as I turn the keys to get the electric motor started. It whirs into life and I manage to spin one hundred and eighty degrees and drive off towards the Green Course without the cart owner noticing.

7

The signage to get me to the first hole of the Green Course is quite confusing and I find myself approaching the tee-off for the Yellow Course once I drive over the west ridge, as the woman at the front desk told me. I take a right after this and follow a winding route until I find myself upon a plateau of ground that resembles a fairway. I'm not sure if I have somehow ended up on the green, but I don't give a fuck anyhow. Whichever way I decide to drive to find the Green Course I know that Robert will be long gone from the first hole and it could be difficult to find him, especially if he is in a bunker or in the rough and not in direct sight.

I stop as I come over a low hill, peering onto the green below at two men standing in and around a sand bunker around twenty feet away from a putting green.

I cannot tell if one of them is Robert; all I can see from this distance is that both of the men are wearing brightly coloured sweater vests over white polo shirts. One of them is wearing a ludicrous shade of purple and the other is wearing an emerald green.

I accelerate and wheel-spin on the dry grass, coming down the other side of the low hill and picking up speed as I drive towards the golfers. I slam the palm of my hand into the middle of the steering wheel, a shrill electronic horn sounding and grabbing the bemused attention of the stupidly-dressed men.

It is now that I can see who they are. The man in the purple is indeed Robert Morrison, standing a few feet into a curving sand bunker, holding a golf club in one of his hands and resting on it like a walking aid.

The man in the emerald green, who stands up on the fairway on a gradient next to the bunker, is Adam Phillips.

He holds a hand up to his face to keep the sun out of his eyes as I get closer, but that doesn't stop me seeing that it's him. I wouldn't be able to mistake him for anybody else with that laughable haircut.

I brake hard and the cart slides around to a stop, one of the front wheels mere inches away from Adam. He jumps back with a yelp, putting out a hand to protect himself from being hit.

I step out and walk towards Adam, who stumbles backwards and falls to the ground. He lifts a hand up to deter me coming at him, and it is then that I can tell he does not recognise me. I stop dead.

"It's your old friend Chris, Adam!" I yell. "Remember this face?"

Adam brings his hand down and squints up at me, the sun now in his eyes. I must just be a silhouette bearing down upon him.

"Chris?" I hear a voice say from behind me. "What's going on here?"

I turn away from Adam to see Robert standing at the edge of the sand bunker, and never before has this man looked so old and decrepit.

He looks so fucking idiotic in his purple sweater vest and beige golfing trousers. But one thing strikes me about him more than ever, he looks tired. Absolutely exhausted.

"You invited me and I'm here," I say. "Ta-dah!"

"Jesus Christ above," Robert says, placing his hand on his forehead. "What's happened to you?"

"What, this?" I say, pointing at my bandaged head.

"Car accident, walked into a door, fell down the stairs, got mugged, hit in the head by a brick. I don't really know, any of the above."

Robert looks over at Adam, exchanging a look with him that implies I've gone loopy. A fucking crackpot, that's what this prick thinks I am.

I'm not the fucking crackpot; both of these tactless cunts lost their minds long before I did. Just look at them, playing golf like a pair of homos before going back to the clubhouse bar, dropping their trousers and sucking each other off.

"Chris, are you okay?" Adam asks, his voice small and feeble.

"I'm fine," I snap. "I'm walking on sunshine. I'm over the fucking rainbow. I'm over the fucking moon."

Adam gets to his feet, dropping the club, which looks like a pitching wedge, onto the ground with a thud.

He must have been stuck in the bunker like Robert, the fucking loser.

"You don't seem fine," Adam says.

"And you would know what fine is, that right Adam?" I sneer. "This whole bullshit act you've got going on, brown-nosing the boss like this so you can get my case, that's fine is it?"

Adam looks over at Robert once again, shrugging his shoulders.

"What's gotten into you, Chris?" the old man asks, his voice breaking up. "I wanted to smooth things over, that's why I invited you down here."

"We're worried about you, buddy," Adam adds.

"I'm not your fucking buddy," I say, shaking my head.

"What?" Adam questions, aggression in his voice. "Have you been drinking?"

"Look," says Robert, "I don't know what you're trying to gain from this, Chris, but whatever you've got going on there's no need to bring us into it. You lost out on the Ramirez case because of your own disregard for its success, it was nothing to do with me."

"You're losing it, man."

"I'm a different person now," I say, stepping forwards. "I'm not a yes-man and I'm not a fucking slave.

"I didn't care about the Ramirez case because that fucker is a paedophile and should be locked up. If you think he deserves representation then you're just as bad as he is. Are you a paedophile, Adam?"

Adam steps forwards as well so that our faces are inches apart. I can feel the toes of his golfing shoes against my feet and his sour breath in my face.

"You're one of my oldest friends," Adam says, "but that won't stop me putting you down."

I laugh in his face, wanting him to hit me.

"That's you all over," I say. "Nothing but talk. It's always the words and never the actions. You're a coward, Adam."

"Fuck you," he says, saliva spraying into my eyes.

"Come on, now," Robert says, not having moved from his place in the sand. "Calm it down, both of you. Let's talk about the situation like adults."

I came here for the old man but now I am completely and utterly preoccupied by Adam's presence.

If only I knew he was going to be here, perhaps I could have prepared something extravagant. I could have brought the chainsaw from the car with me.

I don't take my eyes off his face. I can see his bottom lip trembling, which amuses me. He may be acting the big man but I can tell I'm scaring him, which is understandable. I must look like a hostage who has escaped two weeks of imprisonment and torture.

"I know about you and Jennifer."

He blinks copiously, his lips puckering.

"Sorry?"

You'd better be sorry, Adam. But even that won't help you.

"Don't you think this would be better discussed somewhere private?" Robert implores.

I ignore the old man, tensing my jaw and gnashing my back teeth.

"I know that you've been fucking my wife behind my back."

He looks down at his feet and back up at my face. His lip is trembling twice as much as it was before.

"Bullshit, Chris. No way. You're deluded."

"You want my life so badly and you'll do anything to get it. You want Jennifer and you want my job.

"You've always been jealous of what I have because your life is an empty shell and nobody has ever loved you because you're an egotistical little prick."

Adam shakes his head and looks away from me, holding out his arms and flashing a look of confusion at Robert.

"I have no idea what he's talking about," Adam insists. "He's gone fucking mad."

I take a step back and launch myself forwards at Adam, kicking him hard in the testicles.

He yelps like a dog when its tail has been trodden on, bending forwards and holding his balls with both his hands. He groans, gasping for air.

I see Robert in my peripheral vision climbing out of the bunker.

I look down at the ground at the pitching wedge Adam dropped. I pick it up and grip the end tightly, weighing up the club and watching as Adam staggers around.

"Chris!"

I bring the club behind my head and wait for the right moment before swinging hard, hitting the heavy end of the club against Adam's head with a dull thwack.

He falls to the ground, unconscious, his head slamming against the grass.

I turn to see Robert coming at me, no golf club in his

hands now. He grabs hold of the pitching wedge and tries to pull it out of my grasp, wheezing like a fool, shouting something.

I thrust my head forwards, thumping my skull against his, breaking the lenses of his glasses and sending him falling backwards onto the uneven ground. It hurts a hell of a lot, the wound beneath my bandaged head throbbing intensely.

He rolls down the sloping green, dazed but still awake enough to know he has to get away from me.

When Robert stops at the base of the incline, he looks up at me as if he is a new-born baby and I am the first strange sight of the world he is seeing. He lifts his hands up, begging for mercy without a word. He doesn't deserve it, not at all.

"Please," Robert says. "Don't."

"Don't worry, I'm sure you have life insurance," I mock, raising the club above my head.

His glasses are shattered and hanging off his nose.

"Please," he repeats.

I bring the club down hard and fast, smashing it into Robert's face and breaking teeth, bone and sinew all together.

He cries out, but it only lasts a second, the noise cut off by a choking sound. Blood spurts up from his mouth and covers his face, his greying moustache stained red.

I bring the club back above my head just as quickly and bludgeon him again, this time aiming for the top of his head and not the middle of his face.

I repeat the process until Robert's face is nothing more than a bloody pulp, spewing blood and other fluids.

His face resembles a poor make-up job you would expect to see in a low-budget horror movie. I can see bone and muscle along with pieces of broken glass from his spectacles and two dangling eyeballs beneath the gore.

I strike him a few more times until I am sure that he is dead. Each time the club comes down paired with a revolting wet slap, flicking specks of blood up onto to my clothes.

I drop the club onto the ground and am suddenly aware of my surroundings. I scan all around, glad that there doesn't seem to be another person on this particular hole of the course, which I would hazard a guess at being a par three.

This bunker is situated behind a group of trees on the edge of the course, the gradient keeping this spot low on the green and out of sight, especially for anybody teeing-off from over the hill.

I walk over to Adam lying on the ground, his limbs splayed out, and look at the wound on his head. It's only a small abrasion, but it has leaked blood down the side of his face that stops at the corner of his mouth. His mouth is wide open as he takes slow and long breaths.

I grab him by the ankles, where I notice he is wearing red and white checked socks.

I wonder when he started dressing like such a retard. I pull him along the green towards the golf cart, struggling with his dead weight as my shoes slip on the grass.

Once I get around the back of the cart, I bend down and grab Adam by the upper arms, pulling him up and steadying him as I lean down even further and put my body beneath the bulk of his torso.

I am squatting almost entirely onto the ground as I lift his weight up and onto me with an altered and slightly difficult version of a fireman's lift, his body hanging over my shoulder.

He feels as though he weighs a ton and I swear I can hear my spine creaking.

I place him in the back of the golf cart, carefully dropping him onto his back and leaning him against the bag of golf clubs that belong to the obese man from whom I acquired the vehicle.

I walk around to the front of the cart and get inside, accelerating hard and shifting back towards the hill I came down to the bunker.

The cart struggles to get up there and I only manage to pick up to the speed of a few miles an hour as I get to the top, looking back over my shoulder as I do to see exactly what is left of Robert. All I can see from here is his purple sweater, which is pretty much all that is left of him anyway.

8

I find my way back to the clubhouse without really thinking about the direction I am driving. I pass a few more golfers on their way between courses but none of them look at me as if anything is out of the ordinary.

I suppose as soon as somebody approaches a bunker on a certain par three hole some sort of alarm will be raised, so I need to pick up the pace.

When I get back to the clubhouse there is a small crowd of people chattering amongst themselves and laughing at attempts of humour, ignoring me as I pull up directly outside the entrance. I shut off the electric engine of the cart and jump out, rush around to the back and lift Adam back onto my shoulder with a grunt.

My legs feel like they could buckle and it's most likely because my energy levels are deteriorating due to my lack of eating.

I look down at the ground as I carry Adam into the clubhouse, not wanting to lock eyes with any of the old bastards as I leave Bethpage State Park.

The talking and laughing stops as I approach the crowd and make my way back to the front desk. I can feel their eyes on me as I pant, each step I am taking hurting my legs more and more.

I walk across the polished floors and only look up when I get to the desk a few feet from the exit. I see the woman whom I spoke to earlier continuing to thumb through her novel until I catch her eye. When she looks over at me her face drops and her jaw hangs low, her brow wrinkling so much it makes her look like she's in her nineties.

"Thanks for your help," I wheeze.

Somebody even opens the door for me as I leave the clubhouse, but I don't look up at them or say thank you. It's been much easier than anticipated to leave the golf club without even a question as to why I am carrying a golfer on my shoulder.

Perhaps the ignorant members believe I am nothing more than a good citizen taking my good friend to the hospital after a rogue golf ball hit him on the head.

Yes, that's right. I'll use that if anybody decides to approach me.

I step down onto the gravel and carry Adam over to where the Cavalier is parked. I stoop down and place Adam on the ground, looking through the car to see that it would appear Cassie is still sleeping in the passenger seat.

I take out the car keys and open the trunk. I search around for the packet of cable ties and tear them open with my teeth. I pull out two, kick Adam over onto his stomach and tie his hands behind his back tightly with the cable ties. I do the same with his feet, but I make sure I take off his golf shoes before I do so.

I'll be leaving them here as I don't want Adam to have anything sharp to use to free himself once he wakes up. I take out a roll of tape and tear off a small section.

I grab Adam by the head and slap the tape against his mouth before propping him up against the car. I hold him under his arms and push him upwards into the trunk of the car, rolling him back so he lies in the foetal position.

I slam the trunk and run around to the driver's side, looking back at the clubhouse to see that the woman who had been sitting at the front desk has followed me outside and has brought two of her colleagues with her; both men look like they could be security.

They begin to speed up as I climb into the car and

start the engine, moving the gun and knife I left on the seat down onto the ground beneath my feet. I slam my hand repeatedly on the wheel, honking the car horn.

As I pull away I wonder how my criminal record would read if I was found guilty of all the crimes I have committed in the last few days. It would be fascinating, even for me who has experienced them, and would be the first step to making me a superstar. But that won't happen because I am not going to get caught. I will die in a hail of bullets before I am put behind bars, and that's what will truly make me a superstar.

Oh Jennifer, if you could see me now.

THE EIGHTH TALE - SALIVATE

1

Adam Phillips is claustrophobic, or at least I hope he is. I hope he can feel the walls closing in around him, pinching against his bones like a vice. I hope he starts to hyperventilate and panic, cold sweat running down the sides of his face.

I briefly remember him telling me a story about how he is bad with closed-in spaces because he was locked in an airing cupboard by a few of his friends when he was nine years old.

He was left in there for over six hours and got so distressed that he bit his fingernails down and tore out some of his hair.

At least I think he told me that, but I may have created that myself to give me more pleasure as I imagine him squirming in the darkness, unable to break free from the cable ties digging into his wrists and ankles.

Part of me wishes he had witnessed me killing Robert. Terror comes from a place of great imagination in the human brain, a place where the possibility of an event can be forged into a thought so real you can imagine every scent, sound and vision that leads to what you fear the most.

Adam should be regretful. Adam should be terrified. Adam should be ashamed. Adam should be distraught. Adam should be—

Wait. Is that my cell phone ringing? Where the fuck is it?

Cassie doesn't wake as I lean across her, one hand on the wheel as I slow down, reaching to my jacket on the back seat and fishing out my cell phone.

I look at the screen and see that the call is coming from an unknown number. I wouldn't usually be eager to answer a call like that, but for now I guess I'll make an exception.

It might be Jennifer calling me to say she's sorry.

"Hello?"

"Chris. That you?"

I recognise the voice but it's a lot less bullish than I am used to. The way the voice of a child loses all fervour when their pet dies.

"Yeah, it's me," I respond, knowing full well that driving while talking on a cell phone is dangerous. I'm a mad man, baby!

"It's Beckford."

"Billy, my man!" I bellow. "How's life treating you? To what do I owe the pleasure of your call today?"

I hear him sigh on the other end of the line.

"Listen, Chris. It's urgent. I need to speak with you straight away."

It certainly sounds fucking urgent. I don't think I've ever heard William Beckford sound so serious about anything.

"What's going on?"

"I need to meet somewhere with you, brother. You anywhere near my place?"

I'm not, but I will be in good time. I'm probably speeding.

I wasn't planning to have to take a diversion from my destination, but William Beckford has done a lot for me, however over-the-top and gaudy he can be. He was the one who facilitated my drug habit when it got to its most severe and he was the one who made it possible for me to get a weapon when I had absolutely no idea how I would go about it.

I suppose, with the fucktard Adam in my trunk representing just how disloyal those close to us can be, William has been my only true friend of late.

I wouldn't expect him to screw my wife behind my back; it wouldn't be his style. He'd be too busy getting high and telling somebody about the groupies he used to fuck and the money he used to blow and the blow he used to blow it on.

"I can be," I say. "Give me maybe thirty minutes or so."

The end of the line goes muffled and I hear William say something, probably to one of his skaghead customers.

"Be as quick as you can," William says with deadness in his voice. "You won't be able to meet me at my place, so—"

"No?" I question.

The line goes dead again, but this time I think he has hung up. I look at the screen of my phone and see that the call counter is still going.

"Hello?"

"It's complicated," William says sternly. "I think there's some heat on me from the cops. I've seen a surveillance truck, so don't come to my place. T-there's a restaurant, a few b-blocks from where I live. Can you meet me there?"

He stuttered. That's not like him at all.

"Sure, I'll meet you there."

"As soon as you can?"

"As soon as I can."

He clears his throat.

"The restaurant is Gennaro's, an Italian place near Penn Station on West 30th Street, you shouldn't be able to miss it."

I'm already returning to Manhattan on the Williamsburg Bridge, so I shouldn't be long at all.

"Is everything okay, Billy?" I ask.

He goes quiet again.

"Everything's cushty, mate. See you soon."

He hangs up for sure this time and I look at the time before placing my phone in my lap. It's almost four-thirty, which is later than I expected, but it means that a brief meet with Beckford won't put me too far behind schedule.

He's probably having a paranoid moment and wants

to rant to somebody about the cops following his every move. I would have told him I was busy, but meeting with him gives me a chance of getting hold of some coke, which I could do with right now.

All of this killing is giving me the shakes.

2

Cassie stirs and wakes slowly, rubbing her eyes and gazing out of the window at cars passing us in the opposite direction.

"I thought you were going to be asleep forever," I say, glancing over at her.

She strokes her hair, flattening the ruffled strands on her head.

"I must've been tired."

I finish the cigarette I have been smoking and flick the butt out of the open car window at my side of the vehicle.

"Cigarette?" I offer.

"No, I'm fine. Where are we?"

"Back in Manhattan. I've got to meet up with a friend of mine, somebody I should be able to get some dope from."

"I thought we were leaving. We were in Long Island, weren't we?"

"I met a friend of mine in Farmingdale while you were asleep. He's in the trunk."

"I don't feel comfortable being so close to where Joshua died," Cassie says, ignoring me.

"Nobody saw us, there's no reason to think we're linked in any way. We're fine."

"I want to get as far away from this place as possible."

I sigh, already wanting another cigarette. I look out across the street and see an apartment building I recognise.

We aren't far from Chelsea and I realise I've been

here before. Shit, just three days ago. Everything rushes back into my head and my chest tightens as the cold grip of realisation hits me.

I cannot believe I have let this slip my mind. What a fucking moron. When I left the third-floor apartment I am renting in that building across the street, I told myself to come back in less than a day and now three days have fucking gone by!

"Cassie, wait here," I say, looking over at her. "Keep the engine running, I'll be right back."

She doesn't say anything, just looks at me with a mystified expression on her face. I grab hold of my briefcase, open it and look around in a leather pocket for a set of keys.

Once I have them I turn away and leap out of the car, other vehicles honking their horns as I leave the Chevrolet blocking one whole side of the road.

Cassie is calling after me as I run towards the apartment building but I ignore her.

My heart is pounding heavier than it has all today.

Heavier than when I ejaculated into Cassie's mouth in the coffee shop bathroom.

Heavier than when her ex-boyfriend Joshua was choking me on the dusty ground to within an inch of my life.

Heavier than when I smashed Robert Morrison's face to a bloody stain on a golf course fairway.

I cannot believe I forgot about him.

I worked so hard to make sure that nobody would report him missing and that his absence from his workplace wouldn't seem suspicious.

I did background checks to make sure I had plugged any hole in my strategy and even used my alter ego of Jack Gardener to rent the apartment.

So much fucking work and I've ruined it all by leaving him alone. I told him to remain calm and be patient, because I'd be back before he knew it.

I had intended to get my first meeting with Cassie Jones out of the way before returning to him.

Kidnapping him was a chore: I never expected him to scream so much. I did it late, but when I broke into his home he wasn't asleep, just sitting on his couch masturbating to pornography on his laptop.

Getting him to this apartment near Chelsea was like dragging a large dog to the vets to get castrated, even after I had tied him up and softened him up with some punches. I took a cab and convinced the driver that he was drunk.

I fumble with the keys and let myself into the front door, looking back at Cassie who is holding her hands out, asking me to come back.

Some vehicles behind the Cavalier are trying to weave around it, but cars coming in the other direction are blocking them off.

I rush up the stairs, clumping my feet on the steps as I take them two to three at a time. Once I get to the third floor I take a few seconds to catch my breath. The apartment door is closed, just as I left it, which is a good sign as it suggests that Vincent Ryman hasn't managed to escape or roused enough noise to draw the attention of the neighbours. However, the landlord told me that most of the apartments in this building were currently empty, which is one of the reasons I chose this place as a suitable location.

I unlock the door and walk inside, closing it behind me and pulling the chain across the door. I zip up my hooded sweater to the neck and walk around the corner, move through the empty living area and towards the far bedroom. The door is open a few inches, which, if I remember correctly, is also exactly how I left it.

I step forwards and push open the door, a glare of sun from a gap in the drawn blind at the window hitting me in the face.

I hold up my hand and see a drooping, lifeless figure

hanging by the neck from a rope which is looped around a ceiling fan, swaying softly with limbs draped vertically like eels being displayed at a fisherman's market.

Vincent's mouth is open, his bloated tongue hanging out and his eyes closed. His red hair hangs in greasy strands across the top of his head and his skin is a peculiar shade of grey, dotted blue around his cheeks.

I look down at a wooden stool on its side on the ground, knocked over as Vincent lost his balance and was hanged by the rope.

I gave just enough slack so that he could stand and support himself, which would have been fine for the time I aimed to leave him here, but after almost three days he wouldn't be able to stand any longer, the muscles in his ankles as they stretched for the stool eventually giving way.

The stench is awful and I have to hold my nose. I see a dried pool of dark liquid on the ground beneath Vincent's corpse and expect it to be a mixture of urine and faeces.

There's nothing I can do for him now. He has died simply because of my negligence. If there was one thing he could hold onto as the rope choked him to death, I hope it would be that he helped me. I would never have been able to do everything I have over the last few days without all he told me.

I step over to a low table to my left and pick up a Polaroid camera. I remove my hand from my nose, the stale smell offending me.

I turn on the camera and aim it at Vincent's limp body, clicking a button on the top and filling the room with a bright white flash.

For that split second I see every ghastly inch of this early stage of decomposition, from the sagging skin to the dull blotches revealing pale muscle beneath it.

The picture comes out of a slot at the side of the camera where I pull it out and shake it as it develops. I return the camera to the table and walk out of the bedroom, closing the door behind me.

I stand in the centre of the living room, holding the photograph in the palm of my hand and staring down at it as the image of Vincent's corpse appears, emerging from the fog like a shuffling undead nightmare.

When the photo clears I put it into the pocket of my trousers and return to the front door, take off the chain and leave the apartment.

As I walk down the stairs and return to street level, I wonder when it was that Vincent lost his footing and was lynched. Maybe it was within the first twelve hours, which makes the fact that it slipped my mind not seem so careless.

If he hanged himself after that, then it is fully my fault and I should be held responsible for his death. Fuck, it was down to me whatever way I look at it.

I wrapped the rope around his neck and I strung him up beneath the ceiling fan, knowing as I placed the stool under his feet.

He lived alone and didn't seem to have many friends or any close family, splitting his time between his career and sitting alone in his apartment, watching endless streams of movies in the dark and smoking marijuana.

He wasn't supposed to be part of this. I dragged him into it like a callous brute and abandoned him as a swollen dead body, the life choked out of him and excrement running down his legs.

I leave the apartment building and jog over to the car, knowing that I will never return and unsure as to when Vincent will be discovered. I suppose it will be once the smell gets so bad somebody makes a complaint to the landlord. He'll have to let himself inside and find the source as the telephone number I gave him to contact me was for a sex-line.

Somebody has gotten out of their vehicle and approached the passenger side of the Cavalier, shouting at Cassie through the window and asking her to move the car.

He is middle-aged with light grey hair, his tweed suit making him look a lot older than his years. I walk around the back of the car, squeeze between it and the car I am guessing belongs to this prick, step up onto the curb and punch him directly in the face, watching as he falls to the concrete like a tree falling in the wilderness.

I hear a few gasps from bystanders but ignore them, slide over the bonnet of the Cavalier, open the driver's door and get back inside.

"What the fuck, Jack?" Cassie rages.

I snap on my seatbelt and move the car out of the build-up of traffic, sounding my horn just as much as the irritated drivers who I had blocked off in the road. Fucking people.

"What was that all about?"

"Sorry, honey," I say.

She sighs and crosses her arms.

"Do you live in that building?" she asks.

"Yeah," I grunt. "I had to pick something up."

"I don't understand, Jack. Visiting friends, picking things up from your apartment. What's the point in all of this?"

I honk my horn again, showing my middle finger to a woman in a Jeep who gets in my way.

I feel her eyes looking fiercely at the side of my head. I concentrate on the road ahead, knowing that I am just a few blocks from the restaurant where I will be meeting William.

"We'll escape soon enough, don't worry," I say. "I have some unfinished business to take care of, but we won't take much longer. You're with me, whatever happens, right? Because I need you."

Cassie looks down at her lap, tucking her hair behind one of her ears.

"Of course I am. I think I love you, Jack."

I feel a smile trying to appear on my lips, but I

manage to stop it.

"I love you too, Cassie," I lie.

Oh, Vincent. None of this would have been possible without you.

3

I manage to find a parking space directly opposite Gennaro's, which is a ground-floor Italian restaurant that I don't believe I have seen before, which means I certainly haven't eaten there.

The restaurant's name is displayed in large italic bronze lettering above three windows which are dark due to the closed blinds behind them. Near the glass door of the entrance there are a couple of parasols lying on the ground and a trashcan on its side spilling its contents.

I wonder what motivated William to want to meet at this place. I suppose he knows somebody who works or owns the restaurant and sees it as somewhere private where he can talk to me without worrying about prying eyes and ears.

I'll soon find out, I suppose.

I won't go into Gennaro's completely exposed, however. I've come too far to be doing something as naïve as that.

I pick up the Beretta from between my feet and push it down into my waistband. I also return the switchblade to the inside of my sock where it was previously, hoping that I won't have to use either when I get inside.

I hold Cassie by the sides of her face, kiss her softly on the lips and look into her eyes.

She hasn't broken yet but I can tell it won't take much, so I remind her that I'm here for her by holding her close.

"I have to go into that restaurant and talk with a friend of mine," I say, pointing across the street. "I won't be long. We need to go over some business."

"Okay," Cassie says, seemingly on the brink of tears.

"Not much longer and we can leave, I promise."

She nods.

"I hope so," she says. "I'm so scared."

"It's perfectly natural to be scared, Cassie."

I can see Cassie's lips trembling.

"Stay here," I say. "Lock the doors behind you and wait until I come back."

I place the car keys in her hand.

"Listen carefully, Cassie. I'm pretty sure it's safe for me in that restaurant, but there's a slight chance that it isn't. I can handle myself, but there is something I need you to do for me if I walk into the middle of a shit-storm."

Cassie nods, looking up at me with glazed-over eyes. I place my hand on her thigh.

"If you hear a gunshot, that will be your signal," I say, kissing her once again.

4

I walk up to the entrance of Gennaro's, trying to look into the restaurant through the glare of the late afternoon on the glass. I stand against one of the windows, cupping my hands around my eyes as I peer inside. There are stacks of chairs, empty tables and a bar that stretches along the far side of the restaurant and around a corner towards a different seating area, with far more extravagant furniture and tableware.

I cannot see anybody inside, the only light source coming from the front of this building where I am standing.

I walk to the front door, ignore the sign stating that the restaurant is closed and push forwards, the door opening with a hiss as cold air rushes inside.

I enter and let the door close behind me, my nose filling with an odd smell that resembles burnt hair.

The restaurant is full of cheap tat on the walls and

displayed on every surface possible, including bronze-framed paintings on the walls of various landscapes and portly men who must be of some importance but not to me, small statuettes and hand-painted china plates.

The maroon wallpaper looks like dried blood in this light and the carpet is black, as if I am standing on the edge of space looking around at the stars.

I walk between two stacks of chairs and towards the empty bar. I look at all of the spirit bottles on the back wall, only recognising a couple of brands.

I could sure use a drink, and I hope William could too, because as soon as we're done with whatever he needs to see me about, I'm pouring myself some rum.

I follow the bar around to the sectioned-off seating area, these tables laid with cutlery, napkins and oil-lamps.

There is a window at the back of this area, again with a blind closed over it blocking out much of the light from outside. There is a thin trail of yellow light flowing across the centre of this area, which I follow to a double door just next to the curving end of the bar. The door is open by about three inches, spilling the light from inside.

"Billy?" I say loudly, regretting it straight away.

I should have kept quiet. It just leapt from my mouth like a vulgarity would from a Tourette's sufferer.

I hear a noise coming from beyond the door, which I am guessing is the restaurant kitchen.

It sounded like the clanging of something metallic, perhaps a saucepan. Is William rustling up something for us to eat while we talk? I can't help but feel that I am being overly optimistic.

I feel tension in my chest and arms, my heart thudding irregularly. I lift up my sweater and touch the gun in my waistband with the palm of my hand, reminding myself exactly where it is. I pull the sweater back down and stride towards the kitchen.

I push the double door open and step inside, vivid light irritating my eyes. I squint and see a shape in the centre of the floor, initially looking like a hunched over troll struggling to stand up from the solid ground.

It's then that I notice it is somebody sitting on a chair with their back towards me, their whole body rising and falling with each long breath.

I step forwards and see long lank hair hanging over the back of the chair, which I follow down to see hands tied around it with thin white rope.

I turn around, ready to walk out of the kitchen and get out of the restaurant, when I see a sturdy man with curly black hair standing in the way of the exit. He had been behind the doors as I came in.

His face is red and full of rage as he steps forwards, raising a frying pan in his right hand.

I reach for my Beretta but he's already coming at me and his momentum gives him the advantage he needs, smashing the pan against my head and sending me tumbling into unremitting blackness.

5

Somebody is slapping the side of my face and it hurts like a bee-sting.

I know that opening my eyes will stop it but the darkness feels so warm and reassuring that I want to stay here with it enveloping me.

Another slap connects, this one twice as painful as the ones that came before it, and I open my eyes, blinking in the yellow light and taking in the figures spaced out around me.

I am sitting down on a chair, my hands tied behind my back tightly.

The curly-haired man who hit me with the frying pan is leaning over me, his face inches from mine, looking at me as if he has just caught me raping his daughter.

I would say he is in his late forties, although his dress sense suggests he wants to be considerably younger. He wears a leather jacket and blue denim jeans, both of his hands that hang off the end of broad arms covered in various rings.

I turn my head away from him to see that I am sitting directly opposite William, putting me on the far side of the kitchen in front of the door where I came in.

William is conscious but in a bad way, seeming to have been on the receiving end of a recent beating, which makes his face look like it has collided with a truck.

One of his eyes is closed and puffed out, his mouth and chin soaked in blood. As he looks at me with his mouth hanging open I can see that he is missing some teeth. There's blood in his hair and smeared down his neck. I look down towards his feet, which aren't tied to the chair as his hands are, and see his jacket balled up on the ground.

This damage has been inflicted in the last thirty minutes, because when I spoke to him on the phone he sounded apprehensive but not as though he was missing some teeth after having the shit kicked and punched out of him.

I look beyond William and see another man standing at the door. He is older than the big curly-haired bastard, perhaps in his late fifties as opposed to forties, but about the same height.

He is wearing a grey suit, which matches his slicked-back grey hair, and even from this distance I can see a thick scar running from his hairline down to beneath his ear. He is smoking a cigarette and looking down at the ground.

The curly-haired man turns and says something that I presume is meant for his older counterpart, words that I comprehend to be in Italian, although I don't understand exactly what is said, despite my slight knowledge of the language.

The older man replies in parallel dialect, shrugging his shoulders and finishing his cigarette. He stubs it out in an ashtray on a work surface across from him before saying something else, his words more irate than before.

The curly-haired man says something softly, ending with the English word "sorry".

I'd say the older man is the curly-haired man's superior, the prick standing closest to me just the muscle. He's the one who smashed William's face up, no doubt using the rings on his fingers to cause the mutilation. It was the older man who gave word for his crony to do it.

The crony in question turns back to me, not close enough for me to lurch forwards and rip his nose off with my teeth, but close enough so that I can smell his stale breath.

"I can't believe I knocked you out cold," he says, his accent half and half between New York and Italy. "You went down like a sack of shit."

I look up at him without a word. The smell of burnt hair returns to my nose — I think it may just be the natural scent of this hulking fucker.

I can tell that the Beretta I had in my waistband has gone, which is the second firearm that I've had stolen from me.

"I expected you to be taller," says the older man from across the room, his twang as he speaks English almost identical to that of the curly-haired man.

He walks over so that he is next to William, his hand resting on the back of the chair he is sitting on.

"I expected somebody with a bit more poise," he continues. "Not a scrawny faggot wearing a Nike sweater."

William spits blood from his mouth but it doesn't get to the floor, it just lands in his lap.

"You're an evasive little cockroach," the older man sneers, discoloured teeth appearing from beneath his pale lips. "I never thought it would take so long to find you. You've taken up a lot of my time, and I'm a busy man."

I look at William's single visible eye, the other one hidden behind inflated skin.

I see a fear in it which is more acute than what I saw when Andrei Pasenov threatened him when the Russian arrived for our weapons deal at his apartment, even if it did turn out to be a joke.

These people, whoever they are, are dangerous and I can tell that from what I see in William's face. This isn't a joke, by any stretch of the imagination.

"What's this about?" I ask, my head pulsating.

The curly-haired man walks away from me, and the older man moves over and stands in his place.

"Don't play," the older man says.

He reaches behind, pulls out a weapon and waves it around in my face, the silver barrel pointing at me like a poison arrow. I can't help but flinch and look away, my head turning from side to side violently.

"Do you recognise this?" the older man says.

The gun he is holding is a Colt Python premium American revolver with a .357 Magnum cartridge and a six-inch barrel.

"Of course I do," I say. "It's a gun."

William begins to wheeze, spitting more blood out from his mouth.

"No shit," the older man says. "But it's not just any gun, is it? You could blow somebody's head off with a hand-cannon like this."

I shrug my shoulders, acting oblivious to the effects a weapon like that could cause.

"And that's what you did with this gun here, isn't it?" he continues, his cheeks flushing red. "You blew off my nephew's head in a hooker's hallway."

I remember the moment I shot Gio Rigo in the face, the muzzle flash blinding me temporarily so I didn't see the exact second the bullet collided with his skull.

"I've never seen that gun before in my life," I lie, trying my best to keep my level of deception at a constant. "And I have no idea who your nephew is. Or you, for that matter."

The older man spins the gun in his palm, the movement effortless as if he must be a descendant of a gun-slinging renegade outlaw.

He closes his hand around the barrel and hits me hard in the head with the butt of the revolver. The pain strikes me like an electronic bolt, flashes of white erupting in my eyes.

My head falls back and I feel a trickle of warm blood from beneath the bandage running down between my eyes.

"You inbred bastard!" the older man roars at me, flecks of saliva flying from his open mouth. "You fucking murdered him!"

I shrug again, the blood now reaching the bridge of my nose.

"I think you've got the wrong guy," I say.

He hits me again with the gun, harder this time, and I'm pretty sure it knocks me out but it must only be for a second or two.

It hurts a lot more than the previous one, the pain feeling like a tumour in my head killing off my brain cell by cell. I can't help but cry out in pain, my voice sounding abnormal.

"Don't play games with me," the older man says from between clenched teeth.

He turns and points at William, who appears to be drifting in and out of consciousness.

"Look at the state of your friend," he says. "You think we beat him that badly and didn't get any information from him? He squealed like a pig seconds into his thrashing," the older man pauses. "But he wasn't half as bad as that fucking whore prostitute, no way. She told us what we needed to know before we could even lay a hand on her. Too bad it didn't stay that way."

The curly-haired beast, who is now standing near the door lighting a cigarette, shakes his head and laughs to himself.

"We know everything, Christopher Morgan," the

older man derides me. "Where you live, where you work, your wife's name, where she works, where you took your last holiday. I could go on. You're quite the secretive little fucker, but with the information I pieced together from Mr Beckford and Miss Ross, I've got you all worked out."

He comes closer and thrusts a finger into my face. His slicked-back grey hair is beginning to fall out of place and into his eyes.

"If you kill a member of the Rigo family, you must face the fucking consequences. You're lucky your apartment was empty, because if I'd had my way we'd have your wife strung up here so that you could watch my friend over there rape her, over and over again.

"But don't you worry, we'll get her. I've got somebody waiting for her to get home, and when she does we'll have a lot of fun with her."

The blood is reaching the tip of my nose.

"I'm gunna make sure everybody you love is tortured and killed," he adds.

This old bastard is so deluded by his own hype it is unreal. He can give me the hard sell as much as he fucking wants, but he's oblivious.

I don't give a fuck who he is. He can be the uncle of the pimp I murdered or the President of the United States, I don't care.

"You talk a lot of shit, old man," I say, raising a corner of my mouth in a twisted grin. "I'm not the guy you're looking for. You're not gunna be able to beat the truth out of me cus it isn't in here."

The old man grabs my throat, pushing his bony fingers into my trachea. His fingernails are long and sharp.

"You have identification on you telling me you're Christopher Morgan, a donor card in your wallet," he bites. "Kacey Ross told me that it was you who killed Gio. She had this fucking gun, the murder weapon, in the car she was driving, which she claims she stole from you."

I say nothing.

"You told her you bought this revolver from William Beckford, who happens to be somebody I am very familiar with. So if you're the wrong guy, and this is a case of mistaken identity, then somehow I've made a vast category of blunders, which is unlikely."

He presses his fingernails deeper into my skin.

"I've also got two witnesses who saw you at the apartment of a Naomi Viejo in Brooklyn, where two of my men I sent to pick up Kacey's young son ended up dead. Still think I've got the wrong guy?"

The blood has reached my top lip. I stick out my tongue and taste it, feeling a drop of it roll down towards the back of my throat.

"I'm a cop," I say, almost choking on the blood. "I've been on the trail of Christopher Morgan since Gio's body turned up. After there were reports of gunshots in Brooklyn and two more bodies found, I had to follow it up and forensics found the shells were from the same weapon used to kill your nephew."

The older man loosens his grip on my neck but the rage in his face refuses to falter.

"I tracked him to a motel and that's where I picked up his wallet and cell phone, which he left in a room. By the time I arrived there this morning he was gone and so was his car. Not long after that I received a report stating that a man of his description stole a red Chevrolet Cavalier from a man at a gas station."

The curly-haired man laughs again from across the kitchen.

"Jesus, Gennaro, just shoot this idiot," he says.

Gennaro lets go of my neck completely and turns around to look at him. He points a finger in his direction.

"Keep your fucking mouth shut," the older man retorts.

Gennaro turns back to me, lifts the gun up to the side of my head and presses the end of the barrel into my temple.

"No more bullshit," he says. "Gio was a good boy. He didn't deserve to die like that. You executed him."

I swallow the blood in my mouth.

"When I got the call on Christopher's cell I decided to answer it and see what information I could get from the caller, which isn't a usual practise but I wanted to catch this guy before more people turned up dead.

"When the gentleman opposite me said he wanted to meet here I decided to come along, hoping that perhaps I could find out some possible locations for Christopher's whereabouts."

The gun seems to press harder against my head. I can imagine the barrel piercing my skull without the trigger needing to be pulled.

"So far you've got assaulting a police officer, disarming a police officer, imprisoning a police officer, threatening a police officer with death, and as far as I can tell from what you've told me, two very serious cases of assault: one on this Mr Beckford sitting across from me and the other on a woman named Kacey Ross, who I know is linked to the murders of Gio Rigo and the other two unidentified bodies because it was her apartment where your nephew was found."

I feel the barrel move away from my head.

"You can't take the law into your own hands. I want to catch this bastard just as much as you do but we're getting nowhere like this. I'd very much like to talk to Kacey Ross because it seems she would have a lot of information regarding Christopher and his possible motives and whereabouts."

I see the rage fade slightly from Gennaro's reddened face.

"Got a badge?" Gennaro says.

"In my car, yes," I say. "Parked out front."

Gennaro turns around yet again to look at his counterpart.

"You're not believing this joker are ya?" the curly-haired man says.

"I didn't say that, did I?" Gennaro retorts.

"He's obviously full of shit, even I can tell that. You're losing your touch."

"Keep your opinions to yourself," Gennaro says quietly, his harsh whisper sounding like the hiss of a snake from where I am sitting. "The last thing I need right now is to be pinned to killing a cop. If he's lying he won't have a badge, and then we can kill this fucker."

The two men look into each other's eyes, some unspoken message being exchanged. There seems to be more to the relationship of these two than I first thought.

I had assumed that Gennaro was the big shot and the curly-haired man was the disposable muscle, but there's a considerable amount of tension between them, perhaps represented by years of falling out and a constant fear that they will be double-crossed by the other.

Or maybe they are lovers, I just can't tell.

"Got it?" Gennaro says.

"Sure," his friend replies, rolling his eyes.

Gennaro walks back over towards me but stops near a large gas stove to my right. He places the Magnum on the top of the stove, leans across to some kitchen knives displayed on a magnetic strip on the wall and takes a medium-sized blade from it.

He walks around behind me and pulls the cord around my wrists tight before slicing it with the knife. I feel the blood almost instantly begin to return to my hands.

I feel Gennaro place the sharp edge of the blade against the back of my neck. He leans down and talks into my ear.

"This doesn't mean I believe you," he says, "but I'm a man of principle so I'm going to give you a chance to prove what you're saying is true."

He presses the knife harder against my skin.

"If you've taken me for a ride I'll slit your throat."

He removes the blade and grabs me by the hood of my sweater, pulling me up from the seat and standing me straight, my legs wobbling.

A thought dashes across my mind, urging me to leap forwards towards the stove and grab the Colt Python, but before I have the chance to act Gennaro has already moved behind me and returned the gun to his grasp. He points the weapon at me as he returns the knife to the magnetic strip on the wall, his eyes not moving from me as he does so.

I look down at William who is craning his neck to look up at me, his face unrecognisable as the purple bruising darkens.

He says something, saliva drooling down his chin, but I can't understand him. It's three words, maybe "what the fuck", but I can't be certain.

I regret that he has been reprimanded for my actions, as I have never had anything against Billy Beckford. He was never meant to be scorned by my vendettas, not like this. He was merely an accessory to them when I needed assistance in making them a reality, nothing more than that.

William will recover from his injuries, perhaps with some scarring and hopefully no minor or major brain damage, but I'm not out of this yet.

I have bought myself some time, but it's Gennaro Rigo who holds the loaded revolver, not me.

Gennaro urges me forwards with the gun and returns to standing behind me, moving us past William and towards the kitchen exit.

The curly-haired man shakes his head as we approach, opening a stainless steel fridge door and rooting around inside, now uninterested in this situation.

My nose fills with the smell of cured meat and something else that could be a dairy product that is past its sell-by-date.

Gennaro mutters something in abusive Italian as he

passes his colleague, but the curly-haired man does not respond.

I slow down as we exit the kitchen, cool air against the sweat on my face. I feel the trickle of blood that ran from my head into my mouth drying on my skin.

"Move," Gennaro says, pushing the revolver into my back between my shoulder blades.

"Your friend has a chip on his shoulder," I say, walking forwards. "Does he make a habit of undermining you like that?"

Gennaro says nothing, just pushes harder with the barrel of the Magnum into my spine as we move through the dining area and around the curvature of the bar.

"Makes the both of you look like a pair of fucking mugs," I continue. "If the force knew gangbangers like you two were calling the shots in this part of town it would make my job a lot easier."

"Shut your mouth," the older man says.

I stop, my feet rooted to the floor. We are standing at the front of the bar directly across from the door where I came into the restaurant, daylight flooding in from behind the glass.

"It's a joke really," I say. "Knowing that it's because of dimwits like the pair of you I have to fear for my life every day I am on the job. I mean, you're clearly a fucking idiot, but how can you let a retard like that talk to you with such a lack of respect?"

"Nothing's stopping me hitting you around the head again," Gennaro growls. "Cop or no cop."

"Is it because you're his bitch?" I taunt, ignoring him. "You let him talk that way to you because it turns you on and you know that later tonight you'll be his submissive little whore when he fucks you?"

I slowly turn around and the look Gennaro gives me could cut through glass. He switches the revolver from his right hand to his left and lands a punch directly into my face with his now free hand.

Pain spreads across my nose, my eyes watering and the throbbing in my head now becoming a constant dull ache. I bring my hand up to my nose and hold it, hoping that it isn't broken, only because that would be inconvenient more than anything.

"Shit, that hurt," I say, laughing.

"I'll kill you," the older man spits in my face as he points the Python at me. "I don't give a fuck who you are."

I spit onto the ground.

"So that's another count of assault on a police officer to add to the list," I say. "You're digging your own grave old man, I'm gunna push you into it."

The curly-haired man comes out from the kitchen and around to where we are standing. He looks at Gennaro pointing the gun at me and shakes his head in a similar way to how he did seconds ago.

He holds a bag of chips in his hand and is shovelling them into his mouth at a rapid pace, crunching them up in his mouth as crumbs drop onto the ground.

"You're on my property, asshole," Gennaro says. "How about I see that you're armed when you come in and I kill you in self-defence?"

I shake my head, smiling like a loon.

"No fucking way. Killing a cop post 9/11 gets you nothing short of a lynching, no matter what bullshit defence your mob lawyer comes up with.

"You'll be beyond fucked even if you piss your pants in the courtroom."

The curly-haired man walks behind Gennaro and over to a table in the centre of the room. He pulls out a chair and sits down with a loud exhale.

"This is ridiculous," Gennaro says, his eyes darting around. "You've got to say you're a cop. Aren't there rules about that?"

"Nope, it doesn't work like that. I had a frying pan upside my head before I had chance to say a word."

Gennaro looks down at the ground.

"This guy's good," the curly-haired man says with his mouth full as he crosses his legs over. "He's a storyteller, but I'll be damned if he's a fucking cop. He killed Gio, man, so kill the bastard."

Gennaro looks over at him, his teeth together and the veins in his neck tightening.

"I said keep your fucking opinions to yourself, Joe!" the older man shouts.

Joe places the half-empty chip bag onto the table and holds up his hands as a sign of deference.

"I'm just saying, G. I'm trying to stop you making a mistake. Five years ago you would've whacked this prick without a second thought and now you've given him too much time to construct a bullshit story. It's weak."

Gennaro steps towards Joe and points a finger at him.

I edge back slightly but I know I wouldn't be able to make it to the door if I made a break for it. I don't fancy taking a slug in the back from the Colt Python.

"Jumping in the deep end isn't always the best way to deal with these situations," Gennaro says irately. "It's that meat-head of yours that's got you locked up so many times. Ever thought of that?"

"Don't give me that shit," Joe says. "You would've made the same decisions as me back then and you know it. The years have aged you more than you want to admit."

Gennaro turns back to me, strides over with renewed intent and kicks me hard in the shin, taking me off my feet.

I lay on the ground as the older man kicks me three more times, twice in the stomach and once in the groin. The kicks hurt much more than I thought they would, the old man managing to summon a substantial amount of strength, perhaps out of determination to prove his friend wrong.

"That good enough for you?" Gennaro yells like a beast.

The curly-haired man laughs heartily, clapping his

large hands together.

I feel the barrel of the gun against the back of my head as I cower on the ground.

"Or do you want me to kill him?" Gennaro adds. "Spew his brains out all over this new carpet? Will that satisfy you?"

I look up from the ground and see Joe shrugging his shoulders, the smile on his face the biggest I have seen it.

"Please," I say, trying my best to make my voice sound shaky and distressed. "I've got kids, six of them. Three boys and three girls. Kyle, Brandon, Benjamin, Olivia, Aimee and Samantha. Don't take their father away from them, they need me."

The names slip off my tongue, which is surprising, as I do feel quite afraid.

"You won't get blood and brains out of that carpet, G, you'll ruin it forever," Joe chortles.

The gun pushes harder against my skull.

"Gio was like a son to me," Gennaro says.

"I didn't kill him," I implore. "I'm a cop investigating a homicide. This is just a misunderstanding, and one that I'm willing to forget if you do the right thing."

Joe continues to laugh as if he's watching a comedy sketch.

"Two of my best men were killed as well, you forgetting that?" the older man continues. "They had names too."

I turn my head from side to side, my skin rubbing against the surface of the carpet.

"It wasn't me, I'm a fucking cop!"

"Their names were Marco and Jonathan, but I suppose that doesn't matter, does it? Why should you care about that?"

"I didn't kill them!"

"Bullshit!" Gennaro sneers.

"I'm telling you the truth!"

Joe walks over to where I am on the floor.

"This is more like it, G," he says. "Just like the good old days."

"You guys are so fucking screwed," I say, my tongue pressing against the rough carpet.

Joe sniggers, leaning over me and tapping the side of my face with his sausage fingers.

"Oh, I wouldn't be inclined to agree with that," he says. "I bet when you shot Gio you just expected to get away with it, didn't you? Didn't expect the sharks to come and bite your fucking arms off."

I hear Gennaro laugh this time. I have one last throw of the dice.

"My partner has been sitting outside in an unmarked car since I came in here," I say, saliva gathering under my tongue. "If I was in here for more than fifteen minutes, he's gunna call for back-up. Something I think he would have done a while ago now."

Joe hits me in the back of the head with a fist that feels like a bowling ball.

"We're not buying this cop shit, fucker!"

I spit blood.

"Listen," I gurgle. "You really think I'd come in here alone? It's a high-risk situation, especially with the body count in question. You might as well give yourselves up. Every exit will have been covered by now. Let us take you in."

Joe steps away from me.

"Give me the gun," the curly-haired man says. "I'm killing him, this is fucking crazy."

I don't want this ape to be the person who kills me.

"Give me the fucking gun!"

I look up and see Joe beginning to pace impatiently.

"Just look out of the window," I say. "You'll see my partner sitting in our vehicle across the street."

I turn my head away from the floor and look up at Gennaro, who has stood up straight and is holding the revolver down by his side.

"I don't give a fuck if The A-Team are sitting outside, bitch," Joe barks.

I can hear Gennaro breathing deeply.

"Joe," the older man says calmly. "Go take a look, will you?"

I see Joe put his face into his hands, shaking his head vigorously.

"Jesus, this is a fucking joke," he says.

I remove my head from the ground and move into a sitting position. Joe removes his hands from his face and looks at me as if he's willing my head to explode, his eyes focusing as if he is channelling telekinesis towards my skull.

"Will ya just look out the fucking window?" Gennaro yells, his voice a high squeal.

Joe shakes his head some more and turns around, stomps towards one of the restaurant windows like a rhinoceros and peers outside through a gap in the blinds.

I raise myself up onto my knees while Gennaro watches Joe, so that my head is level with the older man's elbow.

"Well?" Gennaro says impatiently.

"There's a car," Joe says, a narrow strip of light across his face. "Somebody sitting in the driver's seat, can't see them very well from here. It's a red Chevy, looks like a Cavalier."

I'm pushing against the carpet with my feet, my ankles stretching as if I'm warming up before a sprint.

The older man steps forwards slightly before shifting backwards, wanting to go to the window but instantaneously returning to a piece of information I told him in the kitchen.

I can almost hear it click into place in his head and now he knows I'm not a cop.

"What the fu—"

I spring up like a jack-in-the-box as Gennaro turns to me, grabbing his arm hard and pushing the weapon towards the floor.

My other hand grabs his free arm, blocking it off as he tries to push me away. He yells out, no words just a sound, a battle cry that I see alerts Joe at the window.

"Fuck y—"

I thrust my head into Gennaro's face twice in quick succession, feeling his teeth scrape against my skin and the force of my attack loosening the gun in his hand, which I try to twist from his hold.

He won't let go. The old man is a lot stronger than I expected.

I twist and drive an elbow into Gennaro's gut, the revolver firing a deafening shot into the ground a short distance away from one of my feet.

My ears wail from the sound, debris getting into my mouth as I continue to try and disarm Gennaro.

I spin around so that his back faces Joe at the window, his form shielding me as his friend stands hopelessly, looking over at us with his feet rooted to the spot.

I see the change in his face as the fat bastard remembers the Beretta he took from me and opens his jacket to grab the weapon.

He's a bit too quick, however, the gun slipping from his hand like a bar of soap and dropping onto the ground a few feet in front of him.

He leaps forwards, grabs it from the carpet and stands up straight, firing off the gun with what seems like blatant disregard for the health of Gennaro.

Two bullets whiz past my head, smashing bottles of spirits on the bar display behind me. I steady Gennaro with one hand on the lapel of his jacket, blood pouring from a wound on his top lip as another shot is fired, this one hitting my human shield in the shoulder.

Gennaro yelps like a dog, the gun finally coming loose as I kick him backwards away from me, taking the revolver and diving away from Joe's continuing shots and leaping over the bar.

The curly-haired man is shouting something but I can't hear it well, a low rumble growing louder outside the restaurant and muffling his words.

The Cavalier crashes through the window like a juggernaut, glass and brick erupting outwards, twisted metal screeching and a large section of the restaurant wall collapsing.

The car knocks Joe to the ground and I see the front of the vehicle squash him like a bug.

My ears fill with a wall of noise, the car-horn being sounded incessantly, possibly because of the force of Cassie's head on the wheel due to the impact. I hope she's okay.

The restaurant fills with a smog of white dirt almost instantly, the masonry gathering around the car in jagged piles.

I jump back over the bar, leave the revolver on it and walk across the carpet, the smog getting into my eyes.

I step over Gennaro, who is wailing and holding his shoulder, and move over towards Joe's body, which is crushed under the front right wheel of the Chevrolet.

He's dead for sure, no doubt about it. He is lying with his neck bent around, his spine possibly broken, with the weight of the car having crushed his vertebrae.

I rush around to the driver's side and pull open the door, scraping it against broken glass and chunks of broken brick.

Cassie sits with her head against the wheel, both hands gripping onto it tightly.

I pull her back, the persistent car-horn ceasing its noise. I see that she's conscious, her face a pale white and a thin stream of blood flowing from the centre of her forehead.

She looks at me as if she doesn't recognise me.

"Cassie," I say. "You okay?"

She nods.

I look from Cassie to the outside behind the car wreckage. A few people are gathering across the street, peering over like teenagers watching a fight in high school. Some of them are on their cell phones meaning one of them must have called the cops or at least the paramedics. Or they're filming the carnage.

I take hold of Cassie's left arm and put it over my head, allowing her to put all of her weight against my shoulder as I pull her out of the car, her head lolling like the head of a rag doll.

Her face rests against my chest when I start to move around the front of the car, her heeled shoes scraping against the ground. As I move I survey the damage to the front of the Chevy; the bonnet's buckled inwards and the windscreen shattered. It's most definitely a write-off, but if I'm lucky I will still be able to get some use out of it.

I don't have time to find a new vehicle and transfer Adam from the Cavalier to it, let alone all of my purchases from Home Depot.

I approach the passenger's side of the car, the door loose and not fully closed. I don't think it will fall off, but as I open it I have to lift it to make sure it doesn't collide with the ground.

I scoop Cassie up and place her inside the car, kissing her softly on the forehead and closing the door behind her. It doesn't click into place, it just sits in the doorframe.

I taste blood on my lip, perhaps from the wound on Cassie's head or perhaps my blood from my broken face or perhaps blood from Gennaro's mouth when I head-butted him.

There are people now gathering at the back of the car, some of them having crossed the street to look into the restaurant at the destruction.

I can hear a few of them directing questions at me, one man asking if I'm okay and another asking what happened.

I look over at them and shrug my shoulders.

"Women drivers, eh?"

I don't wait for any sort of reaction from them; I just stride across the floor towards the bar and pick up the Magnum.

I turn back and lean down to Gennaro, grabbing him by the collar and thrusting the barrel of the gun into his ribs.

"Get up," I say. "Now."

The colour has faded from the old man's wrinkled face and he looks as if he couldn't get up from the ground even if I threatened to cut his shrivelled cock off.

I hope I don't have to lug this bastard to the car because that really will piss me off.

I am surprised as Gennaro climbs to his feet with dynamism, despite his anguished groans. I don't even have to pull him up, he's standing before I get the chance to threaten him with a bullet.

He looks down at Joe's contorted body under the Chevrolet. He looks away and screws up his eyes, his cheeks puffing out as if he's holding back vomit.

"Walk," I say, pushing him in the back.

He steps over broken glass and brickwork, breathing heavily. I push him towards the driver's side of the car and open the back door, nudging him with the revolver so that he slumps inside.

The car creaks with the extra weight, the front tyre closest to me rolling backwards on its slight gradient.

I close the door behind him as he lies down, wrapping his arms around his body and writhing in pain. It's only a shot in the shoulder, it can't be too bad. What a fucking wuss.

I turn and see one of the men who asked me what happened is close, coming into the restaurant and beginning to assess the situation, looking at the car and its occupants. Nosey prick.

"Hey!" I shout, pointing the Colt at his face. "Back the fuck off!"

He recoils and moves away. There are a few gasps from the others outside as they back up, a middle-aged woman on the phone telling whoever she is talking to that I have a gun.

I look down onto the carpet and see the Beretta that Joe dropped as he was mown down.

I lean down and pick it up, holding both guns out in front of me like a crazed outlaw. I've never felt so fucking dangerous.

I wait until the watching crowd are far enough away from the back of the Cavalier before opening the driver's door and sitting down inside.

Cassie is looking over her shoulder at Gennaro in the back, his face buried into the seat as he whimpers.

"Cassie," I say. "Take this."

I put the Magnum in my lap and give her the Beretta. She takes hold of it and looks down at it with disdain.

It's the weapon she used to kill Joshua. It's a shitty little firecracker and nothing more.

I can't begin to explain how happy I am to have the Colt Python back in my possession.

"If he tries anything, shoot him," I say.

She looks from the gun to Gennaro.

"Who is he?" she asks.

The Cavalier's engine is still running so I put the car into reverse.

"A bad man," I answer.

I rev the engine and look at the dispersing swarm of people in the rear-view mirror.

"I'm proud of you, honey," I tell Cassie. "I knew you could do it."

I lean on the accelerator delicately, moving the car backwards off pieces of wall and levelling the wheels.

I hear a crack, perhaps the breaking of bones, as the front of the car backs up off Joe's body. I get stuck for a second, the clutch growling and the tyres squeaking, but to my relief I am soon free and manage to reverse out of

Gennaro's restaurant. The axles aren't ruined and I know that the Chevy will get me to my destination.

Some woman screams, possibly because she sees Joe's twisted body as I get myself into gear. I drive forwards, the bumper of the car scraping against the ground but not seeming to slow down the Chevrolet too much.

I look at Cassie, her hands shaking as she points the pistol at Gennaro. Her hands may shake, but her eyes are still and focused, convincing me that she's more than capable.

She has already proven everything she will ever need to. There's the corpse of her ex-boyfriend and a destroyed restaurant to prove that.

And if she needs that final push I've got the Polaroid photograph in my pocket.

THE NINTH TALE - VIOLATE

1

I drive around without a solid destination for a few blocks, looking out at the buildings and trying my best to ignore the stares from pedestrians.

After about ten minutes I decide to drive towards a multi-storey car park, the high-rise building catching my eye through the broken windscreen. It looks at least fifteen levels tall.

I pull into the entrance, the toll barrier bumping out of the way as the car bursts through. I'm not driving fast, just at a decent speed to bend the metal obstruction backwards and there isn't anybody manning the entrance.

I drive the wreckage up the first slope, looking around at the parked cars as I approach the each floor.

"Motherfucker," Gennaro mumbles, his face still buried in the seat. "You killed Gio."

Cassie looks at me, confused.

"Who?" she asks.

"The old man is losing his mind. I don't know anybody called Gio."

Cassie turns to me, the gun no longer pointing at the older man.

"Jack, I just want to—"

"His name's Christopher," Gennaro mumbles. "He killed Gio, the fucker. Christopher Mo—"

"Shut your face!" I yell, flecks of saliva spraying from my mouth. "You're fucking crazy, old man!"

He coughs again.

"Fuck you."

I look out of the cracked windscreen again but I can feel Cassie's eyes against the side of my face.

"Keep the gun on him, Cassie," I say calmly.

We reach the top of the car park, level fifteen. I drive up the slope and see that there aren't many cars parked here, just a few dotted around. It's getting late in the day.

I stop the car a little over ten feet away from the barrier at the edge of the car park. I kick open my door and jump out, brandishing the Mangum as if it's part of my body, a silver mechanical hand.

I open the back door and grab Gennaro by the ankle, his legs kicking out like a mule.

"Don't struggle!" I shout.

He ceases kicking and lets me drag him out by the legs, his knees dropping hard onto the asphalt and the rest of his body following like a slab of meat falling onto a butcher's floor.

Cassie gets out of the Cavalier at her side of the vehicle, holding the Beretta in a less than convincing way as she marches over to me.

"What's this about, Jack?" she asks, her blonde hair falling into her face, the trail of blood from the wound on her forehead having dried like black ink.

"Trust me, Cassie," I say, forcing Gennaro to his feet. "Haven't I told you that already?"

Cassie puts her face into her hands, the barrel of the Beretta close to her cheekbone.

"We're gunna get caught," she says, the rate of her breathing increasing. "I knew I needed my head examined, fuck!"

I ignore her words of distress and begin to walk Gennaro over towards the barrier at the edge of this fifteen-storey car park.

He limps, which is strange because his injury is on his shoulder, a bullet taken from the gun of his own man.

"Hands up," I say to him, and he does what he's told.

Cassie leans against the front of the car, my view of the Cavalier from this angle making me aware of the extent of the damage to it.

It looks like it has taken part in a destruction derby.

I hear her starting to cry as Gennaro runs out of room to walk, his feet stopping dead and his arms opening wide like the wings of a bird.

"Turn around," I say.

Gennaro does it, slowly but surely, his face full of terror as we come face to face.

I lower the gun from my waist to down by my side. The old man's shadow falls across the concrete and up to my feet, the sun setting in the distance and bleeding orange light across the New York rooftops.

"I need you to tell me where Kacey Ross is," I say.

Gennaro stares through me.

"I don't fucking know," he says.

"Did you kill her? I need to know."

Gennaro shrugs his shoulders.

"I didn't pick her up, it was Joe."

"And he smashed her face up?"

Gennaro rubs his wound and I notice for the first time that the sleeve of his suit jacket is soaked in blood.

"That's what he told me," the older man says. "I didn't see it. He's got his own methods and they're nothing to do with me."

I look down at the ground, a cold rush of air hitting my face.

Seagulls caw in the distance.

"Did he kill her?" I ask, teeth clenched.

Gennaro shrugs again. I raise the gun level with his gut.

"Tell me."

Gennaro shakes his head.

"No, he didn't. He beat the living shit out of her but she wasn't dead. He even took her to the emergency room."

I breathe in slowly.

"And her son? The boy?"

The Italian looks over my shoulder at Cassie. Her snivels are quiet enough that I can ignore them.

"He was with her. Joe didn't hurt him."

"I've got your word?"

Gennaro raises his hands. His palms are bloody.

"It's the truth."

I imagine Kacey's puffed-up purple face being cleaned up and stitches being applied to the gashes in her head.

"And after the emergency room?"

"I don't know. Joe left her there."

I raise the gun higher, at about the level of his heart.

Gennaro steps back, the heel of his shoe colliding with the brick barrier.

"What, just like that?"

Gennaro nods.

"He told her to say she was beaten up by one of her crackhead clients if asked."

I bite my bottom lip.

"You just let her go?"

He nods again.

"She told us all we wanted to know."

That's it. She's out of my grasp.

She wouldn't go back to her apartment and there's nowhere else for me to look for her, save for Naomi's place in Brooklyn and I don't have the time to be going there, not now.

I raise the gun even higher, pointing it at Gennaro's neck. I might be able to take his head off.

"Listen," Gennaro says, his voice shaking. "Let's talk about this. I may have... overreacted. Gio can be hard work; I know that more than most. He may not have deserved a bullet in his head, but..."

He looks older than his years, a frail skeletal man staring back at me, not wanting to die.

"He did deserve it," I say. "He was violent towards women. And a pimp."

The gun moves from his neck to his chin, up along the bridge of his nose to the top of his head.

"Just think of this as vermin extermination," I say. "I'm doing this city a big favour by cutting down the Rigo bloodline. Reducing drug pushing and prostitution. I should be made Mayor, if you ask me."

Gennaro's trembling hands come up by the sides of his face. He is the second old man of the day to be begging for his life.

"Please don't shoot me," he says.

I hold my breath for a second.

"Okay."

I step forwards and lift my leg, driving my foot into Gennaro's chest. His ribcage feels like an empty box collapsing inwards as I kick him, his body taking flight like a plastic bag caught in an updraft.

I hear his body slapping against the ground below like wet tissue a couple of seconds later.

2

"Jennifer, you sound like a crazy person."

She is shrieking and bellowing, saying words but they are incomprehensible.

She's crying, hyperventilating.

"Calm down, please!" I yell.

She doesn't. More wailing.

"Okay, I'll repeat myself," I say, calmly. I take a breath.

She's silent on the other end of the phone but I can make out a voice in the background.

"I know about your affair with Adam and I'd like the three of us to talk about it. I'm here with him now and he thinks that it's a good idea too."

She doesn't say a word.

"I don't want to fight or scream or yell or strangle the life out of you, I just want us all to work this out."

I realise that I sound like a marriage counsellor.

"Please Jen, listen to me."

I can almost hear the sound of her mouth moving but no actual words.

She's either talking but no sound is coming out or mouthing some words to another party.

"Who else is there?"

The silence on the other end is vast.

"Who else is there, Jen?"

Nothing. Maybe only the sound of her heart thudding in her cavernous chest.

"I asked you a fucking question!" I shout, my throat tightening.

Cassandra hears me from the car across the street and I see her craning her neck around to look at me.

I must cut a forlorn figure standing at this payphone, blood and dust on my once clean and pressed shirt.

"Do you have any idea what you've done?" Jennifer asks, her voice quiet and cracking.

I smile. I imagine Jennifer isn't doing the same.

"The right thing," I say.

She exhales, trembling.

"The right thing," I repeat, slower.

I hear her sobbing. There's a soft, female voice consoling her.

"No police or I kill him, Jennifer," I say. "Come alone and get there quick. I'm not in a patient mood."

I tell her the address of an abandoned warehouse in a run-down industrial complex just off a nearby freeway and make sure that she writes it down.

I have to repeat myself twice as she is blubbering uncontrollably, no doubt shaking as she tries to use a pen.

I hear the consoling female voice again.

"Let me speak to Angela," I insist.

I hear more muffled sounds and then Angela's voice, condescending and cold.

"Chris, this is madness."

I laugh.

"No, Angela. Madness is being single for ten years, you feminist cunt. No police, I mean it. Jennifer comes alone."

I slam down the receiver hard, twice for good luck.

I blow a kiss over at Cassandra but she isn't looking.

3

By the time night has fallen the cover of darkness is a welcome respite from the struggles and cries of Adam in the trunk. I call out and tell him to be quiet but he doesn't listen and when we arrive at the warehouse the Chevy is bouncing like it's in a rap video due to his attempts to escape.

I stop the car and leap out, run to the back of the vehicle and open the trunk, his cable-tied legs thrusting out midway through a desperate kick that is inches away from hitting me in the face. I punch him in the nose a couple of times, grab a fistful of his ridiculous hair and pull him out, his limbs flailing and his fingers clawing at me.

Once out of the car he refuses to get up, staying down on his knees and shaking his head like a petulant child. I give him an open-palmed slap across the face, the noise echoing loudly around the loading-in area where we have come to a stop behind the warehouse. I notice that he's got a huge lump on his head the size of an ostrich egg.

"Jack."

Cassie appears behind me like a ghost, startling me for a second. I slap Adam again, harder this time. He starts to cry.

"Jack," she repeats. "Where are we?"

I've got the revolver out now and part of me is toying with the idea of killing Adam right here, right now. Ending it all in a literal flash, obliterating his brain and eradicating any memory stored in there of my wife's vagina.

The smell, the taste, the feel of it after a recent waxing.

"Somewhere quiet, where we won't be disturbed," I say.

I push Adam's face into the dusty ground and point

the gun at the back of his head. Saliva pours out of his mouth like water from a tap.

"You're gunna do as I say, shithead, or I'll kill you and put your head on a spike," I threaten.

I grab hold of his scrawny neck and force him to stand, which he finds difficult due to his feet being cable-tied together. I nudge him in the back with the Colt, directing him towards the busted back door of the warehouse, half of which hangs from its hinges. He can only shuffle and hop a minuscule distance, which makes the journey from the car to the building take several minutes.

He's trying to talk but he can't get his words out. He sounds like somebody who has recently had the wind knocked out of him.

Once we reach the door I pass Adam and push it inwards with my elbow, gesturing towards Cassie to follow us in. She does so but looks sheepishly behind her, as if half expecting somebody to be watching us.

I guide Adam further into the belly of the warehouse, through a dark and mouldy corridor and out onto the main floor of the building, which used to be the packing area of a factory of some sort. The windows are mostly frosted or smashed in, allowing only a small amount of milky moonlight inside. It lights up the warehouse enough, however, spilling across the dirty ground and up over machinery that has been years, maybe even decades, out of use. A large rusted septic tank, well over twenty feet in length and most likely eight or nine feet deep, is near the far wall.

I kick Adam's legs out from under him and he hits the ground with a heavy thud, wriggling like a maggot as he struggles to move away from me. I stand over him, briefly thinking about taking a piss on his head.

Cassie is staring ahead, lost.

"Cassie," I whisper. "Keep your Beretta aimed at him. If he tries anything stupid, shoot him. In the legs."

She nods and lifts the gun from her side. She aims the weapon at Adam and closes one eye. It looks rather comical.

I return to the Chevy and bring the items I purchased from Home Depot back to the warehouse with me, although it does take a couple of trips. I forget my briefcase and have to go back to get it, which frustrates me.

Once everything is inside I mentally account for each item I need – chainsaw, gloves, gaffer tape, paintbrush, chalkboard paint, drill, blue nylon rope, plywood.

"What's all of that for?" Cassie questions, her gun no longer pointed at Adam.

"This man needs to be taught a lesson," I say, unbuttoning my shirt.

Cassandra watches as I take my shirt off, looking at my bare torso with wide eyes. I look down and see dark bruising that must have been caused by my fall down the staircase at Joshua's place.

"You're hurt," she mutters.

"Yeah," I say, almost laughing. "Can't feel it though."

I point at my head.

"This neither. Just feels numb."

Adam is sobbing quietly as I make a simple sandwich board out of two pieces of the plywood and rope, using the drill to make the holes that connect them.

Adam calls out at the sound of the drill, terrified. It's incredibly satisfying to see him like this. I was planning on using the gaffer tape to cover his mouth again, as the previous tape I put across his lips has come loose, but the sounds he is making are too good to miss.

Once I've linked the plywood together and tied the rope as tight as I can, I used the black chalkboard paint and brush to scrawl the word 'SCUMBAG' on each side in large letters.

"Chris..." Adam groans. "Please."

I admire my work and throw the paintbrush away

over my shoulder. I can't resist a chance to further torment Adam, so I take hold of the half-full tin of paint and pour it over Adam's head and back. He coughs, crawling away from me. I throw the empty tin at his head but I miss.

"Adam, you scumbag," I say. "I want you to wear this."

I point at the sandwich board and smile. Adam wipes away some paint from his face and eyes, looking down at the message I've painted.

"Chris, what the fuck?" he says.

I notice that some of the paint is smeared across my chest. I kick my shoes off and pull my socks from my feet with my thumb.

Adam looks from the sandwich board, up to me and down to the Colt Python in my hand. His mouth upturns and I can see every tooth in the bottom row of his gawp.

"This is revenge, plain and simple," I sneer. "You ruined my life. You took my Jennifer from me. There are some things that a man simply cannot let slide."

Adam looks up, as if pleading to some mysterious force for help.

"When my wife walks in that door she's gunna see you at your weakest and me at my very best," I say. "Then she will know what a mistake she made."

Adam shakes his head.

"Chris, you've gotta listen to me, buddy," Adam pleads. "Nothing's going on with me and Jenny, I swear to you. We've got to get you help, get you better."

His eyes dart over towards Cassie, who looks preoccupied with one terrible thought or another.

"This is Cassandra Jones," I say. "And she's like me. Those she once loved have done her wrong and she's exacted the proper punishment for it."

I point the revolver at Adam.

"Stand up," I order.

Adam shakes his head, refusing.

"Stand up!" I bellow, my voice cracking.

This scares Adam enough that he stands, although he has some trouble doing so. I put the Colt Python in my waistband, lean down and pick up the sandwich board, lift it high and place it carefully over Adam's head.

I stand back to see how clear the word 'SCUMBAG' is, order him to turn around so that I can see the same message on the back, and once satisfied I take out my gun again.

"Help me, please," Adam says, turning his attention to Cassandra. "Don't let him do this."

She stares right through him. It's almost as if she isn't fully present in the moment. I would have preferred that she didn't see this, but she has to be at my side when Jennifer arrives.

I click my fingers.

"Adam," I say. "You're a conniving little prick and I never liked you."

He mouths the word "please" over and over.

"You should've kept your dick in your pants."

I see a set of headlights moving outside the warehouse, a vehicle driving around the side of the building and towards where the Chevy is parked. My throat tightens, but I can't tell if it's because of excitement or fear.

I know that I don't have much time to ensure that Jennifer's surprise is ready, which is quite disappointing as it would have been fun to toy with Adam some more.

"I know you and Jenny have had problems," Adam snivels. "But I'd never, never do anything like that. Not to you—"

I put on the gloves, reach down and grab the chainsaw, then make several attempts to start it to no avail. My heart is pounding and my head is beginning to hurt, the substantial wound clearly still needing medical attention.

"Not to one of my closest friends."

Cassandra drops the Beretta onto the ground. She

looks like a zombie, staring straight ahead without lucid thought.

"I'm scared, Chris!" Adam yells. He begins to cry some more.

I start the chainsaw and lift it up, revving it a few times so that the loud roar it creates can hopefully be heard outside. Adam's moans are drowned out as smoke billows up into my face.

"This is gunna be fucking agonising," I taunt.

I step forwards and push the chainsaw towards Adam, his eyes screwing closed like a kid on a ghost train. The blade stutters as it cuts into his collarbone, cutting into his flesh a few inches before causing him to fall backwards onto the ground. Flecks of blood spray into my mouth that is wide open in a twisted smile.

He screams, his tongue hanging out of his mouth as I pull the chainsaw back over my shoulder and swing it at him like a heavy axe, plunging the razor sharp chain into the side of his neck.

His screams are wet as blood fills his mouth, and I can't help but scream as well, mocking the noises coming from the man that I had once considered a friend.

The chain gets caught but I persevere, having to readjust it several times to ensure that I decapitate him fairly swiftly.

The cuts I make are jagged and messy, blood now covering my gloved hands and arms. There's a considerable amount of it filling my mouth, the metallic taste of it enjoyable somehow.

I see the dark red muscle of his neck coming apart like well-cooked meat, his head dropping from his shoulders with a satisfying wet slap. I rev the chainsaw some more as I watch the severed head roll to a stop, face down a couple of feet away from me.

My bare feet slip on the blood, an unbelievable amount pooling around Adam's corpse. The word 'SCUMBAG' on the sandwich board is almost entirely hidden by it.

I shut the chainsaw off and drop it to the ground. It slips from my grasp easily, lubricated by gore. My hands are steady but my mind is racing.

I look over at Cassandra who has dropped to her knees. Her eyes are closed and covered by her hands. She couldn't even watch.

I look around and notice that I cannot see the headlights from the vehicle I had seen before, the windows no longer catching the bright yellow light. If Jennifer is here, she must have heard Adam's final moments.

I awkwardly position Adam's headless body upright, using the wooden boards to balance him and pulling his legs behind his body to ensure that he stays upwards. He's on his knees, and although most of him is slumping to the left, it's good enough for me. I wipe away some of the blood on the sandwich board to reveal the word 'SCUMBAG' some more. I quickly walk over to Adam's head, picking it up without much thought as to what it really is (although it does feel unexpectedly heavy) and placing it in front of the sign.

I turn it just enough so Adam's face is visible, although it is, of course, drenched in blood. His eyes and mouth are closed, which makes him look strangely peaceful despite the last moments of his life being incomparable fear and suffering.

"Your name isn't Jack Gardener, is it?" Cassandra says quietly, not even able to look at me.

She is biting her lip and heavy tears are running down her face.

She's onto me. Better late than never.

4

"You're right, Cassandra," I admit. "It's not."

Her head slowly turns towards me.

"Why have you been lying to me?" she asks.

She just witnessed an execution and she's worried about me telling her the truth? This girl really needs to get her priorities straight. She's more fucked up than I ever thought she was.

"I had to," I say with a degree of honesty. "I just had to."

Cassandra shakes her head.

"I couldn't have done any of this without you," I say. "You've helped me a great deal. More than I ever thought you would."

She stands up suddenly, probably to run towards me and claw my eyes out or bite me in the face, but she stops dead and looks towards the door.

Jennifer Morgan stands inside the warehouse, alone as I instructed but never expected her to be. She is staring straight ahead, through Cassandra and me, directly at the defiled body of Adam, which lies in an awkward heap of blood and plywood.

She screams and my ears are instantly pierced by the high-pitched sound. It's enough to give me a migraine, but luckily I'm quick enough to run over to her and clasp my hand over her mouth before it bothers me enough that I'll be forced to cut her head off as well.

She's incredibly stupid to actually come here alone; surely she must know that she has signed her own death certificate. Maybe she really did love Adam that much, that she was willing to sacrifice everything if there was a small chance that she could save him. It's weird what love can do to people.

Oh well, that means nothing at all now that Adam's head is six feet away from where it used to be on top of his shoulders.

"Quiet, Jenny," I say into my wife's ear.

Cassandra is walking towards us, her face one of confusion and realisation, her pretty little brain putting together the pieces of my elaborate puzzle.

Jennifer is shaking but not resisting my solid grip on

her face. I make sure she can see the revolver in my hand.

"This is your wife?" Cassandra questions.

Jennifer's dark hair doesn't look like it has been brushed since the last time I saw her. In fact, I think she's wearing the same outfit she had on when she walked out on me.

I smell her, noticing she smells different from the scent she usually has. This time it's garlic and oil, like she's been in a restaurant recently.

I nod, gritting my teeth.

"I know her," Cassandra slurs.

I nod again.

"You sure do," I say. "You've got a good memory, Cassandra. It was well over six months ago when you had your first and only appointment with Jennifer Morgan."

Cassandra's head tilts and she looks back at Adam's corpse. I open my mouth to speak again but Cassandra throws up, a preposterous amount of vomit coming up from her stomach.

Jennifer squirms in my grasp and I turn her towards me, my hand staying firm on her face.

"If I let you go, no more screaming," I say.

She nods, the tears from her eyes pooling around my fingers.

I let go of her mouth and she takes a huge breath, gasping frantically for air. She tries to evade my hold but I twist her arm behind her back and pull her into me.

"Chris," she says, almost too quietly for me to be able to hear. "You're insane. What have you done?"

She bawls like a baby.

"You've killed him!"

Her words are spoken between sobs, mainly inward breaths and not actually comprehensible language.

"He deserved it," I say. "He took what was mine. You both committed the worst kind of adultery. And in my home as well."

She shakes her head some more, her hair bouncing

like a peculiar animal.

"The girl," Jennifer says. "Why the girl?"

Cassandra looks up at me, wiping vomit from her mouth. Her blonde hair looks almost as dark as Jennifer's in this light.

"She was the first domino that toppled," I say. "None of us would be here if it wasn't for her."

Cassandra stands up.

"She came to see me to discuss her marriage," she says. "Told me all about her husband – you – and the way he controlled her. I told her to leave you."

I bite my tongue, but I wish I were biting hers.

"You told her that my wife should file for divorce the first chance she gets, isn't that right?" I say. "You planted that seed of doubt in her mind and let it blossom into a beautiful flower."

Cassandra is angry with me. I can see in her eyes that she is incensed by the deceit. She should've known better.

"But she couldn't do it," I say. "She couldn't divorce me, she was too scared of losing everything she had – the apartment, the car, the endless amount of disposable income. So instead she took out her frustrations with infidelity."

I twist Jennifer's arm harder. She winces in pain.

"I was monitoring Jennifer's phone and emails," I elaborate. "That was how I found out about your little office, the one-hour commitment-free evaluation and that's when I became intrigued with you."

Cassandra wants to kill me. She wants to do what she did to Joshua to me.

"I did some digging, found out a lot about your past," I say. "It got me thinking: how could somebody clearly so damaged think they have any right to tell somebody else what to do with their life?"

Cassandra's lips look dry, almost blue.

"You changed my life forever that day," I say. "And you hadn't even met me. You knew nothing about me, apart from the bullshit that my wife spewed from her mouth."

"You made me kill somebody," Cassandra cries. "I thought you... cared."

She turns away, her arms despairingly reaching up in the air. She whimpers like a dog with a painful bowel condition.

"You made all of this happen, Cassandra," I say. "Without you and your fucking certificates on the wall of your office, my life wouldn't have plummeted downhill like it did. You're to blame, not me."

"You're deluded, Chris," Jennifer says, still crying like an idiot. She squirms some more.

"I knew I needed help," Cassandra says, seemingly to nobody in particular. "I knew I was on the edge, but I thought you were different. You're just like all the rest."

I laugh, but it feels unwarranted.

"The rest?" I question. "The other men?"

Cassandra turns back to me.

"I know a lot about you, Cassandra," I say. "More than you'd ever care to find out about. You've got your friend Vincent Ryman to thank for that."

Her eyes are wide and dark. She looks thin and horrendous.

"V-vincent?" she says.

"I took a good look at your phone and social media records," I say. "It seemed like he was your best friend, the one person you really opened up to. Ironic really, that you ran a psychiatric practice together. Surprising that he'd go into business with a fruitcake like you."

Cassandra doesn't say a word. The Beretta remains on the floor behind her.

"I'll admit, it did take a while for me to get the information out of him I wanted," I say. "But once I did, it was perfect really. I couldn't have asked for more."

"You son of a bitch," Jennifer says. "You've killed a man and you're still playing this sick game. Let the girl go, it's me you want, you monster."

I want to cave her skull in with a rock and pull her brain out of her head.

"Not only do you have a secret history of severe mental illness, Cassandra," I say, "something that should have rendered your qualifications obsolete, but you've also been extremely susceptible to strong male figures in your life. You've got a list of abusive partners longer than your arm. Including Joshua, of course, rest in peace. So, you like the bad boys, huh?"

Cassandra is backing away from me.

"You played directly into my hands," I say. "It was almost embarrassingly easy."

I slip the revolver into my waistband, ensuring that I don't let Jennifer get away from me. I fish around in my pocket for the Polaroid picture of Vincent's hanging cadaver.

I pull it out and hold it aloft. Cassandra squints as she looks at it.

"Vincent is dead," I say. "He hanged himself after what I put him through. That's your fault too."

Cassandra screams, pushing her fingers into her face. Jennifer joins in, both women in unison together in their horror.

I'm a mass-murdering bastard and these bitches are fucking terrified. Fantastic.

5

Jennifer tries to bite my hand that holds the Polaroid but I'm wise to it. I try to break her wrist with my other hand but she spins around, somehow eluding my grasp and managing to scratch at my face.

It doesn't hurt much, but sets me off-balance and I feel the revolver in my pants slip out and onto the ground behind me.

Jennifer starts to run but I kick out my leg and knock

her to the ground.

Cassandra has leapt onto the floor and picked up the Beretta, but I sprint forwards and knock into her back hard, sending her sprawling. She drops the gun and I kick it away from her hands, sending it out into the darkness beneath one of the factory machines.

I grab a handful of her thick, blonde hair.

"I've got a confession," I say. "I wanted to kill you. I wanted to make you suffer like the rest of them. Fuck, I wanted you to suffer the most. But I've fallen in love with you."

Cassandra is crying and pleading. She's seen what I'm capable of and she thinks that she's next.

I look at Jennifer, who hasn't moved from the spot on the ground where she fell. I thought she would have tried harder to get away.

"The police are coming," she says.

I laugh. She's bluffing.

"Angela is outside, in the car," she adds. "I told her to give me five minutes and then call the cops. She told me I was fucking stupid."

I shake my head. I haven't finished yet; the police can't ruin it. I won't let them.

"I thought I could have stopped you killing again," she says. "But you already did, you fucking lunatic."

She looks towards Adam, who looks quite a sight in his current state.

"I never cheated on you with him," she shouts. "There was another man, but never him!"

Another bluff. I pull harder on Cassandra's hair.

"You hear that, Cassie?" I say. "I killed Adam for no good reason."

I laugh emphatically, but it feels so fake I stop halfway through. My face feels like it's on fire.

"My two loves, the one from the past and the one from the present," I say. "Both here together. It's quite magical."

I can hear distant sirens, too far away to be an immediate threat. They're so quiet they sound like bees. The police really are coming. I should've killed Angela as well, the skank.

"It's over, Chris," Jennifer says. "Psychopaths don't get happy endings."

I look deep into Cassandra's eyes. I pull her close but don't feel her embrace me at all.

Is that it? Is all we had gone because I told a few porky pies?

"I wanted to hate you," I say. "But I couldn't. You made it all seem worth it."

I manipulated her, and while originally it was to eventually humiliate her, I ended up turning her into exactly what she always had the potential to be: a take-no-shit redemption-seeking badass, like me. We're meant to be.

"I love you," I say.

Cassandra bites my nose hard, pulling away and taking some of my flesh with it. I scream in pain, using my fist to hit her hard in the side of the head until she lets go. She falls to the ground, unconscious.

My eyes flash white and my nose pours with blood. I see Jennifer scrambling away on the ground towards the door, but I grab her by an ankle and pull her to her feet.

She slaps me, but I turn my head and avoid the full brunt of her attack.

"Now you've done it," I say. "I really have lost everything now."

She screams and curses, spitting and biting and scratching like a crazed beast.

I take off my gloves and pull her towards the large septic tank, which I know from previous visits to this warehouse is filled to the brim with green, festering water.

I slam Jennifer's head against the brown flaking paint and rusted surface, her feet kicking out at me, hoping to connect with a knee or a testicle.

I step up onto the first rung of the ladder that leads up onto the top of the tank, using all of my strength to pull her up with me.

She hits me some more, the bandage around my head now becoming loose. She is biting my back but I can't feel much of anything right now, the adrenaline rushing through me unlike anything I've experienced before from drink or drugs.

The maintenance hatch is already open from my last inspection, and as I look in the stench of the stale water hits me.

I turn and grab Jennifer hard by the throat, squeezing as tightly as I can. I don't want to choke the life out of her yet, I want to hear her final moments from within the tank when I close the hatch and hear her fingernails on the underside of it.

I move to the edge of the open hatch, the bandage now falling completely from my head. My face is soaked in blood – some mine, some Adam's.

The sirens are louder now.

"Chris!"

Cassandra's voice is buoyant. It's almost happy.

"Or Jack, whatever your fucking name is!"

She is standing at the bottom of the septic tank ladder, her hair behind her ears and her arms outstretched. She's holding the Colt Python and pointing it directly at me.

"She's right, y'know," she says.

I'm not entirely sure what she means, but I'm not going to let her get the drop on me.

"Psychopaths don't get happy endings."

She fires the gun and the blast from it is louder than it has ever been before. I try to move Jennifer in front of the bullet but it hits me hard in the stomach, knocking me backwards like a kick from a mule.

I lose my footing and fall head-first into the tank, the water ice cold on my blazing hot skin. The darkness envelopes me and I swallow sour water that has been decaying in this tank for years. I'm not even completely sure that it's just water.

I push up towards the top, ready to leap out and drag somebody, anybody, down into the depths with me. I hit my head hard on the surface of the tank, my arms desperately searching for the open hatch.

I hear the boom of the hatch closing and the rusted creak of the wheel turning on the other side. There's nowhere in the tank for me to catch my breath, not even an inch or two of air for me to cling on to.

My lungs feel tight and the fatal wound in my stomach feels like it is ripping me in two. My watery tomb pulls me further down, the weight of the water crushing my bones.

I am dying but I know that I have done enough. I will live on forever with Cassandra Jones.

I am the cause.

I am the effect.

I am anarchy.

I am chaos.

I am a cool motherfucker.

THE TENTH TALE - TERMINATE

1

A friend of mine died not long after we graduated from college in a motorcycle accident, neck broken.

We'd drifted apart by then, even in those few short months, but the whole aftermath surrounding his death left me feeling despondent.

I think it was then that I began feeling that the human race was something that I was so far removed from that any similarity between their thought processes and mine had been sifted out like grit long ago, back further than I could remember.

I felt grief, but it was temporary, maybe for ten minutes or so, and after that I felt angry - not because he was dead or because a truck driver was doing twenty miles over, and not at myself because I hadn't spoken to him in a number of weeks.

I was angry with every self-gratifying leech who latched onto his death, riding its coat-tails for thrills and making every word spoken about him: how great he was, how kind he could be, how he made them laugh - about them.

Whatever direction the conversation took it came back to 'me, me, me', something like "I can't believe he's gone" or "I sometimes still expect to hear his voice when the front door opens" or "I feel sick".

These bullshit-shovelling people were everywhere - drinks organised in his memory, online forums, laying flowers at the side of the road, the funeral - they just kept popping up like weeds.

One of them said something ridiculous like "at least he died doing what he loved". I almost laughed out loud. Labelling it with 'he lived fast' didn't make it so: he may have loved motorcycles but he didn't love screaming for his mother as he came off his vehicle, smashing his vertebrae and filling his lungs with blood. He wanted to be an accountant, he didn't want his head spun around in his helmet before he had the chance to get married, have kids and make something of himself.

I did a bungee jump when I travelled to Europe in '99. It was great, got my blood pumping, made every inch of my skin feel like popping candy, but I didn't want to die.

What legacy would that have left? Existence and consciousness wiped out while I was dangling from a rope, hanging upside down and roaring like a frat boy. What a fucking waste.

Nobody wants to die, even if they take risks at every turn or insist with every breath that they do.

It's all just a need to feel more alive, cut themselves out of the embryo sac of monotony and claw into the light, to make everything feel more like a wondrous sensory experience and less like a migraine, clouding the world with grey.

When death is immediate and apparent, we all feel the same: lost, scared and confused.

What's next? How am I to be remembered? It's always about that: what impact did I have on those around me to ensure that my memory won't fade away?

What message can I scrawl on the window condensation before it vanishes for good?

There's not much after the slab, after the moment you're identified by your nearest and dearest with a split in your skull or your lips burned off; after your physical form is eradicated you're just a series of nerve receptors flashing in the brains of others who met you, loved you, hated you.

It's too unreliable.

My friend died and everybody tried to give it reason, and once they did they accepted it for what it was - an accident.

He had been driving towards that turn in the road since he was born, his whole life leading to the inevitable and unavoidable conclusion of a broken neck and the skin torn from his back.

There are turns in the road for all of us, some closer than others. I won't be looking in the rear-view mirror when mine approaches. I'll throttle hard.

BEN ERRINGTON

Philanthropist, idealist and possible
borderline sociopath.

Ben Errington is a writer from Bristol, UK. He has
been writing for many years and it was all a bit naff before
he started to put his heart and soul into it, so now it's
(slightly) better. He is also a father, graphic designer and
vocalist in metal band Koshiro.

Printed in Great Britain
by Amazon.co.uk, Ltd.,
Marston Gate.